DEEP DARK SECRETS

KERI BEEVIS

BLOODHOUND
— BOOKS —

ALSO BY KERI BEEVIS

Dying to Tell

To sad endings and new beginnings

In memory of a dear friend and colleague, Fiona.
The world lost a little bit of its sparkle when you passed.
You are missed every day.

And to my good friends, Mr & Mrs Smith, AKA The Smervs.
You are perfect together and I wish you every happiness for the future.

PROLOGUE

DECEMBER 1998

Somebody was in the house.

Lizzie had fallen asleep on the couch, so didn't hear the first thud, but the sound of breaking glass jolted her awake. She hadn't meant to doze off, only intended to close her eyes for a few seconds. The noise had her bolting upright, the textbook she had been reading slipping to the floor as her heart leapt into her mouth. She held her breath, told herself not to panic. For a moment it was just her beating heart and the soft methodical ticking of the grandfather clock. Glancing at the time, she noted it was almost nine. Early still, but it didn't mean it wasn't Nell. Maybe she had cut her date short? She had promised Lizzie she wouldn't be late. Or perhaps it was the Dolans? It crossed her mind briefly that Nell would be in trouble if Mr and Mrs Dolan arrived home and found out she wasn't here. Lizzie was about to call out, wanting reassurance, when she heard a distinctly male cough. She froze.

'For fuck's sake, keep it down.'

The voice wasn't more than a whisper, but it was angry. It wasn't Nell, it wasn't the Dolans, and there appeared to be two of them. She picked up her book, her scrambled brain telling her legs to move. Why weren't her legs moving? The footsteps were now in the hall leading down to the living room, and they were growing closer.

Run.

Her feet finally engaged, the textbook still tightly clutched in her hand as a useless weapon. The kitchen was ahead. There was an archway leading through to the front hallway where she could make her escape.

'Are you sure the place is empty?' A different man's voice.

'I told you it was. They're gonna be gone for hours.'

'So, who does the glass belong to?'

Dear God. In her hurry to get out of the room, Lizzie had forgotten her soda.

Get out, now, before they find you.

She glanced at the archway that led to the hallway and the safety of the front door. Above her, Tommy and Emily slept. If she ran she would leave them alone with two intruders.

'Who the fuck is here? You said it would be empty.'

'Ssssh.'

They were listening for her.

Lizzie made a decision. She tiptoed across to the counter and slid a large stainless steel knife from the block sat next to the oven. She wouldn't let them hurt Tommy and Emily. She crept out into the hallway, her thick socks muffling her footsteps on the wooden floor as she passed the huge Christmas tree decorated in bands of red and silver, its expensive baubles twinkling in the light of the giant chandelier. Her legs were shaking as she took the stairs to the second floor. The rich mahogany of the bannister was decorated with fake holly, winding round and round as it led a path up the staircase. Mrs Dolan always went to town at Christmas and the house was like something on a seasonal greeting card. Onto the half landing and from below came the sound of footsteps. They were in the kitchen now and still arguing.

'There's no car in the drive. Trust me, no-one is home.'

'You can't say that for sure.'

'What about the kids?'

'Sleepover at a friend's. The house is empty.'

'So, how do you explain the soda?'

'Maybe they forgot to clear it away. Listen up. I have more to lose than you do, so stop whining like a little bitch and let's get this done and get out of here.'

Lizzie didn't stop to hear anymore. She needed to wake Tommy and Emily, get them somewhere safe. She opened Tommy's door quietly, thankful it didn't creak, and crossed to the bed where the ten-year-old slept on his belly, comforter half on the floor and one leg of his PJs rolled up to his knee.

'Tommy?' Lizzie set down her textbook and knife on the nightstand and reached for his shoulder, her whisper urgent. 'Tommy, I need you to wake up.'

He opened one eye, stared at her sleepily. 'What are you–?'

'Shush. You have to be quiet.'

'Where's Nell?'

'I'll explain, but first we have to get Emily.'

'But–'

'Nell had to go out. Tommy, I need you to listen.' He was fully awake now and sitting up in bed, rubbing at his eyes.

'There's someone in the house. We need to hide.'

His eyes widened and she could see he had a million questions. He was too young to properly understand and he should be sheltered from this, but there wasn't time. From downstairs came a distinctly male cough.

Tommy's eyes opened wider still. 'Who's that?' His voice was frightened.

'I don't know, but there's two of them and they broke in. We need to get your sister and find somewhere to hide.'

Mercifully he quit with the questions and climbed out of bed.

'Try to stay as quiet as possible. We don't want them to hear us, okay?'

He nodded, clinging to Lizzie's free hand as she picked up the knife and they made their way across to Emily's room. Tommy's four-year-old sister was more difficult to rouse and Lizzie ended up carrying her, quilt trailing on the floor, to the closet where Tommy waited. She ushered Tommy inside and settled Emily down in his arms before returning for the knife she'd left next to Emily's bed.

'What do we do now?' Tommy asked. He sounded frightened. Lizzie returned to him, crouching down. 'I need you to stay here and keep quiet.'

'What about you? Where you gonna be?'

'Do your mom and dad have a phone in their room?'

'Yeah. It's next to the bed.'

'I'm going to try and get it, to call the police. You stay here, okay?'

'You're gonna come back, right?'

'Yes, I'm coming right back.'

As she started to close the door, Tommy caught hold of her hand.

'Lizzie?'

'Yes?'

'I'm scared.'

'I know, baby. I'll be as quick as I can. You hold on to your sister and keep as quiet as possible. Whatever happens, don't come out of the closet. Promise?'

'Promise.'

Lizzie slid the closet door shut and with a deathly grip on

the knife, made her way across the room. Mr and Mrs Dolan's bedroom was at the end of the landing. Barely daring to breathe, she crept down the hallway and into their room. Her relief when she spied the phone on the nightstand was quickly overshadowed by a fresh wave of fear as she heard footsteps on the stairs. She froze, perspiration beading on her forehead, her knuckles turning white as she squeezed the handle of the knife even tighter.

Her eyes darted around the room. The closet was the only option, but it was on the opposite side of the room to the phone. Voices grew closer.

'You're sure you know the combination?'

'Jesus! Yeah, I'm sure.'

Lizzie flew for the closet, pulled back the door and squeezed herself inside, huddling between rows of dresses. She pulled the door shut, holding her breath. They were in the bedroom now. A bead of sweat trickled down her back. The clothes smelt of detergent and a soft musky perfume.

Stay still. Don't make a sound.

The closet door opened, startling both Lizzie and the two men dressed in black. In blind panic, Lizzie leapt out of the closet, lashing out with the knife. She heard an anguished scream but didn't wait to see what damage she had inflicted.

'Fucking bitch. She's getting away.'

Down the stairs, with footsteps close behind her, she ran into the kitchen, her socked feet slipping on the polished floor. As she ran for the front door she felt a hand grab at her hair, yank hard, and she stumbled, falling back and fighting to keep a grip on the knife as the man who had chased her straddled her, pinning her down. Shock registered as she recognised him. She tried to raise the knife, but her strength was no match for a grown man and he easily gained control, prising the knife from her fingers. She reached up, using her now free hand, and speared her thumb towards his eye. He screamed, lashing out wildly, with Lizzie twisting beneath the blows he rained down. As she started choking, horror registered in his one good eye. He raised his hands to his face. They were covered in blood.

Lizzie glanced past him to the stairs, at the decorations snaking up the bannister, to the little boy, his thumb in his mouth, crouched in his pyjamas midway up the steps. Were it not for his frightened eyes, she could have believed he was sitting there waiting for Santa.

Then the picture-postcard scene darkened to black.

1

If there was an award given for bad days, Nell O'Connor figured the one she was experiencing would be in the running. First she had slept through her alarm, then shortly after leaving the motel the engine in her car had overheated and she'd had to wait for a tow truck, then a further two hours at the garage while her radiator was repaired. She couldn't use her card, couldn't risk Caleb tracing her, so she had counted out dollar bills from her precious stash of cash, relieved to have enough left for the ferry crossing. The final setback was on the last leg of her journey when, with less than twenty-five minutes to spare before the ferry departed, she hit a traffic jam on the freeway. There were later ferries, but she wouldn't make it to the bank before they closed.

She tapped her fingers impatiently against the wheel, the radio that had been her constant companion since leaving Chicago now grating on her nerves. Spotting the sign ahead for East Haven, knowing she could cut through the back streets to the ferry port, she hit her blinker. She caught a couple of red lights, but traffic was lighter than on the freeway and she was blessing her decision to cut through, until she caught the tail end of another jam on the main road out of town leading down to the port. Nell glanced at the clock, knew she had about twelve minutes to play with as she drew bumper-to-bumper with the car in front. This wasn't going to work. She was going to miss the damn boat. She swore under her breath, tightening her grip on the wheel. And then she remembered the harbour road that ran down the back of the main street leading to the waterside. It was meant for supply trucks but was generally empty, and was the only chance she had of getting there before her boat left.

Nell slowed the Ford and waited for a break in the traffic to make the turn. She glanced again at the clock and saw she was down to ten minutes. A gap came in the traffic and she seized it, turning into the private road. Mostly she stuck to the rules, but today was an exception. She was familiar with the road, knew it was a four-minute journey straight through. No-one would be any the wiser and she wouldn't miss the crossing.

As she sped past the backs of the shops her gut tightened. Returning to the island brought mixed emotions: nostalgia tinged by regret and, bubbling under the surface, apprehension. Purity had been her home for the first ten years of her life, and, even after her mother had moved them to the mainland, she had continued to spend summers on the island with her aunt. Things had changed though since the last time she had been there and her absence over the years would have done nothing to redress the balance.

Still, it was better than what she was running away from in Chicago.

The car eased round to the right and she began the downhill descent to the waterfront, getting her first view of the ocean. The afternoon sun bounced off the surface, raining sparkles across the swelling green hues of the water. In the distance she spied a couple of sail boats, and knew they were probably filled with tourists staying on the island, hoping to spot a pod of dolphins.

Up ahead a truck pulled into the road, blocking part of the view and Nell pulled into a driveway so it could pass. A few yards before it reached her, the driver hit his hazards and came to a stop outside the back of a bar. Angling his baseball cap low on his forehead, he climbed down from the cab. Nell thumped her palm against the steering wheel as he moved to the back and threw open the doors, beginning to unload crates.

You've got to be kidding me!

The driver had stopped on the narrowest part of the road and there was no way she was going to get past his truck. Frustration bubbled over as she killed the engine and climbed from her car.

'Excuse me.'

The truck driver didn't answer at first, so she tried again, louder. This time he glanced up, a lazy grin on his face. 'Hey, what's up?'

'I need to get down to the ferry. I can't get past your truck.'

The guy glanced at Nell's car then down to the port. He was young, maybe early to mid-twenties, with a swarthy complexion and a goatee. 'You know this is a private road, right?'

'Yes, I know. My ferry goes in about eight minutes. I had to cut through. You need to move your truck.'

'Well, if you know that, you know it's for deliveries only.'

'Yes, I saw the sign. But I told you, I'm running late and I have to be on this ferry. If you could please let me past this once.'

'Sorry, ma'am, rules are rules. The road's private so we don't have to let people through.'

'I get that, but–'

'No "buts". I make an exception for you, I have to start making one for everybody. Now I'm sorry but you're either going to have to turn around or wait until I'm done.' He tilted his hat at her, returning to the back of the truck.

'Wait until you're done? You don't understand. My ferry goes in minutes.' When he ignored her, reaching inside the truck for another crate, Nell grabbed hold of his arm in frustration.

He wheeled around, looking pissed off. 'Look, lady, go wait in your car, okay? I've got a job to do.'

'Why are you being such an asshole? It would take you seconds to move your truck.'

'Because those are the rules, so take your hand off me and stop giving me attitude.'

'Is there a problem here?'

Nell glanced round to see a dark-haired man standing in the doorway that led to the back of the bar, thumbs hooked in the pockets of his jeans. Bar owner, she presumed, hoping she could reason with him to get the delivery guy to move his truck.

'I need to get to the ferry port. My boat goes in five minutes and he won't let me through.'

'You do know it's a private road?'

'Yes, it's a private road, we've covered that. And yeah, I know I shouldn't be driving down here, but seriously, I have to be on this ferry, so a little understanding would be appreciated.'

She was getting snappy and could feel frustration bubbling over into anger, scared it could manifest itself into panic. This wasn't helped by the laid-back stance of the new guy, who stood listening to her rant, shoulder against the door frame, one leg cocked and a lazy half-smile playing on his lips, which suggested she was amusing him.

'You done?' he asked, as she paused for breath.

'What is wrong with you people? Are you seriously finding this funny? I can't believe you're going to make me miss my boat because you're too damn pig-headed to move a stupid truck.' Tears of frustration pricked at the backs of her eyes as her face and neck burned. Nell forced herself to focus on her breathing as the thud in her chest quickened.

The bar owner regarded her, the cocky smile on his face widening. Although his eyes remained on her, he addressed the truck driver when he spoke. 'Fancy a coffee, Eddie? My shout.'

Eddie looked delighted and set down the crate he had unloaded.

'Sure thing.' He tipped his hat at Nell as he passed her, a broad smirk on his face.

'You're just going to leave the truck here?' Nell was talking to the backs of their heads as they disappeared into the bar. 'That's great. Nice one. Thanks for nothing. Assholes,' she yelled after them.

With no target for her anger she kicked the front wheel of her Ford harder than intended, wincing when pain shot up her foot. There was no way she was going to make the boat. The bank would be closed when she arrived and she had no money left to buy groceries. Her heart was racing; the tightening in her chest when it came was sudden and hard, sucking the air out of her lungs.

Oh dear God, not now.

As the vice grip crushed her chest, the trembling started. Her legs too rubbery to stand, Nell sank to the floor beside the car, gripped her knees tightly and forced herself to breathe slowly and deeply through her nose. 'One-hundred, ninety-nine, ninety-eight...' Sweat beaded on her forehead and under her arms as she struggled to control her breathing. She continued to count backwards.

Focus, O'Connor.

'Eighty-six, eighty-five, eight-four...'

She sat like that for close to ten minutes, until the attack passed, aware that she had missed her ferry, and just relieved the street remained empty. Defeated and physically drained, she got into the car and fired up the engine. Michael and Newt were out of town and not back until the weekend. She wished she'd asked for a spare key, instead of insisting she would go straight to the house.

Suck it up, O'Connor. This is just for one night.

Before Caleb she had been happy and confident, embracing each new opportunity, wanting to experience life to the fullest. He had taken those things from her and she had let him.

Stop feeling sorry for yourself. You did it, you left him, and you will get your life back.

As she drove, Nell re-evaluated her mental checklist. The bank was now off the list, so were the groceries. She would call her realtor from the ferry. Chances were they too would be closed by the time she arrived on the island, so she would make arrangements for the key to be left at the house. It was all going to work out.

Caleb, Chicago, it was all behind her. Purity Island was her past and her fresh start all rolled into one. It was time to regroup and start over.

You can do this.

There had been rumours she was coming back to the island, so it shouldn't have shocked him when he saw her in the driveway struggling to get an oversized suitcase out of the trunk of a beat-up Ford. He slowed his car and took a moment to study her as she thumped the case down on the driveway and slammed the trunk shut. She was dressed simply in a dark sweater and jeans that hugged her long slim legs, blonde ringlets escaping from her ponytail. He'd heard she was an artist, something of a big deal, but nothing about her screamed money. Certainly not the car she was driving or the way she was dressed.

He watched her drag her luggage up the driveway, rummage around under a plant pot for the key that had been left for her, and then she was stepping inside the dark house, out of his sight, leaving him with an unsettled feeling. Her return brought up too many questions and although he tried to reassure himself it wouldn't be a problem, things were now out of his hands, and it bothered him.

It's going to be okay. Let sleeping dogs lie. She's none the wiser. The past was the past and Nell O'Connor's return wouldn't disturb anything. But he would keep a close eye on her, just to be sure.

2

Despite being exhausted, Nell barely slept. It didn't help that her stomach kept growling with hunger and, although she had wolfed down half a melted candy bar she'd found in the side pocket of her suitcase, it did little to abate the cravings for food. Luckily, she had contacted the utility companies ahead of her arrival, so at least she had running water and electricity. After a long shower and a glass of tap water she'd flopped onto the bed in what had once been her room, hoping for sleep. It came in fits and starts, the musty odour of the bedlinen, which hadn't been aired in a while, clogging her nostrils, while dreams of the past and the present collided uncomfortably. Finally she drifted off a couple of hours before sunrise, awaking to the sound of birds twittering and beams of light cutting across the bedroom walls. Although she wanted nothing more than to roll over and go back to sleep, she forced herself up, knowing that wasn't an option. Today she was going to be busy, there was no time for self-pity. She showered again, dressed quickly and checked her cell phone, annoyed at the flutter of fear in her belly when she spotted the missed calls and texts.

Caleb.

She had known he wouldn't give up quietly and he had threatened her on enough occasions with what would happen if she ever tried to leave him. She left the phone on silent and slipped it into her purse. First stop was the bank, then she would treat herself to breakfast. Her empty belly was screaming for food and a good cup of coffee.

As she made her way over to the Sizzling Griddle, her mouth was watering at the thought of eggs and bacon. She had spotted the place when parking up outside the bank, standing where one of the old convenience stores had once been.

'Nell O'Connor! Is that you?'

Nell recognised Antonia Richardson as she darted out from behind the counter of the diner to greet her. Her old friend had a few extra lines on her face and her once-naturally brunette hair had been highlighted to ash blonde, but otherwise she hadn't changed a bit.

'My God, it is you! I heard you may be moving to Purity. How the devil are you?'

'It's good to see you, Antonia.' Nell took a self-conscious step back when the woman went to embrace her, but it went unnoticed as Antonia grabbed her in a bear hug. She glanced around the diner. Half a dozen booths were occupied and a couple of the occupants were watching in interest, but most continued with their morning conversation.

'When did you arrive on the island?'

'Late last night,' Nell told her, freeing herself from the other woman's arms.

'I was so sorry about your Aunt Bella and Clarke. It was a shock to us all.'

'Thanks.'

'She'd be pleased knowing you were back.'

'I hope so. How are you doing?'

A loaded question, given Antonia had always had verbal diarrhoea, but it was polite to ask and Nell was keen to change the subject. The pair of them had gone to school together until Nell and her mother had moved away, but they'd kept in touch and hung out during the summers Nell spent with Bella. She nodded and smiled as her old friend updated her on her marriage and divorce, telling her she now owned the diner. The smell of food wafting through from the kitchen was almost too much and as Antonia paused for breath, Nell's belly made an embarrassing grumble. She smiled apologetically. 'Sorry, I haven't eaten since yesterday morning.'

'Oh, you poor thing!'

Antonia ushered her to a table, before disappearing. She returned moments later with a pot of coffee and a notepad to take Nell's order. Nell quickly scanned the menu. 'I'll have eggs over easy, bacon, hash browns and toast please. Oh, and a side of pancakes with maple syrup.' It was greedy, but she didn't care.

Antonia gave her a wide smile. 'Coming right up.'

Alone with her thoughts, Nell poured cream into her coffee and took a sip. It was the first cup she'd had in over twenty-four hours and it hit the spot. The old-fashioned bell above the door rang as it opened inwards and she briefly glanced up at the broad-shouldered, dark-haired man who had his back to her, recognising the Purity Island Police Department navy blazer. She took another sip of coffee and, disinterested, closed her eyes.

'Morning, Chief. You want your coffee to go?' Antonia shouted through from the kitchen.

'Thanks, Antonia, and fix a cup for Tommy too. He had a busy night.'

'Coming right up.'

Something in the man's tone sounded familiar. Nell cocked open an eye. She could see him, his back still to her, making small talk with a couple of patrons who sat near the door. As Antonia came through from the kitchen he turned, affording Nell a side view of his profile: his slightly hooked nose, wavy dark brown hair and stubbled jaw. Her heart went into her mouth as she recognised him as the bar owner who had caused her to miss her ferry. Except he wasn't a bar owner apparently; he was the goddamn chief of police.

Anger bubbled, quickly washed down with embarrassment, as she recalled the encounter. Now, in the cold light of day when she was thinking rationally, she could see she had been clearly in the wrong. He was still an asshole but, she guessed, she had behaved like one too. Feeling contrite, Nell picked up the menu and slipped down in her seat, hoping he wouldn't notice her. She listened to him talking for another couple of minutes, thanking Antonia for the coffee. As he turned to go, she peeked over the menu, accidentally making eye contact with him as he glanced in her direction. The corners of his lips curved as he recognised her.

'I see you made the ferry okay.'

Nell felt her cheeks flame. 'Yes, I did... Eventually.' She forced the words out, wanting the ground to swallow her up.

Just go. Please.

He nodded, amused by her obvious embarrassment, and studied her for a moment, his green eyes intent. She thought he was going to say something else, maybe lecture her for driving down a private road, but instead his grin widened before his attention turned elsewhere. Nell watched from behind her menu as he bid farewell to the customers he'd been talking to and left the diner.

'Isn't he a sweetheart?' Antonia swooned as she arrived with Nell's food. She set down the plates and poured Nell fresh coffee. 'We lucked out when he decided to move to the island.'

He was a mainlander. That figured. 'What happened to

Chief Bristow?' Nell asked, trying her best to sound disinterested as she busied herself unfolding her napkin and shaking salt onto her eggs.

'Oh, he retired about six years back. Chief Cutler transferred over from Portland. I think he enjoys the island life.'

'That so?' Nell speared a piece of bacon with her fork. Her encounter with the police chief had put a brief dent in her appetite, but now the food was in front of her she remembered she was ravenous. 'Shame, I always liked Chief Bristow.'

She finished her breakfast in relative peace, Antonia having other customers to attend. Her belly full and her brain more alert following three cups of coffee, Nell tipped generously and made her way across to the island's main grocery store, where she stocked up on supplies, before heading back to Aunt Bella's house. She supposed she should stop referring to it as Aunt Bella's, as technically it was now hers. Bella had passed away from a stroke at the start of the year followed by her only child, and Nell's cousin, Clarke, who died weeks later in a tragic accident. Guilt crept in, knowing she hadn't made it back for either of their funerals. After she moved from Purity, she had returned every summer to stay with Bella. She should have come home for them. Of course it was easy to say that, now she had left Caleb. In truth, he hadn't given her a choice and deep down she knew Bella's death had been the catalyst for leaving him: the point where revulsion for the woman she had let herself become overtook fear of the consequences.

Monday started the same as any other day.

She generally rose before Caleb, keen to be out of the bed they shared before he awoke. Their house ran on routine, with Caleb liking everything to be a specific way, while Nell functioned like a robot, trying to ensure the whole thing ran as smoothly as possible so she could get him to work and out of the way. Today, it was more important than ever that things went to plan.

After he had left for the office, she was going to leave him.

Everything was in place, she'd run through the details hundreds of times. All she needed to do was be patient, to be compliant, this one last time, and she would be free. Finally.

She walked on eggshells around him constantly, but this morning she was particularly jittery and when she heard him stir, get out of bed and turn on the shower, her heart almost leapt into her mouth.

Pull yourself together, O'Connor. Act natural.

Although she tried, focusing her mind on mundane tasks, fixing his coffee just the way he liked it, pouring out his OJ and scrambling eggs, her hands shook and her legs threatened to buckle under her.

She drew a few deep breaths, setting out cutlery, ensuring each utensil was polished till it shined. All the time his plate was warming in the oven, because one thing Caleb would not tolerate was a cold plate. When he stepped into the kitchen she offered her cheek, her skin crawling at the touch of his lips, and forced a smile.

'Did you sleep well?' She forced herself to ask the question.

'I think I'm coming down with a cold. My chest's congested and I have a sore throat.' Although he was wearing one of his work suits, he loosened his tie. 'Think I have a temperature. Do you think I have a temperature?' He grabbed her hand, pressed it to his head, bottom lip sneering as he stared at her. 'Why are you shaking? You're not about to have one of your dumb fits, are you?'

Nell swallowed hard. 'I'm fine. I'm just cold. Do you want me to get you some Tylenol?'

'I'm wondering if I should take the day off, stay home and get some rest.'

Please God no, don't do that!

'Why don't you have your coffee and something to eat? It might make you feel better.'

He caught her wrist hard and sudden, eyes narrowing. 'What, you trying to get rid of me?'

Nell's bowels knotted, her skin growing clammy. 'Of course not, I just know we have your mother's benefit tonight and how disappointed you'll be if you're too ill to go.'

Caleb stared at her for a moment before releasing her.

'I suppose I should go in. It wouldn't look good if I have to reschedule meetings and then I'm seen at the benefit.' He picked up his coffee cup and sat down at the table as Nell busied herself finishing breakfast. 'Wear the black lace dress, the one with the low back. And make sure you straighten your hair.'

'Of course, Caleb.'

He caught her hand and glanced disapprovingly at her gnawed nails.

'Do you have a manicure today?'

'Yes.' It was a lie, but she needed him out of the house.

'Good. Your nails are an embarrassment.'

It was forty minutes later when she eventually got him out of the house. She waited impatiently, peering out of the upstairs window, watching until his car had turned out of the street. Her shoulders tense, her mouth dry, she moved quickly, getting her suitcase out of the cupboard and filling it with the things she planned to take.

She had never told Caleb that she'd inherited her aunt's house. He knew she had lived with her mom in a small town in Ohio, that her dad had left when she was young, but nothing of her life before. Purity was her sanctuary and in some small way she wondered if her decision to keep her early life private was self-conscious, that perhaps a small part of her had always known this day would eventually come. She had taken the call learning of her inheritance a couple of months after Bella and Clarke had passed, sitting on the news for days, knowing she should tell him, aware there would be terrible consequences if he ever found out that she had kept a secret from him. Her initial instinct had been to put the house on the market and, eventually, she had, aware the money from the sale would give her choices, would help if she ever managed to pluck up the courage to leave him. But as the weeks passed the idea of returning to Purity grew in its appeal and eventually she'd contacted the realtor and removed the house from sale. It took her two weeks of deliberating and plotting, then a further week to pluck up the courage to call her brother and ask for his help. She opened an account with the island's bank, squirrelling money away until she had enough to fund her plan.

Finally had come the task of picking a time to leave. That had been the hardest, and she had put it off for a couple of weeks, terrified Caleb would catch her in the act. Then Saturday night he had been in a randy mood, crawling on top of her as she feigned sleep. They didn't have sex much these days and he had caught her off guard. As she tried to fake enjoyment, feeling sick as he thrust and grunted on top of her, Nell knew she couldn't take this anymore. After he had collapsed into sleep beside her she had known: it was now or never.

Her heavy case packed and sitting in the hallway, she called a cab. While she waited for it to arrive, she went online and booked a one-way plane ticket to San Francisco, using a card she knew he had access to. Her old college roommate Rosie lived in California and she hoped he would assume that was where she had gone. Ready to leave, she watched anxiously out of the window for the cab, panic balling in the pit of her stomach when she saw a shiny red Porsche heading slowly up the street towards the house.

Shit, shit, shit. He's come home.

She was shaking, but before she could think what to do, the car had passed; a dark-haired woman was at the wheel. Minutes later her cab pulled up on the sidewalk out front. Her shaking didn't ease until the house disappeared from view, but even then her nerves were still shot, her shoulders tense. She asked the driver to drop her at a used car place on the outskirts of the city, where she paid cash for the Ford. As she drove out of the lot, heading east, she drew a deep breath. This was her one shot, her one chance to get away. She just hoped to hell she could pull it off.

Bella's guesthouse was situated on the clifftop, three-quarters of a mile from the centre of town. It was smaller than the two hotels on the island, but had always been full over the summer months. In later years, as her aunt's health had failed, the business had closed down and Nell felt a pang of nostalgia as she looked at the old house, awash with the September sun, its white timber framework in stark contrast against the cloudless blue sky. She hadn't realised how much she had missed the place. There was no denying it was run down, with Bella unable to either carry out or afford the necessary repairs, so Nell knew her nostalgia was tinged with guilt. Her aunt had looked after her every summer – she should have been here to return the favour.

Of course, Caleb hadn't been the only one keeping her away from Purity. The place had changed for Nell the night her best friend had died. Lizzie had stepped in at the last minute to cover Nell's babysitting gig at the Dolans' house so Nell could hook up with Cory Spellman. There had been a break-in. Mr Dolan's younger brother, Roy, had been somehow involved and was found dead at the scene; his accomplice had killed Lizzie and fled. Poor little Tommy had watched it happen, but had never been able to ID the murderer.

It wasn't Nell's fault, but she still felt responsible. If she had babysat, Lizzie would still be here. There was no changing that and it was something she would have to live with for the rest of her life. She had never returned to Purity after that summer, but Lizzie's death had left its mark on her and it was not long after that the panic attacks began. Her mother had sent her to a counsellor, a kindly woman who had taught her techniques to deal with them. After that first year they had started to ease, but it hadn't taken long under Caleb's control for them to exacerbate.

Balancing the grocery bags between her left arm and knee, Nell unlocked the front door, the stale waft of mothballs and neglect hitting her. Leaving the door open she made her way past the reception desk and down the long hallway to the kitchen. Behind her came a banging noise and she swung around, heart in mouth as a couple of cans toppled from one of the bags, crashing to the floor. The hallway was empty. Nothing was out of place. She glanced at the open front door for a moment, her mouth dry, half expecting Caleb to appear.

'Hello? Is anyone there?'

There was no response and she immediately felt foolish. Of course no-one was there. She was in an old house that groaned and creaked, and lack of sleep, together with her anxieties about leaving Caleb, were making her paranoid and jumpy. Bending down she retrieved the cans from the floor and slipped them back in the sack. During her grocery trip she had purchased a new coffeemaker. She would get it working, have a cup of coffee to sooth her frazzled nerves, then start giving the house the clean it desperately needed. It was all good.

She had nearly seen him.

As he made his way round to the rear of the house and into the woods, back towards where he had left his car, he grinned at their close encounter and his lucky escape. Of course, he could have told her he was stopping by to welcome her back to the island, but it would still beg the question of how he had gotten into the house and what he was doing there. He didn't want to unnecessarily rouse her suspicions. The less Nell O'Connor knew the better.

If things became a problem then he would take care of it.

3

Alex Cutler could hear the yelling before he had even entered Purity Police Department. He recognised both voices. Jenna Milborn, mad as hell and swearing a blue streak, while one of his deputies, Tommy Dolan, tried to reason over the top of her. Alex knew Jenna's husband, Curtis, was in the holding cell, having received a late-night call from Tommy asking how long he should keep him.

'Let him sweat it out,' had been Alex's response. 'I'll deal with him when I get in.'

Curtis was steaming drunk when Tommy had arrested him and by now would be nursing a monster hangover. Alex purposely took a longer route on his morning run, an extra ten minutes in the shower, figuring he would drag out Curtis's torment for as long as possible.

He pushed open the reception door, coffee cups in hand, heading down the corridor by the front desk towards the main office. Ruby, his receptionist, wasn't in yet and he would have Curtis and Jenna out of the way before her shift started, knowing she'd gone to school with Jenna and would find the encounter awkward.

Jenna rounded on him as he entered the office, hands on hips, her perfume overpowering the room. 'Chief Cutler, please have a word with your deputy. Curtis has been locked up all night and didn't do a damn thing wrong.'

It wasn't the first time the woman insisted on defending her loser husband, and it wouldn't be the last. Alex clocked the darkening bruise on her red tear-stained cheek, careful to keep his temper in check. He handed one of the coffees to Tommy.

'How'd you get the bruise, Jenna?'

'I tripped over the dog.'

'Again?'

'Damn mutt's always getting in the way.'

'And if it wasn't the dog, I guess it would have been the door or the wall or the stairs.'

'What can I say? I've got two left feet.' Although Jenna glared at him, she had the good grace to look away when Alex raised a questioning brow. 'You had no right to keep Curtis locked up all night.'

'One of your neighbours called it in.' Tommy piped up. 'People were worried. Curtis was drunk and mad, and he was threatening you. It was for your own safety.'

Jenna snorted. 'Oh, I know who. That nosy bitch, Polly Rosenberg. She needs to learn to mind her own business. Curtis had a few beers and he gets a little over-excitable is all. It's nothing I can't handle and I sure as hell don't need you interfering in our marriage.'

'So, you're not going to press charges?'

'Why the hell would I press charges? I told you he didn't do this. I tripped over the dog.'

Alex took a drag of his coffee and studied her, sympathy softening his anger. He guessed she had been pretty once; her copper hair framing an angular face, with cheekbones now too gaunt to be striking, her pale blue eyes hard when they had likely once been soft. Harsh lines cut around her eyes and mouth, making her look older than her twenty-eight years. He had only ever known Jenna as Curtis Milborn's wife. He doubted she had been this bitter before she had met him.

'You're gonna have to one day, Jenna. You think you can handle him, but one day he'll take things too far and we won't be around to help you.'

She shook her head defiantly, face twisted with anger. 'You think you know me? You know nothing about me. Now let my husband out of that damn cell.'

Alex gave her a lingering look, frustrated she wouldn't let them help her.

'What you want to do, Chief?' Tommy sounded hesitant. It was uncomfortable for him too. Like Ruby, he had gone to high school with Jenna. 'You want me to fetch him out?'

Alex shook his head. 'No. I'll get him.' He angled a look at Jenna. 'I need a chat with him before he's released.'

Seeing the guesthouse in daylight, beams of sunlight highlighting the dust and cobwebs, the months of neglect, Nell realised it was going to need a lot more than a damn good clean. Carpets needed replacing, walls needed plastering, and the roof needed retiling. It crossed her mind she could always sell the place. There had been a buyer interested when she had taken it off the market. Perhaps she would be better with a smaller house or apartment, something that didn't require so much work? For now, she set about making the place habitable. The kitchen came first and while she set to work with bleach and detergent, the washing machine hummed with sheets and towels. Nell had purchased a radio in town and the station she had tuned in to was knocking out hits from the seventies and eighties, making her feel less alone. Silence reminded her of the home she had shared with Caleb back in Chicago. She wouldn't have it here.

It was dusk when she finally stopped. The kitchen was clean, the groceries stored away, and her bed remade with fresh linen. There was a long way to go, but it was a start. Starving hungry but too exhausted to cook, Nell threw a frozen pizza into the oven and poured herself a glass of wine. While she waited for her dinner she took the stairs to the third floor, which she'd yet to explore. The hallway led to four of the former guest rooms and she gave each a perfunctory glance before making her way up the narrow attic staircase. This room had always been Nell's favourite and although Bella had only used it for storage, the two wide windows built into the roof afforded stunning views out over the ocean. Whenever she wanted to be alone she had snuck up to the attic and climbed out onto the roof. Even as a child she had been able to appreciate the beauty of nature, the forest green of the pine trees cutting a path along the cliff, the pale sand of the beach a stark contrast to the rugged jutting rocks that disappeared into the sea. The ocean never failed to hold her attention and she loved its moods, loved how the calm crystal waves gently lapping against the sand could become wild in an instant. The scent of the sea never changed though, its wonderful saltiness permeating her senses.

She unlocked the door, expecting the room to still be filled with junk. She wasn't disappointed. Junk could be cleared though and this wide airy space would make a perfect studio, especially when the morning sun cut a beam of light across the attic floor. Clearing a path through the junk she found the window covered in a film of dust. Nell traced her finger over it before trying the catch. It took a hard shove, but the window opened and the sound of the ocean filled the room – the salty air mixing with the mustiness – and a thousand childhood memories returned.

With the memories returned the longing to paint, something she hadn't felt in a while.

Before she had met Caleb, Nell had felt a need to tell a story on canvas. He had quashed the free-spirited nature of her artwork and made it all about profit; her work had become a chore to the point where she loathed picking up a paintbrush. The old excitement, the need to create burning inside her, brought a heady rush. By leaving Caleb she had no choice but to sacrifice her career, knowing she had to disappear completely so he could never find her. It didn't mean she had to give up painting though. She could still do it. Do it for herself. And hopefully now she was free of him, the magic would return.

She spent a few minutes at the window, wineglass in hand, watching the sun set against pink hues in the dusky sky, streams of silver flickering across the calm ocean surface. A few boats were still out. It was only September and people would be making the most of the mild weather before winter took hold.

Her belly grumbled, reminding her the pizza was in the oven. Reluctantly closing the window she turned to leave the attic. As she made her way past the boxes she had moved to clear a path to the window, she spotted something on the wall. Curious, she crossed the room and knelt down. It was ink and Nell recognised the writing as belonging to Clarke.

The name *Sarah* was repeated five times, the writing in block capitals becoming more aggressive as it trailed further down the wall. Nell frowned; she didn't remember anyone here with that name. It was definitely Clarke's writing so maybe she was a friend or a girlfriend? Her cousin had always been so awkward and shy around girls though. Perhaps she had been a guest he'd had a crush on, or maybe she had worked at the guesthouse? Puzzled, she went downstairs to get her pizza.

4

The trick was to lure them into accompanying him willingly.

It would have been easy to follow his prey, to grab them when they least expected, but there was no challenge in that, and it made it less of a game. If he wanted them to come willingly, he had to work for it, to charm them. And that brought with it its own satisfaction, a little like foreplay. It also allowed him to see the exact moment where they realised they had been duped, when they understood the flirtation and promise of a fun night was actually a ruse and they were about to fight for their lives. A fight they never won.

He had been doing this for long enough to know the stakes and understand rules had to be followed. He was a careful man who planned everything out meticulously and never cut corners. He had learned the hard way a long time ago that the tiniest mistake could be his undoing. Like a stone dropping into a lake, the ripple effect reached far and could have devastating consequences. He would never make that mistake again.

The lady who would be fighting for her life tonight was called Penny.

He had picked her up in a bar along the marina in a little coastal town called Winchester, learned the guy she was supposed to be hooking up with had let her down, and she was drowning her sorrows rather than returning home alone to her apartment.

Penny was perfect. Slim and tanned, her pretty face framed by a sharp blonde bob. She was nursing a margarita when he started talking to her and he could tell from her puffy eyes she had been crying. He bought her three more margaritas and watched her knock them back while nursing his soda. As the alcohol took hold, Penny's tongue loosened and she told him all about her messy break-up with her ex-boyfriend and how she had joined a dating site, wanting to find someone, only to be messed around by losers, in particular this latest guy, Dan, who she had met once, but who had now let her down twice at the last minute, claiming he had to work late. Lie or no lie, he figured Dan had had a lucky escape. The more she talked the more he realised Penny was self-absorbed, condescending and overly opinionated. Despite being thirty, she liked to play the 'poor little me' card, choosing to blame everyone in her life for her failures. By the third margarita her incessant whiny chatter was grating on him. She was easy pickings and he was going to enjoy snuffing the life out of her.

When she was suitably drunk, enough to dull her rational thought process, but not enough for her to pass out on him, he settled the tab, cash of course, and asked the bartender to call her a cab.

'But it's still early. Why don't we go on somewhere else?'

'I have to work tomorrow.'

Never seem too keen. Always make it their idea.

'Me too. It's not late.'

'Look, you've had a few drinks. Why don't I put you in a cab and maybe we can meet up in a couple of nights?'

The bartender was listening to the exchange, waiting to know about the cab. That was good.

'Come on, don't be a killjoy. Why don't we take the party back to my place? Or yours?' Penny gave him a hopeful smile. It came across as desperate.

'We only met an hour ago.'

'Are you a prude?' She poked at him playfully. 'I'm not.'

'Are you sure it's not the alcohol talking?'

Leaning forward she caught a handful of his hair and pressed her mouth against his. He could smell the alcohol on her breath and kept his lips closed, refusing to let her tongue pass. She was too drunk to notice the slight and stepped back victoriously.

'It's me talking. So, what do you say?'

He made a show of shrugging helplessly at the bartender. The guy grinned back. They both knew Penny was a sure thing. He faked a charming smile for Penny, before winking at the bartender.

'I guess you'd better put a hold on the cab.'

Penny leaned in, traced her fingertip across his moustache then back over his lips. She smiled seductively before leaning in for another kiss.

'I knew you'd come around.'

Smiling back, the anticipation of slitting her smooth throat ear to ear almost too much to bear, he followed her out of the bar.

Banging downstairs awoke Nell.

She had worked hard all day, was dog-tired when she crawled into bed, but her mind had been too alert for sleep. After tossing and turning in frustration for close to an hour she had turned on the nightlight and picked up her book, hoping a few chapters might help relax her. It was because of Caleb she was on edge, she knew that. During the day it was easier to believe her plan of escape was going to work, but come night-time the familiar demons came out to play, knocking her confidence and filling her with self-doubt. She guessed it would be a long while before she stopped looking over her shoulder.

The nightlight was still on, her book on the bed open at the chapter she had been reading when she'd dozed off. At first Nell wondered if she had dreamt the noise, but as she absently rubbed at the cramp in the back of her neck, it came again and she froze, panic searing through her veins. Although she told herself not to overreact, that it was probably something simple and explainable, Caleb's face loomed in her mind. He had told her he would never let her leave him, but she had foolishly tried.

Caleb isn't here. You're being irrational. Go downstairs and you'll see.

Setting the book to one side, Nell threw back the comforter and climbed from the bed, her legs rubbery as she crept towards the door. There was no way she was going to fall asleep until she had checked the noise out. She eased the door open, relieved at the dark silence that met her. Not daring to turn on the light she quietly made her way to the bannister, peering over. The only sound that came from below was the ticking of the grandfather clock. She inched her way down the stairs. As she reached the bottom step the banging came again and Nell almost lost her footing. She clung to the stair rail, recognising the sound as the front door. Nervously edging forward she looked down the hall-way, and nearly lost it when she spotted the door was wide open.

She had locked it before going to bed, she knew she had.

As she contemplated her next move, wanting to lock the door, but scared of what or who might be in the house with her, a figure blocked the doorway. Recognising the cold perfect white smile, Nell froze.

'I told you I would never let you leave me, you little bitch.' Caleb stepped inside the house and kicked the door closed behind him. In his hand he held a knife. As he slowly, tauntingly, walked towards her, he ran his finger along the blade.

Nell willed her legs to work, knew from the look on his face that he was going to hurt her, or worse. As he neared she tried to turn, run back up the stairs. Her legs were leaden and wouldn't support her. He caught hold of a handful of her hair and she lost her balance, falling flat on her face. Caleb roared with laughter, tightening his grip in her hair.

'Clumsy useless Nell, how did you ever think you would outsmart me?'

He smashed her face against the stair edge and the blinding pain had Nell screaming, the metallic taste of blood filling her mouth. She cried out as he dragged her up the stairs by her hair, then they were in her bedroom and he was straddling her on the bed, the knife glinting dangerously.

'Please don't hurt me. Please! I'll come home with you, I'll do anything you want. Just don't hurt me!'

She was trembling uncontrollably, her chest tightening and her breathing growing erratic. The twisted smile he gave as he traced the edge of the knife down the side of her cheek reminded her how much he enjoyed her fear.

'Poor, pathetic, useless Nell. You are nothing without me.' Setting the knife down on the nightstand he caressed her cheek gently with the pad of his thumb before moving his hand down to her throat and gripping tightly.

Nell struggled for air. 'No, please.'

'You betrayed me, Nell. I warned you what would happen if you ever tried to leave me.'

'Please.'

Then his hand was gone and he had hold of the pillow, pressing it against her face. Nell thrashed beneath him, unable to breathe, her screams muffled.

She was tangled in the sheets, sweating profusely, when she screamed herself awake. It took a moment in the darkness to realise it had been a dream: she was alone in the room; the light was off, her book on the nightstand. There had been no banging and Caleb wasn't in the house. He never had been.

Nell flicked on the nightlight, which cast a warm glow around the room. She glanced at the alarm clock. 03.38. Her heart was racing, she couldn't stop shaking.

The night was going to be a long one.

5

Nell worked on the house up to the weekend, leaving only to restock groceries and for a walk along the beach. The kitchen needed remodelling, but it was now clean and functional, as was the main living room, her bedroom and the bathroom she had been using. The attic was still in the process of being decluttered and the dumpster she had hired was already over half full. The size of the project, and knowing she had only touched the surface, had her wondering again if she had taken on too much and perhaps selling might be the wiser idea. Her bones ached from the physical labour and, when she sank into the tub early Friday evening for a well-deserved soak, she contemplated getting in touch with her realtor. The place would make a fantastic home for a family. There was a ton of space both inside and out, and the property's location was far enough out of town to offer wonderful views and seclusion – the nearest neighbour was half a mile away – yet it wasn't too isolated from all the necessary amenities.

As she relaxed in the tub, she allowed herself to fantasise about what she could do with the place if she had the money. It was a pipe dream. Her paintings had sold well, but that had been thanks to Caleb's connections. She no longer had those, and she had left much of the money she had earned, leaving it tied up in joint accounts, and some stocks. It was frustrating, but worth it to escape his control.

Nell thought back to the nightmare she had experienced on her second night in the house. It had felt so real at the time and she hadn't dared sleep with the light off since. Although it had just been a dream, it served as a reminder of what she had escaped.

He was still calling and texting relentlessly. She had been tempted to contact her service provider and ask them to block his number from her cell, but she wanted to keep tabs on him. She knew he would be trying to track her down and she didn't want him ever having the element of surprise, so for the time being she allowed the calls and the messages to come, ignoring all of them.

Thoughts of Caleb had the muscles in her neck and shoulders tensing, making her question if she had covered her tracks well enough. If he ever found her he would likely kill her, she was almost sure of it. Nell forced her mind to refocus. She was free of him and couldn't allow him to still have this level of control. She drew deep breaths, turning her thoughts to those of dinner. She had picked up a lobster on her last trip into town and needed to decide how to cook it. Settling on a risotto she drained the tub and reached for a towel.

A banging door somewhere downstairs startled her. Immediately her thoughts returned to the nightmare. This time she wasn't asleep. Feeling vulnerable in her nakedness she stepped from the tub and wrapped her bathrobe around her, knotting the belt with shaking fingers, aware she had locked the front door before going upstairs. Ignoring the temptation to call out she quietly stepped into her bedroom and crept across to the door. Maybe she had imagined the bang? Although it was the most comforting thought, she knew it wasn't true. The sound of footsteps creaking against the stairs drove that point home. Oh God, he had found her. She swallowed hard, glanced at her cell phone charging on the nightstand. She had to call the cops. As she reached for her phone a voice called out and she jumped almost out of her skin.

'Nell?'

Relief washed over her and immediately she felt like an idiot for being so skittish.

Michael.

As the panic subsided she chided herself for overreacting. It wasn't Caleb. He hadn't found her. This was Purity, an island where folks knew one another and looked out for each other, and it had a low crime rate.

Except for what happened to Lizzie.

She pushed thoughts of her oldest best friend out of her mind and threw open the door, grabbing her brother in a bear hug.

'Hey you.' He scooped her up, seeming pleased to see her. At five ten, Nell considered herself tall, but Michael dwarfed her by a good six inches. With him here, everything felt right.

He released her and held her at arm's-length for an appraising look.

'You're shaking.'

'You scared me sneaking in here.' She swiped at him, tried to shrug it off.

'I called out. Didn't you hear me?'

She shook her head, overcome with relief. 'I was in the tub in a world of my own. Hey, how did you get in anyway?'

'Umm, through the front door.' Michael narrowed his eyes. 'You should really start locking it. I know we're on an island, but you're out here all alone. Anyone could have walked straight in the house. If that asshole shows up here–'

'He won't. He has no idea about this place. Besides, I did lock the front door.' She had, hadn't she?

'You sure? Because I walked right in.'

'Yeah, well...' Except, now Nell doubted herself. How else had Michael got in the house? A little uneasy, she changed the subject.

'What are you doing here, anyhow? I thought you and Newt weren't due back until tomorrow.'

'The hotel was a dive and we couldn't face another night there, so we decided to head home early.' Michael squeezed her arm. 'Plus, of course, there was the bonus of seeing you.'

He was right on that count. They hadn't caught up in over two years, when Michael and Newt had come to visit her, and Nell had missed him. They were half siblings; same father, different mother, Michael the oldest by thirteen years, and aside from their father, who had skipped out years earlier, he was Nell's only remaining relative.

'Newt and I would love you to come by the house this evening. It's still warm out and we figured we'd throw a few steaks on the barbecue, make the most of the weather.'

Nell thought about her lobster risotto. It could wait till tomorrow. Time catching up with her brother was far more precious. Plus, she wanted the chance to get to know Newt better; having only met him the one time Michael brought him to Chicago. 'Sure. That sounds great. You want me to bring dessert?'

'No need. We've got everything covered. Head on over when you're ready.'

He kissed her on the forehead. 'It's good to have you back, Nell.' She knew he was referring to her leaving Caleb, but it was a conversation for another time. Instead, she squeezed his hand. It felt good to be home.

If she was going to Michael and Newt's for dinner, she needed to take something. Of course Michael would wave the gesture away, reminding her it was a casual get together, but still Nell felt she couldn't turn up empty-handed. Wine was the obvious choice, but of the two bottles she had bought on her last grocery trip, one sat empty, while the other was only two thirds full. She'd have to detour into town first. For clothing she didn't fuss, thinking only about the evening temperature. Jeans and a clean T-shirt would do fine. Opting for her favourite red one, she quickly dressed, applied mascara and lip gloss and, after fussing with her hair for a couple of minutes, decided to leave it down. She grabbed her purse, slipped on sneakers and, almost as an afterthought, picked up her denim jacket. She would have it in the car in case the temperature dropped. Leaving the hall light on – knowing how much she hated returning to a dark house – she let herself out of the front door, this time double-checking she had locked it. Satisfied the house was secure, she got into her car and headed into town, heading for the main super-market where she purchased a bottle of chardonnay and a bouquet of daisies and yellow roses for her hosts. She was making her way across the parking lot, had almost reached her car, when she heard a male voice.

'Nell O'Connor?'

She swung around, eyes narrowing at the man standing in front of her. Tall, slim with dark hair curling down to his shoulders, she recognised his face, but took a second to place him. Then it clicked and she immediately felt bad.

'Sam.'

It was the first time she had seen him since Lizzie's death. He had been fourteen at the time, so young to have to deal with such a traumatic experience, and harsh lines around his eyes and mouth showed the burden he had carried. He started to take a step towards her then evidently changed his mind.

'I heard you were moving back, but I wasn't sure I believed it.'

Nell had been dreading this encounter and had secretly hoped Lizzie's family might have moved away so she didn't have to face them. Although they had never blamed her for Lizzie's death, she still carried the guilt, convinced it should have been her in the Dolans' house that night.

'How are you, Sam?' It was a question that felt both insensitive and necessary at the same time. She had to ask. It had been over eighteen years.

'How am I?' He seemed to ponder the question for a moment, staring at Nell almost as if she wasn't there and it was a blank space he was looking at. Then his gaze hardened, his dark eyes locking on hers. 'How do you think I am? Seriously, tell me, Nell. How do you think I am? You put my family through hell.'

Nell stayed silent. He was agitated, angry even, and there wasn't a damn thing she could say to him to make things right. She had said sorry a thousand times over and, even though she still desperately was, it was a word that wouldn't cut it now. Sam's parents had always been so kind to her, never blaming her for what happened, but perhaps they were wrong and she deserved their wrath.

'You should've stayed away. It's been hard enough. We don't need to see your face, reminding us that Lizzie is no longer here.'

Nell clenched the bottle of wine tightly in her hand. 'It should have been me, Sam. Don't think I don't know that. I think about her all the time, I promise you I do. I wish I could go back and take her place.'

'So do I, Nell.' Sam gave her a cold smile and a chill went through her. 'So do I.'

Then he turned away and was gone.

Michael O'Connor and Newton Trainor shared a beach house on the south side of the island; a pretty white stone cottage with pale blue shuttered windows and a wide decked area spilling onto the beach, perfect for entertaining. Michael was the labourer, able to build and plaster and generally restore the property – which had a couple of years back been little more than a neglected shack – but Newt had the designer's eye. It was his creative streak that had been responsible for giving the cottage its warm and homey feel, from the stringed lanterns woven into the overhead framework of the decking, to the scattered colourful cushions, to the various plants strewn around both inside and outside the house, one of which Teddy was currently cocking his leg up against.

Alex clocked him in the nick of time and called out to him.

'Teddy! No!'

The mutt glanced his way with a guilty look and skulked away from the plant, relieving himself on the sand before returning to the deck with a contrite look on his face. Tongue panting, one blue eye, one brown eye, both looking guilty, he rested his head against Alex's leg and gazed adoringly at his master.

Newt shook his head. 'That dog is a law to himself.' He glanced at Sasha, lying quietly in the corner, occupied with one of the dog chews Michael had given them on arrival. 'Now that one I get. This one, you've got your work cut out with.'

'Yeah.' Alex took a slug of his beer, narrowing his eyes at Teddy, before ruffling the fur behind his ears. 'But he'll be worth it.'

He had acquired the dog just over a month ago when visiting the pound in East Haven, only intending to drop off a cheque, but having been suckered into meeting the latest residents. Teddy had been found wandering the streets, no tag and no chip, a fifty shades-of-everything dog with crafty eyes and a dopey smile. His shaggy grey-and-white coat had been trimmed, but it didn't make him any less scruffy. Alex was sold. He didn't need another dog, already had Sasha – who he'd adopted from the same shelter four years earlier – but he found himself reasoning that she would like a canine companion, that Teddy was such a goofball maybe no-one else would take a chance on him. And so the cheque was exchanged for the mutt currently sitting in front of him, and again he wondered what the hell he had been thinking, though he knew deep down Teddy had already wormed his way in and wouldn't be going anywhere.

Right now he had caught the scent of the steaks Newt had thrown on the barbecue and raised his nose to the air, looking thoughtful.

'Don't you even think about it, buddy.'

Newt chuckled. 'Can you watch this for a minute? I need to make the cocktails.'

'Cocktails?' Alex asked dubiously.

'Nell is coming over. I want her to try my strawberry daiquiris. You want one.'

'No.'

'You sure?' Newt teased.

'Trust me, I'm good with my beer. But go make your fancy drinks. I've got you covered.'

'Thanks.' Newt waved the tongs at Teddy before handing them over. 'And you, stay away from my steaks. Touch them and you're going on the barbecue.' Teddy looked up with eyes full of an innocence Alex had already learned was an act.

Out on the decking alone, he took time out to appreciate the moment. He had been an islander now for five years, but watching the sun setting across the ocean was a view he would never tire of. Here with this backdrop, good friends, his dogs and a few steaks on the barbecue, this was it. For him, nothing else mattered. Flipping the steaks, he took another sip of beer, hearing the sound of the doorbell chime above the low soulful voice of Stevie Wonder feeding through the speaker system. The barbecue had been thrown as a sort of welcome home thing for Michael's sister, Nell. Alex had never met her, but Michael talked about her often. He knew she had left the island years before and was an artist living in Chicago. Michael had made it clear over the years that her boyfriend was bad news. Apparently she had finally ditched the guy and was moving into the guesthouse she had inherited from her aunt. The place had stood empty since Clarke Golding's death and Alex had been up there on more than one occasion to deal with kids trying to break in. He glanced at the patio doors, wondering if this was her, his heart sinking when he recognised the shrill girlish giggle of Autumn Eastman and realised this was another set up.

Despite Alex's protestations, Michael and Newt had decided between them that he needed to settle down and over the past year there had been sneaky matchmaking attempts to pair him with various women. None of them had worked. He was quite capable of getting a date when he wanted one, and preferred to keep things casual. Autumn worked at one of the hair salons in town. She was a sweet girl and Alex knew she had a crush on him, but he wasn't interested in any kind of romantic liaison with her. Michael was supposed to be his best friend. He seriously needed to stop doing this.

The moment he had been enjoying ruined, he faked a smile as Autumn stepped onto the decking, daiquiri in hand, closely followed by Newt. Annoyed as he was, he couldn't bring himself to be mean to the girl, though it didn't stop him shooting Newt a look over her head.

'Hey, Alex. How are you?' She was petite and buxom, the pale sundress she wore swamping her small frame. He could tell she was also nervous, from the way she giggled after the question and tucked her hair behind her ear in a self-conscious gesture.

'I'm good, Autumn. You?'

The doorbell rang again and Newt conveniently excused himself, a grin on his face. Alex made small talk with Autumn as he continued to flip the steaks, realising that for the moment he was trapped. As she sidled closer, so did Teddy, until eventually he was nuzzled up against her leg. Autumn stepped back, as if she had been scalded by the flames.

'Oh my God, what was that?'

Alex glanced down. 'Just Teddy, my dog.' Teddy grinned up at her and Autumn hesitantly took a step back, eyeing him warily.

'He's kinda big. Does he bite?'

'Only when he's hungry.'

'Seriously?' Looking alarmed Autumn took another step back, tripping over the hem of her dress. With a thud she fell back, landing on her ass and Teddy immediately moved in to lick her face. As he slobbered over her, paws up on her pale sundress, Autumn squealed in panic.

'Teddy. No!' *Fuck!*

When the dog ignored him, Alex grabbed him by the collar and yanked him back. He held his free hand out to Autumn. She took it while eyeing Teddy warily. 'He's fine. I was joking. He's a big softie.'

Autumn didn't look convinced.

'Everything okay out here?'

'It's fine.' Alex turned to Michael, aware Autumn still had hold of his hand. Beside his friend stood the blonde woman he'd had a run in with on the mainland. Michael had his arm draped around her shoulder and a proud smile on his face.

'Alex, I want you to meet my sister, Nell. Nell, this is my best friend, Alex.'

She was not what he had imagined. He had figured the blonde for a tourist. Never in a million years had he expected her to be the sister Michael talked so much about. They shared the same fair hair – though Michael's was starting to grey – but that was where the similarities ended. Michael was like a lumbering bear; heavyset and tall, with a ruddy complexion and aquiline features, while Nell was softer. She had height, but was slim in build with a pale angular face and wide-set amber eyes. She looked younger too, maybe early thirties, closer to Alex's own age. They hadn't gotten off on the right foot, but hell, she was Michael's kid sister, and he would try to look past first impressions. Pulling his hand free from Autumn's iron grip, he offered it to Nell. 'Welcome home. Michael's told me a lot about you.'

It was clear from Nell's reaction she was equally surprised, flustered even.

'This is Alex?' she questioned her brother, though she took Alex's hand.

'Yeah, you guys are gonna get along great,' Michael assured her, oblivious to any tension between them.

'And I'm Autumn, Autumn Eastman,' a voice beside Alex piped up. 'I cut everyone's hair. Nice to meet you, Nell.'

'You too.' Nell smiled at them both, though she still looked uncomfortable.

'Alex is our police chief,' Michael continued. 'You might want to bring him up to speed with things, you know... just in case.'

'Michael! Everything is fine.'

'How can you be so sure? You're in Bella's house and you're all alone out there. I worry.'

'You have no need to.'

'Is there a problem?' Alex figured Michael's concern was with the ex-boyfriend. In his experience, if there was trouble it was generally a husband or boyfriend.

'No!'

'Yes!'

Nell and Michael glared at each other.

Newt chose that moment to stick his head out of the door.

'Who's up for another cocktail?'

Nell shook her head at her brother, looking relieved at the chance of a subject change. 'He's not going to let me rest until I try one of those daiquiris,' she said with a hint of a smile. 'I'll bring you one out. Anyone else want one?'

Autumn held out her glass. 'I'm about empty.'

Nell glanced briefly at Alex as he studied her, trying to figure her out. 'I'm good.'

As she disappeared into the house he raised a brow at Michael.

'Wanna tell me about it?'

His friend shook his head. 'We'll talk later.'

∾

The last guest timed his arrival as Michael was serving up the steaks. Nell had kept herself busy by offering to help Newt in the kitchen. She was still reeling from her encounter with Sam Kent, the expression on his face and the bitter words he had spoken playing like a show reel in her head. He had been so angry at her and she didn't blame him. What she had said to him, about wishing she could go back and take Lizzie's place, she had meant every word.

She was also keen to stay out of everyone's way. Michael hadn't warned her that there would be other dinner guests. It was stupid to feel overwhelmed by such a small thing, but she had expected it to just be the three of them. Plus, of course, one of those guests was the guy – the police chief – that she'd picked a fight with before even arriving back on the island, and who, it transpired, just happened to be her brother's best friend. It seemed Michael was intent on involving him in Nell's private business with Caleb. Something she intended to make clear she was not happy about as soon as they had a moment alone. She understood his concerns – was already scared enough, knowing what Caleb was capable of – but she didn't want everyone on the island knowing about her psycho ex-fiancé.

She had just finished chopping up tomatoes to go in the salad when the doorbell rang.

'That'll be my brother, Luke, and Stacey,' Newt told her.

Nell's heart sank at the thought of more new people to have to deal with, but she forced a smile on her face. Newt had been nothing but welcoming to her. As he was busy getting potatoes out of the oven, Nell wiped her hands on a towel and went to get the door.

There was no couple, just one guy who stood on the front step, more smartly dressed than the rest of them in a suit and tie. He gave her a wide grin. 'Nell, I'm guessing.'

'Hi, yes. You must be Luke?'

'I am.' He held up the bottle of champagne he carried in one hand.' I thought we could celebrate, given we're all together and soon to be related. Well, you know. Your brother, my brother...'

'Sure thing. Come on in. Newt said you were bringing–'

'My girlfriend, Stacey? She's not coming. Long story; don't ask.' He stepped into the hallway and gave Nell an impromptu kiss on the cheek. 'Anyway, nice to meet you, Nell. So, where's that brother of mine?'

Nell followed him through into the kitchen and watched him greet his brother with a fist bump, before finding room in the already rammed refrigerator for the champagne.

'Stacey?' Newt questioned.

'Not coming,' Luke told him, loosening his tie. 'She stormed out on me.'

'You didn't have to dress up especially for us you know.'

'I didn't, smartass. Some of us have to work late. Hence the fight with Stacey.'

'Again?'

'What can I say? She has a temper.'

Newt rolled his eyes at Nell. 'Drama queens, the pair of them.'

'Ha, that's rich coming from my high-maintenance gay brother.'

Luke's comment was met with a chuckle and a high five. 'Touché, little brother.'

Nell watched, amused by their banter.

'So, who else is coming?' Luke asked, picking up one of the daiquiris from the counter and taking a sip. He glanced up at Nell over the rim of the glass, his eyes a vivid light blue, framed by thick dark eyebrows. Like Newt, he was olive-skinned, though had a full head of almost black hair, which only served to accentuate the lightness of his eyes. Newt's hair had mostly receded and what was left was almost white in colour.

'We're all here,' Newt told him. 'You were the last to arrive. Michael's out back with Alex, and Autumn Eastman is here. We found out she has a crush on Alex, so Michael suggested we invite her.'

'He doesn't appreciate your matchmaking attempts, you know.'

Newt grinned. 'Only because we haven't managed to find the right girl for him yet. The night is still young. Give Autumn a chance. She might grow on him.' He grabbed the dish of potatoes. 'Come on, give me a hand here. It's time to eat. Nell, salad. Luke, plates.'

Nell followed Newt outside to the large rectangular table positioned towards the edge of the decking. The evening had cooled a little with the disappearance of the sun, but it was plenty warm enough for her to sit outside in her T-shirt. Across the expanse of beach which separated the cottage from the ocean, waves lapped gently against the sand. Autumn had positioned herself close to Alex, and sat intently hanging on to his every word as he talked with Michael; Nell chose a seat on the opposite side of the table. She had assumed they were a couple, but according to Newt and Luke, Alex was single. Not for long it seemed, if Autumn was to get her way.

'Hey, guys,' Luke greeted them, giving Michael a warm hug and raising a hand in greeting at Alex and Autumn. He took the seat next to Nell and immediately dived into the basket of bread.

'No Stacey?' Autumn sounded disappointed. 'She promised me she'd be here.'

'Sorry.' Luke shrugged, looking a little uncomfortable. 'She changed her mind.'

Conversation flowed easily during dinner, giving Nell the

opportunity to get to know the people in Michael's life a little bit better. She learned Newt and Luke had moved to Purity when Luke was still in high school. Their parents had died when Luke was a baby and Newt was in his teens, and they'd been raised by their paternal grandmother until she passed away, when Newt had taken over the role of Luke's surrogate father. She had only met Newt once before, when Michael had brought him to Chicago, but they had instantly hit it off. There were no airs and graces with him, he just wanted to please everyone. He was principal over at the local kindergarten, while Luke shared a home near the harbour with his girlfriend, Stacey, and worked as a junior partner in a law firm in East Haven.

Alex had moved to Purity five years ago, taking over from Chief Bristow when he retired, and he lived further along the beach from Michael and Newt. He said little of his life before Purity, but Nell understood he had been a cop in Portland before moving to the island.

He had his two dogs with him: Sasha, a beautiful German Shepherd, and Teddy, a bumbling buffoon of a shaggy dog. He virtually attached himself to Nell's leg at the table, eagerly wolfing down the bits of steak she kept sneaking him under the table.

The jury might still be out on Alex, but she was already falling for his dogs.

Then there was Autumn, the hairstylist. She was younger than the others; Nell guessed from her conversation topics that she was in her early to mid-twenties. A nice girl, but her flirtations were getting her nowhere. Alex was polite and friendly, but it was obvious he wasn't interested in her in a romantic way. He had a dry sense of humour and, although Nell didn't want to find him funny – still hadn't quite forgiven him for their first encounter – she found herself smiling at a few comments he made during dinner, noting most of them went straight over Autumn's head. She could tell he had an easy friendship with her brother and that he meant a lot to him, and for that reason she would give Alex a chance. Michael had always looked out for Nell and she could see he did the same for his friends. She watched him throwing back glasses of wine and whiskey, their father in her thoughts. Although Michael was nothing like Mick O'Connor – the drinking was just while socialising with friends – she worried about him heading down the same path.

Hypocrite, she told herself, glancing down at the beer she was drinking.

Blessedly, Michael had dropped talk of Caleb for the evening, so Nell was annoyed, when clearing away dishes, to have Alex follow her into the kitchen and broach the topic.

'So, I'm guessing the thing Michael is worried about is your ex-boyfriend, am I right?' he asked, dumping empty glasses into the sink and turning to face her.

Nell glanced up from where she stood, scraping leftover food off the plates into the trash. 'He's been talking to you about me?'

'He's your brother. Of course he talks about you. He's worried.'

'No, he's overreacting. There's nothing for him to worry about.'

'You seem pretty certain about that.'

'I am.' Nell hesitated, unsure how much Michael had told Alex. 'Look, I left Caleb back in Chicago and it's not like I wrote him a note saying where I had gone.'

'Does he know about your aunt's house, that you inherited it?'

'No, I never told him.'

'But he knows your brother lives here?'

'They only met once and it was a couple of years ago. He

showed no interest in Michael at the time. I doubt he even remembers his name.'

Alex cocked a brow. 'You sure?'

'I am,' Nell lied. Truth was she was terrified of Caleb finding her. Alex didn't need to know that though. She barely knew him and didn't want everyone seeing what had really happened in her relationship. She went for nonchalance. 'Anyway, it's over. I broke up with him.'

'Well... technically you didn't break-up with him, you snuck out on him while he was at work. I'm guessing he's gonna be pissed.'

Nell's jaw dropped. Michael had a lot to answer for, blabbing about her personal life to his friends. 'Don't you dare judge me,' she snapped, cheeks burning with anger. 'You know nothing about my relationship or what it was like. I had no choice but to "sneak out" as you kindly put it. Caleb is not the kind of person you break-up with face-to-face. If I had tried, he wouldn't have let me leave.'

She expected Alex to apologise for overstepping the mark, but instead he leaned back against the counter, insolently, arms folded, and gave her a pointed look, one brow cocked and a sly smile on his handsome face.

'What?'

'You pretty much just admitted it. He wouldn't have let you leave. So why are you so sure he won't figure out a way to track you down?'

She realised she had walked into a trap, revealing far more than she intended. 'Why are you so sure he will?' she countered.

'Because I know this situation: possessive controlling boyfriend or husband; sometimes even wife or girlfriend. It's my job. Don't shut your brother out when he's only trying to help. And keep your wits about you.'

'I am,' Nell insisted, but her temper was already dissipating.

She was fast learning it was difficult to stay mad at Alex. He was poking his nose into her private business and being brazen about it, but the wide, almost cheeky smile he turned on whenever he stepped too close to the mark and the teasing glint in his eyes, suggested he was too laid-back to ever take himself too seriously. That said, she didn't doubt his concern was genuine, no doubt due to both his friendship with Michael and his job.

'Have you thought about having the locks changed on your aunt's house?'

'It's on the list. Why?'

'The place stood empty for a while and we've had trouble with kids breaking in. If they managed to, so could someone else.'

'I'll take it under advisement. Are you always this interfering?'

His smile widened into a devilish grin, dimples cutting into his cheeks. 'It's my job to be.'

Nell shook her head, ignoring the flutter in her belly. He might be able to charm the pants off Autumn, but she didn't fawn so easily. 'I don't remember Chief Bristow poking his nose into other people's business this much,' she muttered wryly.

'Well, then I guess you should be glad he retired and I took over.' There it was again, that appealing sardonic humour. He was certainly nothing like Chief Bristow; that was for sure. Of course, the former police chief had seemed like an old man even when Nell had been a kid, whereas Alex was maybe in his mid-thirties. The former chief had been a kind man, if a little gruff around the edges, but he had always been a figure of authority. Alex, she guessed, would be more approachable.

'Are you guys having some kind of private party in here?'

Nell glanced up as Luke bounded in. He opened the refrigerator and pulled out the bottle of champagne he had brought with him.

'You planning on drinking that all yourself?' Alex asked wryly.

Luke grinned. 'Tempting as it is, I'm driving tonight, so a small glass for me to toast Nell's homecoming. We need some glasses!'

Nell looked in the cupboard, pulling out one of a set of kitsch flutes with pink flamingos painted on the side of them. 'Really, Michael?' she muttered to herself.

Luke's grin widened. 'Ha, I'd like to blame your brother for those, but I have to take responsibility. They were a joke gift I bought when they moved in together. I have to say I'm touched they kept them.'

Nell smiled to herself as she gathered up the rest of the glasses and followed the boys outside. It was easy to like Luke and she found herself glad Michael and Newt had returned home early from their vacation and decided to hold their impromptu barbecue.

She hadn't planned on drinking much over the course of the evening, but Newt kept topping up her glass and before she knew it she was a little drunk. Luke offered to give both Nell and Autumn a ride home and they left before midnight, with Newt promising they would have everyone over again soon.

Autumn seemed disappointed Alex hadn't asked to see her again. Like Nell, she'd drunk quite a few of Newt's cocktails and she babbled incessantly about him on the journey to her apartment.

Luke, ever the chivalrous gentleman, escorted her up to her door, making sure she was safely inside, before returning to the car to drive Nell home.

'She kept asking me if I thought he liked her,' he said,

screwing up his nose as he got back into the driver's seat. 'Is it bad I said yes?'

'Well, I guess she did put you on the spot and you didn't want to hurt her feelings,' Nell rationalised.

Banter with him was easy on the drive out to the house and Nell found herself telling him all about her dilemma over what to do with Bella's guesthouse, though she stopped short of telling him the reasons behind her move back to Purity Island. Michael had already blabbed to Alex and it was likely Newt was in the loop; the fewer people who knew about Caleb and why she had left, the better.

'Well, I guess it depends on what you plan to do with the house?' Luke reasoned. 'Do you want to hold on to it for sentimental reasons? If so, I understand. But do you need all that space? It's a big house and will cost a lot to maintain.'

'My thoughts exactly, and I'm not sure I can afford the work it needs.'

'It would make a great family home though if you could get the money together.'

'Yeah, it would. Except I don't have a family and it's just me rattling around inside the place. I know it holds a lot of memories, but I'm still kind of inclined to sell it. Free up some capital and get somewhere smaller.'

'Sounds like you've already reached a decision.'

'I'll sleep on it one more night.'

Luke dropped her outside the front of the house, killing the engine and starting to open his car door.

'It's okay. No need to get out,' Nell said, stopping him. 'Ten steps and I'm inside.'

'Well, as long as you're okay.'

'I'm sure. But thanks for the ride. I appreciate it.'

'Any time.'

On impulse she leaned across and brushed his cheek with a brief kiss. 'Goodnight, Luke, and thanks again.'

He waited until she stepped inside before driving off. Waving goodbye, she closed and locked the door, glad she had left the hall light on. Slipping out of her sneakers, she headed down to the kitchen, fishing in the refrigerator for a bottle of water. She double-checked all the locks before heading upstairs.

It had been a good night and for the first time Nell felt confident in her decision to return to Purity. Although Caleb had never been far from her thoughts, it hadn't stopped her enjoying herself. Closing her bedroom door behind her, she pulled her T-shirt over her head, throwing it on the bed, and stepped through into the bathroom, turning on the shower. As the old pipes of the house groaned and the water heated, she kicked off her jeans and looked around for the grip she needed to pile her hair up. Spying it on her dresser in front of the window, she made her way back into the bedroom. As she clipped her hair up, she glanced out into the road. A car was parked at the end of her drive. Was Luke still there?

What if it was Caleb?

She quickly stepped back from the window, conscious she was in her bra and panties, in full view of whoever it was. Clicking off the light she returned to the window.

Sam Kent sat in the driver's seat of the car, staring up at the house.

Nell sucked in a deep breath. What the hell was he doing out there? She recalled their earlier exchange: 'I wish I could go back and take her place.'

'So do I, Nell. So do I.'

Momentarily she debated what to do. Should she go outside and confront him, ask him what the hell he wanted? Maybe call the police? He wasn't breaking the law though, he was just parked in the street outside her house. As she wrestled with what next, Sam started his engine and pulled away. Nell shuddered with relief and reached for her bathrobe, deciding before she stepped into the shower that she would first go downstairs and check, for a third time, that all of the doors were locked.

Through the window she watched his tail lights disappear into the night.

7

The last person Luke expected to see when he arrived home from the barbecue was his girlfriend, Stacey. After everything that had happened earlier, he had believed it was over for good, so when she appeared in the doorway of the bedroom as he was removing his tie, a scowl on her face as she tapped the toe of her stiletto on the wooden floor, he took a step back, eyes widening.

'I thought you were gone?'

'You hoped I was gone, you mean.'

'Don't twist my words, Stacey. You know it's not true. I love you. I never meant for this to happen.'

'Well, you sure have one hell of a way of showing it! Did you have fun at the barbecue with your brother and his friends? Did you tell them why I wasn't there?'

'I told them you're jealous and possessive and you've never trusted me. Though I think they already know that. What happened tonight was your fault, Stacey. Don't try and play the victim. You have no idea how much you've hurt me.'

'I hurt you?' She took a step towards him, throwing her head back laughing when he took a step back. 'I can smell perfume on you. Who is she this time?'

Luke put his hands to his head, sighed in exasperation. 'You're crazy. There is no other woman. It's just you. It's always been you.'

'So, why can I smell her? Who the fuck is she, Luke?'

'She was no-one. You were supposed to be at the barbecue, Stacey, remember?'

When Stacey remained silent, he continued.

'Autumn was there, but you already knew that, because she was disappointed when you didn't show, and Michael's sister, Nell, has moved to the island. You would like her. She's living in Bella Golding's guesthouse.' He didn't add that Nell had been a pleasant surprise. Pretty, blonde and so very different to her brother. Stacey didn't need to know that.

'And you want her, don't you?'

'I don't! She's Michael's sister for Christ's sake.' Luke let out an exasperated sigh. 'I'm not sure what it is you want from me, Stacey? I don't know what I can give you anymore.'

'Are you asking me to leave?'

'You know I don't want that. I would give anything to fix what happened tonight.'

Stacey studied her manicured nails. 'I think it's a little too late to make things right.'

'So, you are leaving?'

She didn't answer, gave a cat-like smile and sauntered out of the room.

Luke sat down on the bed, rested his head in his hands and sucked in a deep breath. She was the only woman he had ever truly felt anything for, and he meant every word, knew he would give anything to fix the damage.

He finished undressing, slipped into bed and turned out the light, part of him hoping she would join him. She didn't and, as

he waited for sleep to pull him under, he wondered if she had
ever loved him.

She had been gone four days.

Four days, during which Caleb Sweeney had experienced
many different emotions. The first had been white-hot rage. He
had arrived home from work early Monday evening, stepping
into the townhouse they shared, irritated immediately when he
couldn't smell food cooking in the kitchen. Nell had known they
had plans, that they had to eat early so they could attend his
mother's museum benefit. When he found the kitchen empty,
the work counter clean, intimating she hadn't even started
preparing the meal, he stormed upstairs expecting to find her in
her studio, having lost track of time. She hadn't done that in a
long while, having learned the consequences the hard way.

Clearly it was time for a reminder.

He pushed open the door to the studio, surprised to find it
empty. Her tools were all in place, but there was no canvas being
worked on. Feeling a trickle of fear, he had gone into the master
bedroom. The bed was neatly made, with cushions evenly scattered across the pillows. He had called out to her then, irritation
building into anger when there was no reply. As the mist built
inside him, pounding his head, he had raced from room to room
wondering where the hell she was, promising himself she would
pay dearly for scaring him this way. She knew the rules, knew he
didn't tolerate having them broken.

As he sunk onto the edge of the bed, trying to deliberate
where she might have gone, his attention was drawn to the
closet and he noted the door to the room was slightly ajar, the
light on inside. Aggravated she would leave it this way when she
knew he needed order in his life, he got up, the anger building.

What the hell was she playing at?

He had flung the door open, half expecting to find her inside, but not prepared to find it empty of the majority of her clothes. The pretty dresses he had spent a fortune on were still mostly in place, but the everyday shirts, sweaters and T-shirts she favoured were all gone.

Panic clawed its way up his throat as he pulled open drawers, noting her jeans were missing and all of her underwear, then went through into the bathroom where the shelf that held her perfumes and creams now stood empty. Back downstairs to the hallway closet; her jackets no longer hung beside his, and her boots were gone, along with those ugly sneakers he hated to see her wear. Fear and anger balled together into furious rage and Caleb thumped his fist into the closet door, smashing through the wood, before sweeping his arm over the hallway table, knocking the china figurine he had paid a four-figure sum for, along with various picture frames, to the floor. It smashed into pieces and he kicked the table over, watching impassively as it landed on top of the shards.

Furious with Nell for daring to disobey him and with himself for trusting her not to, he skulked through to the living room and snatched up a decanter full of bourbon, and poured himself a large glass.

That fucking bitch.

He pulled out his cell phone and dialled her number, almost beside himself with rage when it went through to voicemail. She knew never to ignore his calls. He left a foul-mouthed rant, laden with threats and warnings, offering her the chance to return without consequence by midnight.

She never called back, never walked through the door and as her deadline approached, Caleb poured more bourbon, eye on the clock, plotting in his head the ways he would make her pay when he finally got his hands on her. He had drunk himself into oblivion that night, the alcohol blurring rage into sorrow. How could she do this to him? He had tried to give her everything. All she had to do was follow the rules.

When he woke early the following morning, having slept on the couch in his suit, he was hungover and ashamed. He had called her, this time leaving her a contrite voicemail, apologising for his last message and begging her to come home. He stared at his phone for over an hour, expecting her to call. Even at his most despicable he had always been able to win her around with an apology. It was while he was in the kitchen putting on the coffee pot that his phone rang and he practically leapt over the back of the couch to retrieve it from the cushion, new levels of irritation searing through him when he realised it was his secretary reminding him he had an eight o'clock appointment.

He barked at the woman to cancel it and not to disturb him for the rest of the day, flung the phone back down on the cushion and paced, hands balled in tight fists, wanting a target for the fury building deep inside of him. In an attempt to calm himself he went through to the bathroom and splashed cold water on his face. Staring into the mirror above the basin, he grimaced at his reflection. His dark brown eyes were bloodshot, his cheeks and shaven head pink with rage, even his neatly trimmed goatee looked unkempt, while the suit he had slept in made him look as rumpled as a tramp.

Nell had a lot to answer to. She was responsible for this.

Needing to take action he had called the bank and the credit card companies as soon as they opened, had her funds stopped, put a call in to the police, tried to report her as a missing person, losing his rag with the officer he spoke to when he was told it was not possible because technically she was not missing.

He called her friends, their mutual acquaintances, sucking in his anger and playing the role of the concerned doting fiancé. No-one had seen her, or if they had they weren't saying. Nell, it seemed, had disappeared without a trace, and Caleb couldn't help but suspect she had been planning this for a while. Over the next twenty-four hours he systematically tried to cut her off, leaving only her cell phone connected, aware it was the only medium he had to reach her. He spoke with the phone provider, demanded they track her cell and give him the location, raging when told this wasn't possible. She was out there somewhere and she would have to know he was looking for her. He would eventually find her. At a loss over what to do he continually called and texted her number, hoping against hope she would eventually relent and answer. The calls and messages ranged from sorrowful to enraged, and he offered up all kinds of bargains and threats, contradicting himself in every message.

Having already dealt with the banks, he turned his attention to her buyers, making it clear to everyone who had contact with Nell on a professional basis that they were not to deal with her direct and must alert him if she tried to approach them.

It was going through bank account and credit card statements online that he discovered the charge for the flight ticket to San Francisco, noting it had been purchased the day she had left. He remembered she had a friend who lived there, an old college roommate.

What the hell was her name?

Nell had already deleted and blocked him on Facebook, but he checked her other social media accounts, eventually finding her name on Nell's old Myspace page. Rosie Garcia. He managed to locate the woman, calling and e-mailing her; livid when she didn't respond. Hopping on a flight the next day, he showed up at her apartment. Rosie hadn't been pleased to see him, her knucklehead boyfriend stepping in when the confrontation threatened to get ugly. She told him she hadn't seen Nell and hadn't had any contact with her in the past couple of years. Caleb hadn't believed her but left the apartment, checking into a hotel down the street from where he discreetly stalked Rosie for two days, eventually concluding she was telling the truth. If Nell had gone to San Francisco, she hadn't made contact with her old roommate.

From San Francisco he flew straight to Ohio, heading for the town where he knew Nell had lived with her mom, but it was a fruitless exercise. Robin O'Connor had passed away and there was no family left there. Still, he stopped by the house where she had grown up, visited the high school she had attended and the diner where he knew she had worked, hoping against hope. With Ohio giving nothing he returned home frustrated, arriving back at the townhouse late Friday night.

He remembered there had been a brother, Michael, an older guy who had visited once with his boyfriend. Caleb hadn't liked him, remembered only that he drank cheap beer and told bad jokes. He wished now that he had taken more notice of who he was and where he had come from. Despite having nothing to go on he spent a couple of hours googling Michael O'Connors, irritated that the man had such a common name. Frustrated he was getting nowhere, he eventually threw his iPad on the couch.

It felt as though Nell had disappeared without a trace, but he knew there had to be a clue – something that would lead to her location – and he would rip the place apart until he found it.

8

Nell ran her fingers back through her hair in frustration as she stared at the calculations on the page. She had spent the past hour working out her finances, knew the money she had squirrelled away to see her by for a few weeks was already dwindling fast. She was going to have to start looking for a job. She had known she would have to find one eventually, that the money wouldn't last forever, but she had hoped to buy a little more time. It was also yet another reason to put the guesthouse back on the market. Deciding she needed to clear her head, she headed downstairs and grabbed her purse from the kitchen counter, figuring she would walk down to Michael's to fetch her car.

The temperature was cooler than the previous day thanks to a light northerly breeze, but the sun was out, burning bright in a cloudless sky that contrasted against the vivid blue-green swell of the ocean. Sail and fishing boats were out in abundance, bobbing on choppier waters. Nell took the path along the main road, enjoying the view through the trees of this more rocky area of coastline; her route took her down a steady incline through lush woodland until the road snaked to the right and she could see the rooftops of the houses on the outskirts of the town.

Weekends were busy on the island, a mix of locals, holiday-makers and day trippers, and the main ferry ran every couple of hours. The streets nearer to the town centre would be busy, but for now she got to enjoy the solitude of the near-empty road, the only noise coming from the birds in the trees, the distant sound of waves hitting the rocks, and her own sneakered feet beating against the asphalt.

She was about fifteen minutes from Michael's when she heard the sound of a car in the distance, approaching from behind. As it neared, the engine slowed, and Nell glanced round.

The window was wound down and Luke Trainor grinned up at her from the driver's seat as he pulled the car up alongside her.

'You walking down to get your car?'

'I am. Figured I'd better not leave it too late.'

'Hop on in. I'll give you a ride.'

Nell had been enjoying her walk, but if Luke was heading in her direction she figured she might as well catch a lift with him.

'How's your head?' he asked, as she closed the passenger door.

'Not too bad. I think I was lucky though. Your brother was a bit heavy with the rum. Autumn knocked back more of those daiquiris than I did, so I doubt she was feeling great this morning.'

'She was a little unsteady on her feet when I dropped her off last night.'

'You've been in work?' Although Luke was dressed casually in jeans and sweater, she noted he'd moved his briefcase from the passenger seat when she had climbed in the car.

'Yeah, I had a few bits I needed to finish up in the office. I've just dropped some papers off with one of your neighbour's, Bob Pilgrim.'

Another name Nell remembered. She pictured the face of the cranky old farmer, recalling he had scared the hell out of her and Lizzie one time when they had accidentally trespassed on his land while hiking through the woods. 'I'm surprised he's still around. He had a hell of a temper on him, I'd have thought he'd have given himself a heart attack by now.'

'Still has. Hence why I didn't keep him waiting for his papers. Not one of my favourite clients.' Luke glanced across at her. 'So, did you wake up with a fresh perspective about what to do with the house?'

'Yes, I think I'm gonna put it back on the market. I thought I'd go talk to the realtor after I picked up my car.'

Luke nodded. 'Well, I'm happy to handle the legal side of things for you. Twenty per cent discount?'

'That would be great. Thank you.'

Nell toyed with telling him about Sam Kent, but if she told him about Sam then she would have to get into the whole thing about what happened to Lizzie. Chances were he already knew the story; almost certainly he would know about Lizzie's death. It was early days and she didn't know Luke well enough yet, plus the conversation between them had so far been light. She didn't want to ruin things. She would visit the realtor, get the house back on the market, and look for somewhere more manageable in town. Once she was out of Bella's house, she'd no longer have to worry about Sam Kent. No need to burden anyone with what had happened.

Luke pulled his car up outside Michael and Newt's cottage, killing the engine and following Nell out of the car. Michael had already heard them arrive and stood on the front door step, beer in hand, waiting for them. He didn't miss the look that Nell shot him.

'Hey, it's Saturday afternoon. I'm just kicking back and relaxing.' As though to make his point, he took a healthy swig and grinned at her.

'I never said a word.' Nell pecked him on the cheek, brushed past him into the house, noting the three empty beer bottles already stood on the kitchen counter, her thoughts immediately going back to their father. She kept her concerns to herself though, determined not to become a nagging sister.

Newt came in from the decking, greeting her with a hug and a kiss. 'Hey, Nell, Luke, great timing, I just put the coffee pot on.'

As the four of them sat on the back deck chatting, Nell decided to bring her brother up to speed with her decision to sell the guesthouse. She had assumed he would favour the idea of having her living closer to town, so she was surprised by both his reaction and his proposal.

'You don't want to do that.'

'I don't? Why?'

Her brother shared a glance with Newt. They both looked excited.

'Listen, Newt and I have been wanting to talk to you about something.'

'You have?'

'Yes. We know the guesthouse is run down and needs a lot of work, but we have a proposition for you.'

'Go on.' Nell was intrigued.

'We want to help you renovate the house and reopen it as a guesthouse.'

'You want to reopen it?'

'Yes. Of course, the final decision is with you. It's your place, but we have savings, enough to do the work needed and then some more. Plus, of course, I have the contacts to do much of the work. Your guesthouse, but we go partners on the business. We could put in a pool and a hot tub, make the place fancy. There's too much potential there to sell.'

'Wow.' Nell needed a moment to take it all in. She had no idea Michael had been harbouring these ideas. 'It's a big project to take on.'

'It is, but between us we could do it.'

'And who would run it?'

'You would, with our help. Newt has been thinking about a career change for a while. He's pretty good in the kitchen. I can look after the upkeep of the place and any maintenance issues, and we can always look at employing extra help if we need it.'

'You've been giving this a lot of thought, haven't you?'

Newt nodded. 'We talked about doing this a couple of years ago, if the right property came along. When you inherited the guesthouse and first put it up for sale, we discussed making you an offer then, but we couldn't get enough cash together. Then you decided to move back and Michael suggested the partnership.'

Nell's head was reeling and she needed more time to fully process what Michael and Newt were proposing. She glanced at Luke, wondering if he had known about his brother's plans.

The look on his face suggested he hadn't, as he seemed as surprised as Nell at the sudden turn of events. 'I never realised you wanted to do this,' he said to Newt. 'I thought you loved your job at the school.'

'I did love it... still do at times, but this is something I've been thinking about, wanting to do for a long time. I think we could turn the guesthouse into something special. What do you say, Nell?'

Bella would have approved, Nell thought, and it would be a fitting legacy to her aunt, but it was a hell of a project to take on. She needed to give the proposition some serious thought. It wasn't something she could make a decision on instantly.

'It's something to consider. I need time to think it over though. It's a big commitment and I don't want to take it on unless I'm sure I'm doing the right thing.'

'Completely understandable,' Michael agreed. 'Take all the time you need.'

'It's weird, you know, being back in the house, but Bella and Clarke not being there.'

'I guess it would be. You're up there alone, so the house is going to feel empty. I wish you would come and stay with us for a while, just until you decide what to do. I don't like you in that house alone. If Caleb…'

'Caleb won't find me,' Nell insisted through gritted teeth, annoyed that Michael was openly talking about him in front of Newt and Luke. She guessed Newt knew all about her past relationship, though he had been polite enough to keep his nose out, but Luke didn't, and much as Nell liked him, she still barely knew him. She could tell from the look on his face he was intrigued to know more about who Caleb was.

'By the way, I've been meaning to ask you. Who is Sarah?' she asked, changing the subject abruptly, fighting to keep her tone light.

'Sarah?' Michael's brow furrowed.

'I was up in the attic and her name is scrawled on the wall. It looks like Clarke's writing.'

'Sarah?' Michael repeated, looking at Newt and Luke. Luke shrugged his shoulders, shaking his head, while Newt pressed his finger to his lips looking deep in thought. 'It's quite a common name. There are a few Sarahs on the island.'

'Wasn't there a Sarah who worked for Bella a few years back?' Newt nodded to himself. 'She was a pretty girl with long blonde hair. You must remember her, Luke.'

'Vaguely, though it was a long time ago.'

'Yes, I remember her,' Michael agreed. 'She worked with

Bella one summer and then ran out leaving Clarke alone. Bella was real pissed about the whole thing.'

'She was looking after Clarke?'

Michael nodded at Nell. 'Yeah, Bella was in hospital and had left Sarah to look after the guesthouse and keep an eye on Clarke, but she took off and went back to the mainland. I heard rumours that she had been offered another job.'

'So why would Clarke write her name on the wall?'

'Maybe it affected him, being left alone like that?' Newt suggested. It was possible, Nell thought. Clarke had Asperger Syndrome and his reactions had sometimes been extreme.

'Or perhaps it was another Sarah?' Luke chimed in. 'Maybe Clarke had a girlfriend or a crush?'

'Yeah, I guess.'

'Why are you so interested?' Michael asked.

Nell shrugged. 'I'm not really. I was just curious when I saw her name. Guess we'll never know who she was.'

Nell drove home instead of going into town, her original plans now shelved while she considered Michael and Newt's proposal. Her head was filled with reasons for and arguments against, and her mind was spinning by the time she pulled into the driveway. The first thing she did once inside was put on the coffee pot and grab a pen and notepad. She created 'for' and 'against' columns and started filling them. Restoring the place in honour of her aunt was top of the 'for' list, but the amount of work involved was the top 'against' and she wasn't sure how well Michael had really thought this through. She had spent enough summers with Bella to see how much work was involved in running the guesthouse. He hadn't. And yes, she would have him and Newt to help her, but she still wasn't convinced they realised how much of their time it would take.

But then there was the attic room which she longed to turn into a studio. If she sold the place she would never have that. She added 'attic' to the 'for' list.

Money was a concern, but Michael had assured her he and Newt had the financial side covered. She would need to know what kind of figure he was talking about and have to be sure there was enough in the pot to do all of the work necessary, as it was something she was unable to contribute to. For now, she put 'money' on the 'against' list, but with a question mark against it. Just until she had ascertained how much everything was going to cost. She tapped the pen against the notepad impatiently, annoyed her brain was struggling to work. What else was there to consider?

Deciding she needed some fresh air, she grabbed her jacket. A walk along the beach would clear her head and help her refocus. She crossed the road at the end of the driveway, and went through the thicket on the other side to the steep stone steps she knew led straight down onto the shore. When she had been a kid, Nell had spent a lot of time on this beach, loving that she generally had it to herself. Because it wasn't well signposted, most of the holidaymakers didn't know the pathway existed, and those who did tended to favour the less rocky beaches closer to town.

As she made her way down the steps, careful not to lose her footing on the looser stones, old summer memories flooded back. From fishing in the rock pools with Clarke, to sharing her first kiss with Matthew Johnson under the stars, after she had snuck out of her bedroom window to meet him. Then there were the times she and Lizzie had come down here, generally dreaming and planning their futures, talking about boys and proms, and how Lizzie was going to be a famous photographer, while Nell would find success through her paintings. Only one of them had lived long enough to see those dreams become a reality.

One of the first paintings Nell had sold had been of this stretch of beach, capturing the sun setting over the ocean, bathing the rocks and the water in shades of gold. It had always been one of her favourite pieces.

Right now the sun was setting again, but this time burning orange in a sky full of pink. Nell walked down to where the foamy waves lapped gently against the sand. There was a chill in the air and further along the coast she could see the last of the fishing boats heading back towards the island. It was the middle of September and in another few weeks the waters would be far quieter as winter took hold. Reaching down for a handful of pebbles, Nell took aim with each of them, throwing them as far as she could into the water. Her thoughts returned to Michael's proposition. Could they make it work?

Although the guesthouse was out of town, Bella had always attracted a lot of business. People were drawn to the old building with the fantastic views. If they restored the place to its former glory, would the tourists come back? Michael and Newt had big plans, wanting to put in a pool and a hot tub, landscape the gardens and revamp the rooms, giving the place a more sophisticated upmarket feel. It was a lot of work, but the potential was there, and if they pulled it off Nell wouldn't have to worry about finding work elsewhere.

Deciding she was going to take the plunge and accept Michael and Newt's offer she reached down for another handful of stones. The waves had washed a large pile of seaweed ashore and she pushed it back into the water with her sneaker, her toe hitting something heavy.

Assuming it was a rock, Nell reached down to pick it up and set about freeing it from the seaweed. As the green gooey plant fell away, she found herself staring at a woman's face. The skin was grey, the eye sockets empty and what was left of her mouth appeared to be open in horror. The neck had been severed neatly and the woman's body was nowhere in sight.

Nell screamed and took an unsteady step back.

Bile rose in her throat as the head, now dislodged from the seaweed, rolled a couple of feet across the sand and came to a lazy stop. Disgust burned through her and, dropping to her knees, she puked until her guts were empty. When she was done she pulled her cell phone from her jacket pocket with trembling fingers and called the police.

Her body shaking, tears burning, she sat back on her haunches and glanced warily around the empty beach. She was alone, except for the eyeless face staring up at her.

9

Tommy Dolan was the only officer available and it was with some reluctance he headed down to the beach where Nell waited with her gruesome find. He hadn't spoken to her in over eighteen years; he had been a kid when she had left, and her return to the island had awoken memories he had tried so hard over the years to bury.

She was sat on the rocks when he arrived, chin resting on her knees and her arms hugging her legs. For a moment she was sixteen again, still slender with blonde loose curls falling around her face.

Nell had always been Tommy's favourite babysitter. She only visited during the summer, but she was carefree and fun, and as a ten-year-old, he had idolised her, thought she could do no wrong. He had convinced himself that had it been her and not Lizzie in the house the night of the murder, things would have worked out differently. She would have known what to do and no-one would have died.

But Nell hadn't been there, she had left him and Emily alone with Lizzie, and he had watched the man who had broken into the house with his uncle stab Lizzie in the throat with one of his mother's kitchen knives.

Everyone had expected Tommy to be able to name Lizzie's killer and Chief Bristow had grown frustrated with him when he couldn't even offer a description. He had to live on the island; Tommy must have known who he was. But the man had worn a baseball cap and Tommy had only ever seen him from behind. He had felt useless, unable to give the adults the information they so desperately needed from him.

His parents had taken him to a child psychologist, hoping to unlock memories, but it had been to no avail and his mother had grown fearful for Tommy's safety, aware he was a witness and that the killer could come back for him. They had lived under police protection for a while, but Tommy never remembered, and the killer was never caught. Eventually life had moved on.

Nell should never have come back, but here she was, and she was living in her aunt's old guesthouse. Everything about her return made Tommy uncomfortable. It felt like the safe cocoon he had wrapped himself in might start to unfurl. He wished she had stayed away.

She heard his approach, got to her feet as he neared the bottom of the stone steps, and brushed her palms on her jeans; her face was deathly pale in the dusky light and she was visibly shaking.

Tommy wasn't sure how to greet her, wasn't even sure she would recognise him after all these years. He supposed he should have kept it official, but the situation was awkward. Everything about this was awkward.

'Hey, Nell.'

She hadn't recognised him, but the familiarity of his greeting had her looking closer and he saw the moment realisation dawned.

'Tommy? Jesus, Tommy, I can't believe it's you.'

For a moment she looked as though she wanted to hug him, but then something, it looked like regret, passed over her face and she looked plain uncomfortable. Nothing about this situation was easy and Tommy wished to hell the chief was here right now. Alex was off duty, but Tommy had left him a voicemail. Purity was a small island community with an almost zero crime rate. He was going to want to know that a head had washed up on the beach.

For now he tried to focus on the job, keep Nell on the professional and away from the personal. 'Dispatch said you found a head?'

'I, yeah...' She looked green around the gills, like she was going to puke, as she pointed across the sand towards the sea. 'Over there.'

As she appeared reluctant to go near it, Tommy approached on his own, flashlight on in the fading light, grimacing when he spotted the head lying on the sand. When he had received the call, he had initially figured it as a prank. This kind of thing didn't happen in Purity. Someone was playing a joke. But then he had been informed of the caller's name, and knew if Nell was involved it would be no joke. He couldn't help but wonder if her return to the island was responsible for this. Bad things seemed to happen around her. It was as if she attracted trouble.

He slipped on latex gloves, careful not to disturb any evidence. While he would have liked to think this was some kind of horrific accident, he could tell from the clean cut that a knife had been responsible. Which suggested someone had intentionally done this to the victim, and begged the question, where was the rest of the body?

∽

Nell was numb all over and still couldn't stop shaking. She watched Tommy work from a distance, finding it hard to believe the grown police officer before her was the same little boy she had once babysat. She still pictured him at ten years old, but here he was, all grown up, his thick tawny brown hair still neatly cut in a similar style he'd had as a boy, his eyes that deep pool of blue she remembered, but his scrawny little frame now matured into a man's. He had been a beautiful looking kid and that beauty had carried through into adulthood, though she was certain he must be broken a little on the inside. He had witnessed his babysitter's murder. It wasn't something a ten-year-old would forget easily.

She made her way closer to where he worked, her legs rubbery, though was careful to keep her distance from the head.

'I didn't know you had joined the police,' she said to him, reaching for normality, annoyed her voice was sounding reedy and that she couldn't stop her teeth from chattering.

His shoulders tensed, but he didn't turn around. 'Yeah, a few years back.'

'Do your mom and dad still live locally?'

He nodded.

'And Emily?'

He got up from the ground, turned to face her, looking annoyed.

'You might want to go back up to the house. I have work to do here and I need to concentrate. I'll come take your statement in a while.'

He was being formal, cold even, and Nell got the impression she made him uncomfortable.

'Yeah, okay, sure.' She forced a smile. 'I'll be there whenever you're ready.'

He nodded, turning his back on her. Nell watched him for a moment, feeling the need to try and close the distance between them, but not knowing where to start. The words not coming, she turned and made her way unsteadily back up the stone steps. When she reached the top she glanced down to where Tommy was bent down in the sand, flashlight on, his silhouette now barely visible against the darkening sky.

Back in the house she felt vulnerable and alone. It was stupid as she'd been living here almost a week and had spent a lot of time by herself, but it hadn't felt as big, empty and unwelcoming as it did right now. Rubbing the goosebumps on her arms she went from room to room turning on lights. In the kitchen she flicked on the radio, trying to make the place feel homey. Aware she had touched rotting flesh she went to the sink and washed her hands under the burning water until they felt raw. Hugging her cold body, she relented and turned on the heating.

She wondered how long Tommy would be down at the beach. How long it would be before he knocked on the door wanting to take her statement. Restlessly she paced, wringing her hands together, not knowing what to do while she waited. She felt cold to the bone, probably the shock of what she had stumbled upon. Whose head was it and where was the rest of the body? It had looked cleanly cut, like a piece of meat. Had it been an accident or had someone cut the woman's head off intentionally? The skin around the nose and mouth had been chewed – by fish or crabs, she supposed. Nell hadn't wanted to remember that detail, but it was one of the first things she had spotted, and the image of the gnarled lips and the eyeless sockets was clear in her mind.

Where was the rest of the woman and what had happened to her? She shuddered, not sure she wanted to know the answer.

Glancing at her wristwatch she noted she had only been home fifteen minutes. It felt longer. Although she was tempted to go upstairs and run a hot shower to take the chill off her bones, she wasn't sure how long Tommy was going to be. Instead she filled up the coffee pot, thinking it would be polite to offer him a cup when he showed up. While she waited for the water to boil she went upstairs, cleaned her teeth to get rid of the taste of sick, and ran a washcloth over her face. Back in the bedroom she looked out of the window to see if she could see any sign of him. Her view of the beach was obscured by trees. His car was still parked on the road, but he was nowhere.

She went back downstairs, made a coffee, paced some more, toyed with calling Michael, but dismissed the idea. So, she had found a head on the beach. What would he be able to do about it? Nell laughed to herself. It sounded almost hysterical.

She picked up her coffee, realised she had let it go cold, and poured it down the sink.

Come on, Tommy.

Would it be awkward when he came to take her statement? He'd seemed so distant towards her. Sam Kent blamed her for what had happened to Lizzie. Did Tommy blame her too? Nell tried to push the thought from her mind, told herself she was being paranoid, but was she?

Focus on something else.

She thought about turning on the television, but knew she wouldn't be able to concentrate. Maybe she should make something to eat. She had forgotten all about dinner. No point though as she had no appetite. The discovery of the head had taken care of that. Her throat felt sore from when she had thrown up, and her belly was empty. It was so cold in the house. Why couldn't she warm up?

Had the woman died on the beach where Nell had found her head, or had it washed ashore from somewhere miles away? Again, a detail she shouldn't be thinking about.

A knock at the door had her jumping in her skin.

Jesus, O'Connor. Pull yourself together.

Hastily she made her way down the hallway, unlocked the door and pulled it open and, expecting it to be Tommy, was surprised to find herself face-to-face with Alex.

'Hi.'

'Can I come in?'

He was out of uniform, though he wore his badge on the belt of his jeans and a firearm holstered on his hip.

'Sure, yes, of course.' Nell stepped back and let him pass. 'I thought you were going to be Tommy.'

'He's still down on the beach helping the medical examiner.' He turned to face her as she closed the door, green eyes sober. 'Are you okay?'

'Yes, I'm fine. Cold... does it feel cold to you? But I'm fine. I put coffee on a while back, but it'll be cold now too. I'll make a fresh pot.' She was aware she was babbling as she headed down the hallway to the kitchen, Alex following behind her. 'I guess you want to take a statement, right? That's why you're here? I'll make coffee and we can talk.'

'Nell, sit down.'

When she ignored him, Alex caught her by the shoulders and guided her to a chair.

'I was going to make coffee.'

'I can make the coffee. Sit.'

'I'm fine.'

'You're ice cold and you're shaking. You're in shock.'

Nell attempted a laugh. It sounded delirious. 'I'll be okay, honestly.'

She started to get up, but Alex gave her a warning look and she thought better of it. He took off his jacket and slipped it around her shoulders.

'Cups are in the cupboard next to the sink,' she pointed out, trying to be helpful as he went to fill the coffee pot. She tapped her foot impatiently, fighting the need to fidget, and slipped her arms into the jacket, hugging it against her, grateful for its warmth.

'In here?' He opened the cupboard, rummaged around, and instead pulled out a glass and a half full bottle of brandy. It had been one of Bella's bottles. Nell rarely touched the stuff, but hadn't gotten around to throwing it out.

'This will be better,' he told her, uncapping the lid and pouring a generous measure.

'Really?' Nell screwed up her nose. 'Coffee's fine.'

Alex pulled up another chair and sat down at the table next to her. He handed her the glass.

'Drink,' he ordered.

She stared dubiously at the molten liquid, opened her mouth to protest again and received another pointed look. Hesitantly she took a sip from the glass. The brandy burned her throat as she swallowed, hissing as it touched the pit of her empty stomach.

'And again.'

With a sigh she did as she was told. 'Has anyone told you you're bossy?' she grumbled, but kept hold of the glass, not wanting to admit the brandy was pleasantly warming her belly.

'You want me to call Michael?' he asked, ignoring her question.

'No, he doesn't need to be here. It's not a big deal.'

'Okay.'

Nell shook her head slowly. 'Shit, that came out wrong. I didn't mean it's not a big deal. Of course it is. Jesus fucking Christ, there's a head on the fucking beach. A woman's head. What the hell?' She took another, much larger, gulp of the brandy, and choked this time as she swallowed.

'I'm fine, I'm fine.' She held up a hand when Alex reached for the glass. 'Seriously, I'm okay. I've never seen, touched, a dead body... head, whatever, before. It's taking a little while to process. And thank you for offering to call Michael.' She hesitated, finding it hard to ask for help. 'Maybe you're right. I do need him here.'

Alex nodded, pulled out his phone and made the call.

Nell heard her brother's deep voice blustering on the other end of the line as he learned about what had happened, her heart sinking a little. He was going to wrap her up in cotton wool. She so wanted a chance to reclaim her independence, rebuild her confidence, but dammit, she didn't want to be alone tonight.

Alex ended the call. 'In case you somehow managed to not hear any of that, he's on his way.' There was the faintest hint of humour in his tone, a warm glint in his eyes. He had been patient with her, and was now trying to put her at ease and lighten the moment, and she appreciated that. She drew a deep breath and told herself to relax.

'I guess you've seen some pretty bad stuff before, huh?'

'Back in Portland, yeah, but nothing like this here.'

'How did she... Could it have been an accident?'

'We'll have to wait on the report from the medical examiner, but no, it wasn't an accident.'

'Which means someone did that to her.' The glass shook in Nell's hand. Annoyed, she set it down on the table and hunkered down into the jacket, trying to get warm. 'You think it's someone on the island?'

'It's too early to say. Can you talk me through what happened? You were on the beach. How long had you been down there?'

Nell told him about her visit to Michael's and how she had gone for a walk down to the beach to clear her head and think things through. 'There's not much else to say. I was by the water and spotted something stuck in the seaweed. That's when I...' She broke off, needing a moment, the woman's face clear in her mind. She wondered if that was how it was for Tommy with Lizzie. Did he see her face every time he closed his eyes?

'How is Tommy doing?' she asked.

'Tommy?' Alex raised a brow. 'It's his first homicide, but he'll be fine.'

'It's not his first brush with death though.'

'I know. Lizzie Kent's murder was one of the main reasons he joined the police department.'

'We know each other from way back, Tommy and me.'

Alex said nothing, his expression neutral as he waited for Nell to continue.

'Come on, I know you know. Lizzie Kent was my best friend. I was the one supposed to be babysitting that night. It should have been me. Even if Michael or Tommy never told you, you're the chief of police. You know.'

'And your point is?'

'Things seemed weird with Tommy, down on the beach.'

'Really? You're gonna make this about the past? You just found a dead woman's head. He has never dealt with anything like this before. It surprises you things were a little weird?' Alex shook his head, seeming bemused by the path of the conversation. 'If you were hoping for some big happy smiley reunion, it wasn't going to happen tonight, Nell.'

'No, it wasn't like that. He wouldn't even look at me. It was like he blamed me for what happened to Lizzie.'

'What is it you want me to say? That it could have been you that night? Yeah, it could've, but it wasn't. It was Lizzie; wrong place, wrong time, end of story. We all make choices, we all make mistakes, hell I know I have, but that's life. You have to accept them and move on. Tommy is grounded and he's a good guy. He's passionate, hard-working and his heart is in the right place. He hasn't seen you in close to twenty years and when he finally does you meet under difficult circumstances. Cut him a little slack, okay?'

Much as she didn't want to admit it, he had a point. Nell probably was reading far more into their encounter than she should. Her brush the previous night with Sam Kent hadn't helped her paranoia, but Sam had reason to resent her, Tommy not so much. She was shaken as hell about the head, so she doubted it was a walk in the park for Tommy. He'd just been focusing on his job.

'Are you always this annoyingly right?' she asked, forcing a smile in an attempt to lighten the moment.

Alex laughed, his wide appealing grin suddenly back, wiping the seriousness off his face. 'Yeah, most of the time.'

'I'm sorry I got whiny on you.'

He gave her arm a squeeze. 'It's okay. I'm going to cut you a little slack too under the circumstances.'

They were silent for a moment.

'Michael and Newt want to renovate this place and turn it back into a guesthouse.'

'And is that what you want?'

'Yeah, I think it is.'

A loud crashing sound came from outside, making Nell jump. Instinctively she reached out and grabbed Alex's arm.

'What was that?'

He was already on his feet, heading towards the back door, changing instantly from casually laid-back to hard and alert, all trace of humour gone. 'Wait here,' he ordered, gun drawn, when she got up to follow him.

She was too jittery to sit, so she stayed where she was, watching anxiously as he quietly turned the lock, eased the door open, and stepped outside.

This was Purity. It was supposed to be a safe place to live. Statistically it was.

Tell that to Lizzie. And there's a woman's severed head on the beach across the road. It didn't get there by accident.

Still, she was overreacting, Alex was overreacting.

Even though she tried to convince herself it was true, when he didn't reappear after thirty seconds, panic clawed its way up her belly and into her throat.

'Alex?'

Nell waited a beat and when there was no answer, called again. The half whisper of her voice cut into the quiet night air, met only with silence. A wave of hot clammy nausea washed over her, making her head spin. She gripped the counter to steady herself as the pounding started in her chest.

Oh God, no, not now, not again.

'One-hundred, ninety-nine, ninety-eight...'

She slipped to the floor, her back against the counter, and drew her knees against her chest.

Breathe, damn it, O'Connor. Focus on your breathing.

Her brain wasn't receiving the instructions, her breathing growing faster and out of control.

Focus.

'Eighty-four, eighty-three, eighty-two...'

'Nell?'

'Seventy-nine, seventy-eight, seventy-seven...'

Alex dropped to the floor beside her.

'It's okay, you're having a panic attack, but it's going to pass. You're going to be okay.'

His voice was low, his tone calm. 'Focus on your breathing, Nell.'

'I can't. I can't... breathe. Seventy, sixty-nine, sixty-eight...'

'You can. Your brain is trying to trick you. Breathe with me, in through your nose and out through your mouth, slow and steady.' He took hold of her hand. 'Repeat it with me. In through your nose, out through your mouth, in through your nose and out through your mouth.'

'In through my nose and out through my mouth, in through my nose and out through my mouth.' Nell gripped Alex's hand tightly and tried to focus on doing as he instructed.

'It's just a panic attack. It can't hurt you. In a few minutes you're going to be okay.'

Eventually her breathing steadied, but he didn't rush her, waiting patiently until the attack had fully passed. They sat in silence for a few moments.

'Did you see anything?' Nell asked eventually. She was too exhausted to feel embarrassed. She still had hold of Alex's hand, needing the physical connection.

'There's a broken flower pot underneath the window. Whoever or whatever knocked it over has gone. It might've been kids, or more likely raccoons.'

She recalled he had told her there had been problems with some of the local kids trying to break into the house, though had hoped they would leave it alone now it was occupied again.

'So, how long have you been having the panic attacks?'

'They started after Lizzie's murder. I had them under control for a while, but they've got worse over the past couple of years.' Since Caleb, she thought, but didn't say. She had a feeling Alex had already figured that out. 'Michael doesn't know. Please don't tell him.'

'They're nothing to feel embarrassed about.'

'I know, but I am. They make me feel so weak and useless.'

He gave her hand a squeeze. 'I don't think you're weak and useless. Do you know how many people suffer from panic attacks? The number would surprise you. You can't help how your body reacts. The trick is learning how to control them.'

'You sound like you know what you're talking about.'

'My mom used to have attacks. You should talk to Michael. He would understand.'

'No, it'll be another thing to stress him out. Please don't say anything.'

Alex was silent for a moment, his jaw tightening. 'Okay, I won't tell him, but if he asks, I won't lie either.'

'That's fair enough, I guess.'

'There is a compromise.'

'Which is?'

'I'm going to give you my cell number. If you won't go to your brother when you need help, you come to me. Do we have a deal?'

It was Nell's turn to be silent. She barely knew Alex, hadn't even liked him at first, but she had to accept her first impression of him had been wrong. He had just seen her at her weakest and he had stayed by her side, helped talk her down. Caleb had used her panic attacks as another way to humiliate her, loving the extra power it gave him over her. She had misjudged Alex and it meant a lot that he wasn't going to shoot his mouth off to Michael about the attacks. He said he wanted to help her and she believed the offer was genuine.

'Okay, we have a deal.'

In the bushes to the side of the house he watched Michael O'Connor arrive, then a few minutes later he saw Alex Cutler leave and make his way back across the road to the crime scene. He heard the door being bolted shut, though knew that Alex was right, the locks were weak and he could easily still get in the house.

He had heard a lot of the early conversation from where he had been crouched in a cramped position beneath the single-glazed kitchen window. But then he had been foolish enough to move, accidentally knocking over the plant pot and alerting them to his presence. After Cutler had come outside looking for him, he didn't dare risk approaching the house again. Still, he had heard enough and what he had heard made him unhappy.

It was time to give Nell O'Connor a scare she wouldn't forget.

10

Jenna Milborn stood in the line for the checkout and glanced at her reflection in her powder compact. She had tried her best to disguise the bruise on her cheek, but it was still clearly visible in the harsh lights of the store. Hearing laughter from the next checkout, she glanced up to see Melissa Reynolds and Ginny Cook whispering and looking in her direction. Her cheeks flushing, she snapped the compact shut and dropped it back into her purse.

They might laugh and think they knew her, but truth was they didn't have a clue.

Curtis Milborn was a brute of a man and one with a particularly ugly temper when he had been drinking, but he was her penance. Years ago, Jenna had had big dreams and hopes for the future, but it had all been taken away from her in the blink of an eye. She had done bad things and now she had to pay for them. Each time Curtis hit her, the pain softened, and while she didn't go out of her way intentionally to goad him, she knew she deserved every punch. Of course, she still had enough pride to try and hide her bruises, still went along with the charade of pretending her husband hadn't given them to her, though that was more to protect him. People didn't believe her; she could see it clearly on their faces. Chief Cutler had been trying to get her to press charges for the past couple of years, but she never would. Curtis was her cross to bear and she had learned to accept that.

The checkout line moved forward, and she loaded her groceries onto the conveyer belt: bread, milk, eggs, carrots and a couple of six packs of Coors Light, Curtis's favourite beer. Another snigger came from the next checkout and Jenna fixed both women with a glare. They had been in the year below her at high school. Back then Jenna had been popular and pretty, and she'd had barely a care in the world.

How had it gone so wrong?

Back then she had been dating Luke Trainor. He had been the love of her life and she had truly believed they would get married and start a family. Luke would get a good job and they would live in a nice house. Jenna would have expensive clothes and pretty things, her life would be perfect. Part of it had come true – well, for Luke it had. He had the job and the house. He just had it with someone else.

Jenna had seen his girlfriend, Stacey, a few times, though didn't know her to talk to. She was younger, perkier and prettier, drove a flashy car and was always immaculately dressed. Things had fallen apart for Jenna and Luke straight out of high school. These days they seldom spoke. Jenna wondered if he viewed her with the same disgust and ridicule Melissa and Ginny did, and thought bitterly about how unfair it was that his life had gone on to be so perfect while she struggled to exist from day to day. She drummed her fingers impatiently against the conveyer belt as the woman in front paid for her shopping, chatting away to the store clerk, oblivious to the line forming behind her.

'Isn't it terrible? Speculation is she was killed in East Haven, though I don't think anything official's been released yet.

Someone tried to hide her body at sea, but her head washed up here.'

Jenna tuned into the conversation, her mouth dry.

'They say Michael O'Connor's sister was the one who found it.'

'Yeah, I heard that. Wasn't she friends with the girl murdered in Don Dolan's house?'

'Really?'

'She was originally supposed to be babysitting that night.'

'Isn't she living in Bella Golding's old place?'

'That's the one. I guess that girl must have a talent for attracting death.'

Jenna ran a shaky hand through her hair, her blood running cold. This was the first she had heard about a murder victim's head washing up on the beach. When the hell had this happened? And Nell O'Connor was back on the island, living in her aunt's old house. Jenna vaguely remembered her from years back, knew she used to spend her summers with Bella. So much had happened since then.

As the woman in front picked up her groceries, Jenna moved to the front of the line. She forced a smile for the cashier, but inside her world was unravelling.

The head was identified as that of Penelope Maher, a thirty-year-old dental nurse from Winchester, a large coastal town twenty-five miles south of East Haven. Alex met with the Winchester County Sheriff, Sid Talbot, on Monday afternoon, hours after the formal identification of their victim. Talbot was accompanied by one of his detectives, Hunter Stone, who, it was agreed, would work with Purity Police Department on the Maher case. Talbot was a burly gruff man in his early fifties. Alex knew of him, was aware he had a reputation as a straight-as-an-arrow, plain-talking, but fair, man who preferred action over conversation, something which had seen voters favour him in the past four elections. Meanwhile, Stone was a familiar face, having worked in homicide with Alex when both of them had served as detectives in Portland.

'Priority has to be trying to find the rest of the body,' Talbot commented, glancing out to sea, as they stood on the beach where Penelope Maher's head had washed ashore. The light breeze blew through his thick hair, the sunlight accentuating the rich copper colour that had earned him his nickname, Red. He had been keen to view the crime scene first and foremost, even though it was unlikely to yield any new clues. Still, Alex got that. If it had been one of the island's citizens on the mainland he would have wanted the same.

'Coastguard has already been alerted and we have teams out trawling the waters,' he advised. 'The ME has her in the water two days tops, and we're focusing on an area about three miles south of Winchester.'

'Family has been notified this morning. Parents and younger sister are flying out from St Louis later on tonight. I'll bring them over tomorrow.'

Alex nodded at Stone. 'It's going to be tough on them. They'll want answers.'

'Hopefully we'll have some to give them soon.' Stone raised his sunglasses and rubbed at the bridge of his nose. 'I plan on speaking with Penny's friends and work colleagues when I get back. See if we can start to piece together her last-known movements.'

'The woman who found her lives locally you say?'

Alex glanced back in the direction of the guesthouse, though it was mostly obscured by pine trees, and ran a hand over his unshaven jaw. 'Nell O'Connor: sister of a friend of mine,' he told Talbot. 'She lives up on the cliff over there.'

'Not a pleasant find.'

'She was pretty shaken.'

And he could tell that had pissed her off. Nell was friendly, but guarded, and his first impression of her the day their paths had crossed in East Haven was that she was a stuck-up princess who believed the world owed her a favour. Learning she was Michael's sister had forced him to put his judgement on hold and he now realised he had her wrong. She tried to put on a brave front, but the panic attack he had witnessed had exposed her vulnerability, hinting at hidden scars; he found himself intrigued at the layers that might lie below.

'Unsurprising,' Talbot commented. 'Kind of thing like that'll give you nightmares.'

The Medical Examiner's office was their next stop. Violet Marsden, who had lived on the island for all of her sixty-three years, talked Talbot and Stone through the report she had already shared with Alex. The head had been severed cleanly, most likely with a cleaver or similar-style knife.

'There's no chance this was a tragic boating accident?' Talbot wanted to know.

'The victim's head was severed post death, Sheriff.' Violet told him. 'It's difficult for me to tell what the actual cause of death was without the rest of her body, but it wasn't decapitation. She also has residue of tape around her mouth and in her hair, which suggests she was being held against her will.'

'So, he kills her in Winchester then dismembers and dumps the body out to sea,' Stone mused, rattling the change in his suit pants. 'Needs to have a boat.'

'More than half the folk living in Winchester own a boat,' Talbot muttered gruffly.

'We have to narrow it down then.' Stone flashed a smile at

Violet, dimples cracking in ebony cheeks. He was a lady's man, tall, slim and sinewy, with a shaved head, neatly trimmed goatee and a dapper wardrobe. 'Do you have anything else for us, Ms Marsden?' To the outsider who didn't know him he appeared too smooth, too arrogant, but Alex did know him and was aware that beneath the slick guy persona was a more-than-capable cop.

If anyone could help him catch Penelope Maher's killer, Stone was the man.

'Very little at this stage,' Violet told him. 'Bring me the rest of Miss Maher and I might be able to give you more answers.'

Lizzie's smiling face stared out from her sophomore yearbook picture. This was how Sam remembered her: happy, full of life, her dark hair falling in soft waves around her shoulders. At the time the photo was taken she was his big, slightly dorky sister. He had been fourteen, had only just started his freshman year, and didn't want her cramping his style. Only now could he fully appreciate how special his sister was. She had been a grade-A, hard-working student with a promising future ahead of her, and her easy-going, kind nature made her popular with everyone. She never judged, never bitched and refused to fall into any of the high school cliques, accepting everyone for who they were.

She had so much to offer and it had all been taken away from her in the blink of an eye.

Although she hadn't held the knife that killed her, Nell O'Connor had been responsible for putting Lizzie in the house that night. She was the one supposed to be looking after Tommy and Emily Dolan, the one who was meant to be babysitting. Instead she shirked on her duties, persuading Lizzie to cover for her so she could sneak off with her boyfriend.

If Lizzie had refused, if she hadn't have been Nell's best friend, she would still be alive. Instead she was gone forever, and Sam's family was destroyed.

Beautiful, clever, kind Lizzie had died, while average, irresponsible, selfish Nell had gotten to live.

The injustice of it stank, and seeing Nell back on the island, strolling around and acting as if nothing had ever happened, was too bitter a pill to swallow. Yes, when confronted, she had given false platitudes about how sorry she was and how it should have been her that night, but her words rang hollow. If she had meant what she said she would have stayed away and never returned to Purity.

After he ran into her at the grocery store, Sam had driven out to the old Dolan House. It stood in a secluded position, out on the old coastal road, surrounded by forest and suffering from years of neglect. Once this had been the most upmarket part of the island, but Lizzie's murder had changed everything. Everyone associated the area with her death and no-one wanted to live in the house where she had met her gruesome end.

Sam hadn't visited the place in a while. He tended to purposely avoid this part of the island. But he had sat in front of the wrought iron gates the night he ran into Nell O'Connor, and drank half a bottle of vodka, bargaining with the Devil and wishing to hell he could have his sister back, begging Him to take Nell in Lizzie's place.

He was normally a law-abiding citizen, but Nell's return had tipped him over the edge. After drowning his sorrows and shedding tears for his sister, Sam had driven back into town completely wasted. It had been stupid, and he was sorry he had done it, but at the time he hadn't been thinking rationally, just as he hadn't been thinking straight when he had pulled up outside Bella Golding's old house and had watched Nell through the lit bedroom window.

She had said she was sorry, that she wished she could swap places with Lizzie, but it wasn't true. She acted as if she didn't have a care in the world.

Lizzie was gone and Nell didn't give a shit.

That made Sam mad as hell. He just wasn't quite sure what to do about it.

11

Nell stayed with Michael and Newt over the weekend before returning to the guesthouse on Monday, needing time alone to process everything that had happened.

Feeling restless and not up to concentrating on any specific task, she paced from room to room, made countless cups of coffee, toyed with going for a walk to clear her head, dismissing it almost immediately following what happened the last time she had done that, before flopping on the couch with her iPad. She checked her e-mail, spotting six messages from Caleb; she didn't open any, instead moving them to the folder she had created in his name, thinking it would be wise to hold on to them in case anything ever happened. Done with her e-mail she logged on to Facebook, safe in the knowledge that he wouldn't be able to contact her there as she had already deleted and blocked him. As an additional precaution she had also culled her friends list, leaving just the handful of people she knew she could trust. She commented on a photo Michael had posted, a goofy selfie he had taken with Newt when they were both clearly under the influence.

On a whim she looked up Luke and Alex, saw they both had

accounts and spent five minutes stalking their profiles. Alex's settings gave nothing away, she guessed because of his job, but Luke's was like a glossy catalogue with pictures documenting his perfect relationship with Stacey, the pair of them smiling out from dozens of photos and gushing about how much they loved each other. Nell rolled her eyes, fully aware from her relationship with Caleb and the sickly posts he used to put up to tell the world how much he adored her, that Facebook was all for show. Not that she thought Luke was beating up on Stacey, but she was aware there were cracks in their relationship. Her finger hovered over the friend request button for a moment, but caution won over. Too soon.

For some reason her thoughts turned to Sarah, the girl whose name was graffitied on the attic wall. Who was she? There would be no way to Facebook stalk her without her full name. Setting her iPad to one side, Nell headed upstairs. There were boxes in the attic that contained all of Bella's paperwork for the guesthouse: bills, receipts, tax returns and employment records. Sarah's details would be documented somewhere. It took a couple of hours of reading through yellowing pages, but Nell finally found what she was looking for.

Sarah Treadwell had been employed at the guesthouse in the summer of 2005. Was she the Sarah who Clarke was referring to? Armed with the name, Nell went back downstairs and did a Facebook search. There were dozens of Sarah Treadwells though, with thirty-plus living in the States.

Frustrated, Nell grabbed her car keys and headed out. Michael should be home from work shortly. He remembered Sarah and would be able to give her a description. Maybe that would help narrow her search?

Michael was kicking back with a beer when Nell showed up.

'Hey, I was about to call you.' He opened the door wide, catching her in a hard hug as she breezed in. 'Is everything okay?'

'Everything's fine. I just figured I'd stop by and see my big brother.' She eased back and he didn't miss her frown as he picked up his beer.

'What?' he demanded.

'Today isn't Saturday,' she commented drily.

'And? I just like to have a beer to relax. What are you, the fun police?'

'Just a concerned sister.'

'Well, you've no need to be.'

'Okay.'

Michael narrowed his eyes, his hackles raised. 'Okay? What's that supposed to mean?'

'It means "okay". Subject dropped. You brought it up first.'

'Your look started it.'

'Just forget it, Michael. I didn't come here to pick a fight.'

He immediately felt bad, remembering everything she had been through over the past couple of days. 'Sorry. Were you okay in the house last night?'

He hadn't wanted her to go back, and had already called her twice over the course of the day to check up on her.

'I was fine. Actually, I came here to ask you something.'

'Yeah, what's that?'

'Sarah Treadwell was the girl Bella employed, the one who skipped out, right?'

Michael's brow furrowed. 'Yeah, Sarah Treadwell, that was her name. How did you find that out?'

'From Bella's old files in the attic. I've been trying to look her up on Facebook, but there are several Sarah Treadwells. I thought you might recognise which one she is.'

'Maybe. Why do you want to know though? It was years ago.'

Nell shrugged. 'Her name is written on the wall in the attic. I guess I'm just being nosey.'

'So, what's the plan? You find her and send her a friend request?'

'Funny guy. I just want to know what happened to her.'

'Okay, Nancy Drew.' Michael shot her a look, but took her offered iPad, and scrolled down the list, ruling several of the girls out immediately. He clicked on a handful of profiles that had pictures of pets, but eventually was able to dismiss them all. 'None of these girls are her.'

'You sure?'

'Yeah, she was a pretty girl. I'd recognise her. Maybe she doesn't have a Facebook account.'

'I guess not.'

Nell seemed distracted, which had Michael wondering why finding Sarah was such a big deal to her. Maybe it had something to do with finding the head? Perhaps she needed something else to focus on to take her mind off the traumatic experience?

No more had been said about the guesthouse proposal. After the gruesome discovery both Michael and Newt had been fussing over her and it hadn't felt like an appropriate topic to raise. Maybe now was the right time?

'So, you given any more thought to what we talked about the other day?' He kept the question casual, his belly knotting, annoyed at how big of a deal her answer was to him.

Nell picked a peach from the fruit bowl on the counter and rubbed it on her jeans before taking a bite. 'Yeah, I have actually.'

'And?'

Her lips curved. 'Okay, let's do it. Let's renovate the guesthouse.'

Michael felt excitement swell in his gut. 'You're serious?'

'Sure, why not?'

He hadn't been convinced she would go for it given her measured reaction when he first made the suggestion, and he had been certain finding the head would put her off the idea completely. Now he found himself studying her, wondering if there was a catch. 'This is definitely what you want, right?'

'It is. I've had a couple of nights to sleep on it and I think we can make it work. I can't afford the repairs myself and, while it was tempting to sell up and move to somewhere smaller, I kept feeling guilty, as I'm sure it's not what Aunt Bella would have wanted. Besides, I was going to have to start looking for work, so this is ideal. I do have one request though.'

'Which is?'

'I want to keep the attic space. Have it as a studio. The lighting through the windows is fantastic. I know I can no longer paint professionally, but I can still paint for me, right?'

She gave a sad smile and Michael felt a fresh rush of anger for what she had been forced to give up. They had talked about it, but Nell didn't dare risk trying to sell her paintings in case Caleb was able to track her down. Michael hated that the asshole had taken that from her.

He had only met the dude once, but he hadn't warmed to him. Of course, he had been polite, not wanting to piss off Nell, but he got the impression Caleb knew how he felt – that the feeling was mutual. He wanted Nell to himself, didn't want her family poking their noses in. He was a smooth operator, slick as a snake, with a controlling personality and a toothpaste smile that never quite reached his eyes. Michael couldn't for the life of him understand what Nell saw in the guy. He guessed Caleb had wined and dined her, impressed her with his connections to the art world, sucked her in and then made it difficult for her to back out.

She had told him a little about Caleb's controlling nature,

but refused to open up about whether he had ever physically hurt her. Michael had his suspicions and if he found out they were true, he would personally fly to Chicago and break his legs.

'We can do that. The space is huge. Why don't we convert the whole top floor, so you can live up there? It would give you your own privacy away from the guests.'

Nell smiled and he could see she immediately liked the idea. 'You'd do that for me?'

'Of course we would. Why don't you stay for dinner? Newt will be home in a while and we can talk more.'

'Sure, okay.'

They worked together in the kitchen for the next hour, radio on, both singing and goofing around as Nell diced vegetables and Michael prepared the meatloaf. He had really missed this. During the summers that Nell visited, Bella had invited him up to the guesthouse for dinner once a week and he treasured the time he got to spend with his kid sister. Helping prepare dinner in that big kitchen with Nell and her cousin, Clarke, had been some of the best times of Michael's life.

He finally had his sister home and he wasn't going to lose her again.

Dinner was in the oven when Newt finally arrived home. 'I've brought another guest for dinner,' he announced, dragging his brother in behind him.

'No Stacey again?' Michael questioned, opening the oven door and pulling out the meatloaf.

'Sore subject.' Newt told him, giving Nell a quick kiss on the cheek. 'And the reason why he's having dinner with us. They had another fight, Stacey's stormed out, and I found my brother here sitting in front of a big glass of Scotch, about to drown his sorrows, so I figured I'd better bring him here.'

Truth was Newt was worried about Luke. The fighting with Stacey seemed to be getting worse and it was sending his brother into a downward spiral. He rarely drank, so to see him suddenly hitting the bottle so heavily was a concern. Luke liked to pretend to the world that he had the perfect life and, it was true he had a good job and an extravagant lifestyle, but it was all a front. Things hadn't been easy for either of them after losing their parents and they had struggled to get along with their grandmother, a strict eccentric woman who saw them as a burden. Newt knew things hadn't been easy for her either, that she had been widowed young and left to raise their father and his brother on her own. She resented having to do it again with Newt and Luke, never made them feel welcome, constantly criticising and picking at them, yet showering their cousin, Jane, with affection and gifts whenever she came to visit. It had been tougher on Luke, who was younger and more vulnerable, and Newt couldn't always be there to protect him. He had been twenty-two and fresh out of college when their grandmother had passed away, barely an adult himself, but he had taken on the responsibility of looking after Luke himself, determined to give him the childhood he had been denied.

For the most part things had been great since then, but Enid Trainor had knocked Luke's confidence and although Newt did his best to build it back up, pushing Luke through college and encouraging him to chase his dreams, his younger brother was given to bouts of depression and self-doubt. Stacey was a firecracker and it seemed just recently she and Luke had been permanently at each other's throats. That wasn't a good thing. When Luke was up, he thought he was omnipotent and was the life and soul of the party, but when he was down he quickly became detached from reality and risked going off the rails.

He was sullen and quiet as they sat down to eat, his mood smothering the room, and Newt could tell Nell was shocked by his change in personality having only seen fun Luke on their previous encounters. Newt and Michael tried their best to cover the awkward moments of silence as Luke pushed his food around the plate like a sullen teenager, looking like he would rather be anywhere else. He perked up slightly when Michael brought up the subject of the guesthouse. Although Newt was concerned for his brother, he found it difficult to contain his excitement once he knew Nell was on board with their proposal, and by the time they had finished dinner and were clearing the plates away, even Luke was joining in with the conversation.

'I can't believe we're actually going to do this.' Michael was just as excited as Newt and could barely keep the grin off his face.

'You won't regret this, Nell,' Newt assured her, hoping she wouldn't have a change of heart further down the line. He knew she had been through a lot and it had already been a big step for her to leave Caleb and return to Purity. While he really wanted this, he was conscious that they had to be careful not to push her.

It was after nine when she got up to leave. 'Did you want a ride home, Luke?'

Newt had suggested Luke stay over with them, not liking the idea of him returning to his empty house and pouring a drink. He saw him waver for a brief moment.

'I think I'm gonna crash here, but thank you.'

'No worries. If you want some company some time or to talk through stuff, just let me know.'

'Thank you, I appreciate that.' Luke was thoughtful for a moment. 'How do you fancy dinner tomorrow night?'

Newt saw the brief look of panic on Nell's face. Her offer had been kind, but had Luke misread it? He was about to step in when his brother smiled.

'Just to talk,' he assured her. 'And get to know each other better since we are practically related.'

Nell still looked a little flustered, but she relaxed slightly. 'Umm, okay, I guess so.'

'Shall I come up to the guesthouse around seven?'

'I... I guess, yes, okay.'

Newt and Michael walked her out to the car.

'Don't let him hoodwink you into dinner,' Newt urged her. 'He's harmless, but I know you don't know him well enough yet. If it's too much too soon, just say and I will tell him no.'

'He just wants to be friends, right?'

'Yeah, and he knows he would have me to deal with if he tried anything on.'

'Steady up, Mr Macho.' Newt rolled his eyes at Michael before turning back to Nell. 'It's a bad idea. I'll tell him no.'

'No, don't do that.' Nell smiled, though it looked a little forced.

'It's okay. He's your brother and I know he's in a bad place right now. Maybe dinner will cheer him up.'

'If you're sure it's okay.'

'It will do me good to start socialising more. Honestly it's fine.'

'If you change your mind you'll let us know, right?' Michael questioned.

'I won't change my mind. It's just dinner. And like Luke said, we're practically related so we should get to know each other better.' Nell opened the car door. 'I've just remembered I have Alex's jacket with me. He lives near here, right? I can drop it off on the way home.'

'Yeah, he's a couple of minutes along the coast road.' Michael gave her directions. 'I'm not sure if he'll be there or not. I know he's busy with the case at the moment, but you can leave it on the deck if not. Or give it to me and I'll drop it off tomorrow.'

'No, it's fine. I may as well call in on my way home.' Spontaneously, Nell reached out and gave them both a hug.

'What was that for?' Michael asked, sounding surprised.

She grinned and kissed his cheek. 'It's for being there for me, both of you. You have no idea how much it's appreciated.'

Newt raised a hand as she reversed out of the driveway. It was going to be fine. It was just dinner. Luke needed cheering up and Nell was right, it would do her good to start socialising, and it would hopefully help rebuild her confidence.

Still, he intended to have a word with his brother beforehand, to remind him to be on his best behaviour.

12

Nell pulled up outside the modest two-storey white wooden house Michael had given her directions to. She killed the engine and stepped from the car, Alex's jacket in hand. His Jeep was out front, but there were no lights on in the front windows, suggesting perhaps he wasn't home after all. As she made her way up the pathway to the front door, a timer light flashed on, highlighting the neat front yard. From inside came the sound of excited barking.

Most likely Teddy, she thought to herself, grinning as she imagined the large scruffy bag of fur going nuts inside.

She rang the doorbell, and waited a minute, her thoughts turning back to dinner.

Luke had shocked her tonight and she had barely recognised the man who had sat down at the dinner table as being the same person she had laughed and joked with a couple of days ago. The split in his personality had initially unsettled her, reminding her of Caleb and how dangerous that could be, but it wasn't fair to compare him to her ex-fiancé. Luke was upset because his girlfriend had walked out on him. It was only natural he was going to be a little quiet.

She had put forward the offer to talk because she felt sorry for him, so he had thrown her when he had managed to turn the gesture into dinner. Initially her belly had knotted in fear at the idea, but she quickly berated herself, annoyed at her overreaction. There had been nothing romantic in his suggestion and the dinner would probably do them both good.

Nell was sick of being afraid. It was time to start rebuilding her confidence.

She tried the doorbell again. When there was still no answer, she followed the path that led down the side of the house and up the wide wooden steps onto the deck. It was simple and uncluttered with a wooden bench and a barbecue the only furniture, while various plant pots were scattered around the edge. The location was perfect, offering a prime sea view, and although it was dark, the rising moon seemed to nestle between rocks, casting a silver glow over the ocean. Leaving Alex's jacket on the bench seat, Nell pulled her phone from her purse and activated the camera. She leaned over the wooden railing and spent a few moments snapping at the view, trying to capture it as best she could in the hope she would be able to later recreate it on a canvas.

In the distance on the beach she spotted a figure running across the sand, close to the water's edge, silhouette dark and distinctly masculine against the sparkling waves. She snapped another couple of pictures. As the figure neared, she realised it was Alex. Nell waited patiently as he jogged towards the house. He hadn't spotted her standing in the shadows and as he approached the top of the steps, he yanked his T-shirt up over his head, giving her a full-on view of his lean, toned belly, a smattering of dark hair trailing down from his navel and disappearing into the waistband of his sweatpants.

Her eyes widened, the 'Hi' she was about to greet him with catching on her tongue.

Enjoying the view, she continued to watch as the T-shirt dropped to the floor and he turned to grab the towel that hung across the railing at the top of the steps, rubbing it over his face and hair with his back to her, muscles flexing in broad shoulders. The damp material of his sweatpants clung to a well-toned butt and narrow hips.

Something stirred inside her and for the first time in a long while it wasn't fear.

Teddy picked that moment to hurl himself against the French doors, letting out an almighty bark. Nell jumped, stepping back into one of the plant pots, and Alex spun round, looking ready to pounce.

'Jesus! Nell?'

She lamely raised a hand in greeting. 'Hi.'

'What are you doing here?'

'I, umm... I brought your jacket back and I was admiring the view.' She glanced again at his naked chest and, realising her choice of words, felt herself flush. 'The sea view I meant. I didn't mean... I was enjoying the view... of the ocean,' she clarified, wishing the ground would swallow her up.

Oh good God, O'Connor. Zip it now.

Alex studied her for a moment, his dark hair damp and curling, clinging to his forehead and the nape of his neck. Realisation dawning, he slowly grinned. 'Okay.'

Seeming amused, he picked his T-shirt up from the decking, slipped the towel over one shoulder and headed across to the French doors. As he unlocked them a joyous Teddy bounded out, jumping up first at Alex and then heading over to greet Nell. Sasha followed, her approach far calmer as she gave Nell's hand a cursory sniff. She made a fuss of them both as Alex disappeared inside, not sure if she was supposed to follow or not. There was no dignified way out of this situation. Nell had just been caught red-handed checking him out. As she considered the possibility of quietly sloping off back to her car, he called to her.

'So, are you coming in or are you just gonna stand out there?'

No. There was no dignified way out.

Hesitantly, Nell stepped inside and found him in a galley kitchen at the back of the main living room. She was relieved to see he had put on another T-shirt.

'Do you want a coffee?'

'Sure.'

She glanced around the room, taking in the space. It was light and airy, unfussy, but homey. A wide corner couch took up part of the room, facing a flat-screen TV. One wall was filled with shelves. They mostly contained books, with a few ornaments, plants and picture frames.

'Have you lived here long?' she asked, uncomfortable and needing to make small talk to try and put things back on a more even level.

'Five years. You take milk?'

'Please. What made you decide to move out here? City life not exciting?'

'Something like that.'

'Had you been a cop for long before you moved here?'

Alex brought two cups through, and handed one to Nell, stepping into her personal space. 'Do you always ask a lot of questions when you get flustered?' he asked directly, eyes intently focused on hers, awaiting a reaction. He was close enough that she could smell his scent, feel his breath warm on her face. She felt another stirring inside, recognised it this time for exactly what it was. Lust.

'I'm not flustered!' She snapped the words a little too defensively, taking a step back as she felt her cheeks flame. 'I was making conversation.'

'Okay.'

Okay? What was that supposed to mean?

He was looking a little smug, which cranked her irritation level up a notch. Fair enough, she had been checking him out, and okay, yes, she would concede she found him attractive. But so what? It was irrelevant. Forget the fact he was her brother's best friend, he was also the chief of police, plus, of course, she wasn't looking for romance, a fling, hot sex, whatever. After everything she had been through with Caleb, she wanted a break from men, period. She had simply come here to return his jacket and suddenly things seemed different between them. On their previous encounters she had been Michael's sister and a witness who had found a severed head. He had been so good with her that night, kind and patient, helping her through the panic attack. Tonight was different, and the air crackled with unexpected tension.

'The woman I found... has she been identified yet?'

It was a pertinent question, one Nell was curious to know the answer to, and it also moved the conversation back into safer territory. She had spent much of the past two days thinking about the head on the beach and who the victim was. How she had ended up dead.

Had it been a random attack or had the woman been killed by someone she knew and trusted?

Nell thought back to Caleb. There had been times in their relationship where she had wondered if he would one day snap and go too far. It was scary how he could go from calm and rational to crazy-angry in the blink of an eye.

'We have an ID, but it's not public yet. Her folks are flying out tonight. They're coming over to the island in the morning.' He moved past her as he talked, and whistled to Teddy and Sasha. Both dogs trotted in, Sasha moving with the grace of a panther, Teddy bounding behind like an oversized baby goat. Alex closed the French doors, moved to sit on the couch, and stared up at her, amusement in his green eyes, seeming to find her embarrassment entertaining.

Nell remained standing, still feeling awkward. She held her cup with both hands and took a slow sip of her coffee. 'Do you think you'll find the rest of her?'

'We're trying.'

She understood he was limited on what he could share with her. It was an active investigation and still in the early stages. 'I can't even begin to imagine how her family must be feeling.'

As she spoke she broke away from the scrutiny in his gaze and glanced out of the French doors towards the ocean. Knowing the rest of the woman's body was out there somewhere, a shiver ran down her spine.

'You tell Michael yet about the guesthouse?'

Alex's question broke her thoughts. 'Yeah, I actually just came from his place.' She turned to look at him before eyeing the couch. Tentatively she took a seat, perching on the far corner.

Not too close.

'He's pretty excited. I think it's something he and Newt have wanted to do for a while. They have a ton of plans.'

'I know he is and it will make him feel easier knowing you're not always up in the guesthouse alone.'

Nell shot him a look bristling with irritation. 'I'm thirty-four years old. I don't need my brother to babysit me.' Her reaction was unnecessary, especially as Alex had already seen her at her weakest, but she stuck out her chin defiantly anyway, needing to create a boundary between them.

'He worries about you.'

'I know, and I appreciate it, but I need my own space too. It's been a huge thing for me coming back here and I need time to put my life back together.'

'Your ex was an asshole.' It wasn't a question, more an observation.

'He was used to being in control and getting his own way,' Nell said diplomatically. She wasn't up for a conversation about Caleb's true nature. 'This is a fresh start for me and I can't do it with Michael breathing down my neck.'

'He's terrified this Caleb guy is going to figure out where you are, so cut him some slack, okay? He's just looking out for you.'

'I know, but as I told you before, I was careful. Caleb won't find me.' At Alex's half-cocked brow, Nell sighed. 'Why do I get the feeling I have two of you looking out for me now?'

Alex studied her for a moment, but didn't answer the question.

'It's getting late,' he said eventually, getting up and lifting her cup from her hand. 'You should go home.'

Nell's jaw gaped. One minute he was inviting her into his house, the next he was asking her to leave. 'You're kicking me out?'

'I have an early start tomorrow. Our dead girl's folks are going to be here on the first ferry.'

'Sure.' Nell understood. She didn't envy the task he faced. Still, she felt there was something else behind the sudden decision to get her to leave. But she didn't push it, thanked Alex for the coffee and fished her car keys from her purse.

'You get those locks sorted yet?'

'It's on the list.' And it was on the list as a priority. Nell just didn't have the cash available to pay out for a locksmith. Pride had so far stopped her asking Michael for the money, but she guessed it wasn't so bad now they were partners. And she would feel far safer in the house once all of the doors and windows had new locks.

Alex gave her a frustrated look. 'So you keep saying.'

'I will get it done this week, I promise.'

As she stepped out onto the porch, he caught hold of her arm.

'Nell?'

She turned, brow raised.

'I want you to text me when you get back, so I know you're home safe.'

When her brow arched higher, he glared at her. 'Just humour me, okay? I have a murdered woman in the morgue and until I figure out what happened, I'm not taking any chances.'

'Sure thing, Dad.'

His lips curved and he lightly skimmed his fingertips down her arm. Nell felt her belly quiver. Annoyed, she tried to ignore it.

'Text me.'

She forced a smile. 'Will do.'

Nell pulled up on the driveway of the guesthouse fifteen minutes later and fished her phone out of her purse, firing off a quick message to Alex.

'Home safe. No-one hiding in the bushes.'

She knew the tone of the message was facetious, but couldn't help it. Something had awoken in her tonight and it left her feeling unsettled.

Stepping out of the vehicle she took a moment to draw in a deep breath. The air was fresh with the mingled scent of pines and the salty sea air, a familiar fragrance conjuring a dozen warm memories; she took a moment, let it flood her senses. Despite her gruesome find on the beach and the encounter with Sam Kent, she couldn't bring herself to regret the move back to Purity. Everything about it felt pretty much right.

She unlocked the front door and stepped inside, annoyed

she had forgotten to leave the hall light on. She'd been so certain she had.

Flicking the switch, light flooded the passageway. She bolted the door behind her and headed to the kitchen for a bottle of water.

She hit the light switch and let out a gasp, her eyes connecting immediately with the photo frame sitting on the counter.

Lizzie's smiling face from her sophomore yearbook photo stared back at her.

Nell sucked in a breath, panic rising inside her. It had to be a joke, a sick joke.

She glanced around the kitchen. Nothing else seemed out of place, no-one was hiding in the shadows waiting to leap out at her. On shaky legs, she crossed the room to the back door, tested it, not quite sure if it was relief or another knot of fear she felt when she found it locked.

Someone had been in her house, someone had left this on purpose for her to find.

Her thoughts went to Sam Kent. He was pissed she had come to the island. Had he done this? Her first reaction was to call Alex, but she stopped herself almost immediately. He had already seen her at her most vulnerable and tonight something else had shifted between them. Nell wasn't ready to acknowledge what it was. Instead she planned to ignore it.

Placing the picture frame face down on the counter, she grabbed a large knife from the drawer. Clutching it in both hands she did a room-by-room sweep of the first floor, flicking on light switches and checking behind furniture and curtains, making sure all windows were closed and locked before exiting each room. Satisfied no-one was hiding in the shadows she made her way upstairs and performed the same check on the second and third floors and the attic room, until she was finally satisfied she was alone in the big house.

Her legs still felt like jelly as she returned to the kitchen ten minutes later. She released the shaky breath she was holding, setting the knife down on the counter next to the downturned picture frame.

It was a prank, a stupid prank, she told herself as she got her water from the refrigerator then calmly made her way across the kitchen, leaving the light on and heading back upstairs, the knife back in her hand.

It was a precaution and she refused to let the picture bait her. Lizzie's death, while tragic, had been a random incident.

You keep telling yourself that. You know it's your fault she's dead.

Nell quashed down the annoying inner voice, twisting the key in the bedroom door and locking herself inside. She kicked off her shoes and set the knife and bottle of water down on her nightstand before getting undressed, the whole time feeling as though someone was watching her. Crawling into bed she reached for the lamp, flicked it off then back on.

With the warm glow from the bulb still lighting the room, she closed her eyes and attempted sleep. It was a good hour before she finally drifted off and in her dreams she saw the photo frame with Lizzie's innocent smiling face. And then her friend was climbing out of the frame, standing before her, her throat slit wide, blood pouring from her mouth and her dark eyes accusing. She pointed a finger.

'You did this to me, Nell. This is all your fault.'

13

It had been the simplest of things that eventually gave Caleb her location: the laptop.

Caleb and Nell seldom used it these days, favouring tablets and cell phones, and its only real purpose was to store details and transactions for all of Nell's buyers. Caleb had fired it up in a last ditch attempt, wanting to be sure he hadn't missed anyone, had pored over the list for the best part of a couple of hours, annoyed when it offered nothing. He had been about to shut the laptop down, when he had on a whim logged online and scrolled through the favourites list, checking every link methodically. Amazon had been her downfall. Nell must have forgotten to log out of her account the last time she had used the laptop and when he checked her most recent purchases, made only days ago, he saw the new shipping address.

It was for a guesthouse on Purity Island.

He googled the place and saw it was a popular fishing and tourist haven off the northeast coast of Massachusetts. At first it made no sense. Why would she run away to a tiny island?

Maybe Amazon had the shipping address wrong.

He made a martini, went back to the laptop and did some more research. The guesthouse had been owned by a woman named Annabella Golding. Perhaps Nell had taken a room there.

Then as he sipped his drink he remembered that there had been an Aunt Bella.

Nell had been distraught when he refused to let her attend the funeral. At the time Caleb had taken little notice, assuming the woman came from her hometown in Ohio.

Had she lived on Purity Island?

More research showed that Annabella Golding had passed away earlier in the year, followed a few weeks later by her son, Clarke. Typing in Nell's name with Purity Island yielded no results, but it did bring up another familiar name: Michael O'Connor.

It was the oafish brother who had come to visit them with his nerdy boyfriend. He had wanted little to do with either the brother or the boyfriend and, having tolerated a weekend in their company, had put a stop to further visits. Nell didn't need her past. Only her present and future, which was right here with him.

The hot-white rage he had been experiencing simmered into cold calculating anger and a need for retribution. She had tried to trick him, make a fool of him by throwing him off scent with San Francisco, wasting his time. He had no idea she could be this devious. This island had something of his and he intended to get it back.

Slowly, methodically, he began to plot his next move, packing a case on Monday night and making his way to the airport early Tuesday morning. Two flights and a hire-car drive later, he could see the place in the distance through the railings of the ferry: he felt nothing but contempt for what it had stolen from him. He had warned Nell before that he would never let her leave him, but she hadn't listened, hadn't believed him.

Now, when he found his fiancée, he would make her pay.

14

Luke had been looking forward to his dinner date with Nell all day, relishing the opportunity to get to know her better. After a full day in the office he caught the ferry back to Purity, letting himself back into his empty house and getting ready, trying his damnedest to forget the last bitter argument he'd had with Stacey.

'You're never here. You pretend you're working late, but I know what you're really doing. How many women have there been, Luke? How am I supposed to forgive you for what you've done?' He had tried to reason with her, to rationalise, but she was verging on hysteria and there was nothing he could do to calm her down.

When Newt had shown up unexpectedly on Monday evening and found him on his couch, a glass of Scotch in his hand, Luke had told him that Stacey had walked out. Truth was, he didn't know if he would ever see her again, and he wasn't sure if that left him devastated or relieved. He pushed thoughts of her from his mind as he dressed in a pair of black jeans and a blue shirt. Dabbing cologne and slicking his hair back, he glanced in the mirror and smiled to himself. He was back on track and everything was going to work out fine. Collecting his keys he let himself out of the house.

He stopped by the grocery store en route to Nell's, picking up a bottle of white wine and a colourful bouquet of flowers. Turning the aisle to the checkouts, he stopped short, spotting Jenna Milborn up ahead. Luke would have liked to turn and sneak off in the opposite direction before she clocked him, but she was too close, her cart filled with beer – no doubt for her loser husband. As he stood debating over whether he should acknowledge her, Jenna glanced up and made eye contact, a wide smile stretching across her face before tears filled her eyes.

'Luke?' she murmured, as though barely daring to believe he was there.

His heart sunk, knowing the charade they were about to go through.

Jenna had been his high school girlfriend and had never accepted the fact they were no longer together. She seemed to forget the things that had come between them and had worked some romantic notion into her head that everything would be okay if they were still together.

'I tried to call you,' she told him, one big wet tear spilling down her bruised cheek, pulling a line of inky mascara with it.

He knew and had ignored her, knowing he had nothing to say to her and not wanting to give any kind of encouragement. He had enough on his plate at the moment without having to deal with Jenna. 'I've been busy,' he said instead, knowing he couldn't tell her the truth.

'We need to talk.' She bit into her bottom lip. A long time ago he had found it sexy, now he found it irritating.

They didn't need to talk. The past was the past and he had told Jenna this so many times he couldn't understand why she was unable to get it into her stupid head.

'We've been over this, Jenna. You need to get past this.'

'I try, I do, but it's so hard.'

More tears spilled down her cheeks and Luke glanced around, worried she might make a scene. He looked at his watch, annoyed she was holding up his evening plans with Nell and also edging him into a corner.

'Look.' He softened his tone. 'I have some place to be, but come over tomorrow after work and we'll talk, okay?'

It would be the quickest way to get away from her. Every so often he had to go through this merry dance with her.

She looked hopeful. 'You promise?'

'Yes.' He doubted, hoped even, that Stacey wouldn't be around; he didn't want to add fuel to the fire. 'Come over about six, okay?'

'Okay.' She reached out, squeezed his arm and he clocked the fading bruises all the way from her wrist up to her elbow.

'I have to go. I'm running late.'

He hurried away, the cloying scent of her cheap sweet perfume lingering behind him. Quickly he paid and left the store. As he made his way back to his car he wondered for the hundredth time how he had gotten himself into this mess. They had been so young at the time. Jenna had been the prettiest and most popular girl in high school and that had attracted him, but he had never really felt anything more for her than lust, and although she put out for him, her lack of willingness to try anything new had eventually killed what few feelings he did have for her and he had grown bored.

Biting down on a sigh, he climbed into his car and dumped the flowers and wine onto the passenger seat. He had been looking forward to dinner tonight, but his run in with Jenna had ruined his mood.

Pull yourself together, he ordered, glancing in the rear-view mirror.

Telling himself everything was going to be okay he pulled out of the parking lot and hit the coast road, heading up to the guesthouse.

The day had started early for Alex, with Hunter Stone bringing Penelope Maher's next of kin over on the first ferry. It was never an easy task meeting with relatives of a murder victim. They reacted in many different ways, but every one of them was bound by an overwhelming grief and a need for answers.

Penny Maher's family were no different. Both parents were a mess, blaming themselves and holding out hope the police had gotten it wrong. Their daughter, Claire, was the strong one. Despite her young age she was the glue holding her family together, the one who was alert enough to focus and ask the right questions as her parents crumpled. Alex wished he had more he could tell them. The investigation was still in an early stage and without the rest of Penelope Maher's body, the medical examiner was limited on information.

Stone had been investigating Penny's last movements and the dating website angle. He had managed to locate Dan, the guy Penny was supposed to have had a date with, but found out it had been cancelled last minute. He had a solid alibi and the restaurant where they had reservations claimed no-one ever showed up for the table that had been booked. Stone was working on the assumption Penny may have gone on to a bar after being blown out, but still had several on his list to check.

After Stone and the Maher family left, Alex spent the rest of the day out on the water, working alongside the coastguard as they widened their search area, looking for the rest of their victim. It wasn't until dusk that the search was finally called quits for the day and he returned to shore tired, frustrated and in need of a drink. He called up Michael, who agreed to meet him in one of the harbour side bars, where they spent a couple of hours drinking beer and shooting pool, talking about anything that wasn't murder related. Michael's enthusiasm about the guesthouse was palpable and he was keen to share his ideas. Alex guessed his excitement had as much to do with having his sister back on the island and going into partnership with her as it did for the fancy pool and hot tub he had planned.

'She stopped by to see you last night, right?'

'Yeah.' Alex lined up his cue and pocketed a red ball. 'I keep telling her she needs to get the locks sorted on the house.' He glanced over at Michael as he moved round the table, selecting his next shot. 'You'll get on to it, right?'

'Yes, yeah, of course. I didn't realise it was an issue. Leave it with me and I'll make sure it's done tomorrow. Dammit. She's so certain that Caleb won't find her here, that she's covered her tracks well enough. The guy's intense though and I'm worried he's not going to give up until he's tracked her down.'

Alex could see Michael was concerned. Nell too, even though she was reluctant to talk about it. He guessed things had been bad in the relationship, and didn't think she was the kind of woman who would go to such effort to cover her tracks unless she was really scared. Each time their paths crossed he saw a different side to her. Saturday night after her gruesome find, she had been shaken to the core, the panic attack he had witnessed leaving her vulnerable and exposed. Then last night she had shown up at his place and the air had taken on a different edge. Alex hadn't pushed her. He knew she had felt it as clearly as he had, but he also understood she was fragile and needed space.

He had already decided he found her intriguing; vulnerable yet tough, friendly but guarded, those amber eyes giving little away yet at the same time revealing more than she wanted to show. Last night that intrigue had spilt over into attraction and he was still figuring out how he felt about that. For the past five years he had kept his romantic liaisons short and sweet, cutting things off if they ever threatened to get serious. It was easier that way, less complicated, and the reason why he had made the move out to Purity; needing to regroup and rebuild his life after it had been ripped apart. Nell had only been there a week and had somehow managed to knock the simple everyday order of his life onto its ass.

He didn't need the hassle of falling for his best friend's sister, knowing that because of who she was and what she had been through, it couldn't ever just be sex, which was a problem as it made things complicated. He no longer had the energy for complicated.

The Caleb angle bothered him too. Alex tried to convince himself it was purely because Michael was worried that he was concerned in his role as police chief for one of the island's citizens. He knew only what little Michael had told him, that the guy came from money and had made a name for himself in the art world, and that he had tried to cut Nell off from her family, attempting to control every aspect of her life.

'You think he would actually hurt her?'

Michael shrugged, the frustration clear on his face. 'I don't trust the guy – I know, from what little I've managed to pry out of her, that he's got a mean temper. And he's got these dead-looking eyes. She tries to make out she's okay, but I'm not so sure. My sister's no pushover, but she stayed with him for a long time and the one time I saw them together she didn't seem happy – looked frightened even. So, I'm figuring he had some kind of hold over her. He's the kind of guy who likes to own things and I can't see him letting her go without a fight.'

'Get the locks changed,' Alex urged, missing his next shot and stepping back to let Michael have his turn at the table. He picked up his beer and took a healthy swig. 'If this guy does show, you don't want him walking straight into the house.'

Meanwhile he intended to do his own checking up on Caleb Sweeney, to find out exactly who he was dealing with. If this asshole did ever wind up on the island, he'd be ready for him.

15

I t was a warm evening for late September and Nell set the table on the balcony leading out from the main living room and overlooking the ocean, hoping the temperature would hold up while they ate. With an abundance of fish in the refrigerator she had made a clam bake and the baby clams, along with mussels, lobster and crabs, were boiling away in the pot on the stove when Luke showed up, full of apologies for being late.

She had kept herself preoccupied in the kitchen, fighting her nerves over the dinner, promising herself she wouldn't cancel, so she hadn't even noticed the time, but it was irrelevant anyhow. It was a casual dinner and there were no hard or fast rules. Caleb had been big on timing and her life had been governed by a clock for long enough. She'd taken back control, intended to have a fresh start – and that meant no more rules and no more rigid time-keeping.

'It's fine,' she insisted. 'It's just dinner – and it's not even ready yet.'

'I brought wine,' Luke announced, handing her the bottle. 'And these are for you.'

Nell glanced at the colourful posy, the feeling of sickness in her belly. She had received flowers from Caleb over the years, but always as an apology when he had gone too far. When things had been really bad the reparations had come in the form of an expensive gift: a piece of jewellery or a new purse. The flowers Luke presented her with were simple and inexpensive compared to the elaborate bouquets from Caleb, and she wanted to believe in the sweet innocence of the gesture, chiding herself for even considering he might expect something in return.

'You didn't have to bring me flowers.'

'You're cooking me dinner so I don't have to stay home alone. It's nothing, really.'

'Well, you haven't sampled my cooking yet, so you may want to hold off on the thanks till you've eaten,' Nell said dryly, hunting out a vase from one of the kitchen cupboards. She found a pretty yellow pot shaped like a watering can, filled it with water, arranged the flowers quickly, and sat it on the windowsill. It instantly brightened the kitchen.

Luke chuckled. 'I'm sure your cooking will be better than the two-day-old pizza I was going to heat up.'

It was good to see him smiling and it helped put her at ease. 'Do you want some of your wine, or would you rather have a beer?'

Luke glanced at Nell's beer bottle. 'I'll take one of those, please.'

'I thought we could eat out on the balcony as it's still quite warm,' she told him, opening the refrigerator and swapping the wine for a bottle of beer. She popped the top and handed it to him.

'It's too dark now to enjoy the view, but you can hear the waves against the rocks. I've been sitting out there in the mornings while I drink my coffee – it's a pretty good place to start the day.'

'Sounds good. You're really settling into the house, aren't you?'

Nell gave a wistful smile. 'This place holds so many memories. I can't believe only a couple of days ago I was considering selling it.'

'You seem happy with your decision.'

'I am. I was so uncertain what to do. Staying didn't seem the right decision and financially I couldn't have afforded the work that needs doing, but selling felt wrong too. Michael and Newt's solution – it feels right. And the best bit is I get to do it with my brother.'

'I'd love a tour of the place – see what you have planned. I've driven past so many times over the years, but I've never been inside. Maybe after we've eaten you can show me?'

Nell glanced at the simmering pot. 'Dinner's going to be another ten minutes. I will now if you like?'

'Great.' Luke's smile widened.

'How's things with Stacey?' she asked, leading him out of the kitchen and into the main living room. She was still a little uncomfortable here with him alone, and the topic of his girl-friend kept things on a definite friend level. His vivid blue eyes turned doleful at the mention of Stacey's name, and she immediately regretted mentioning her.

'Not great.' He gave a sad smile. 'Truth is, I don't know how much longer I can carry on with her this way. It's tearing me apart, but I still love her.'

'I'm sorry I brought it up. I shouldn't have mentioned it.'

'No, it's okay. I do still love Stacey and she was... hell, she is, a great girl, but her temper and jealousy issues. Man, I don't think I can deal with it. I keep thinking it's over, that I'm gonna get home one day and she'll be gone.'

'I'm sorry, Luke. I know it's not easy.'

'Michael mentioned you left your fiancé.'

Damn it, Michael.

'Things hadn't been right there for a long time.' Nell shrugged, intentionally keeping her tone breezy. 'We'd been engaged forever and it wasn't going anywhere. I was unhappy, so I made the decision to leave.'

Luke gave her a half nod, the look in his eyes suggesting they shared a connection. Nell quickly changed the subject. 'Anyway, onto happier matters! This is the main living room in case you haven't guessed.'

If he was aware that she was uncomfortable he didn't let on, playing along with the charade, and she gave him brownie points for that. It wasn't Luke's fault she was a little jumpy and anxious, and if she could get over tonight it would be a major step forward. She showed him the large conservatory, which her aunt had used as a sun porch for guests, telling him about Michael's plans to convert the area into a pool and pointing out the patio that was intended for the hot tub; she led him up to the second floor, all the time wondering if he knew more than he was saying. Michael had blabbed to Alex, so chances were Luke knew too.

Not that Michael knew everything about her relationship with Caleb. There were plenty of details she hadn't shared, and now she was glad because she was still annoyed at him for talking to Alex, having already learned her brother's best friend wasn't into charades and called it as he saw it. Alex might come across as laid-back and charming – and he had shown her nothing but kindness and support when she had her last panic attack – but those deceptively laconic green eyes missed nothing, and that unsettled Nell. It also unsettled her that she had been unable to stop thinking about him.

She kept the tour of the bedrooms as brief as possible, closing the last door on the third floor, intending to head back downstairs.

'What's up there?'

Nell glanced at the narrow staircase leading to the attic. 'Just the attic room. It's mostly junk.'

'Can I see?'

'I guess so.'

She was conscious of him behind her on the stairs as she opened the door and flicked on the light. 'Like I say, it's mostly junk.'

'This is where you're going to have your studio, right?'

'Yeah. Well... actually, it's going to be more than a studio. When we open to the public I'm going to live up here. Michael is going to put in a bathroom and fix it all up. You see that window?' She pointed across the room. 'It has the best views of the whole island. That window is my inspiration.'

Luke nodded. 'For your painting, I get it.' He glanced around, frowning. 'Hey, that's what you were talking about the other day, right?'

Nell glanced at the graffiti on the wall that Clarke must have done, rewriting the name Sarah repeatedly. 'Yeah. Weird huh?'

'A little I guess. Probably some girl he had a crush on at school.'

'You went to school with him, didn't you? You'd have been about the same age.'

'Your cousin was in the year below me. I didn't really know him.'

'And you don't remember any girls called Sarah from school?'

'It was a long time ago. I think there might have been a couple.'

'Or, of course, it could have been the Sarah who worked here – the one who let my aunt down.'

'Yeah, maybe.' Luke shrugged. 'I guess you'll never know.'

'I guess not, though I do like a good mystery to solve.'

Luke studied her, his piercing eyes boring right into her. Feeling uncomfortable she broke away from his gaze. 'Come on. Dinner's probably ready,' she said lightly. 'You've had the house tour, so let's go eat.'

She was right about her cooking; Luke had tasted much better, though he was too much of a gentleman to tell her, so he complimented her on the dish, made a point of finishing his plateful, politely declining seconds, all the time wondering how someone could make seafood taste so bland. The food might have been mediocre, but he had to give Nell credit: her company wasn't. She had been a little uncomfortable when he had first arrived and he'd picked up on her nerves. They had him curious, wondering what kind of number her ex had pulled on her to make her so on edge. She was a woman with secrets and he wanted to know what made her tick. He turned on his charm though, and over the course of the dinner she gradually relaxed, the conversation becoming easy and her self-deprecating humour coming through. It pleased him to have this opportunity to get to know her better; it certainly beat sitting around in the house wallowing over Stacey.

'You like it on the island?' Nell asked, bringing through dessert. Luke eyed the plates warily, concerned dessert could be something else she'd made herself.

'I cheated and bought from the store,' she told him, as though reading his mind, setting the slices of New York cheesecake on the table.

'Store-bought is always good,' Luke assured her, picking up his fork and tucking in. He took a swig of the beer he was still nursing, wishing he could have another, but knowing he had to drive home.

'I do love it here,' he said between mouthfuls, answering her earlier question. 'I get to work in East Haven, but keep a house here on the island, so the way I see it I have the best of both worlds. And Newt is here too. Family is important.'

'It must have been difficult losing your parents so young.'

'I was a baby when they died. It's been just Newt and me for a while now.'

'You were raised by your grandmother, right?'

'Yeah, until she passed away, then Newt took care of us. It was his idea to move here.'

He tried to breeze over the subject, but bitterness roiled in his belly at the mention of his grandmother.

What is wrong with you, Luke? Can't you ever do anything right?

I don't know what terrible thing I did to deserve having to raise you, boy.

Why can't you be more like Jane? She's no trouble at all.

He took another sip of his beer, the image of his cousin clear in his mind. Prissy, stuck-up Jane with her pale hair and perfectly ironed clothes. She always said the right thing, always knew how to tease a smile out of their witch of a grandmother: the only grandchild Enid Trainor ever wanted. He hadn't seen Jane in years, and wondered where she was now. She wouldn't stick her nose up at him now if she could see what a success he had made of his life.

'It was great spending my summers on an island. Endless days on the beach and out on the water.' Nell's voice cut through his thoughts and he glanced up. She had traded her beer for a glass of the wine he had brought and she took a slow sip, staring out from the balcony into the blackness. 'All of my friends had boats; they were a bigger deal to them than getting their first car. Do you have a boat?'

'I do, though I don't get out on the water as often as I would like.' He forced a smile and pushed the image of Jane from his mind. 'Newt and I had never even seen the ocean before we moved to Purity, but it didn't take long to convert us to water babies.'

'This place'll do that to you. We'll have to go out on the water one day.'

Luke's smile widened, thinking he would like nothing more than to take Nell out on his boat. Maybe if circumstances were different.

'Yeah, perhaps we can.' He shovelled a mouthful of dessert in his mouth. 'I know you lived with your mom in Ohio, but you never mention your dad.'

The shutters went down almost immediately, the soft expression on her face replaced with a scowl. 'I haven't spoken to my father in years. He left Purity when I was a kid,' she answered tersely.

'You don't know where he is?' Luke pushed.

'He never left a forwarding address, but it's fine. I have no need to see him.'

Okay, so no love lost there, Luke noted. He wasn't the only one with family issues. 'Sorry I brought it up.'

Nell took another sip of her wine, a faraway look on her face. He could tell she was trying to push thoughts of her father from her mind.

In the bushes in front of the balcony, a twig snapped loudly, followed by the distinctive sound of footfall crunching against the ground.

Nell jumped to her feet, straining to see out into the night, her hand tightening on her glass.

'It's probably an animal,' Luke told her, trying to offer reassurance, though he didn't believe it himself. The noise sounded human and he felt his hackles rising.

When she didn't sit, he got to his feet. 'Why don't you wait here and I'll–'

He gasped loudly, unable to finish the sentence as pain seared through his shoulder and he fell back down into his chair.

Nell's eyes widened as she looked down at him. 'Jesus, you're bleeding.'

Luke focused on her face, on those wide expressive eyes staring at him with concern. He heard frantic scuffling in the bushes, tried to look up, but his vision blurred and a wave of nausea swept over him. Nell was applying pressure to his shoulder. He saw her fingers were red.

She pressed his hand against the cloth, her pale face briefly swimming back into focus. 'Stay here and hold this against the wound,' she instructed, her tone reedy but determined. 'I'll call 911.'

Luke had passed out before she left the balcony.

16

Two pellets had been fired from the air rifle, the first was embedded in Luke's shoulder, while the second had bounced off the wall next to the French doors and was recovered from the balcony floor.

An ambulance had taken Luke to the ER to have the shot removed while Nell stayed back to give Alex a statement. She was pale and shaken, but the panic hadn't taken hold of her this time, probably because she had quashed it down with anger. When Michael arrived fifteen minutes later, it only served to darken her mood. As Nell hadn't called him and, as he wore a pissed off expression of his own, Alex figured he must have learned of the attack from Luke and Newt.

'Jesus, Nell, what the hell happened?' he demanded, rubbing his hand over his cropped hair. 'Are you okay?'

Nell pushed him away when he attempted to fuss around her, getting to her feet and pacing the length of the kitchen. 'I'm fine. Luke's the one you should be concerned about. Some asshole shot him.' She scowled at her brother then at Alex. 'Seriously, who the hell hides in the bushes and takes potshots at someone with a damn squirrel rifle? I mean, what had Luke done to deserve that?'

Alex didn't bother to point out the bullet that had hit the wall had landed closer to her than it had to Luke and it was likely she had been the intended target. She was already tightly wound, on the verge of losing it, and not thinking straight. She didn't need to know that piece of information right now and neither did Michael, who was likely to steam off into town on a hunt for vengeance.

Luke, it appeared, had been unfortunate enough to get in the way. Nell had already talked Alex through the scene on the balcony after the ambulance had taken Luke away. Gauging from where she had been standing, from the fact Luke had stood up unexpectedly, there was no doubt in Alex's mind the shot had been intended for Nell. But for what end gain? As it had been an air rifle, not an actual gun, it suggested the intention had been to frighten her, not cause serious harm. As it happened, the pellet had caught a blood vessel in Luke's shoulder, causing a more-than-serious wound; if he had been hit in the head the consequences could even have been fatal, despite the weapon only being an air rifle.

Alex had been off duty when the call came in, and had not long been home from the bar. Tommy had called him, assuming he would want to know, and he was right. Someone was trying to spook Nell, and Alex would have been annoyed if Tommy hadn't put him in the picture. As he had only had the one beer, he decided to take the call himself.

'So, who the hell did this?' Michael demanded, frustration fraying the edges of his temper.

'You didn't see anyone lurking around the property or even across the road?' Alex had already asked the question once, knew he faced Nell's wrath for repeating himself, but was also aware that in the shock of the moment it was easy to miss things.

'No-one; I would have said if I had seen anyone. It was just Luke and me. Someone was in the bushes, we heard a noise, but couldn't see who it was, and by then it was too late.'

She ran her fingers back into her hair and he could tell she was annoyed with herself that she couldn't give him anything further. Someone had been outside the house on Saturday night, Alex recalled. At the time he had put it down to animals or kids, but now he wasn't so sure. It was a big step between breaking and entering an abandoned property, and causing someone actual bodily harm.

This was the second time Nell had been forced to call the police since returning to Purity, the first being when she had found Penelope Maher's head on the beach. Was there a connection? It seemed unlikely given Penny had most probably been murdered on the mainland, her body dumped at sea and tides carried her in the direction of the island. It had almost certainly been purely by chance that she had washed up on the shores of Purity.

Regardless, it was still an angle needing to be investigated. As did Nell's connection to Lizzie Kent's murder. Alex hated to drag it up, especially since Nell had already spoken of her guilt and had accused Tommy of reacting coldly towards her. At the time he had pretty much dismissed her, but now he wondered if there were people on the island who harboured a grudge about her return. Possibly even Lizzie's killer. He had never been caught and it had long been suspected that he was an islander.

The ex-boyfriend was top of Alex's list though. He had already planned to run a check on him in the morning. Crazy ex tracks down his missing girlfriend and sees her having dinner with another guy; it was a scenario he could see happening. And even though there was nothing in it, the relationship between Nell and Luke purely platonic, Caleb wouldn't have known that.

Hell, even Alex had felt an unwelcome stab of irritation at

the cosy-looking scene, much to his annoyance. Nell was a free agent and nothing had happened between them. She was free to have dinner with whomever she wished.

'So, what happens now?' Michael asked. He had started pacing the room, same as his sister, though they were on different sides. Alex remained centre, leant back against the counter, arms folded and eyes watchful, aware of the tension bouncing off the pair of them.

'I have a couple of guys outside sweeping the area and dusting for prints. Hopefully we'll find something.' He raked a hand back through his hair. 'Aside from Saturday night, is this the only trouble you've had?' he questioned, addressing Nell.

Something flickered across her face; uncertainty, apprehension, and she wavered for the briefest second before answering. 'Yes, I mean, no trouble.'

Her eyes were focused on the door to the hallway, avoiding his. She was lying.

'You're sure?' he pressed.

This time she met his gaze head on, her chin tilted defiantly. 'I'm sure,' she said tightly.

Alex didn't push it for now. He shot Michael a look. 'I take it you're going to stay here tonight?'

'Of course.'

Nell opened her mouth, Alex suspected to protest, but then she closed it again. While she wasn't crazy about having her brother hovering over her, he figured she preferred it to the alternative of being alone in the house.

'Keep the doors and windows locked and the curtains drawn,' Alex instructed.

'Got it.' Michael glanced at Alex. 'I need to head down to the beach house and grab an overnight bag. Are you okay to stay here until I get back?'

'Sure. Nell and I aren't done here, so take as long as you

need.' Alex made a point of catching Nell's attention and shooting her a look, wanting her to know he was on to her. Her expression turned wary and she quickly looked away.

Michael was too spiked on adrenalin to notice the exchange. 'I'll be back in half an hour.'

'I'll see you out.' Nell was quick to follow him down the hallway to the front door, seeming keen to get away from Alex's scrutinising stare.

He waited patiently in the kitchen and was still standing with his back to the counter, keeping his pose deceptively casual, when she returned a few moments later.

'I'll put the coffee pot on,' she announced, refusing to make eye contact and heading straight past him.

'So, what happened that you're not telling me about?' He adjusted his position enough to keep her in his line of vision. Beneath the tumbling blonde curls her shoulders tensed at his question.

'Nothing's happened. I already told you.' She kept her back to him, her tone light.

Another clear indication she was lying. He had only met her a week ago, but it was long enough to know she had a feisty streak. If she was telling the truth she would have been pissed the moment she was doubted.

'Michael's gone. Whatever it is, it's between you and me.'

'Nothing happened.' She repeated the words, but this time they were clipped and there was a defensive edge.

'I know you're lying and I will figure it out, so you may as well tell me.'

Although his tone was calm, reasonable even, the harsh words hit and she whirled around at the accusation, glaring at him with flaming eyes, heat rising in her cheeks. 'Dammit, Alex, I told you nothing happened, so drop it okay?'

'I'm trying to help you and I can't do that unless you let me.'

He pushed away from the counter, went to her, purposely keeping his movements slow, relaxed, not wanting to spook her. Her fists were balled tightly, a frown line creasing her brow. Her expression turned from annoyed back to wary as he took hold of her hands.

'You're cold,' he noted, closing his palms over her knuckles.

Her fists remained clenched, but she didn't pull away. They were close in height, with a couple of inches between them, and she raised her chin a notch, putting them on level, eye to eye, gold on green, the look she gave him challenging.

'You're pissing me off.' She tried to sound annoyed, but the tremor in her voice gave her away.

'Ditto.' He held her gaze, refusing to back down, close enough for the scent of her perfume to infiltrate his senses and to notice the tiny scar beneath her left eye. 'I know you think you have to do this all by yourself, but you don't. You have people here who care about you, who want to be there for you. Don't shut them out and make this into some kind of you-versus-the-world bullshit. Luke is in the hospital because someone fired an air rifle at you both. If you have any idea who that could be or why, you need to tell me. I'm the chief of police, Nell. I can help you. You just need to trust me.'

At the reminder of his job role, she broke eye contact briefly, took an appraising look at his hands covering hers then glanced back at him, eyebrows raised, questioning. 'Do you always get up this close and personal with your cases?' she challenged.

'Nope.' His lips curved slightly, and he released one hand, reaching up to brush a stray curl back from her face, allowing the pad of his thumb to graze her cheek.

Nell sucked in a breath, her eyes widening and betraying her momentarily, before the frown returned. Annoyed at how she had reacted and, he suspected, with him for not biting when he was supposed to, she let out a sigh and pushed him away.

Muttering and cursing to herself, she went to the storage cupboard in the corner of the room. He watched as she stepped inside, rose on tiptoe to reach the top shelf, all the time trying to avoid how the loose floral top she wore had risen, showing off the curve of her back.

She returned with a picture frame, stopped in front of him and held it out, her chin raised stubbornly. 'This was in the house when I got back last night.'

Alex took the frame, recognising the girl in the photo instantly as Lizzie Kent.

'In the house where?' he questioned.

Nell gave a tight smile. 'Right here, on the kitchen counter.'

'And the place was secure? No doors unlocked, no windows open, no sign of anyone breaking in?'

'No.'

Alex nodded, annoyance bubbling beneath the surface because she was only telling him this now. 'Why didn't you call me?'

'I... It was late.'

It was a lame excuse, but he let it slide. Getting angry with Nell would only push her away. Someone had been outside tonight, taking shots at her and Luke. The picture had to be connected.

'So, do you have any idea who might have left this?'

She was silent and he could see the debate in her eyes of whether or not to tell him. 'Sam Kent was parked outside the house on Friday night.'

'Okay.'

'I ran into him at the grocery store on the way over to Michael's. He... He wasn't happy to see me back on the island.' Nell glanced up at Alex, resignation now in her eyes. 'I don't know why he stopped by the house. He didn't get out of the car, just sat there for a while. But then he drove off and I figured that was it.'

Alex nodded. Sam Kent was a loner, but a hard worker. The loss of his sister had hit him hard and, even though nearly two decades had passed; time hadn't appeared to heal the wound. There had always been sadness in Sam, but Alex had never seen anger. He was a law-abiding citizen, quietly coming and going, minding his own business. It was a huge stretch to get from sorrow to assault, but he believed Nell. She had a lousy poker face and he could easily tell when she tried to hide things from him. Sam had been outside her house on Friday night; he didn't doubt it.

'You should have told me this sooner.'

'His sister is dead because of me. I figured he deserved a little slack.'

'Yeah, he deserves a little slack, but breaking and entering, taking a shot at someone with an air rifle? That's in a different league.'

'Presuming it was definitely him.'

'You think it's someone else?'

Nell was silent for a moment. 'No,' she eventually admitted. 'I guess not.'

'When Michael gets back here I'll go have a chat with him.'

'Alex?'

'Yeah?'

'Go easy on him, okay? Please?'

'You don't owe him anything, Nell.'

'It doesn't matter that I don't owe him. He's been through a lot, lost a lot. His family, they don't need this, and I don't want to make things worse.'

Alex smiled, though it was without humour. 'It seems to me it's already too late for that.'

'Jenna?'

When his wife didn't answer immediately, Curtis Milborn turned down the volume on the TV and yelled louder. 'Jenna, fucking come here when I'm talking to you.'

He heard the sound of footsteps on the stairs and his mouse of a wife appeared in the doorway wringing her hands together.

'Sorry, Curtis, I didn't hear you.'

She had been crying, rings of red around her eyes and her make-up a mess. Not that it was unusual. It never took much for Jenna to start blubbing her eyes out. He took a final drag on his cigarette, stubbed it out in the overflowing ashtray and held out his empty can. 'Get me another beer.'

Dutifully she took the can and scurried off. Curtis stared at the empty doorway, contempt on his face.

He recalled the first time he had asked Jenna out. She had been fresh out of high school and not long broken up with that arrogant son of a bitch, Luke Trainor. Jenna had been so pretty back then, and Curtis had barely believed his luck when she agreed to a date. He had been just shy of his thirtieth birthday at the time, still had aspirations of hitting the big time and getting off this shitty island. Scoring a date with a pretty girl twelve years his junior made him feel invincible.

At first he had treated her like a princess, spending what little money he did have in an attempt to impress her. Looking back, she had been self-pitying and dull even then, but he hadn't seen it, convincing himself he had landed the top prize. He had been quick to march her down the aisle and it wasn't until they had been married for a few months that he started to recognise her for what she was, realising that he had been duped.

That was the story of his life. Every time he thought he had something good, it either slipped away or turned out to be a waste of time.

Jenna returned to the living room with another beer. She looked pale and shaky as she handed him the can, quickly turning on her heel to leave the room.

'Jenna?' Curtis rolled the beer between the palms of his hands, fury balling itself in his chest at the temperature of the can. 'Why have you just given me a warm can?'

She glanced back apprehensively, eyes widening. 'I put them in the refrigerator as soon as I got back from the store, I promise.'

'Well, maybe if you'd have gotten back sooner my fucking beer would be cold.'

'I'm sorry, Curtis, there was a long line.'

Curtis hurled the can at her and she ducked as it skimmed her head.

'Don't answer me back. Do you need me to come and teach you a lesson on how to chill my beer?' He got up from his chair, took a menacing step towards her.

'Please, Curtis. I'm sorry.'

Just seeing her standing there all pathetic made him want to beat the crap out of her. She started to sob, which just served to irritate him further.

'I'll go see if there's another.'

'You've ruined the moment for me now. Look how you've made me all angry. If there was a cold one you should've brought it to me in the first place.'

He lunged at her suddenly, reaching for her arm, frustrated when she darted out of the room and fled for the stairs.

'Don't make me come up there after you, Jenna.'

He heard the bathroom door bolt shut, rage boiling in his gut as he flew up the stairs after her. 'Open the door, Jenna. OPEN THE FUCKING DOOR!'

She couldn't stay in the bathroom forever and when she came out he would be waiting. She wouldn't ever serve him warm fucking beer again.

17

Tommy Dolan couldn't quite decide if he had lucked out or drawn the short straw going to the hospital to take a statement from Luke Trainor. As a nurse led him down the corridor to the bed where Luke was recuperating, he decided there had only been short straws. He hadn't been up for another encounter with Nell O'Connor, was cursing her when the call had come in, wondering how one person was able to attract so much trouble, and he'd breathed a huge sigh of relief when Alex had put himself back on duty and responded to the situation.

Of course, it left Luke to Tommy, an encounter he didn't relish either.

The pair of them had gone to high school together, though Luke had been a year ahead of him. As a teenager Tommy had thought he was pretty cool, envied him even. Luke was captain of the football team, dated Jenna Campbell, and had tons of friends. He didn't really know Luke to talk to, but passing him in the hallways of school, where he was always surrounded by a crowd, was enough to make sixteen-year-old Tommy Dolan aspire to be like him.

Of course, sixteen was a long time ago and he had learned

there was a lot more to life than being popular in high school. Luke and Jenna had broken up when Luke went away to college and their lives had carved different paths in the interim years, with Jenna marrying Curtis Milborn and becoming a pathetic shadow of her former self, while Luke had graduated and returned to the island with a shiny new car and a flashy wardrobe. He always seemed to land on his feet, could talk his way in and out of most situations, and had a good job with a law firm in East Haven, but to Tommy he never looked happy or seemed satisfied with his lifestyle, bimbo girlfriend and his big bank balance.

Tommy no longer aspired to be like Luke Trainor, and seeing everything he represented only irritated him.

It had initially surprised him to find out Luke had been having dinner with Nell, particularly as he figured Luke's girlfriend, Stacey, would not approve. Tommy had only met her a handful of times, but knew she had a reputation for having a jealous streak. He supposed as Luke's brother was in a relationship with Michael O'Connor, it gave him some common ground with Nell, but he couldn't help wondering if there was more to it. Nell was pretty, there was no denying that, and Tommy knew Luke had always had an eye for the ladies. Word had it she had fled a bad relationship back in Chicago. Was Luke trying to play on her vulnerability?

He shrugged off the question, guessing it was none of his business if it was true. Luke could flirt with whoever he wanted, and he didn't care what Nell did, as long as they both stayed out of his way.

The nurse hauled the curtain back and Tommy faked a smile for the patient, nodding at Newt Trainor who sat by his brother's side.

'Thanks for coming.' Newt leant forward to shake his hand.

'Tommy,' Luke greeted him. His usually olive

complexion was pale, and Tommy could tell he was grimacing against the pain in his shoulder, which had been bandaged up.

'Luke, Newt.' Tommy kept his eyes on Newt Trainor, though was aware of Luke staring at him. He got the impression Luke knew he didn't particularly like him. Their paths seldom crossed, and he was happy to have it that way. He pulled up a chair and took out his notepad.

'Is Alex not coming?' Luke questioned.

Tommy knew both Trainor brothers were friendly with the chief, so guessed it was only natural they would assume he might be here.

'He's still at the house with Nell.'

'Oh, okay.' Luke hesitated. 'How is she? It's all a bit of a blur from when I was shot. I imagine she must have been pretty shaken up.'

'I wouldn't know. I wasn't there,' Tommy replied bluntly.

There was an awkward moment of silence, which Newt Trainor was quick to try and fill.

'Michael is going to stay with her tonight,' he assured his brother. 'He says she wasn't happy about it, but I think he's making the right decision.'

'That's good. She shouldn't be alone. I take it there was no trace of whoever shot me?' Luke's eyes were intently on Tommy, waiting for a reply.

'No, but we're working on it. What can you tell me about what happened tonight?'

Tommy listened as Luke spoke, making notes, his focus on the notepad, keenly avoiding his piercing blue stare. He finished taking the statement, asked a few questions, smiled tightly as he flipped shut the notebook and capped his pen. Luke hadn't seen anything and his statement wasn't going to be any help in catching whoever shot him.

He got up, pushed back his chair, eager to be on his way. 'We will be in touch.'

Newt nodded, the stress of the evening clearly etched on his face.

'Thanks, Tommy. We appreciate you coming down.'

Tommy briefly made eye contact with Luke, his tight smile becoming a scowl. 'We will be in touch,' he repeated. Without another word he turned and walked out of the ER.

Sam Kent lived on the east side of the island, a mile out of town, in a neat unassuming red brick house on a quiet residential street. His car was in the driveway. Alex pulled his Jeep to a halt alongside the curb, noting the lights in the house were all off. He glanced at the dashboard clock, which flashed 22.11, guessing Sam was either in bed or wanted it to appear that way.

He felt the hood of Sam's car, noted it was cold and hadn't been driven recently, then made his way up the pathway to the front door and rang the bell. While he waited for an answer he surveyed the front yard. It was low-key, understated, much like Sam. Alex knew him well enough to exchange pleasantries with, but other than that their paths didn't cross. Sam kept to himself, held down a job working on one of the island's fishing boats, and had never married. He was still close to his parents, worked hard, was seemingly mild mannered, and by all accounts had never gotten over his sister's death.

Had he held a grudge against Nell over all of these years or had her return to the island sparked something inside him?

Of course, there was no conclusive proof he had been responsible for the picture or for firing the air rifle, but he was the most viable suspect at this point. Alex planned to tread carefully, but if he found out Sam was responsible for harassing Nell and trying to harm her, for putting his friend in the hospital, he would come down on him hard.

He rang the bell again.

This time he saw the flicker of a light through the pane of glass in the door and heard footsteps in the hallway.

The door swung open a few inches and Sam peered out. He looked half asleep and his breath reeked of alcohol. His eyes bugged as he recognised Alex. 'Chief? What you doing here? Are my parents okay?'

'Your folks are fine, Sam. Can I come in?'

'Is something wrong?'

'Why don't we go inside and talk?'

'Umm... I guess, okay.' Sam rubbed his eyes and took a step back so Alex could enter. He looked a little uncomfortable as he closed the door. Not necessarily in a guilty way, more he seemed unsure how to act with an unexpected visitor. 'So, um, do you want something to drink?'

'I'm good.'

'Okay, well the living room is through here.' He gestured ahead and lead the way down the hall to a simply furnished room with an oversized TV playing quietly in the background and a single couch.

Judging by the rumpled state of the cushions and Sam's creased T-shirt and mussed hair Alex suspected he had been asleep when he had arrived. The half-empty bottle of vodka on the floor suggested that sleep had likely been alcohol-induced.

He ignored Sam's gesture to sit down, preferring to remain standing.

'Can you tell me where you were tonight, Sam, between the hours of seven and ten?'

'Where I was?' Sam seemed surprised by the question. 'Why do you want to know?'

'Can you answer the question?'

Sam frowned, looking confused. 'Sure, I've been here.'

'You've been home all evening?' Alex pressed.

'Yeah. I mean I finished work just before seven, called in the grocery store on my way home, but yeah, I've been here having a drink and watching TV. I was actually asleep when you rang the bell.'

Alex didn't bother to apologise. 'So, you've seen no-one. No visitors who can corroborate your story?'

'No, it's just been me.' Sam sighed and shoved back a handful of hair. 'What's this about please, Chief Cutler? Why all the questions? Am I in some kind of trouble?'

'Someone was out at Nell O'Connor's place earlier tonight firing an air rifle. Luke Trainor was hit and is in the hospital.'

Alex watched Sam's reaction carefully as he processed the information. He didn't seem overly surprised, certainly didn't seem concerned.

'Okay. And you think that person was me?'

'Do you own an air rifle?'

'No.'

'But you did run into Nell a few nights ago?'

'Yeah, at the store.' Sam's tone turned bitter. 'Last person I wanted to bump into.'

'Because of what happened to Lizzie?'

'Do you blame me?'

'Nell says she saw you parked outside her house later that night. What were you doing there?'

'It was a shock running into her like that. I didn't know she was home. I went for a drive, ended up out that way.' Sam's expression became guarded. 'I didn't do anything, I never harassed her and I wasn't even on her property. Last I remember, pulling over in the road outside someone's house wasn't a crime.'

'I never suggested it was.' Alex kept his tone lighter than he felt. Losing his temper wasn't going to help the situation. 'You showed up outside her house though and you've made it clear you don't like her, so I'm sure you can understand why I have to talk to you about tonight.'

'Don't like her? I hate the bitch. She killed my sister.'

'Roy Dolan's accomplice killed your sister.'

'It should have been Nell.' Sam spat the words, the fury coming quick and sudden, and his eyes flashing black.

'Is that what you think Lizzie would have wanted?' When Sam didn't answer, Alex continued, 'It shouldn't have been either of them. What happened to your sister was terrible, Sam, but Nell didn't kill her. Don't punish her for something that wasn't her fault.'

'Who else am I supposed to blame? How easy do you think it is for me having to see Nell walking around here again, while Lizzie lost everything because Nell was too irresponsible to babysit?'

'So, you've never made a mistake before, never regretted a decision?'

'Not one that's ended up costing someone their life. You can't make me forgive her, so please stop trying.' Sam scowled at Alex. 'Do you have any further questions for me, Chief, because unless you plan on arresting me, I'd like you to leave.'

Alex gave him a measured look, aware he could reason with Sam all night and never get him close to changing his mind. The jury was still out on whether he had fired the air rifle. Sam had no witnesses to verify his whereabouts and he certainly had the grudge, but he made no secret of it, plus he had seemed genuinely shocked to see Alex on his doorstep tonight.

The level of hatred the man felt towards Nell still bothered him though. He had a temper and Alex intended to keep him on his radar.

'No more questions for now but stick around, as I may be

back.' As he was heading out to the Jeep, his cell rang. It was one of the deputies he had left working the scene at the guesthouse. 'How you getting on, Kyle?'

'We've lifted a print. It was on a matchbook we found lying on the ground in front of the balcony. I checked with Miss O'Connor and she confirmed it's not hers.'

It was a start. 'Anything else?'

'Not yet, but we're still looking.'

Alex ended the call feeling hopeful. If the matchbook didn't belong to Nell – and he knew Michael and Luke didn't smoke – then there was a reasonable chance their shooter had dropped it. He thought back to Sam Kent and couldn't recall ever seeing him smoking and hadn't spotted any ashtrays in his house, but it didn't mean the matchbook wasn't his. Hopefully when they ran the print it would offer up a lead.

Caleb Sweeney sat in one of the seafront bars nursing his second martini and musing over the events of the evening, letting the numbness of the alcohol soothe the burning rage he felt inside.

Rage at this point would get him nowhere. He needed to take time, reassess the situation.

He had arrived on the island early evening and intended for his visit to be a brief one. Being a thorough man, he had already studied online maps of the island and knew where Nell's aunt's house was located. His plan was for them to catch the late ferry back to the mainland and make it back to the airport in time for the midnight flight back to Chicago. Confident things would work out the way he intended he had already purchased two tickets.

He hadn't expected there to be any difficulties and his bad mood had lightened slightly as he turned the hire car onto the coastal road he knew led to the house. His flight had been on time, the car in place waiting for him at the airport, and the ferry crossing smooth. Nell had betrayed him, so he anticipated a little resistance on her front, but he was certain with the right amount of persuasion he would quickly make her see sense. There was no need for any ugliness tonight, as long as she took responsibility for her actions and set about making things right.

The good mood had lasted until he turned the corner in the road, spotting the guesthouse up ahead, and the sporty Camaro pulling into the driveway.

Caleb had slowed the rental car as he approached the property, eyes on the tall, dark-haired man who had exited the Camaro, on the flowers and wine in his hands. Before the man had reached the front door, it had opened and there she had stood, so pretty with her blonde hair loose and spilling over her shoulders it had almost taken Caleb's breath away, and then she was accepting the flowers and ushering the man inside the house. Struggling to breathe, he had pulled his car to a halt a little further up the road, spent a few minutes trying to get his emotions under control as burning rage rose deep inside him, threatening to overwhelm him.

The bitch was with another man.

She hadn't just left him; she was seeing someone else.

Red mist blurred his vision, the pain searing through him almost intolerable, and it had taken every ounce of control to stay in the car, when his fists wanted nothing more than to beat the man's face to a pulp, then to wrap his fingers around Nell's throat and choke her until she couldn't breathe, hurt her the way she had hurt him.

She belonged to him and him alone.

Instead he thumped the steering wheel, yelled and cursed until his face was red and he had worked up a sweat. In his chest his heart raced furiously. He had wasted time and money on her irritating little game, having to come all the way to this pissant island, and now he was here she was rubbing his nose in it by cavorting with another man. She'd pay for this.

He had toyed with hiding the car somewhere off the road, walking back to the house and staking-out the property, trying to get a measure of what he was dealing with, but he knew the fury he felt was too fresh, too raw, and he may not be able to keep his emotions in check, so could end up doing something he may regret.

If he burst in on Nell and her guest, things would turn ugly, he could end up arrested and she would be drawn further out of his reach. He needed time to think, to figure out the best time to approach Nell when she would be alone. If Caleb Sweeney was anything, he was organised and meticulous, and if he was going to get his fiancée back he was going to have to come up with a foolproof plan.

Needing time to think and to clear his head he drove further along the coast road, following the route as it snaked through trees before descending towards the beach. On a whim he pulled over into a clearing where rocks jutted down into the sand a few feet below.

A walk along the beach would help clear his head, help him think.

By the time he had returned to the car two hours later, the sky had darkened, the rise and fall of the tide had picked up, and he was a little calmer. He decided he would drive back via the house, see if the man's car was still there. If he had gone then he intended to get Nell, but if he was still there then Caleb would check into one of the hotels in town for the night and return for Nell in the morning. It annoyed him he had paid money out for flights that couldn't be used, but he would deal with Nell over that later. The only important thing at the moment was getting her back.

This time when he approached the house there was a hive of activity. He spotted the police Jeep first, then the ambulance; both had anxiety curling in his gut and his hands tightening on the wheel.

Had something happened to Nell? Was she okay?

The anger swelled as he spotted the Camaro still at the house, but this time it was mixed with fear and panic. What if Nell was hurt or dead?

Without her his life meant nothing.

Wanting to stick around, but knowing it would be a bad idea, he had forced himself to drive past the house again and head back into town. There were two hotels on the island and he made his way straight to the Purity Oaks, having read it was the better of the two; they still had a few rooms available. He had checked in for the night, showered, ordered room service, and pushed the food around on his plate, before giving in to restless pacing, the confines of the plush room closing around him like a cage.

Eventually he had grabbed his jacket and headed out. He didn't want company, but needed the distraction of other people around him. Following the route down to the harbour he wandered aimlessly along the front, not seeing anyone around him: his sole focus on Nell, on both her betrayal and the ambulance.

He wouldn't rest until he knew she was first okay and until they were off this damn island and on their way back home.

'Hey, watch it!'

Caleb had snapped back to the present, focusing on the angry face in front of him. The guy had coffee down the front of his shirt. Not in the mood for confrontation, he pushed the man out of his way and carried on walking, ignoring the indignant protests behind him.

He spotted a bar up ahead and, needing a drink, he had ducked inside.

Draining the glass he caught the bartender's eye and pushed it forward. 'Another martini.'

The man nodded and started fixing the drink.

Two women entered the bar, their chatter annoyingly loud. They took the booth behind where he sat and as one giggled shrilly, Caleb snatched up the glass the bartender had set in front of him, and took a generous sip.

'Did you hear Luke Trainor is in the hospital? Nasty accident tonight.' One was asking.

'Really? Is he okay?'

'My sister's a nurse. She texted me. Apparently, he was shot with an air rifle.'

'Noooo way? How the hell did that happen?'

'He was having dinner with Nell O'Connor, out at her place.'

Caleb had been about to turn around, ready to warn the two women to keep their voices down. His shoulders tensed at the mention of Nell's name.

'He was having dinner with her? What about Stacey?'

'Are they still together? I haven't seen her about lately.'

'You think she's left him? Why the hell would she leave him? The woman needs her head tested. So, he's seeing Nell O'Connor?'

'Looks like it. Cops are out at her place now. Funny how she seems to attract trouble.'

'Yeah, I guess she does. She's certainly keeping the chief busy.'

'First there's Lizzie Kent's murder, then the head on the beach, now Luke getting shot. Things have certainly livened up here since she arrived back.'

Caleb listened intently. So, something had happened up at the guesthouse tonight. It seemed Nell's dinner guest had been shot. Who the hell had been out there and what was their endgame? The women had mentioned a girlfriend, Stacey. Ex-girlfriend possibly, but had she been the one to take the shot? Things were more complicated than he had anticipated. While that both frustrated and annoyed him, it was also intriguing. With the guesthouse a crime scene, he was going to have to tread carefully and that meant a change of plan. It was likely the cops would be swarming the place for the next few days and it was best for him to keep a low profile. In the meantime, he intended to find out everything he could about this Luke Trainor and his girlfriend, Stacey. It irritated him knowing Nell was so close and yet there was nothing he could do about it, but he could live with that.

Caleb Sweeney was a cautious and orderly man. Yes, he may have a temper, but he measured things carefully. If he had to wait a few days for Nell, then so be it.

18

By Saturday morning Nell was starting to go stir crazy. It had been four days since the shooting incident that had put Luke in the hospital and, even though nothing else had happened since, Michael was acting like her bodyguard, refusing to let her out of his sight. She appreciated him being with her and knew she couldn't have been left alone in the house after everything that had happened. And she didn't want to appear ungrateful, especially after he had called in the locksmith and a local security company to fit an alarm. She just wished he would give her a little breathing space, instead of taking charge, making decisions without consulting her and keeping tabs on her every move.

Heading down to the kitchen Saturday morning in need of coffee, she grimaced hearing his familiar jovial whistle. She loved her brother, but it was all getting too much.

'Hey, you're up.' He greeted her with a huge grin and way too much enthusiasm for eight thirty in the morning. Since she had been back, Nell preferred to ease her way into the day and generally avoided all forms of communication until she had downed at least two cups. Ignoring him, she went to the coffee pot, grateful at least that he had heated it up and she didn't have to wait.

'You want waffles?'

'No, I'm good.'

'I picked up maple syrup. Or I have blueberries if you prefer.'

'I'm not hungry.'

She poured her coffee and hoped to make a quick escape back upstairs.

'I thought we could go over some of the ideas I have for the guesthouse this morning.'

Nell paused. 'This morning isn't a good time. I was planning on painting.'

'Okay then, how about this afternoon? You take the morning to paint, it will do you good to relax and take your mind off things, then this afternoon we can sit down and–'

'Jesus, Michael. Just stop, okay?' Nell slammed her cup down on the counter, her head spinning. 'I can't do this. I can't have you shadowing me like this.'

She met his eyes and inwardly flinched at the pain in them.

'I'm not shadowing you.' He spoke quietly, hurt evident in his tone. 'I'm worried sick by what happened Tuesday night and I need to know you're safe, okay? I'm sorry if that's too much for you to handle, but you're my sister and I love you, care about you. If anything happened, I... I couldn't forgive myself.'

Although she was still irritated, Nell's tone softened. 'Look, I'm sorry. I really appreciate you staying with me the last few nights. I know you care and you are trying to help, I do, but you need to give me space to breathe.'

'You want me to go back to the beach house?'

'You can't give up your life and babysit me forever. What about Newt? He needs you too.'

When he continued to waver, she put her arms around him, gave him her most beseeching look. 'The locks are secure, you've installed a fancy alarm system. If it makes you happier I will call you every night and morning to let you know everything is okay.'

Easing himself out of her embrace, Michael turned his attention back to breakfast. Although he said nothing, Nell could tell he was chewing the suggestion over. Truth was, after everything that had happened, the idea of being alone in the house terrified her, but she knew she would have to take the step at some point.

'Sit down, Nell. Eat these waffles I made.'

'I told you, I'm not hungry.'

'Sit,' he ordered. 'Eat the damn waffles. If you do, I'll move back home.'

'You will?'

'I will. But first we are going out tonight?'

'Out? Out where?'

'There's a party in town. Remember Stephanie Richardson?'

'Yeah, I ran into her sister, Antonia, on my first day back on the island.'

'Well, it's Steph's fortieth birthday. Her husband and Antonia are throwing her a surprise party down at Maloney's. They said to bring you along. There will be dancing, there will be alcohol. After the stress of the last few days it will do both of us good to get out and have some fun. What do you say?'

Nell hesitated. She remembered Antonia's older sister, had always liked her, but a party was going to bring her into contact with a lot of the townsfolk. She had planned to ease herself back into life on the island gently. But maybe it was time to reacquaint with old faces. Plus, Michael was right, it would do them both good to let their hair down. She had promised herself a fresh start and that meant jumping in with both feet.

'Okay, why not?'

It was a beautifully mild day and Nell spent much of it painting, enjoying knowing the canvas she was working on was for her and her alone. There was no longer anyone dictating how and what she should paint, and casting a critical eye over each finished piece. Her thoughts turned to the party and apprehension knotted her gut at the thought of having to deal with a room full of people. She had promised Michael she would go and knew it would probably be good for her confidence. Over the past few years, her only social engagements had been the stuffy cocktail parties and benefits Caleb had dragged her to. Slowly, methodically, over their first eighteen months together, he had managed to isolate her from all of her friends. It had been so gradual Nell hadn't even realised it was happening, but eventually the calls and the invites had stopped coming and when things started to get bad with Caleb, she found herself alone.

She would never make that mistake again.

With no-one to confide in, no-one to tell her otherwise, she had started to believe the things he told her, even feeling responsible for being the cause of their many fights. It wasn't him, he would tell her. No, he was the patient one, the suffering one, while she was always the guilty party. It made her cringe to think back to how worthless he had made her feel.

As the sun started to set, she downed tools and headed for the shower, debating over what she should wear. Jeans were her safety blanket and while she was tempted to stick with them, it was a birthday party. Maloney's was hardly upmarket, but it wasn't spit and sawdust either. Back in Chicago she had a closet full of beautiful dresses Caleb had bought her and insisted she wear to various functions. Nell had left them all behind except one she had chosen and paid for herself.

Self-consciously she appraised herself in the mirror twenty minutes later, the silky blue material of the dress hugging her curves and leaving her feeling exposed and vulnerable. Unsure what to do with her curls, she tied them back in a loose low knot, put diamond studs in her earlobes and slipped her feet into a pair of strappy heels. When she reached the foot of the stairs five minutes later, Michael glanced up, jaw falling open.

'Good God. What have you done with my sister?'

The apprehension returned. 'Is it too much?'

'Hell no, baby, you look beautiful.' He leaned in, kissed her on the cheek, before offering his arm. 'Shall we?'

The party was in full swing by the time they arrived with cars crowding the parking lot. Michael had driven, but planned to leave his pickup at the venue and collect it the following morning. With no space close to Maloney's, he found a roadside spot. Nell felt the apprehension returning as they walked down the road towards the bright lights and jovial sounds coming from the bar. She clutched tightly at the bottle of champagne they had stopped to buy for Stephanie on the way.

Her nerves must have been palpable because Michael took her hand as they headed up the steps to the front entrance and gave it a squeeze. 'It's gonna be fine,' he assured her. 'We'll have fun, I promise.'

As the door opened, the noise and the heat from the crowd hit them. The place was rammed, with several folk queuing at the bar, while others had already hit the dance floor and groups were gathered either standing around or having taken over one of the tables.

Nell spotted Antonia and Steph standing chatting under a large pink 'HAPPY 40TH BIRTHDAY' banner. She was glad to see they both wore dresses and felt more relaxed about ditching her jeans. As they glanced over, she raised a hand in greeting.

'Go mingle,' Michael shouted over the band, who were playing an enthusiastic cover of *Sex on Fire*. 'I'll get you a drink.'

He swatted her on the butt, pushing her forward towards the sisters.

'Nell, you came!' Antonia, all perky in pink, sounded over-joyed, flinging her arms around her. 'Steph, you remember Nell O'Connor, don't you?'

Steph was the chalk to Antonia's cheese, her dark hair softly curled and the red dress she wore, understated, but feminine and flattering.

'Yes, sure I do. It's good to see you, Nell. I heard you'd moved to the island. Thanks for coming tonight.'

'Happy to be here. Oh, and happy birthday.' Nell thrust the bottle of champagne at Stephanie, earning herself another Richardson hug.

Technically she wasn't sure if happy was the right word. She was still a little anxious and hoped Michael wouldn't take too long at the bar. She needed both the drink and her brother for support. She forced her smile wider and made small talk as best she could over the noise of the band with Stephanie and Antonia, before they were mobbed by fresh newcomers bearing birthday wishes and gifts. Easing away, Nell glanced around the room, looking for other familiar faces.

Come on, Michael.

Across by the doors leading out to the deck she spotted Alex, his attention firmly on the woman he was engaged in conversation with. She was pretty, Nell noted, with long auburn hair, her curves wrapped in a sinfully tight black dress. Alex was leaning in close and whatever he said made the woman laugh and move even closer, so her breasts were brushing against his arm.

Jealousy stabbed at Nell's gut, immediately followed by irritation. Why should she care who Alex was flirting with? She certainly had no dibs on him. Still she watched, annoyed at the jealousy still bubbling away under the surface.

'You having a good time?' Michael asked, rejoining her. He handed her a beer.

'Yeah, it's great,' Nell lied. 'Who's that with Alex?'

She asked the question as casually as possible, telling herself it was innocent curiosity.

Michael glanced over to where she was pointing. 'Oh, that's Mia Grayson. She's a doc over at the hospital. She and Alex used to have a bit of thing.'

Used to?

Michael didn't elaborate, and Nell couldn't bring herself to push it. Besides, it was none of her business.

'Come on, I'll introduce you.'

Nell protested as Michael took her arm, but the words were lost beneath the drone of the loud music. She didn't want to meet this Mia person. Coming to the party had been a bad idea.

'Hey, buddy.' Michael slapped Alex on the shoulder.

The redhead looked annoyed at being interrupted. Her gaze moved briefly over Michael before settling on Nell, who was trying to stay discreetly behind him. Alex turned, grinned at Michael and also clocked Nell, his eyes widening as they skimmed the full length of her then slowly moved back up to linger on her face. 'Wow, what happened to you?' A sly wide smile dimpled his cheeks and Nell blushed furiously. The redhead didn't miss his reaction, and her expression darkened as she took hold of his arm proprietarily and glared at Nell.

Michael threw an arm around his sister, pulling her forward, oblivious to everyone's reaction. 'Nell, this is Mia Grayson. She works over at the hospital. Mia, this is my younger sister, Nell.'

Nell forced a smile and a hello as the woman appraised her.

'Nice to meet you, Michael's little sister.'

There was no warmth in her tone and she didn't offer her hand, instead keeping it possessively on Alex's arm.

'I figured Nell needed a night out,' Michael shouted to Alex over the band. 'So I talked her into coming along.'

'Good call,' Alex agreed, his focus still entirely on Nell.

She thought back to their last encounter, the night Luke had been shot, when Alex had crossed the line between professional and personal. At the time it had both unnerved and flustered her, as she presumed he wanted something more from her than she wanted to give. Seeing him tonight with Mia knocked home that it hadn't been about her. He was obviously a tactile and flirtatious person with everyone and she had misread the situation. It should have relieved her, so why did it leave her disappointed?

The band kicked in with the first beats of *Uptown Funk* and Nell started tapping her foot. Screw Alex. She had come out tonight to have a good time. Watching him flirting with a snooty redhead hardly measured up. 'We should go dance,' she yelled to Michael, forcing a bright smile on her face. 'You promised me dancing, remember?'

'I did.' Michael seemed delighted. 'Keep an eye out for Newt,' he instructed Alex. 'He's supposed to be meeting us down here.'

The floor was packed, but Nell found a space, dragging her brother along behind her. For the next hour she lost herself in the music, all thoughts of Alex, of Caleb, of Lizzie, of Luke's shooting and the dead woman's head pushed from her mind as she melted into the sea of sweaty bodies, enjoyed the enthusiastic vibe of the crowd and the beat of the band. Michael was a willing participant and he threw himself around, slightly out of sync with the music, swinging her clumsily around. They stayed on the floor until the band had finished their set and the music was replaced by a DJ who kicked his set off with a ballad.

'Drink?' Michael suggested.

Nell nodded, her throat parched as she followed him from the dance floor.

She had missed this: out having fun, dancing and letting her hair down. She'd really missed it. Caleb would have pitched a fit if he had seen her in a place like this and it had her wondering why it had taken her so long to leave him.

Newt arrived as Michael handed Nell another bottle of beer, full of apologies he was running late after stopping by to drop off groceries for Luke.

'How is he?' Nell asked as her brother ordered Newt a drink. Luke had been discharged from the hospital the morning after the shooting, and she had been to see him a couple of times, knew he was frustrated with the injury to his shoulder.

'He's still in pain,' Newt told her. 'The doc's given him some stronger painkillers. He was going to come along tonight, but they've wiped him out. He was asleep on the couch when I left him.'

'I'll stop by and see him again in a couple of days.'

'I'm sure he will appreciate that.'

Michael rejoined them and Nell left them to talk while she went in search of the restroom. She glanced in the direction of doors that led to the deck, noting Alex and Mia were no longer there. Looking round the bar, she couldn't spot either of them. Maybe they had already left together? The thought took the edge off her good mood and disappointment and jealousy balled uncomfortably in her belly at the thought, making her a little nauseous. She shouldn't care, and was mad at herself that it was bothering her. Alex owed her nothing and she wanted nothing from him. Still that little ball gnawed away inside her gut, calling her a liar.

The restroom was blessedly empty and after peeing, she spent a few moments appraising herself in the mirror hanging over the sink. The bar was warm and she was hot and sticky from the dancing, her skin flushed; her hair was still up, though a few loose tendrils had escaped the knot she'd tied.

She was retouching her lip gloss when the door opened and a woman entered. She didn't spot Nell at first, seemed distracted, her palms splayed over her face before she shoved her hands back into her copper coloured hair.

Nell narrowed her eyes. 'You okay?'

The woman visibly jumped, glancing up wide-eyed at the sound of Nell's voice. She seemed flustered, embarrassed. Clearly she had thought the bathroom was empty.

'I'm fine.' The words were clipped, to the point, an automatic conditioned response and she glanced at Nell warily before averting her eyes and disappearing into a stall. She didn't look fine and something in Nell's gut had her lingering, waiting for the woman to emerge. When she did she threw Nell another quick glance, still wary, but this time irritation also showing because Nell was still there. As she stepped up to the sinks, Nell clocked the fading bruise on her left cheekbone and bile rose in her throat, recognising the injury for what it was.

'It's a good party, don't you think?' It was a lame opening line, but Nell needed to start a conversation.

'Sure, it's great.' There was no enthusiasm in the words, the woman's tone flat.

'I don't think we've met before. I'm Nell O'Connor. I recently moved to the island.'

'I know who you are.'

'You do?' Nell arched a brow, not recognising the woman before her. She was slightly younger though, which could explain it. 'What's your name?'

'Jenna, Jenna Milborn. That's my married name. You'll remember me as Jenna Campbell.'

The name was familiar, and Nell's gaze narrowed as she tried to place the woman.

'You babysat for me one summer.'

'I did?'

And then she remembered. Tina Campbell had been a nurse and a single mother. Jenna was her daughter. She recalled her as a bubbly outgoing child, always with a beaming smile on her face. She would only be twenty-seven, twenty-eight, but the years hadn't been kind to her, with harsh lines around her eyes and mouth, her coppery hair falling dully around her shoulders.

'I do remember you. You went to school with my cousin, Clarke Golding, didn't you?'

'We were in the same year, but I didn't really know him.' Jenna focused her attention on the mirror, turning her back dismissively on Nell as she touched up her make-up, carefully reapplying powder over the bruise.

'So, you're married?'

'That's what I said.'

'Milborn you said? You're married to Curtis?'

'Yup.'

Nell remembered him. He was a few years older than her and she recalled him as a show-off with a big mouth and a hot temper. It looked like he hadn't changed. Jenna's eyes briefly met hers in the mirror and she scowled, realising Nell was watching her. Looking uncomfortable, she snapped the powder compact shut, slipped it back in her purse and turned on her heel. 'Look, nice as this walk down memory lane is, my husband is out there waiting for me.'

The husband who gave you that shiner, Nell thought, but kept the words to herself.

It was clear from Jenna's stilted answers she didn't want to talk to her and so Nell followed her out. She spotted Curtis, one hand on his hip, the other holding a full glass of beer, as he looked around the room for his wife. The years had been even less kind to him, his once thick hair badly receding and his gut spilling over the top of his jeans. His mouth was contorted into an ugly scowl as Jenna approached and, even though Nell couldn't hear their conversation, she could tell from the way he spoke to his wife that he was annoyed with her.

Jenna kept her head lowered, clearly used to being put down. Nell watched for a moment, her stomach sick as she recognised herself in Jenna. How many times had she gone through this same scenario with Caleb? Had other people looked at her with the same pity with which she was now viewing Jenna?

She glanced around the bar, spotting Michael and Newt at a table talking with a couple of guys she didn't recognise. There was still no sign of Alex or Mia. Stephanie and Antonia were busy on the dance floor, surrounded by people. Nell skimmed the crowd, noting the place was still packed. Her eyes briefly passed over a man, tall, muscular, shaven head, staring right at her.

Caleb.

Fear spiked through her, turning her blood cold. Frantically she glanced back to where she had seen him, but he was nowhere.

Impossible. He had just been standing there. How could he disappear?

Nell grabbed hold of the back of a chair and held on to it for support, her legs shaking, and forced herself to draw a couple of deep breaths. She couldn't have a panic attack, not here, not with all these people. Counting under her breath, she glanced round the room, trying to take in every detail, every partygoer. There was a guy in a pale shirt, bald and stocky, making his way to the bar. He bore a passing resemblance to Caleb.

You're losing the plot, O'Connor. He's not here.

She wanted to believe it was true, but was she sure?

The whole Jenna thing has you freaked out. You were thinking about Caleb and now you're convinced you've seen him. A trick of the eye.

It made sense, she knew it did. If he had been here she would have known and there was no way he could have snuck out without her seeing him again. The vice-grip eased in her chest, though she was still trembling, and with each passing second she began to feel more stupid about her overreaction, as well as irritated he still had such a hold over her. She didn't want to be scared of Caleb, but the truth was he terrified her. Needing fresh air and a few minutes to pull herself together before she rejoined Michael and Newt she pushed her way through the crowd to the terrace.

Out on the decking it was blessedly cooler, a light breeze drifting off the ocean and soothing her hot skin. With no-one to disturb her, the noise from the crowd and the music slightly muted, she was able to think clearly, to process her encounter with Jenna Milborn and her ridiculous fantasy that her ex had been in the bar.

She leaned over the railing, staring out into the darkness beneath.

A mere fifty yards away, hidden from sight in the shadows, Caleb Sweeney was sat in his hire car.

Watching her.

19

She was finally alone.

Still Caleb sat in his car, waiting, half expecting someone to join her on the deck. It would have been easy to approach her, but if she didn't listen to reason or tried to make a scene, things might turn ugly, and he couldn't take the risk of anyone walking out on them. Since the shooting incident, her oaf of a brother had barely let her out of his sight. Caleb knew he was in the bar, so was aware he had to be careful.

At least the new love interest hadn't been around. He had done some digging and knew Luke Trainor was home recuperating from his shoulder injury. Nell had been to see him a couple of times, always accompanied by Michael who, he had since found out, was living with Luke's brother. He supposed that kind of made Luke and Nell family; he had tried to rationalise with himself that perhaps they were friends and not involved. It didn't make sense that they were having cosy dinners together though, or why he had brought her flowers. There had been no sign of the woman Luke was supposed to be living with and he wondered if she had perhaps left him?

Maybe he had ditched her for Nell?

The idea made Caleb's blood boil. The thought of another man with his hands on Nell was almost too much to bear.

It was good to see her dressed up. Since she had been back on the island, Nell had barely been out of jeans and T-shirts, her hair either loose or scraped back. Tonight she had made an effort. He remembered the blue dress. It was demure, not revealing too much flesh, but he loved how the silky material hugged her breasts and the curve of her ass, leaving plenty to the imagination.

God, she was so beautiful. He ached with the need to be able to touch her, to unzip her dress. He glanced at the bar, noting she had been outside now a good couple of minutes and was still alone, caution wrestling with the overwhelming urge to have her in his arms, to feel her beneath him.

He missed her so much. To hell with it.

Quietly he eased the car door open, eyes warily glancing round as he started to cross the parking lot, the gravel crunching beneath his feet. She stood against the railing, looking out to sea, her hair blowing gently in the breeze. She looked distant, caught up in her own thoughts, and Caleb wondered if in these quiet moments she was thinking about him.

He had almost reached the staircase leading up to the deck when another figure stepped out from the shadows, heading towards her. Caleb balled his fists as the anticipation of needing to touch her, talk to her, slipped from his grasp – the frustration of the situation making him want to scream. He fought to control his temper.

Bide your time. The right moment will come.

Quietly he slipped back to the car.

Listening to the soothing sound of the waves washing against the shore, Nell didn't hear the approaching footsteps, and she started slightly when Alex was suddenly beside her, mirroring her pose as he leant against the railing.

'Jeez, you made me jump.'

He cocked his head and gave her a quizzical glance. 'How come you're out here? I thought you'd still be on the dance floor.'

'I needed some fresh air.'

Alex's eyes narrowed. 'Did you have another attack?'

'I'm fine; I honestly just needed some air. How come you're out here?' she countered. 'I figured maybe you'd left.'

'I had to take a call.'

'Is everything okay?'

'Yeah, I was going over a couple of things with Hunter Stone, the detective working Penny Maher's murder.'

He didn't elaborate and Nell didn't ask, understanding there was only so much he could disclose about a case. She couldn't believe it had been a whole week since she had stumbled across the head, but then so much had happened in the interim with finding the picture of Lizzie in her house, agreeing to go into business with Michael and Newt, and Luke being shot. And she had only known Alex a week. It felt longer.

She wondered where Mia was, but was reluctant to ask.

'Where's Michael? Is he still inside?'

Nell rolled her eyes. 'Yeah, he's with Newt. We talked earlier and he's going back home tonight.' She was quiet for a moment. 'I take it you have no leads on who shot Luke?'

'We ran the print on the matchbook, but there are no matches in the system.'

'But you've ruled out Sam Kent?'

'We don't have his prints on file. I'm keeping a close eye on him, Nell, I promise, but unless he puts a foot wrong there's nothing I can do.'

'Michael still doesn't know about the picture. You promised you wouldn't tell him.'

'I haven't said a word.' Alex let out a frustrated sigh. 'You should tell him though. He deserves to be kept in the loop.'

'He worries too much already.'

'He has good reason. I hear he's had an alarm system installed.'

'Yeah, and the locks have all been replaced.'

'That's good. You should cut Michael some slack. He's only trying to do what he thinks is best for you. If it were my sister I'd be the same.'

'You have a sister?' Nell was curious. He had never mentioned family before.

'Yeah, I have a younger sister and an older brother.'

'And are you and your brother overprotective pains in the ass when it comes to your sister?'

Alex considered the question and smiled. 'Yeah, we are.'

'Where do they live?'

'My brother, Joe, is in Philly and my sister, Cassie, is back home just outside of Portland.'

'Is that where you grew up?'

'It is.'

'Do you miss them?'

'Sure, sometimes. We still see each other though.' Looking amused, he shifted his position so he turned to face her. 'You're full of questions tonight.'

'I'm just making conversation. You were the one who came out here to join me. Besides, my brother keeps telling me you're his best friend, so I figured I should get to know you a little better.' She kept her tone light, teasing even.

Alex's grin widened, cutting deep dimples into his cheeks. His green eyes glinted dangerously, and Nell was aware she suddenly had his full, undivided attention. Part of her brain, the rational part, warned her she was treading on dangerous ground, but another part wanted more. She felt her belly flip and wondered how many women had been seduced by his wickedly appealing grin.

Mia certainly had, which had Nell wondering why Alex was out here with her.

'What happened to your friend from earlier?' She had promised herself she wasn't going to ask, but the question slipped out.

Alex narrowed his eyes slightly. 'Friend?'

'The redhead. Michael said the two of you had a... thing.'

'Mia? We did, about four years ago. Now we're just friends.' His grin widened further, amusement clear in his eyes as he understood where the question had come from. 'So, you were asking Michael about Mia? Why the interest? Were you jealous?'

His directness made Nell's cheeks flush. 'Of course not.' She snapped out the words a little too defensively. 'I was just curious.'

Her denial only seemed to amuse him further.

'You know you're pretty when you get flustered,' he told her, easing closer and grazing his knuckle over her cheek.

Nell somehow managed to hold both her ground and his gaze.

'I'm not flustered,' she protested, swallowing hard as his focus dropped to her mouth. She could feel the heat radiating off him, and was aware of her own body reacting in turn.

'And the jealousy thing is sweet. I'm flattered.'

'Don't be. I told you I wasn't jealous.' She raised her chin stubbornly. 'You must think an awful lot of yourself to–'

'Nell?'

'What?'

'Can you stop talking for two minutes?'

Nell opened her mouth to protest, but no words came out as

Alex caught her off guard, cupping her face with both hands and leaning in to kiss her, gently at first, his lips soft against hers, then deepening as she responded, one hand slipping down to the small of her back, pulling her against him. He slid his tongue into her mouth, deftly exploring, his mouth devouring hers. Caught up in the moment, Nell yielded, slipping her arms around his waist as she felt herself melt into him. She allowed her hands to roam down over the cute tight butt she had drooled over before, then back up over the hard muscles of his back and shoulders and into his hair. He tasted of honey and whiskey, his mouth hot and seducing, and as he changed the angle of the kiss, becoming harder and more urgent, a moan escaped from deep within her.

Alex's lips curved against hers as he broke the kiss, though he kept his arms linked around her. 'Well, that took the edge off things,' he announced, green eyes locked on hers. He lightly traced one hand down the length of her back before he released her.

Nell took an unsteady step back on shaky legs, still reeling. She had never been kissed like that before, though had no intention of sharing that fact with Alex, who was already looking at her like the cat who had gotten the cream.

'No need to look so pleased with yourself,' she told him, trying for prudish, though she made no attempt to stop him as he settled his hands on her hips and leaned in for another kiss. As she tried to steady her feet she felt her left heel disappear beneath her, realised too late it had slid down between the planks on the decking. As she attempted to pull her foot free, the heel slipped further, becoming trapped and pulling her foot down with it.

This time she grunted against Alex's mouth, using him as an anchor as she tried to stop herself from falling over. As she broke the kiss, he moved his mouth down to nuzzle her neck, the roughness of his stubble tickling against the curve of her shoulder.

'Alex. Stop. I'm stuck.'

'Huh?'

'My heel is caught in the decking.'

'Your what?' He lifted his head, finally spotting the awkward angle at which Nell was leaning against him. 'Oh my God, you've got to be kidding me!' A wide grin broke out on his face.

'Can you help me get free please? It's not funny.'

He chuckled, looking amused. 'Yeah, it is, Nell. It's definitely funny.'

'Just help me, okay.'

'Okay.' He stole another quick kiss, ducking when she tried to swipe him away. 'Talk about ruining the moment,' he grumbled, dropping down on his knees and giving her foot a test yank. 'Yeah, you're stuck. Damn it, you're a walking klutz, O'Connor.'

One hand around her ankle, the other under her shoe, he tugged harder and Nell almost lost her balance again. She steadied herself by catching hold of his shoulders.

'I knew there was a reason why I rarely wear these shoes,' she muttered, her face heating, a little embarrassed. This was hardly her finest moment.

Alex glanced up, a sly smile on his face. 'Just for the record, they work for me.'

'That's great, but unless you can get me free they're going in the trash.'

'Okay, we need to get your foot out of the shoe. The heel's jammed tight.' Alex unfastened the straps and helped Nell wiggle her foot out of the sandal.

Relieved to be free, she scooted down beside him as he yanked at the embedded shoe.

'Here, let me try,' she told him impatiently.

'You think you can do better?'

'Maybe.' Nell grabbed hold of the shoe, pulling hard. It was wedged tight. 'Damn it.'

'You're gonna snap the heel off if you yank it too hard,' Alex commented as he watched her, still looking thoroughly amused.

Ignoring him, Nell tried again, cursing a string of expletives when his prediction came true, the sandal breaking away from the heel, sending her careening backwards. She landed inelegantly on her butt, half a shoe in her hand.

Alex sat down beside her, looking at her with a solemn expression. 'Oops.'

'It's not funny,' Nell fumed, as the corners of his lips curved. 'Now what am I supposed to do? I can't walk around with one shoe.'

When he burst out laughing, she swiped at him with the ruined sandal, annoyed he was finding the situation funny, but also fighting the urge to laugh herself.

Damn it, O'Connor. You sure know how to make an impression.

It didn't escape her that had she been with Caleb he would have found her moment of clumsiness irritating and would have berated her, even humiliated her, for it.

She could hear his voice in her head.

'Good God, Nell. Can't we go anywhere without you being an embarrassment?'

Alex wasn't embarrassed by her. Amused, yes, but not embarrassed, and that made him all the more attractive. The whole situation was so ridiculous, and he was right, it was funny, she thought, trying her hardest to keep a straight face, but failing miserably as she gave in to the laughter. Once she started she couldn't stop, tears rolling down her cheeks, her sides aching. Just as she thought she had her giggles under control, an exchanged glance with Alex had the laughter starting afresh.

'There's a lot to be said for sneakers,' she muttered, wiping at her eyes, cheeks aching. 'Sneakers wouldn't do this to me.'

'Are you always this accident prone?'

'Tripping over invisible stuff is my party trick.'

'I'll bear that in mind.'

They were silent for a moment and while her nerves were still present, Nell was aware of the sexual tension bouncing between them. 'I suppose I should call a cab,' she said a little reluctantly. 'I can't go back inside with one shoe.'

'Or we could go back to my place.'

She caught her breath, a trickle of apprehension creeping in as she glanced at Alex. 'Your place?'

'It's a ten-minute walk,' he reasoned, 'and we can cut along the beach, so you don't need to worry about shoes.'

'And once we get there?'

'Then I'll ply you with alcohol and try to charm my way into your panties.'

If he had been serious, Nell would have slapped him and ran a mile, but his deadpan tone and the look of mock innocence on his face instead had her bursting into another fit of giggles.

Alex grinned, reaching across to brush a loose curl back off her face. 'How about we figure it out as we go, okay?'

Caleb had been the only man in her life for six years, controlling her, belittling her and making her feel inferior, and when she had left, Nell had promised herself a break from men. This was too soon, and she should walk away now. The temptation Alex offered though was difficult to resist and the more time she spent around him, the more attractive he became. He was kind, made her laugh and she trusted him, but most of all she wanted him. Deciding it wise not to overthink things she drew in a deep breath and took the step off the cliff. 'Okay.'

Caleb had returned to his car, but remained parked in the lot, watching them.

He recognised the man, knew he was the island's police chief, Alex Cutler. At first he wondered why he was talking to Nell, assumed it was business, and was curious if it had anything to do with Luke Trainor's shooting. Then his worst nightmare had come true as he watched the pair of them embrace, understanding that the relationship between them was far from professional. First, she had shared an evening with Trainor, now she was kissing Cutler. His fiancée had turned into a filthy whore and he couldn't help but think her behaviour was intentional, designed to hurt and humiliate him.

She didn't know he was here on the island, but Caleb didn't let that little detail stop him from twisting and turning the facts, as in his mind he was the heartbroken boyfriend, so utterly destroyed, while Nell was a scheming slut who had used him and cast him to one side. She had told him she loved him, but the bitch had lied.

It took every ounce of control he had to remain in the car. Cutler was the police chief and this made things more difficult. Caleb Sweeney had a reputation as an upstanding citizen and he couldn't afford to fall foul of the law. But the fact remained Nell had hurt him, had broken him, had betrayed him in the worst possible way, and he could not let that go unpunished.

As he watched them step down from the deck, walking along the beach talking and laughing, tears of grief and rage filled his eyes. As they disappeared, hands linked, into the distance he buried his head against the steering wheel and sobbed until his heart was empty.

The pain twisted his insides, unbearable and cruel – the love he had felt for Nell crossing the line into pure hatred. He began to plot his revenge.

20

Luke spent much of the night on his couch, having emptied the best part of a bottle of Jim Beam, while the TV played quietly in the background. The bourbon, he had told himself, was purely for medicinal purposes. He had painkillers and was taking them regularly to help numb the throbbing ache in his shoulder, but the alcohol helped dilute it further. It also helped to dilute the reminder of what an awful fuck-up his life was at the moment.

He was spinning out of control, and given how normally he was so organised and meticulous, it pained him to have such disorder in his life; that there wasn't a damn thing he could do about it was frustrating as hell. The whole terrible mess with Stacey, together with the physical pain from being shot, had knocked him for six, stealing control away and making him feel as though he was on an inevitable collision course that could only end one way.

He wasn't a big drinker, at least hadn't been until recently, preferring to stay sober and in charge of his reactions. Sitting around led to far too many thoughts, all of them negative, and he wanted the blessed relief of being able to forget his problems. Newt had stopped by earlier and tried to persuade him to come along to Mahoney's for an hour, telling him it would do him good to get out of the house and be with friends, even if it was only for a short time. Luke had declined, not in the mood for company.

Newt hadn't been impressed when he found out Stacey wasn't around, and was annoyed when Luke told him she was staying with a friend for a few days on the mainland. He had hoped seeing her boyfriend shot would have brought them closer together, not pushed them further apart, and he made his views clear to Luke, suggesting maybe it was time to end the relationship if she couldn't be there for him. Luke had let his brother rant, aware he had no idea how bad things were with Stacey.

Newt looked out for him, always had done since their parents had been killed. Even as a child he had tried to protect Luke from their grandmother's wrath. He felt a stab of anger at the thought of Enid Trainor; he knew she was responsible for the insecurities that had plagued his early childhood. Nothing was ever good enough, no matter how hard Luke had tried to please her, and it became worse when Newt went to college. When the old witch had died, and Luke had moved in with Newt, it had been the happiest time of his life. Newt was the one constant, the only person who had ever really been there for him.

He feigned sleep until his brother had left then spent an hour trying to figure out what the hell he was going to do about Stacey. She had always been wild and unpredictable, perhaps something he should have considered before moving her into his home, and her hot temper and paranoid jealous streak should have been a warning that things between them could only ever end badly.

It didn't stop the regrets or the fact he missed her. How was he going to fix this?

When no solution came his thoughts turned to Nell. She had stopped by to see him a couple of times during the week, and he knew she felt guilty about what had happened. So far there were no leads on the shooter and it begged the question: had Luke been the intended target or had the gunman meant to hit Nell?

Alex suspected the latter and Luke was curious as to who on the island might want to hurt her. He guessed Sam Kent was the most logical suspect. Michael was up in arms at the shooting and about Nell's safety. Luke knew he had been staying at the guesthouse the past few nights and had already changed all the locks and put in a swanky alarm system. The second time Nell had been to see him she had brought him a basket of fruit and some homemade soup. Luke had thanked her and waited until she left before sniffing the soup suspiciously and pouring it in the sink. He was already suffering with his shoulder and sure as hell couldn't cope with her cooking. The basket of fruit had been a nice touch though.

The more he saw of her the more he wanted to get to know her more intimately. She was definitely his type: blonde, slim, pretty, and she presented contradictions that he found appealing, a feisty edge protecting a vulnerability he had only seen hints of. She was the kind of woman who he thought could challenge him. Luke suspected this ex of hers had come close to crushing her spirit, but Nell appeared strong enough to have fought back. She was guarded and hesitant, fragile even, but also a survivor, which made her all the more fascinating. It was complicated though, and there was no conceivable way he could see it would work. Besides, Stacey had to be his primary focus. She was his girlfriend and the one he needed to take care of. He poured himself a large glass of whiskey, wallowed in self-pity for a while, letting the dark liquid burn in his empty belly.

Newt said Michael had taken Nell to the party. Of course, there was a high possibility Jenna would be there and if one blessed thing had come out of the shooting, it was that she had left him alone. Luke knew she was a mess and it was inevitable he would have to have a conversation with her at some point, but at least it was one less problem to worry about for now, which was good. He sure as hell didn't have the energy needed to deal with Jenna Milborn right now.

He drained his glass and poured another whiskey, the alcohol starting to take effect.

As he started to drift off into a drunken sleep, Jenna's face lingered in his mind, hard and broken, so different to when they had been high school sweethearts. He was popular, she was popular, and their relationship had just kind of happened. They had parted ways after high school, but still they remained tenuously bound. Luke knew she was fragile and could easily break, so he kept a close eye on her, gave her a shoulder to cry on and an ear to listen to when every so often things became too much, all the time hating the way she looked at him with longing. At times he loathed having to go through the merry dance, and had considered on more than one occasion severing the tie, but it wouldn't be easy.

Her face morphed into Stacey's, who was sharper and had more spirit than Jenna, her dark hair always glossy and her eyes always alert and never missing a trick. Luke had tried to keep her happy, moving her into his home when she lost her job and funding her expensive lifestyle. She never trusted him though, always suspected he was lusting after other women.

It wasn't true.

Liar, a little voice whispered in his ear, as Nell O'Connor's face took Stacey's place. Nell had complicated everything with her return to the island. She was his friend's sister – hell, his brother's boyfriend's sister – and he had no business wanting her, especially after everything with Stacey. But it didn't stop the craving.

Nell was off limits. She had to be. But as he finally drifted off to sleep, it was her that stayed in his mind.

Nell knew she should have called Michael, or at least texted, to let him know where she was and that she was safe, but she had been so caught up in the moment it had slipped her mind. Alex had told her they would figure things out as they went along, and she fully intended to take things slowly, but that plan went out of the window less than five minutes after they arrived back at his house, and it had mostly been her own doing.

Teddy and Sasha had been pleased to see them and Nell had preoccupied herself making a fuss of both dogs while Alex fetched glasses and a bottle of wine. The look he had given her as he'd crossed the room to where she sat on the couch, a wide sexy smile curving his lips, worn jeans clinging to lean hips, and his hair still dishevelled from where she'd been running her fingers through it, had Nell turning to liquid. She was already nervous; had silently questioned a dozen times on the walk back along the beach if she was making a mistake. Sex was something she no longer enjoyed and, even before Caleb, she hadn't been the type of person to engage in one-night stands.

Of course, nothing had to happen. She trusted Alex, knew he wouldn't push her, but truth was, the part of her that wasn't scared wanted him, and so she had tried not to overthink things, going to him and taking the wine and glasses, setting them down on the table, giving in to the need to touch him, to taste him, to have his body against hers again, figuring that for tonight she would take and not ask questions. He hadn't complained at her advances, his mouth on hers hungrily, and they had tumbled onto the couch, necking like teenagers, hands roaming over clothes, kissing and nibbling bare flesh. Nell fumbled at the buttons on his shirt, undoing the first four before deciding to pull the shirt straight over his head. As Alex reached for the zipper on her dress, her cell phone began to ring.

He paused for a second, glancing at Nell.

'Ignore it,' she demanded, pulling his head back down and kissing him. She wanted him so badly, but the nerves were still there and she was scared that if they stopped now she might lose her courage. She shifted slightly beneath him so he could get the zipper fully down, running her hands down the taut muscles in his lean back. His bare flesh was hot under her fingertips. The cell stopped ringing and she wriggled out of the top of the dress, eager to be free of it.

The phone pinged, a text being delivered, and she glanced at it in annoyance.

Alex paused. 'It's probably Michael wanting to know where you are.'

Or Caleb, Nell thought, though his calls and texts had stopped over the past few days; something that both bothered and relieved her. Alex was probably right about it being Michael.

She sighed. 'I meant to text him.'

Before the words were even out the cell started ringing again.

'Shit, Michael.' She reached for her phone, poking out from the top of her purse from where it sat on the coffee table, checked to be certain it was him before answering.

'What are you going to tell him?'

Nell cut Alex a look. 'It won't be that I'm currently half naked on your couch. Just be quiet, okay?'

Alex grinned as she answered the phone, ducking his head to kiss her neck.

'Hello?'

Michael's voice came booming out of the phone. 'Where the hell are you?'

'I had an accident with my shoe, so I decided to leave the party.'

'You left? Without telling me? Where are you? Back at home?'

'No, no. I'm not there.'

'Well, where the hell are you? You're worrying me, Nell.'

'I'm fine. I'm with Alex.'

'Alex? Why are you with Alex?'

'It's all good.' Nell arched her back as Alex deftly worked her bra strap.

'Where are you? At his place?'

'Umm, yeah. We cut back along the beach.'

'You should have told me. I was worried.'

'I'm sorry, it slipped my mind.'

'Newt and I are now leaving. We'll swing by and pick you up, give you a ride home.'

Free of the bra, Nell lost focus on the conversation as Alex closed his mouth on her left breast. 'What was that?'

'I said we're coming to pick you up.'

'No, no, God, no, you don't need to.' Her voice raised half an octave, as his tongue teased her nipple.

'Why? What's wrong? What the hell's going on?'

'I'm fine, everything is fine. I'm going to stay here tonight.'

'Nell?'

'I'll call you in the morning.'

'NELL!'

She ended the call, dropped the phone on the floor, this time letting out an audible gasp as Alex continued to torment her breast.

The phone immediately started ringing again.

'Jesus, Michael!' Nell growled, ignoring it.

'I told you we should have talked to him before we left.'

When the call rang off there was a three second period of silence before Alex's phone began to vibrate.

'Don't answer it,' Nell urged. 'I already told him where I am.'

Alex arched a brow. 'We both know if I don't answer it he'll show up here in ten minutes.'

As annoyed as she was, Nell figured he was right.

Grunting, Alex shifted his weight, reached in his pocket for his cell phone, and sat up, shoving his free hand back into his hair.

'Yeah?'

Nell studied him as she waited, his handsome face currently wearing a slight frown, drawn dark brows over those expressive green eyes, the aquiline nose and unshaven jaw.

'Yeah, she is.'

Broad shoulders, toned chest smattered with a few dark hairs, flat belly with the wisp of more dark hair disappearing into his low-riding jeans.

God, her brother had terrible timing.

'No, it's fine... Yeah, I'm sure.' There was another pause.

'Oh, I won't, I promise.' Alex glanced down at Nell and grinned wickedly. 'Got it... Yeah, okay... Night.'

He killed the call and threw his phone on the coffee table.

'You won't what?'

Alex settled himself back down on top of her, his weight pinning her to the couch, and his lips curved an inch above hers. 'Let you out of my sight.'

'He hasn't figured it out yet, has he?'

'Nope, he thinks you're staying here because you didn't want to be alone tonight.' Alex admitted. He blew out a breath and looked momentarily distracted. She could tell from the frown on his face it bothered him to be lying to her brother.

Not that it was a lie. They just hadn't told Michael why she was here. Alex might be Michael's best friend, but this was all new. It could be a one-night stand and fizzle out or perhaps it was the start of something. They deserved time to figure things out without anyone else interfering. Right now, she didn't want to think any further than tonight.

'Hey, earth to Alex.' She ran her fingers up into his hair, guided his mouth back down to hers, distracting him from thoughts of Michael with a slow lingering kiss, savouring the taste of him. 'I'm the only O'Connor you need to be focusing on right now. My brother can wait.'

He chuckled at that, hands slipping down over her hips and the tops of her legs, easing underneath the silky material of her dress and pushing it up her thighs, green eyes locked on hers. 'That shouldn't be too difficult.'

As he kissed her, a wet nose nuzzled against Nell's shoulder. She heard panting, felt something wet roll against the side of her neck and turned as a large slobbery tongue licked her across the face.

'Teddy!'

Pleased she had acknowledged him, Teddy nudged the ball he had dropped and gave a big doggy grin, willing her to play.

'Dammit, Teddy!' Alex growled, grabbing the ball and throwing it across the room. As Teddy bounded after it, toenails scraping against the floor, he glanced down at Nell, and they both burst out laughing.

'We're not having a lot of luck here,' Nell commented as the dog returned, dropped his ball, and waited in anticipation.

'You wanna go upstairs?'

Nell was silent for a moment, the niggling doubts still eating away at her. Alex wasn't Caleb though and it scared her how much she wanted him. She sucked in a breath, tried not to over-think things. 'Yeah, I do.'

Alex's grin widened. 'Good.'

Teddy could wait. Michael could wait. It could all wait. For now, all Nell wanted was to lose herself in the moment, forget everything that had been happening, and have this one night to herself. She figured she would work the rest out in the morning.

Luke awoke to the scent of her perfume. As he stirred himself awake, his mouth rough from the taste of Jim Beam, his head pounding, he cranked open one eye, glancing at the clock on the TV, aware from the thumping pain in his shoulder and the dull ache in his neck that he had dozed off on the couch.

The perfume lingered and he scrambled to sit upright, hope surging through him. 'Stacey?'

At first, she didn't answer, and he wondered for a moment if perhaps he was dreaming, then came the familiar sound of heels clicking on the wooden floor echoing through from the bedroom. He bolted upright, heart in mouth, the mixture of alcohol and pain sending a wave of nausea shooting through him and for a moment he thought he might pass out. He gripped the arm of the couch and drew a deep breath.

'Stacey?'

He tried again, this time staggering into the hallway and through to the bedroom they had shared. Stacey stood in the centre of the room emptying her clothes into a suitcase from a drawer. She had her back to him, her long dark hair in a loose braid and her shapely rear snug in her favourite tight-fitting white jeans.

'Don't say a word,' she said sharply. 'I'm not interested in anything you have to say. You're responsible for this and you've got to live with the consequences.'

'I miss you.'

'You should have thought about that before you did what you did.'

'Please can we talk?'

'It's over, Luke. Accept it.' Finished with her clothes, she began to gather up her bottles of perfume and toiletries, piling them on top of the strewn garments in the already overloaded case. 'I have nothing more to say to you and I want you to leave me in peace.'

He couldn't let her leave like this. They had been together for four years, which had to count for something.

'Please. Let me try fix this.'

'It's final, it can't be fixed.' Stacey's tone was calm, but he could hear the edge. 'What's done is done. At least now you won't have to worry about me knowing about the women.'

'There are no women! The only one I care about is you.'

'Liar. You had dinner with Michael's sister the other night.' Stacey turned in time to see Luke's jaw drop. Her tight smile said it all. 'Don't even bother to deny you want her.'

'Nell and I are friends. Her brother is dating my brother for God's sake.'

'Who are you trying to convince, Luke?'

'You, because you're crazy. Nell means nothing. You're the only one I want. Why can't you believe me?'

'Because I know better. You're in denial and I can't be here anymore.'

Glancing around the room, seeming satisfied she had everything she needed, she pulled down the lid of the case and sat on it to weigh down the contents and force the zip around. As she heaved it off the bed, it made a scraping noise against the wooden floor.

When Luke blocked the doorway, Stacey let go of the case, jammed her hands on her hips, the gold bangles she wore jangling on her wrist.

'Don't make this difficult, Luke. You know it has to be this way.'

'Don't leave me. Please.'

'Get out of my way.'

When he didn't budge, she scowled at him, blue eyes flashing furiously. 'If you want a last fight I will give you one. It won't end well though.'

Luke stared at her. He had loved her, still did love her, but Stacey was right. It couldn't go on. It was time for him to try and move forward with his life.

'I hope you find happiness,' he told her quietly, stepping to one side to let her pass.

She grabbed hold of the case and dragged it past him into the hallway towards the front door, then she was gone, disappearing into the night. Feeling numb, Luke scrubbed a hand over his face and went back through to the living room to fix himself another drink.

———

21

Sunday brought grey skies full of ominous dark clouds that threatened to pour. Alex rose before the rain hit, slipping out of bed and shrugging into jeans and a sweatshirt, leaving Nell sleeping as he took Sasha and Teddy for an early morning walk along the beach. As he threw the ball for them and watched Teddy gambol frantically into the surf, he reflected back over the previous evening and Nell O'Connor.

He hadn't intended on sleeping with her last night, hadn't actually planned on making any kind of move until he was clear in his head what he wanted from her and what he was able to offer in return, but then she had shown up at the party looking so damn pretty in that blue dress, and had knocked his world off its axis. When he had found her outside looking lost, he had thrown caution to the wind. Things had escalated quicker than he had anticipated, but the truth was he couldn't bring himself to regret any of it. As he had told her before they left Mahoney's together, they were going to have to figure it out as they went.

Alex wasn't sure how Michael was going to react. His friend knew about his past back in Portland and also knew of his reluctance to settle down. Although Michael was forever trying to fix him up on dates, how was he going to feel knowing Alex was sleeping with his sister? There was no doubt in his mind he intended to sleep with Nell again. In fact, he liked knowing she was back at the house asleep in his bed more than he cared to admit. Thoughts of her still on his mind, he whistled to the dogs, keen to get back. As he entered the bedroom ten minutes later, two cups of coffee in hand, he took a moment to study her sleeping frame.

She had rolled across the mattress and lay on her belly, the sheet having slipped down to expose the arch of her back, her breasts mashed into the mattress, one arm above her head and a tumble of curls spilling over the pillow. In the sliver of light cutting across the shadowy room he noted the slim scar that ran down over her hip and his gut tightened.

It could have been the result of an old injury, possibly even dating back to childhood, but doubt was in his mind. Had Caleb Sweeney put the mark on her?

He set the coffee cups down on the nightstand, sat down on the edge of the mattress and ran his fingertips lightly down her back and over the scar. She stirred beneath his touch, turning her head and staring up at him through sleep heavy eyes the colour of whiskey.

Alex smiled at her. 'Hey.'

He hadn't been sure if in the cold light of day her guard would be back up, but she seemed relaxed, reacting to his greeting with a lazy smile.

'You're up early?'

'I took Teddy and Sasha out before it rains. I've made you coffee.'

'Thank you.'

Nell scooted up, bringing the sheet with her to demurely cover her breasts, which had Alex grinning.

'What's funny?' she asked, narrowing her eyes as she picked up the coffee cup.

'Nothing.' He leant across and kissed the tip of her nose. 'You're beautiful.'

Her cheeks flushed, and she studied him warily over the top of the cup, clearly uncomfortable with receiving compliments. He guessed Caleb hadn't paid her many of those.

'It's gloomy out,' she commented, staring at the open French doors.

'Yeah, I think it's going to storm. It started raining as we got back up from the beach.'

'Talking of storms, have you heard from my brother yet?'

'Not yet. I'm sure it won't be long.'

Nell smiled. 'I'm surprised he hasn't shown up yet with the cavalry to escort me home.'

Alex chuckled, though knew the reason Michael hadn't shown up was because he trusted Alex to look after his sister. The thought brought with it another niggle of guilt, which he was quick to quash down.

'I'm working this afternoon. I'll drop you off on the way.'

'This afternoon?' Nell questioned, her tone amused as she added slyly, 'How do you propose we kill time until then?'

'I have a few ideas.'

'Well, I only have my party dress with me.'

'You won't need your clothes.'

Nell took another slow sip of her coffee then set the cup back down on the nightstand. Eyes locked on his she dropped the bed sheet. 'Guess I won't need this either then.'

'You're a damn tease, O'Connor,' Alex muttered, leaning in to kiss her as she yanked at his sweatshirt, pulling it up over his head. Discarding the shirt on the floor he pushed her back on the mattress, arms tightening around her, not wanting to admit how right she felt.

Outside the rain started to fall more heavily, the breeze picking up and pushing the door back on its hinges. The storm was on its way.

He dropped her back at the guesthouse just before one, insisting on going inside the house before leaving, wanting to be sure for himself the new locks were effective, and he didn't miss her eye roll as he got out of the Jeep, hunkering down in his jacket and chasing after her through the pouring rain.

'I have a swanky alarm system now, remember?' she told him as they took cover on the small front porch that barely sheltered the two of them.

'I know, but I'll be happier when I've checked it for myself.'

She shook her head as she unlocked the door, seeming amused.

'Michael's gonna be pissed that you've stolen his bodyguard role,' she joked, punching in the code for the alarm.

Alex noted the model and was pleased to see Michael hadn't cut any corners. He had spent a decent amount of money on it and gone for a sophisticated system. 'He can keep it, but until I figure out who's been harassing you, you're gonna have to deal with me too, okay?' When she pouted at him he snaked an arm around her waist, pulling her in close and planting a quick kiss on her lips, teasing a smile out of her. 'I'm gonna take a quick look around before I go, okay?'

Nell wavered and he saw the battle for control, and knew she found it difficult to ask for help. Truth was, alarm or no alarm, he had no intention of leaving her alone until he was certain she was safe.

'I guess it wouldn't hurt,' she agreed, swallowing her pride. She hovered close behind him as he did a perfunctory check of the first, second and third floors, making sure all of the rooms were empty and the windows locked.

'Is that the attic?' Alex asked, glancing at the narrow staircase that led to the top floor.

'Yeah, I've been using it as my studio.'

She followed him up the staircase and into the room. Alex nodded, taking in the wide open space. A canvas sat in front of the window and he recognised the scene on the painting, the full moon perfectly positioned between jutting rocks and casting slivers of silvery light across an ocean of midnight.

'Hey, this is from my deck, right?'

'It is.'

He caught hold of her hand and stepped closer. 'It's perfect.'

The compliment actually made her blush, which he found endearing given she was already an established artist. Keeping hold of her hand, he walked around the room, checking out the space, frowning when he spotted the graffiti on the wall.

'Did you do that?'

'I think my cousin, Clarke, did. I don't know who Sarah is supposed to be. I found employment records for a Sarah Treadwell, who helped out my aunt back in 2005. I'm thinking it could be her.'

'The writing is pretty aggressive. Maybe Clarke didn't like her.'

'Michael says she disappeared, leaving Bella in the lurch. Just packed up her stuff and left one night when she was supposed to be looking after Clarke. I've tried facebooking and googling her, but haven't had any luck.'

'Why do you want to find her?'

Nell shrugged. 'I don't, I guess. It just bothers me a little that she disappeared and no-one ever heard from her again. Plus, she must have stirred some pretty strong emotions in Clarke for him to write her name all over the wall.'

'I'm sure she's fine. People bail on temporary jobs all the time. Your cousin was probably just pissed at her for ditching him.'

Satisfied the house was empty, Alex followed Nell downstairs.

'Keep the doors locked as a precaution, okay? You don't know who might be lurking around.'

'What if I want to go outside?'

He glanced out of the kitchen window at the teeming rain and raised his brows. 'Then you might want to have a towel handy for when you come back in,' he suggested, his tone sardonic.

Nell's lips curved. 'Do you want a coffee before you go?'

He glanced at his watch, noted the time. 'I should get going. I'll pick one up on the way into the office.' Tucking a stray curl behind her ear that had escaped her ponytail he pulled her in for another kiss, this one deep and lingering, reluctant to break away when she slipped her arms around his waist and snuggled in close. 'I'll call you later, okay?'

Nell held on for a moment before letting go, her wide golden eyes locking onto his. 'Okay.'

Alex made a pit stop on the way to the office to get his usual coffee to go from the Sizzling Griddle. Antonia was behind the counter, though looking worse for wear, her normally bright eyes bloodshot and her hair scraped back in an untidy bun.

'You left early last night,' she commented genially as she brewed Alex's coffee.

'Something came up,' he told her, non-committedly, his thoughts still on Nell.

'Well, whatever it was seems to have put you in a peachy

mood. You just walked in here looking like the cat that got the cream.'

Alex chuckled, though declined to elaborate. 'Did Steph have a good night?' he asked, changing the subject.

'Oh, yes, she loved it. She had no idea what Marty and I had been planning, so it was a total surprise to her...'

He listened to Antonia as she chattered away, patiently waiting for a pause in her conversation to pay for his coffee, then stopped to talk briefly with a couple of the regulars before heading over to the police department.

After checking in with the deputies who had taken the nightshift, ensuring there had been no problems, he picked up his messages from Ruby before going into his office and calling Hunter Stone.

'I think we may have found our guy,' Stone told him without preamble.

'Go on.'

'Bartender recalls our vic bawling her eyes out over a guy who had stood her up. He says she was drinking solo, drowning her sorrows, when another guy came in and made a move on her. The pair of them left the bar together.'

'Any cameras in the bar?' Alex asked, sipping at his coffee.

'Not in the bar, but there's one outside. The owner is pulling the tapes and I'm going down there to view the footage this afternoon. Hopefully we'll get a headshot of our guy, but even worst case scenario, the way the camera is angled should give us an idea of which direction they headed off in.'

It sounded like a breakthrough and one that was overdue. With poor visibility due to the stormy weather, the recovery search on the water had been postponed for the day, so it was good to know the wheels of the investigation were still turning. After chatting for another fifteen minutes, Alex hung up, with Stone promising to call later that afternoon with a progress report. There was nothing more he could do on the Penny Maher case for now, so he turned his attention to Luke's shooting, which led to the other question: who was trying to terrorise Nell? He looked at the two names he had jotted down on his list: Sam Kent and Caleb Sweeney. Both had motive and Sam hadn't even tried to hide his dislike for Nell. There were no two ways around it – he blamed her, held her responsible even, for Lizzie's death.

He had the motive all right, but try as he might Alex couldn't link him to the shooting at the guesthouse. He claimed not to own an air rifle and, although his alibi was slim, there was no evidence to suggest he was lying.

Sweeney was a whole different ballgame. He had motive, he had history, and Alex tended to agree with Michael: he wasn't going to stop trying to track her down.

Alex had looked into the guy and knew, on paper, he was a model citizen. Sweeney had been born into money, the eldest son of an investment banker and an art dealer. Ironically, his mother served as director on the board of a charity for battered women, and Caleb was known as one of their most generous benefactors. A call to an old friend now based in the Chicago PD, and who dug a little further, painted a picture of a man who was used to getting his own way, who smiled for the cameras, but as soon as they were turned off, belittled those around him, and who, interestingly, had been the subject of an assault allegation in his college senior year. The woman in question had gone to the police accusing him of beating her up when she turned down his advances after a date. Charges had initially been pressed then quickly dropped with the woman's character coming under scrutiny and rumours flying around that she was unstable and trying to set him up. Sweeney had walked away from the incident as the victim, while the woman had been vilified. Alex had her name and number, and had tried to call her a couple of times, but had yet to reach her. He had resorted to leaving her a message and hoped she wouldn't be too spooked to call him back.

He had also called Sweeney's office and garnered from his secretary he was out of town on business. The information made him pensive, particularly as the woman wasn't prepared to reveal where. She asked if he wanted to leave a message, but he had declined, figuring he would try again in a few days. If Sweeney was on the island he was lying low. Alex had checked with both of the hotels and knew neither had a guest staying under Sweeney's name. From everything he had learned about him though, Sweeney was the kind of man who wouldn't react well to seeing his fiancée having dinner with another man. It was plausible he could be the shooter.

Outside of Kent and Sweeney, it was hard to think who else would have a grudge against Nell.

Sam's parents had never held her responsible for their daughter's death and it was difficult to imagine their stance changing eighteen years later. They were both in their late sixties and had always struck him as good, kind people. It was difficult to picture either of them hiding in the bushes with an air rifle.

Nell had mentioned Tommy's cool reaction to her, and Alex had dismissed her at the time. While he couldn't for one second see Tommy being responsible for pulling the trigger – hell, he had even been on duty at the time of the shooting – he had never spoken with him about how Tommy felt over Nell's return to the island. It was a conversation perhaps worth having.

Alex had been eighteen at the time of Lizzie Kent's murder and in his first year of college, but he remembered the case, knew it had been in the headlines of the east coast press for several weeks. Roy Dolan had been found dead at the scene, but his accomplice had escaped after murdering Elizabeth Kent and had never been caught. Tommy was the only one who had seen him, but the police had never been able to get a useful description out of him.

Alex called him into his office. Tommy had been first on the scene with Penny Maher's head and was working his first murder investigation. There was nothing unusual about wanting to check in with him to see how he was coping and it gave Alex the chance to casually bring Nell's name into the conversation.

'I guess it must have been a little weird seeing her on the beach.'

Tommy shrugged. 'It's been a long time and it's odd her being back. We were kids when we last saw each other.'

'Did seeing her bring back memories about what happened to Lizzie?' Alex asked the question casually. This wasn't an interrogation.

'A few, yeah. Seeing her that first time on the beach was strange. I guess it always was going to be weird though. I'm sure things will get easier.'

Alex nodded.

Tommy had been ten when he had watched Lizzie die and it was difficult to know how deeply things had affected him. It had been easier for his sister, Emily, who was now away at college. She had been too young for the tragedy to leave its mark.

'I heard Nell is planning on reopening her aunt's guesthouse.' Tommy's voice broke through Alex's thoughts.

'Yeah. Michael and Newt are going to help her renovate the place.'

'Okay.'

'You seem surprised.'

'I guess I am a little. I'm still shocked she came back.'

'Why's that?'

'Well, Lizzie was her best friend. She has to feel guilty about what happened. And she has her career back in Chicago. I figured she'd want to sell up the house and forget this place.'

'Do you think she should feel guilty about Lizzie?' Alex asked, curious.

'I'm surprised she came back is all,' Tommy said, ignoring the question. 'What are they planning on doing to the place? Do you know?'

'It needs a lot of interior work and I think they're going to put in a pool and a hot tub.'

Tommy nodded, but didn't comment. He seemed a little distracted. It was obvious Nell being back bothered him more than he was admitting. Alex thought back to his conversation with Nell before he had left the guesthouse. 'You used to be good friends with Nell's cousin, Clarke Golding, didn't you?'

The change in conversation caught Tommy's attention. 'We hung around a bit as kids. Why?'

'Do you remember a girl called Sarah Treadwell? She worked at the guesthouse about twelve years ago.'

'No, it doesn't ring any bells.'

The instant response had Alex looking up. Tommy's face was drained of colour.

'You sure about that?'

'I'm sure.' Tommy gave a tight smile. 'Is there anything else?'

Alex regarded him. He was lying. 'No, we're all done.'

He watched Tommy leave the office before adding Sarah's name to his list. Nell had a gut feeling about Sarah Treadwell and he couldn't help but wonder if, perhaps, she was on to something.

22

Michael and Newt had shown up within forty minutes of Alex leaving and Nell must have been smiling like a loon because Michael immediately picked up on her mood. She played along, not saying much, wanting to keep her night with Alex under wraps until she figured out if there was anything substantial there between them. Nell had always believed sex to be overrated, but Alex had changed her mind on that last night, and despite repeatedly telling herself it had just been a bit of harmless fun, she hadn't been able to stop thinking about him.

Michael and Newt took her out for lunch then they spent the afternoon shopping for home furnishings, Newt in his element as he and Nell debated over colour schemes and styles for the guesthouse, while Michael dragged his heels as he followed them down the aisles, more interested in getting the actual labour underway.

'You know there's no point buying cushions and lamps until we've fixed the plastering and redecorated,' he grumbled.

'Well, of course,' Newt agreed. 'But we still need to be looking for ideas.'

In the end they bought paint and brushes, the plan being

that Nell could start decorating the rooms on the third floor which required little more than a spruce up. Meanwhile, Michael would work on the plastering required on the second level.

They called in to see Luke after the shopping trip and found him sitting on the couch looking hungover and watching reruns of old TV shows on cable.

'You need to get out of the house,' Newt told him, casting a critical eye over the sweatpants and old T-shirt his brother wore. The room was dark, the curtains still drawn and the air was pungent with the smell of stale Chinese food.

'Stacey came by and got the rest of her stuff last night,' Luke announced, not bothering to look up from the TV. 'She's gone.'

'I'm sorry,' Nell told him, thinking that had to suck. Here she was, barely able to keep the smile off her face thanks to Alex and the poor guy had just had his heart broken.

That said, she couldn't help wondering if it was for the best. She had never met Stacey, but the girl sounded like hard work and from what Michael and Newt had said, Luke was better off without her.

Still, Luke had been shot and dumped in the same week. It was hard not to have sympathy for him.

'You're coming back with us to Nell's,' Newt ordered. 'Sitting around here wallowing is only going to drag you down further.'

Luke protested, but only a little. Nell suspected he secretly wanted the company.

While Newt dragged him off to get showered and changed, she and Michael opened curtains, turned off the television and cleared up the empty bottles of liquor and the barely touched cartons of takeaway.

'Where does he keep the vacuum?'

'I think it's in the laundry room, down in the basement,' Michael told her, heaving the sack out of the trash. He pointed to a doorway that led off the kitchen. 'I'll go down and get it if you give me a second to take this out.'

'It's okay, I can get it.'

Nell opened the door, flicking on the light and peering nervously down the stairs. She berated herself for the nerves and forced her legs to move down the steps, ignoring the fact they were shaking. This was Luke's house. She was no longer in Chicago. There was nothing to be scared of here.

At the foot of the stairs she found herself in a large room that housed a washing machine, tumble dryer and a large chest freezer. The bulb overhead flickered and she glanced nervously up at the door, her imagination getting the better of her as she envisioned the light dying and the door slamming shut. She rubbed absently at her left arm, the one she had fractured in the fall down the stairs. It had long ago healed, but the mental scars were still there.

Memories can't hurt you. Caleb can't hurt you anymore.

Still, her mouth was dry, her palms clammy, as she stepped further into the room. The cool dankness, lack of natural light and the slight mustiness of the air mixing with detergent and bleach into the scent of the unwelcome memory.

'I trusted you, Nell, and you betrayed me. Do you have any idea how worried I have been?'

Her crime had been going out with friends for a drink and losing track of time. Caleb had an important meeting early the next morning and needed his shirt ironed. She'd arrived home just after one in the morning, a little tipsy and oblivious to the eighteen missed calls and texts on her phone. They had fought, because back then she had given as good as she had got and wasn't going to let a man tell her what she could or couldn't do.

The trip down the stairs had been her fault, or so she had been conditioned to believe. Yes, Caleb had shoved her, but he hadn't meant for her to fall. He was trying to get her to go downstairs and iron his shirt. It was her stupid fault for being so clumsy and losing her footing.

As she had lain at the foot of the stairs, writhing in pain, he had stepped over her to get his shirt, his face twisted in anger as he shouted at her. Everything was her fault, the night out, returning home late, not answering her phone and, now, falling down the stairs, meaning he didn't have a clean shirt.

He had locked her in the laundry room that night, ignoring her pleas for help, leaving her on the floor in the dark, crying at the pain in her arm. She had stayed there until he returned after his meeting the following day, when he had made her apologise and promise to never let him down like this again, before taking her to the ER.

When they had returned home he had bought her flowers.

Nell shuddered at the memory, so angry at herself for staying as long as she did, for letting him treat her that way. A hand touched her shoulder and she jumped.

'What are you doing down here?'

She turned to see Luke standing behind her. He looked annoyed.

'I was looking for your vacuum cleaner. I'm sorry.'

He studied her before the frown on his face softened. 'It's not a problem. I'm the one who should apologise. I'm tired, hungover and feeling sorry for myself. I'm not the best company at the moment.' His expression turned to one of concern. 'You okay? You look like you've seen a ghost.'

'I'm fine.' She drew in a shaky breath and forced the smile back onto her face. 'Like you, I'm just tired.' Not exactly a lie.

He nodded, eyes still on hers as he fetched the vacuum for her from beside the chest freezer. 'You're sure?'

'I'm okay, honest. I've never been a fan of basements.'

'Let me guess – you saw too many creepy movies as a kid?'

He was looking fresher, dressed in jeans and a clean shirt, his hair combed back.

'Something like that,' Nell agreed, keen to get back upstairs.

'Come on. Let's finish getting this place cleaned up and get back up to the guesthouse. Your brother's cooking tonight.'

As she started to walk back up the stairs, he caught hold of her hand, gave it a squeeze, and she glanced back down at him.

'Thank you. Thank you for being here for me and for being a good friend. I appreciate it.'

'No problem,' she smiled, pulling her hand free when he held on a second too long. 'Come on. They'll be waiting for us.'

Back at the house, Michael showed off the new alarm system to Luke, while Newt and Nell went through to the kitchen with their purchases. They had settled for a soft grey paint for the bedroom walls, with the intention of adding colour through the bedding and curtains. Nell packed the paint and brushes away, while Newt began chopping up the various ingredients for dinner.

Nell had just put on the coffee pot when the doorbell sounded.

'I've got it,' Michael shouted through.

'I still like the duck-egg blue comforters,' Newt commented as he chopped tomatoes.

He and Nell had spent twenty minutes of their shopping trip debating over bed linen, much to Michael's chagrin, with Newt wanting the blue, while Nell favoured a set in daffodil yellow she felt would brighten the old house, making it homely and welcoming.

'How about we compromise and go for blue in some rooms and yellow in the others?' she suggested.

'Yeah, I guess we could do that.' Newt glanced at the kitchen door and lowered his voice. 'Listen, Nell, I just wanted to say thank you for being cool with Luke tagging along for dinner. It means a lot.'

'You don't have to thank me. He's your brother, and welcome here any time.'

Newt set down the knife and turned to Nell. 'He's not in a good place at the moment and I worry about him.'

'He's going through a rough time. I've never met Stacey, so it's not fair of me to judge her, but it sounds like he's better off without her.'

'You're right, he is. I know he appears confident and outgoing, but things weren't easy for him after our parents died. He went off the rails badly once before and I really worry it's going to happen again.'

'Was this recently?' Nell had already picked up on Luke's mood swings and knew Stacey was responsible for causing them, but still she was curious.

Newt glanced at the door again and when he spoke his voice was barely above a whisper. 'I shouldn't really say, as we don't talk about it, but you are Michael's sister. It was a while back, just before we moved to the island. Luke was in high school and living with me at the time. He had some trouble with one of our neighbours. She was a single woman, desperate for male attention. He was just fifteen, but a good-looking kid, and he had no idea how to deal with things when she made advances towards him. Of course, he turned her down, but she became bitter about it, started making up stories about him, generally trying to cause trouble. No-one believed her because they knew of her reputation, but it affected him badly, really knocked his confidence.'

Nell was shocked. Luke had struck her as so confident and easy-going. 'That must have been awful for him.'

'He struggled for a while. After our parents died we lived with our grandmother, but she didn't make things easy, especially for Luke, and she continually picked at him and criticised him. After all the problems with her and then this woman, it tipped him over the edge. His grades were failing, he was getting in fights at school, and he was constantly depressed. He deserved a fresh start and that's why I made the decision to move here. Since things have been bad with Stacey he's been on a downward spiral again, and it worries me.'

'What worries you?' Luke stepped into the kitchen, a bright smile on his face.

Newt picked up his knife, turning his attention back to the tomatoes. 'If yellow will be too full on.' He glanced at his brother's blank expression. 'We're discussing colour schemes for the bedrooms.'

'Okay.'

There was a moment of awkward silence before Nell heard more voices and she glanced up as Alex followed Michael into the kitchen. His eyes met hers, his lips curving into a slow sexy smile, and she felt her heart lurch into her mouth. She berated herself for her overreaction, annoyed that he looked relaxed and unflustered, giving nothing away of their night together to the others, while she felt it was written all over her face.

'I'm making coffee, do you want one?' she offered, needing to busy her hands.

'Sure.'

His gaze continued to linger on her face for a moment and Nell felt her insides pool. Unable to stop herself from smiling, feeling like a teenager with a foolish crush and wishing to hell the others weren't here right now, she turned her attention to making coffee as the men talked.

'You're still working?' Newt asked.

'Yeah, I'm hoping to finish up about eleven. I've been out on a call and thought I'd stop by and make sure everything was okay here.'

'Shame, you could've stayed for dinner. I'm making shrimp creole.'

Nell stirred cream into the coffee and handed round the cups. Alex took his, his hand lingering over Nell's briefly; her belly lurched.

'We probably owe you dinner for last night,' Michael joked to him.

'You do?'

'Yeah, I don't know what you did to my sister last night, but you managed to pull the stick out of her ass. She's in the best mood I've seen her in for ages.'

Alex choked on his mouthful of coffee, while Nell felt her face flame.

'Dammit, Michael,' she fumed.

Enjoying the fact that she was biting, Michael's grin widened and he snuck a hand around her waist. 'Just saying it as it is. I've missed teasing my sister.'

'Have I missed something?' Luke asked, those intense blue eyes looking from Michael to Alex and then settling on Nell.

'No, you haven't missed anything,' she told him, stepping in quickly before Michael could say anything else. 'Nothing at all. My brother thinks he's being a comedian.'

'Trust me, he is so not a comedian,' Newt joked.

Michael grinned, taking a playful swipe at Newt's head before looking at Nell, eyes sobering. 'Are you going to be okay here tonight? I don't mind staying.'

In truth, Nell was dreading being in the house alone, but she had to take the step at some point. She forced a smile. 'I'll be fine. I have a fancy new alarm system and new locks. No-one is getting in. You go home with Newt.'

'You stayed with Alex last night because you didn't want to be alone. I don't mind staying another night.'

'You stayed with Alex?'

Nell glanced at Luke, colour heating up her neck as his eyes narrowed, brow knotting to a frown. His eyes darted to Alex then back to her, his gaze suspicious.

'It was nothing.' She kept her tone light, refusing to look at Alex. 'I broke my shoe, his place was close, and it was easier just to crash there. Michael is right, I'm still a little spooked about being here alone.'

'Which is why I think you should let me stay another night.'

'I'm working the late shift so I'm gonna stop off and check on Nell when I finish.'

This time Nell did look at Alex. 'You are?'

He met her gaze, green eyes unreadable. 'That a problem?'

'No. No problem at all.'

His lips curved, and Nell's belly flipped again. 'Good.'

Newt was preoccupied with dinner, while Michael seemed oblivious to the sparks between them. Luke didn't miss a trick though, watching the exchange intently.

He knows.

Nell willed him not to say anything, not ready yet for Michael to find out what she had been doing at Alex's last night. If he found out there would be pressure to define what had happened between them. At the moment they were just having a good time, no commitment, and she wanted to keep it that way, at least for now.

As they set the table later for dinner, she half expected Luke to say something, but he thankfully stuck to lighter topics. The three of them left after they had eaten, Michael doing his whole 'dad' routine, reminding Nell to lock the doors, keep her phone on her and let him know if there was any trouble. She appreciated the concern, giving him a hug before kissing Newt and

Luke goodbye. Luke lingered for a moment, as though there was something he wanted to say, but whatever it was, he seemed to have a change of heart. 'Goodnight, Nell.'

He knew about Alex and her, she was sure of it. She watched him join Michael and Newt in the car and waved them off, wondering if she should have broached the subject, and hoping he would keep his mouth shut. Locking the front door, she glanced at her watch. She poured a glass of wine and headed upstairs, planning to indulge with a soak in the tub. Although Alex had said he would call her, they hadn't made plans to see each other again. Knowing he would be stopping by after work had her stomach somersaulting in anticipation.

As the water ran she drew the curtains and started to undress. Outside it was raining again. Her phone beeped on the nightstand and she glanced at the screen. There were two texts, one from Michael checking she had her phone with her, the other from Alex saying he'd be there just after eleven.

Smiling, she replied to both.

She pinned up her hair then took both her wine and phone into the bathroom. Setting the glass down on the side of the tub, she found a mellow playlist on her cell phone and set it on the shelf, lighting the two candles beside it before killing the light. Enjoying having some time to herself she sank into the water, soaped herself down then rested her head against the edge of the tub. Relaxing to the sound of Al Green, she drifted off to sleep.

Fifteen minutes later she was jolted awake by a loud bang coming from downstairs.

Nell shot up in the tub, water splashing over the side. Her heart went into her mouth. Was someone in the house?

She held her breath, listening for another sound. When the only noise came from the still-sloshing water, her thumping heartbeat and John Mayer singing through her phone, she began to wonder if she had dreamt it. Maybe her imagination was playing tricks on her.

Still, she was too tightly wound to relax. Pulling the plug she climbed from the tub, reached for her towel and turned on the light, blowing out the candles. Picking up her glass of wine she took a generous sip and ordered herself to chill.

She was stepping back into the bedroom when the bang came again, this time loud, decisive and repetitive, and she froze, glass clutched tightly in her hand. This time she recognised where the noise was coming from. Someone was banging on the front door.

Nell glanced at the time on her alarm clock. It was only nine thirty. Alex had said he wouldn't be over before eleven. Michael had a key. There was no reason for anyone to be outside banging on the front door.

Fingers trembling, she set down the wine glass on the nightstand and, slowly pulling back the curtain, glanced down towards the front door. Although the porch was partially hidden she couldn't see anyone on the front step and saw no vehicle parked in the drive.

Her belly knotting, she went back into the bathroom, grabbed her phone and called Alex.

He answered after two rings.

'You okay?'

'You're still at work, right?'

'Yeah, why?'

'Someone's outside knocking on the door. I was reluctant to answer if it wasn't you.'

She heard him go from relaxed to alert. 'Is there a car outside?'

'I can't see one?'

'The doors are locked?'

'Yeah, I locked them before I came upstairs.'

'And the alarm is set?'

'Yes!'

'You definitely can't see who it is?'

'No.' Nell glanced out of the window. 'I'm looking right now and I can't see anyone.'

Another loud bang had her jumping and she almost dropped the phone. This time it came from the back of the house. 'Shit!'

'Nell?'

'Whoever it is has gone round back.'

'Stay in the house, keep the doors locked. I'll be there in ten minutes.'

He had hung up before she had a chance to reply. Nell grabbed her bathrobe, feeling vulnerable.

The doors are locked and the alarm is set. You're fine.

Part of her was tempted to stay in the bedroom, wait for Alex to arrive, but a niggly little voice from the irrational part of her brain kept picking away.

What if the alarm is broken? What if someone is breaking into the house right now?

Her robe belted and her cell phone still clutched in her hand she gingerly opened the bedroom door, glancing down the landing to the stairs. The house was silent, the only noise coming from Bella's old grandfather clock, which was ticking in the hallway below.

What if it's Caleb?

Nell shuddered at the thought, hating that she felt so scared. She had come home wanting to be strong and brave, to build herself up, but her legs were shaking, her insides knotted so tightly she could barely breathe. At the top of the stairs, she took a moment, annoyed with herself that she was too frightened to go downstairs in her own home.

There had been no further noise since the banging against the back door. Maybe whoever it was had gone.

Nell looked at her phone. It had been four minutes since she had called Alex. Maybe she should go lock herself in the bathroom?

Get your butt downstairs, check the doors and grab a knife.

She psyched herself up and shakily descended the stairs, determined she was going to be brave, mad at herself for falling to pieces over something so stupid. As she reached the hallway, she glanced at the front door, relieved to see it was still locked, then down towards the kitchen, cursing she hadn't drawn the blinds and that anyone outside could see right into the house.

There was no other sound apart from the ticking clock. Maybe whoever had been outside had gone, realising they were unable to get in the house.

Go draw the blinds and get a knife, then wait for Alex.

She forced herself to walk down the hallway to the kitchen, drew a shaky breath before quickly crossing to the window and yanking down the blind. Feeling a little less vulnerable now she knew no-one could see in, Nell opened the knife drawer, grabbed the largest blade and gripped the handle tightly. She glanced over at the back door. It looked secure, but she needed to double-check.

As she crossed the kitchen the window rattled behind the blind. Whoever was outside was banging against the glass. The knife slipped from her fingers, clattering against the floor. She retrieved it quickly with trembling hands as the banging came again, this time closer to the door.

She hurried across, needing to reassure herself it was locked.

As she reached the door, yanked at the handle to check, a face pressed up against the glass and she screamed, her heart leaping into her mouth. The glass was frosted, but she could see a white mask. He stood with his face pressed against the glass, gloved hands either side, palms splayed, as he stared through the door at her.

Nell stood frozen to the spot, the knife gripped in one hand, her phone in the other, too terrified to move as she stared back at the black eye holes in the ghoulish white face, then the man shrieked loudly, a ghoulish high-pitched banshee cry that sounded like mad laughter, and he pummelled his fists against the glass in the door.

Startled, she let out a yelp and backed away, hitting the counter. Her legs so rubbery she didn't dare use them. She sank to the floor and crawled behind the counter out of sight of the door, the knife still tightly gripped in her hand.

After what was probably only a few seconds, but felt much longer, the banging ceased and everything went quiet. Still she remained on the floor, squeezing her eyes shut, not daring to move. Barely able to breathe, she listened to the slow perpetual tick of the grandfather clock.

The attack hit hard and sudden, the vice-like grip in her chest stealing her breath, her head pounding, vision blurring. Sweat beaded on her forehead and rolled down her sides as a wave of nausea swept over her. She began counting, desperately trying to gain control of her breathing, the panic increasing as her tightening chest worsened, convinced she was going to black out.

The front door bell chimed, making her jump. Her hand clenched even tighter on the knife.

She heard Alex's voice. 'Nell, it's me. Open up.'

Letting out a shaky breath she tried to pull herself up and failed.

'Fifty-four, fifty-three, fifty-two...' The bell sounded again.

'NELL?'

Nell gulped for air and tried again, holding onto the counter for support. Her legs were shaking badly, her head swimming, and she sank back to the floor.

Her cell phone started to ring in her hand. It was several seconds before she managed to activate the call.

'Nell?'

'Alex, I...'

'Nell, listen to me, can you open the door?'

'I tried... I can't move.'

There was a pause. 'You're having an attack. Nell, talk to me.'

'I... I can't breathe.'

'Yes, you can. Your brain is trying to fool you. Slow and steady like before, and in through your nose, out through your mouth. Tell me what else you feel.'

'My chest, it hurts. I'm gonna pass out.'

'You're not going to pass out. It just feels like you are.'

'It's making me dizzy and I feel sick.'

'Focus on your breathing.'

'I can't.'

'One breath at a time, slow and steady. You've got this, Nell.'

'I'm trying.'

'Where are you? Are you upstairs?'

'In the kitchen.'

'I'm just a few feet away.'

'Oh God, the man... there's a man.'

'He's gone, I've already checked. It's just you and me, and you're going to be fine, I promise. The attack feels real, but it isn't. Keep breathing, keeping talking to me. You've got this.'

It was several minutes before she felt steady enough to get to her feet and, although the tightening in her chest had eased, her breathing under control, her legs were still rubbery as she made her way down the hallway. She disabled the alarm, unbolted the latch and pulled open the door, stepping back to let Alex in.

He glanced at the knife she was still holding, eased it gently from her fingers and laid it on the reception desk then cupped her face, eyes studying her carefully. 'Are you okay?'

'Yeah, I'm...' Nell paused, drew in a shaky breath. Who the hell was she kidding? She had just experienced one hell of a panic attack, which had left her drained, and she couldn't stop shaking.

'No, I'm not,' she admitted. 'I will be, but I need a little while.'

She didn't protest as Alex wrapped his arms around her, letting herself sink into him and holding on tightly, needing the physical contact.

'I saw him,' she whispered. 'His face was pressed up against the door. He was wearing a mask, but I saw him.'

Alex held her close, one hand stroking her hair, the other rubbing her back. He kissed her gently on the forehead.

'Whoever it is, I will get him. I promise you.'

23

He stared down at the girl on the table in front of him. Her wide blue eyes were full of tears, the look in them pleading. She wasn't supposed to be here. This wasn't part of the plan. He had deviated, acted on a whim. And he was royally kicking himself, because he was smarter. He was supposed to know better.

To hunt successfully, rules had to be followed, routines adhered to. There was no room for spontaneity. Acting on impulse led to sloppy mistakes and that was how people got caught.

He had been spontaneous once before, twelve years ago, and was still paying for the mistake he had made that night, still trying to clear up the mess he had caused. That night had been his Achilles heel and, as he attempted to rectify the problem, clear up the loose ends, he found himself slipping on his usually high standards.

Penny Maher should have been routine, but he hadn't been fully focused, had still been reeling from Nell O'Connor's return to the island, worrying she could be the catalyst for his whole world unravelling.

Needing to relieve frustration he had gone hunting, but his emotions had gotten in the way, and he hadn't been thinking clearly when he disposed of Penny's body. The key was hiding them well enough that the fish would have time to take care of any evidence. With no body, it was a case of a missing person, and he was always careful with his victims, making sure he picked women who lived alone, where he could stage it to look as though they had left of their own accord.

Sometimes the police bought it, other times they suspected foul play, but never did they cotton on that a serial killer was playing in their backyard.

He had fucked up with Penny and then his emotions had caused him to lose his temper and he had completely lost his head, revealing his true self and killing again, and, in doing so, managing to break every single code he lived by.

For years he had followed the rules he had created: always hunt away from home, always leave plenty of time between kills, never let emotion get in the way, and always get rid of the evidence.

But he had screwed up. Penny's head had been found and she was now the subject of an active murder investigation.

While there was little chance of her being linked back to him – he was always careful to cover his tracks – it bothered him the waters were being trawled as they searched for the rest of her body. It was impossible to know what the fish had eaten and what they had left to rot on the bed of the ocean, and the discovery of other victims would spark a major manhunt.

It also caused a problem as he was unsure what the hell to do with the other body he needed to get rid of, not daring to return to his usual dumping ground.

There was a certain irony Nell had been the one to discover Penny's head and he couldn't help but think in some twisted way it was a sign. She was trouble though, that one, and he had enjoyed scaring her tonight a little too much. He would have liked to have taken things a little further and probably would have done if Alex Cutler hadn't shown up.

Nell was supposed to be business. She was simply a problem that had to be dealt with. But truth was, she was to blame for the midnight trip into East Haven and it was her fault there was a pretty blonde currently strapped down to his table.

He had slunk away from the house, his bloodlust yearning, the volume cranking up a notch in his head, threatening to consume him. It always started slowly, like a trickling of water, but as the pressure built, the craving growing, the rush of water came faster, overpowering. The only way to relieve the pressure was to kill.

He hadn't been thinking clearly when he had seen her, and had attempted to charm her with his usual practiced lines, but something must have been off about his delivery tonight, perhaps something not quite right with his smile, because it hadn't worked and she had blown him off. Frustrated, he had followed her from the bar, thinking it had to be fate when she headed into the parking lot where his car was and clicked her keys at a vehicle parked half a dozen cars away. He'd glanced around, noting the lot was empty and the corner where both their cars were parked was in the shadows, the overhead street-lamp not working, and as she went to get in her car, he had grabbed her from behind, smashing her head against the door.

She had been unconscious for ages and he was beginning to worry maybe he had hit her head a little too hard, perhaps she wouldn't wake up, but she had eventually come around, slowly realising the gravity of the situation. He always loved that bit. The moment where he could see in their eyes that they under-stood how much trouble they were in.

As he teased her with his knife, running the smooth end of the blade across her belly, enjoying the look of terror on her face as she awaited the first cut, the rational part of his brain kicked in, reminding him she shouldn't be here, that in terms of screwing up, he had gone off the scale.

He knew nothing about her, and for all he knew, she could have a husband or boyfriend waiting at home who would report her missing before morning. And although he was fairly confident he hadn't been seen, he couldn't be certain. Add to that he already had a body he needed to deal with, and the problems kept adding up. He never should have taken her – he realised that now – but of course it was too late to let her go. She had seen his face and she would go to the police.

Yes, he had made a terrible mistake. Another one he would have to live with. He hadn't been thinking clearly and the woman on his table would be another problem to deal with in the cold light of day.

She was here now though and when he had finished with her the pressure in his head would ease, allowing him to think clearly and figure out what the hell he was going to do.

He flipped the blade, the cold sharp steel carving a thin trail of ribbon red across the woman's navel. She bucked on the table, pulling against her bonds, her whimper caught behind the tape covering her mouth, and fat tears spilled down her cheeks.

Running his finger along the bloody knife, he smiled down at her. 'How about we get this party started?'

24

'I want to get a gun.'

Alex cut a glance at Nell, immediately disapproving of the idea.

'You don't need a gun.'

'If I have one I'll feel safer.'

'You ever fired one before?'

'No.' She raised her chin stubbornly. 'I was thinking you could teach me.'

They were down on the beach, making the most of the fading daylight and what had been a slightly cooler, but still bright and sunny day, as Sasha and Teddy dived in and out of the surf, chasing each other in circles.

The events of Sunday night were behind her sudden desire to get a gun, he understood that. Whoever had been outside the house had achieved their goal of frightening her, and he knew she hated that. Four nights later, she was still too scared to stay alone in her own home. A gun might make her feel safer, but it was still a bad idea, especially with her panic attacks.

Alex had been staying with her, though was always early to rise, needing to get back to walk the dogs and wanting to escape before Michael arrived. He and Nell had yet to define what they had between them and by an unspoken pact, had been keeping things quiet.

Tonight he was working late and had persuaded her to stay over at his place. Although she would be alone, he felt happier leaving her knowing she had the dogs for protection, as well as the security of closer neighbours. It also didn't hurt that Michael and Newt were just a five-minute walk along the beach.

Neither of them knew about Sunday night's intruder. Nell hadn't wanted to worry her brother and, while that rested uncomfortably with Alex, a small selfish part of him knew Michael would be hovering over her if he knew, making it impossible for them to spend any time together.

He was doing everything he could to find out who was responsible for harassing her, and come dawn, he had completed another sweep of the perimeter of the house, though found nothing.

Sam Kent still sat top of his list and Alex had put one of his deputies in plain clothes and ordered him to follow Sam at a distance. That had been three days ago and so far Lizzie's brother hadn't put a foot wrong. Likewise, there had been no further incidents at the guesthouse – though that was probably because the place had been buzzing during the day as the renovations began. With her brother around during the day and Alex with her at night, Nell was safe. She didn't need a gun.

'You do realise that by carrying a firearm you're more likely to be killed during an attack than if you're unarmed?' he pointed out, not liking the idea at all.

'You carry one.'

'Because I'm a cop and it's my job. I've been trained how to use it.'

'So, you could train me.'

'It's not just about knowing how to fire a gun, Nell. If you found yourself in a situation where you had to shoot someone, could you actually pull the trigger?'

'Could you? Have you?'

'I have once,' Alex admitted. 'Armed guy holding up a gas station; he had hostages and was threatening to shoot them.'

'Did you kill him?'

'I punctured his lung, but he survived and was able to stand trial.' He caught hold of Nell's hand and pulled her round to face him. The evening breeze was blowing through her hair, her cheeks glowing and her amber eyes burning bright as she looked at him. 'If you have a gun and you're in a situation where you need to defend yourself, if you hesitate to pull the trigger, that's how you end up dead.'

'So, I wouldn't hesitate.'

Alex cupped her face with his free hand, tracing the pout of her bottom lip with the pad of his thumb. 'That's what bothers me. I worry that you would.'

Her eyes hardened slightly, annoyed he wasn't backing down.

'I'm going to get a gun,' she sniffed. 'You can help me with that or I can figure out how to use it by myself.'

He relented on Friday.

Nell had said she was going to get a gun, with or without his help, and Alex knew she wasn't bluffing. If he couldn't stop her carrying, he figured he would rest more comfortably if she at least knew how to use the thing.

He had stopped by the guesthouse, found Michael out on a supplies run and Nell upstairs in one of the third-floor bedrooms, two steps up a ladder, wearing jeans and a checked shirt, hair scooped back in a red bandana, her blonde curls spilling out of the back, as she carefully applied emulsion to the coving. Loud music was playing on her phone, and she was wiggling her ass between strokes to the sound of Blondie. Slipping quietly into the room, he waited until she had dipped her brush back in the tin, before grabbing her from behind and pulling her down into his arms. Momentarily startled, she lost her grip on the brush, the brief look of panic on her face bubbling into laughter as she realised it was him. Still, she gave him a swipe as he righted her on her feet.

'You idiot, sneaking up on me like that. I could have stabbed you with my paintbrush.'

The room was a soft pale grey and offset nicely against the brilliant white coving.

'You look like Axl Rose,' he commented, touching the bandana.

'My homage to the eighties,' she told him dryly, nodding to the phone as Debbie Harry sang 'One Way or Another', linking her arms around his neck and leaning in for a kiss. 'Is this a social visit or are you here on business?'

Alex reached up and rubbed at the smudge of paint on her nose.

'It's a little of both actually.' When Nell cocked a brow, he elaborated. 'We'll head over to the mainland and get you a firearm tomorrow then we'll go to the shooting range and I'll teach you to use it.'

'Really?' Her face lit up.

'I'm not going to pretend I'm happy about it,' he cautioned. 'If it were up to me, you wouldn't have a gun at all. I figure you're going to get one with or without my help though, and I want to be sure you know how to use it.'

'Thank you.' She hugged him tightly. Holding her close against him, his hands roamed down over her butt.

Footsteps in the hallway, the creak of the floorboard then a loud cough had both Alex and Nell looking up. Michael stood in the doorway watching them, his jaw agape.

'Why have you got your hands on my sister's ass?' he demanded.

'Michael, don't overreact,' Nell urged, pulling away from the embrace, clearly startled by his sudden arrival. 'There's something we need to talk about.'

Michael ignored her, turning in the doorway, hands on head, clearly thinking things through, the pieces slotting into place.

'Seriously, really?' He disappeared into the hallway.

'Michael?'

Alex pulled her back. 'Let me go talk to him.'

He followed his friend out of the bedroom and found him pacing the landing, his face flushed. 'How long?' he demanded, as Alex pulled the door closed behind him, leaving Nell inside.

'Since Saturday night,' Alex admitted, figuring honesty was now the best policy.

'You're sleeping with her?'

'I am.'

Michael's face turned a deeper shade of red and he swore under his breath. 'And you didn't think to run that piece of information by me?'

'I'm thirty-four years old!' Nell's voice came from the other side of the door. 'I don't need to get a permission slip from you, Michael. I can sleep with whomever I want.'

'Stay out of this, Nell.'

'Stay out of it?' She yanked the door open. 'It's about me. How about you stay out of it?'

She stood with her hands on her hips, eyes flashing angrily at her brother, her face almost the same shade as the ridiculous bandana on her head.

'Look, stay here.' Alex eased her back inside the bedroom and closed the door. He needed to diffuse this situation and getting caught between two hot-headed O'Connors wasn't helping.

'Walk with me,' Michael demanded, storming off towards the stairs, not waiting for Alex.

Down on the first floor he started pacing. Alex leant back against the bannister at the foot of the stairwell, the calm against Michael's storm.

'You know what she's been through. I told you she's not in a good place. She came back here for a fresh start, not to get her heart broken. She doesn't need this.'

'What makes you think I'm going to break her heart?'

'Because that's what you do. I've watched how you operate for the last five years.'

'How I operate?'

'With women. You suck them in, have your fun then decide you don't want the commitment.'

'That's not how this is.' Alex didn't bother to point out the irony that it was Michael who had been pushing his female friends on him for the past couple of years, trying to convince him that he just needed to meet the right one.

Michael stopped pacing momentarily and stared at Alex, his eyes sober. 'So what, you're telling me you're in love with her?'

'We're still getting to know each other.' Alex answered the question as honestly as he could. Hell, he had only known Nell for a couple of weeks. It was far too soon to be throwing words like 'love' around. 'I care about her,' he eventually conceded. 'I care about her a lot. This is more than just sex.'

He was grateful both of Michael's labourers had made themselves scarce when they had heard both of them come downstairs. The last thing he wanted was an audience.

'Does she know about Portland? Have you told her?'

'Not yet.'

'Are you going to tell her? She deserves to know that you

won't ever commit to her, just as you wouldn't commit to Mia or Charlotte or Allison.'

Alex felt the edges of his temper bristle. He was under no obligation to tell anyone anything about his past. It was his personal business. If he told Nell, it would be on his terms. 'I'll tell her when I'm ready.' His tone was harder than he had intended and he deliberately softened it. 'And don't write her off as another Mia or Charlotte or Allison. She means more to me than that. I know she's your sister and you're looking out for her, but I promise you I wouldn't have slept with her if I didn't think there was a chance it might become more serious further down the line. I'm not going to lie to you and tell you I'm in love with her. It's too soon. She's just out of a bad relationship; I'm figuring out how to do this again. We need a little time, okay? Just give us some space and let us work this out together, please.'

His words seemed to placate Michael some. He still didn't appear thrilled with the idea, but he no longer looked like he wanted to punch Alex in the face, which was a start.

'You break her heart, I'll break your face.'

'Really, you're throwing movie lines at me?' Alex couldn't help but break out in a grin, recognising the quote from one of Michael's favourite films, *Some Kind of Wonderful*. When Michael glowered at him, not quite back at the joking around stage yet, he added sagely, 'I won't break her heart. I promise.'

'Have you two kissed and made up yet?'

They both looked up to see Nell peering over the bannister on the second floor.

Alex wondered how much she had heard. She gave nothing away as she came down the stairs, giving her brother the evil eye.

'Not yet,' Michael said gruffly. 'But we'll get there. Give me a little time to get used to the idea, like Alex wants me to give the pair of you. I'm still pissed off that you both kept it a secret from me.'

'Well, maybe if you didn't act like such an overprotective dad all the time, it might have been easier to tell you the truth.'

Michael's nostrils flared at that. 'I do not act like an overprotective dad. A concerned big brother, yes, and you should be grateful I have your back.'

When Nell pouted, looked ready to retort, Alex caught hold of her hand. 'Instead of blaming each other, why don't we sit down and talk like adults?'

Michael scowled at the idea. 'I have to get on with the plastering. It's getting late.'

Muttering to himself under his breath he skulked off up the stairs. Alex watched him go. Michael was supposed to be his best friend and he had lied to him. While he knew he would come around, that he just needed a little time, it still made him feel shitty.

'He'll be okay. Just let him brood for a bit, eat some ice cream and quote a few more movie lines.'

Nell's comment had Alex smiling, though he almost immediately sobered, curious as to how much of their conversation she had overheard. 'How long were you listening?'

'A while,' she admitted. 'I heard enough.'

'So you heard Michael mention about Portland?'

'I did.' His expression had obviously turned wary, because she squeezed his hand. 'But don't worry; I'm not going to ask.'

'Nell... I–'

She raised a finger to his lips; cut him off.

'I said I'm not going to ask. You'll tell me when you're ready.'

'Okay.'

She gave a wistful smile that was tinged with sadness, regret even.

'We both have our secrets, Alex. How about we carry on

figuring things out for now? We can talk about the past when the time feels right.'

Caleb had been forced to return to Chicago, much to his chagrin. His mother was throwing a charity benefit on Friday night at which he was the guest speaker. Despite his best attempts to get out of the evening, Bitsy Sweeney Brooks was not a woman to be trifled with and she flattened every one of his excuses before telling him in no uncertain terms that he would find a way to be there or suffer the consequences. Caleb may have been a thirty-eight-year-old successful businessman in his own right, and almost twice the size of his diminutive mother, but she was the only woman who could make him quake in his boots.

She had never liked Nell, had thought her too common for her son, too much of a free spirit. The pair of them had locked horns a couple of times early on in the relationship, back in the days when Nell had thought it was acceptable to question his mother. Bitsy had told him that he would never be able to control a woman like her, that eventually she would betray him. Of course, he hadn't listened, had tried his damnedest to tame Nell, to correct her when she erred, determined to prove his mother wrong. And for a long while he had believed he had her under control. Ultimately though, his mother was right, and Nell had betrayed him. Bitsy didn't yet know that her future daughter-in-law had left. Caleb hadn't told her, unable to face the gloating and the lectures. Nell would be expected at the benefit tonight though and he would have to conjure up an excuse to avoid his mother learning the truth.

With much reluctance he had made his way back to the mainland early Friday morning and flew home. While it was an inconvenience, he guessed it could be for the best. He had spent a good portion of the week drinking himself stupid from the mini bar in his room, ordering in food, and generally feeling sorry for himself as he tried to formulate a plan. On the occasions he had ventured out, wanting to keep tabs on Nell, he had found her with either the police chief or her brother. So far there had been no opportunity to catch her alone and to be honest – at this stage he wasn't quite sure what he would do if he did.

He had initially come to the island planning on dragging her back home to Chicago, but after seeing her with Cutler on Saturday night he had experienced such a level of rage, grief and betrayal, he had wanted her dead. He was still figuring out if he wanted her back or wanted her gone for good, veering between both depending on his mood and the amount of booze in his glass. The only thing he was completely sure of was that he wanted retribution.

And when the time was right, he was going to get it in spades.

25

As they drove away from the shooting range, Nell wasn't quite sure if she had won or lost the battle to own a firearm. They had purchased a gun, a Glock 9mm that she had selected after trying the grip of a few, but Alex had insisted on both paying for it and registering the gun in his name. The deal he proposed was that once she had learned to shoot it, he would transfer the papers to her name and hand over the weapon. It had seemed like a good deal, until they arrived at the shooting range and Nell had missed every shot badly.

She wanted to be mad at him, but he had been patient with her, had tried to help her, and it was likely she would have lost her temper a whole lot sooner if he hadn't been there with her, saying the right things when she started to get annoyed with herself, making her laugh when the anger threatened to spill over into tears of frustration.

When they had left the shooting range he had refused to hand over the weapon, and, although she protested, she couldn't actually blame him. He also promised that they would return in a couple of days for another practice. Deep down she knew it was her fault she had blown it, but still she couldn't help but feeling like she had been hoodwinked. She shouldn't have let him pay for the damn gun.

As they approached the turn off for East Haven heading for the ferry port, Nell recalled their first encounter. At the time she had thought he was a pompous ass and was seething with him for causing her to miss the ferry. How quickly things had changed.

'I was so mad at you that first time we met,' she told him, recalling the incident.

Alex shot her a sidelong glance. 'You weren't flying high on my radar either.'

'I missed my ferry because of you.'

'I know. But you got a later one.'

'By which time the bank was shut, I had no money and had no food. I was starving all night and wishing all kinds of bad stuff on you.' Nell grumbled, remembering the hellish night. Her lips curved as she recalled their next encounter. 'I figured you owned the bar. I nearly choked on my coffee when you walked into the diner the next day.'

Alex chuckled. 'The bar's owned by a friend of mine. And yeah, your expression was priceless when I saw you in the diner. To be fair, I had you pegged as a stuck-up tourist and it knocked me for six when Michael introduced you as his sister. You weren't what I was expecting.'

'No?'

He turned briefly to look at her, a sly wide grin on his face. 'Nope, not at all.' He slipped one hand off the wheel, onto her thigh, and left it there as he returned his attention to the road.

Their first encounter on the mainland had happened over two weeks ago, but it felt much longer, and it was crazy how quickly things had escalated. Part of Nell wanted to put on the brakes, slow things down. She wasn't used to jumping in with both feet and feared the spark between them that had flared so quickly could just as easily die out. She had heard Michael's words that Alex didn't commit, told herself it didn't matter as they were both consenting adults and she would enjoy the ride, not let herself get sucked in too deeply. But she had also heard Alex tell her brother it was more than just sex, and, much as it annoyed her, she found herself wanting to believe that.

Things felt right with him, comfortable. If they ended suddenly, would she be okay with that?

One day at a time, O'Connor. Just take it one day at a time.

She placed her hand on top of his, ordering herself to relax. One day at a time.

Jenna Milborn was in the liquor store, on a supply run for Curtis, when the chief walked in with Nell O'Connor. She heard them laughing, glanced up, a bottle of Wild Turkey in her hand, her heart sinking, hoping she could pay and get out of the store before they spotted her.

Curtis had run out of whiskey late last night and Jenna wore the marks of his frustration in a line of ugly bruises around her neck. He had choked her so hard that for a moment she had thought he might kill her and for a second she had hoped he might, thinking it might be for the best, an easy way to escape her problems. And it was no less than she deserved. She had always known that one day she would have to pay for her sins.

Fear had overtaken guilt though and when he had eventually released her she had crawled into the spare bedroom, locked the door, and sobbed herself to sleep. She had tried to cover the bruising with a scarf, but it kept slipping down, and she didn't want the chief to see, knowing he would likely start ragging on her to press charges, would probably arrest Curtis, and then she would face a fresh new hell.

Nell O'Connor knew too; she had seen it in her eyes that night at Maloney's. She sure as hell wanted nothing to do with Nell and wished the damn woman had never moved to the stupid island. Nell was trouble and the fact she was cosy with the chief only unnerved Jenna further.

She quickly filled her basket with the bottles of liquor, frustrated to see two other people in the line at the checkout. As she waited her turn, she played nervously with the scarf, using the overhead mirror to try to pull it higher to disguise the bruising.

Panic clawed at her gut as she saw the chief and Nell had joined the line behind her. They hadn't spotted her, or if they had they didn't let on, seeming too caught up in each other. Jenna ducked her head and fussed around digging in her purse.

'I was thinking we should go out tonight.'

'Out?'

They were talking quietly, but she was close enough to pick up on their conversation.

'Yeah, out. Your brother knows about us now, so we don't have to keep sneaking around.'

'You want to go on a date?'

'Yeah, I do. Let me take you out to dinner.'

So they were involved with each other? Jenna didn't know whether to laugh or cry. Could this situation get any worse?

'Jenna?'

Hearing Nell say her name, feeling the touch of a hand on her jacket, sickness crept up from her stomach. Slowly Jenna turned, wishing she could leave the store, but knowing Curtis would go nuts if she arrived home empty-handed.

'Sorry,' Nell was apologising. 'I didn't realise it was you standing in front of us.'

'It's fine.'

She noticed the chief's eyes narrow on her neck, and fought to resist the urge to fiddle with the scarf as Nell insisted on making small talk, wishing the damn line would hurry up and move and the stupid woman would shut up, realising from Jenna's monosyllabic replies that she didn't want to have a conversation with her.

The chief let Nell do the talking. Jenna could sense he was annoyed, and hoped to hell he would stay quiet and not question her about the bruising. Thankfully he didn't say anything. She just hoped he wouldn't decide to pay a visit to Curtis.

Eventually the line moved and she quickly paid for the alcohol, not replying to Nell's goodbye or bothering to look back, desperate to get out of the liquor store.

In her car she leant her head against the steering wheel, tears pricking at the back of her eyes. When one fell, she brushed it away furiously.

Why was this happening? After all of these years, why now? Damn Nell O'Connor.

Pull yourself together, Jenna. Maybe it will be okay?

Except she knew it wouldn't. Everything was starting to unravel and she needed support.

Instead of driving home, she headed out on the lower coast road, turning into a quiet street of middle class suburban houses. Spotting the car in the driveway, she pulled up alongside the curb and drew in a shaky breath.

He wasn't going to be happy with her visit. She knew she was about to break the vow they had made to never talk about the incident. But damn it, that was before Nell came home and everything went to hell. He had to be sharing the same concerns, and have the same fears.

She rang the bell, stomach knotting as she waited for him to answer. He lived alone and the house was too big for one person, but she figured he could afford it.

Footsteps sounded in the hallway, she heard the lock turn and then the door opened.

Tommy stood before her; he was wearing his police uniform and she guessed he was getting ready to head into work.

Concern knitted his brow, but she could also see the wariness in his eyes. 'Jenna?'

'We have to talk.'

'This isn't about Curtis, is it?' he asked, sounding resigned, already knowing it wasn't.

'I know we said we would never mention it again, but I'm scared, Tommy. I'm really scared. Everything is falling apart.'

'It'll be okay.' Even though he spoke the words, she could tell he didn't believe them himself.

'No it won't. It's all going wrong.' Fresh tears filled her eyes. 'What the hell are we going to do about Nell O'Connor?'

Tommy Dolan's sixteenth birthday was when he first started to shine.

The nightmares about Lizzie's murder had pretty much stopped, he got his driving licence and his parents bought him his first car. He made it onto the high school football team, and finally girls were starting to notice him. He had gone from being a cute freckle-faced ten-year-old boy to a gangly, slightly awkward teen, but now his shoulders were starting to fill out, his features softening and becoming more handsome, and he had lost the brace he had been stuck with since his thirteenth birthday.

The one girl he lusted after though was unfortunately out of his reach. Jenna Campbell was a junior, same as him – and so, so pretty with her copper hair and her cornflower eyes. She smiled at Tommy, always said hello if they passed in the hallway, but he knew she was totally besotted with her boyfriend, Luke Trainor, who was a senior.

Tommy was a little jealous of Luke, but also envied and admired him.

Luke was so laid-back, so cool, and he always had loads of

kids flocking around him. He hadn't lived on the island long, had moved here with his brother, and the day he started at the high school, he had everyone eating out of the palm of his hand. He and Jenna had started dating within weeks and Tommy, who had secretly had a crush on her since he was a freshman, had watched his hopes of ever getting to kiss her, go up in smoke.

Eventually he moved on, dating various girls in his year, gradually bailing on his old friends, his confidence soaring as his popularity grew.

He was a few weeks shy of his seventeenth birthday and feeling invincible the summer Sarah Treadwell arrived on the island.

Sarah was voluptuous and pretty, with hair the colour of champagne. She was older – Tommy had heard someone say she was in her early twenties – and apparently married, though separated from her cheating husband, and she was looking for work.

Bella Golding took her on, giving her a temporary job at the guesthouse, and Tommy, along with most other red-blooded males on the island, fell in love.

He had grown up with Clarke Golding, though seldom hung around with him these days as Clarke was just too odd, but he was a ticket to Sarah, so Tommy started stopping by the guesthouse on a more frequent basis, quick to offer assistance if Sarah looked like she needed a hand. She was always nice to him and Bella seemed happy that he was back on the scene and looking out for her son. He tried to help out with odd jobs around the property where he could, wanting to be seen as pulling his weight and someone who could be relied on.

Everything about the summer of 2005 was perfect. Until Luke Trainor started sniffing around.

Sarah was a tactile person, and it was easy to read too much into the way she touched Tommy's arm when she spoke to him, always giving him her full attention when he talked, and how she laughed whenever he told her a joke. Although she was six years older, he had managed to convince himself they had a connection, but then one day he had seen her in town buying groceries, and the bag she carried to Bella's car split with cans and vegetables spilling onto the ground.

Tommy had gone to help, but Luke had appeared from nowhere, beating him to it, and then he was there fixing Sarah with his toothpaste smile as he played the knight in shining armour and she was touching Luke's arm, giving him her undivided attention and laughing at his jokes.

Tommy had been furious. Furious with Luke for thinking he had the right to flirt with Sarah when he already had Jenna, with Sarah for flirting back, and with himself for being so gullible and believing she actually liked him in the first place.

He was also furious because he knew that he couldn't compete with Luke, who was a year-and-a-half older and had just graduated high school, whose body had already matured into that of a man's and who only, it seemed, had to look at girls with those intense blue eyes to have them falling at his feet.

Although he continued to hang around the guesthouse, Tommy cooled a little towards Sarah, his teenage mind twisting things to believe she had led him on.

Luke continued to date Jenna, acting as if nothing had happened, but Tommy saw him and Sarah together a number of times towards the end of the summer. They were never doing anything they shouldn't, but he could tell from their body language and the way they looked at each other when they spoke that they were flirting, and he didn't doubt for one second that there was more going on that he hadn't seen.

He didn't believe Jenna realised what was going on, felt sorry for her as he knew she adored Luke and didn't deserve to be treated this way. He certainly knew if he was lucky enough to have a girlfriend like Jenna Campbell, he would worship the ground she walked on and never take her for granted. Jenna was already reeling, knowing that come September Luke would be heading off to college and she would only get to see him in the holidays. If she found out he was cheating on her, it would break her heart.

It crossed his mind that perhaps Sarah didn't know about Luke and Jenna, that maybe Luke was pretending he was single, though it was a stretch. Everyone on the island knew about Luke and Jenna. Still, he brought it up in conversation one Saturday afternoon after helping Sarah as she unloaded sacks of groceries from the car.

'I guess you're going to miss Luke Trainor when he heads off to college next month.' He kept his tone casual as he took the heavier of the paper sacks.

Sarah didn't answer for a moment and he glanced at her, saw the wariness on her face. 'What makes you say that?'

'I thought you two were close.'

'We're not. I barely know him. I mean... Yes, I know him to say hello to, but that's it.'

She seemed flustered, wouldn't look at him.

Liar, Tommy thought.

'My mistake then,' he told her sarcastically, hating the fact she couldn't even be honest with him and disliking her for it. He had thought Sarah Treadwell was better than that. 'I'm sure his girlfriend, Jenna, will miss him though.'

Sarah gave a tight smile. 'I'm sure she will.'

Tommy knew he should have let it drop. Luke would be out of everyone's hair in another few weeks and with him gone from the picture things could easily change. Sarah would likely soon forget him, and the separation could even take its toll on Jenna, who still had another year of high school and shared many of the same classes as him. It was that last thought that was playing on his mind when he saw her leaving the grocery store a few days later, head down, busy texting.

'Tommy, I'm sorry, I didn't see you,' she apologised, as he sidestepped out of her path. She had her sunglasses on so he couldn't see those lovely pale blue eyes that always made his belly flip, but she was beautiful all the same, her legs tanned and toned in the little black mini skirt she wore, her copper hair plaited.

'It's okay, I should watch where I am going,' he lied, having intentionally placed himself in her path.

She smiled at him and his world wobbled. Damn she was pretty.

'Can I give you a hand with your groceries?'

'Sure. I'm over here.' Jenna handed him a couple of sacks, fished for her car keys with her free hand and clicked at her teal-coloured Beetle.

'How have you been, Tommy?' she asked as they crossed the parking lot. 'I feel like I haven't seen you in ages. You haven't been down the beach much this summer.'

'I've been okay. I've been over at the guesthouse helping Bella a bit.'

'That's nice of you. I can't believe we're about to start senior year.'

'The summer has gone quick.'

'Too quick,' she agreed, the smile dropping off her face. 'I can't believe Luke will be gone in a few weeks.'

Jenna pulled open the passenger door, deposited her sack on the seat, while Tommy shuffled uncomfortably on his feet, thinking he should keep his mouth shut, but knowing it wasn't going to happen.

'Maybe that's for the best.'

She turned to face him, her expression hard to read behind the sunglasses. 'Why would you say that?'

Tommy shuffled some more. He had planned this conversation out in his head a dozen times, but the next line, the one where he told Jenna plainly that Luke was cheating on her, didn't come.

'Tell me what you know, Tommy!'

'I shouldn't have said anything.'

'But you did, and you obviously had a reason for saying it, so what is it?'

'You know Sarah Treadwell, who works at...' Tommy trailed off as Jenna's bottom lip wobbled.

'That bastard. I knew I was right to suspect.'

'You know?'

'I've had my suspicions. I didn't want to believe them.' A tear rolled down Jenna's cheek from below the sunglasses. 'Oh, Tommy.'

'He doesn't deserve you, Jenna. You're too good for him.' Tommy fumbled awkwardly in his pocket for a handkerchief, taken by surprise when Jenna flung herself against him. He tentatively put his arms around her as she sobbed against his chest, loving how she fitted against him and the sweet scent of her perfume assailing his nostrils. 'I shouldn't have told you.'

She looked up at him, her sunglasses now pushed back on her head, and her eyes still full of tears, shining a stunning azure blue.

'No, don't say that, Tommy. You were right to tell me. I deserve to know. You're the only good friend I have.'

Her words warmed his heart and he squeezed his arms tightly around her, feeling fiercely protective. 'I'd do anything for you, Jenna.'

His words brought a watery smile. 'I know you would, Tommy. I know.'

～

She called in on that favour two nights later, waking him after midnight with a text.

Tommy fumbled for his phone, his heart skipping a beat when Jenna's name flashed up. Rubbing his eyes, he opened the message.

When you said you would do anything for me, did you mean it?

Tommy hesitated briefly before replying.

Yes. Everything OK?

I saw them together tonight.

I'm sorry Jenna. I am. What can I do to help?

There was a long pause before Jenna's next text flashed up.

Help me get the bitch. Will you do that for me, Tommy?

Tommy's fingers hovered over the keys. He wasn't quite sure what Jenna had in mind, but he knew she was hurting, that this was his one shot to impress her. He fired off the reply and pressed send.

I will.

27

Sam Kent hit his blinker, slowing as he approached the turn off to his house. A quick glance in the rear-view mirror showed him that the Buick three cars behind was also signalling, which, although was what he had expected, still had him scowling in irritation.

He had first noticed the tail two days ago, though suspected he may have been followed for longer. He recognised Dwight Halloran, one of the deputies in the Purity Police Department. There was nothing unusual about that. Halloran had been in plain clothes, to any unassuming bystander he was off duty, and it was a small island, so it was inevitable that Sam would run into him on occasion. Except, Halloran appeared a few times too often to make it seem like coincidence.

Initially Sam had told himself he was being paranoid, but paranoia had made him alert and he had started looking out for the deputy, quickly realising that he was definitely being followed.

When Halloran disappeared, obviously off shift, he kept his eyes peeled, eventually recognising Kyle Mathis had taken over. Mathis was smarter, blended into the crowd more easily. Had he been the only tail, Sam may not have noticed him at all, and that unnerved him, had him thinking back over his movements from the past few days.

Chief Cutler didn't trust him, had figured he had something to hide, and Sam guessed he couldn't blame him. He was cussing himself for shooting off his big mouth the night the chief had shown up on his doorstep.

He hadn't been able to help himself though, his emotions still running high with Nell O'Connor's return.

He should have kept control, played it cool about Nell without revealing how he truly felt about her. But then that had always been his problem. He couldn't ever quite control the rage that burned inside of him. The psychologist his parents had sent him to see over on the mainland had recognised that and knew that the bitter feelings over the injustice of Lizzie's death had scarred him deep. Sam tried his best to keep the pain hidden, but Nell's return had tipped him over the edge. He had barely been able to sleep, continually playing out fantasies where it was Nell, not Lizzie, who had died that fateful night eighteen years ago.

Still it infuriated him that he was being followed. The chief had no proof that he had done anything wrong, but, although the temptation was there to storm into the police department, file a grievance about the way he was being treated, he was smart enough to realise that by figuring out he was being tailed, he could play the cops at their own game.

He parked up, went inside, and spent an hour cooking dinner, showering and changing his clothes, periodically glancing out of the window to ensure Dwight was still in place.

When he left the house it was under the cover of dusk, the TV was still playing in the living room, the table lamp on, and the blind drawn, enough to convince anyone snooping that he was home and having a lazy night in front of the television.

Leaving his car parked in the driveway he headed out of the back gate, making his way down the alley that joined the main road down to where he moored his boat. Less than five minutes later he was heading out of the harbour, feeling a small sense of satisfaction at being able to shake his tail so easily.

Cutler thought he had him figured so easily. He had no idea.

The walls and ceilings had been plastered, the rooms repainted. Over the past few days Nell, Michael and his team had been working hard on the guesthouse and their efforts were starting to show. With the bedrooms now all in good decorative order, Nell and Newt had been into town, shopping for bedding, furniture and accessories, and, while the superfluous stuff didn't interest Michael, he had to admit the finished rooms looked the business.

The plastering now complete, he was keen to turn his attention to the pool, and planned to start on pulling up the concrete floor of the conservatory first thing in the morning, which was why he was en route to the storage unit he rented to fetch his jackhammer.

As he drove, thoughts inevitably turned to his sister. The whole Alex situation still grated on him and although he had worked himself down from furious to irritated, he was still giving Alex a wide berth, and couldn't help but be a little sulky around Nell. The past few days they had mostly kept out of each other's way as they worked, sniping at each other if their paths did cross, and on the occasions Alex had stopped by, Michael had been quick to duck out of the way, not ready yet to accept there was anything going on between his sister and his best friend.

He tried to convince himself it was because he was looking

out for Nell, but truth was it was as much because he was pissed off at being kept in the dark.

Annoyed with himself he cranked up the stereo, letting the sound of Springsteen fill the truck as he pulled into the site where his storage unit was. There were twelve units in total and Michael rented the one furthest back in the lot. As it was gone eight thirty and already dark, he wasn't surprised to find the site empty, knowing the few businesses that also used the units daily would have long packed up and gone home. He drove to the back of the site, pulled up alongside the unit he rented and killed the engine. As he climbed from the truck, still humming *Hungry Heart*, his mind flitted back to his sister.

He assumed she was with Alex, as she had been pretty much every night since he had found out about the two of them. He knew this because he had detoured past the guesthouse most evenings and seen Alex's Jeep outside. While that still vexed him, it also gave him comfort, knowing that at least he didn't have to worry about Nell being up at the house all alone. He promised himself he wouldn't drive past there tonight on his way home, but knew it was a promise he'd likely break. He might be pissed at her, but she was still his sister and it mattered to him that she was safe.

Finding the key on his keychain, he turned his attention to the door, immediately noticing it was slightly ajar.

He had locked it, right?

Unease washed over him like a wave. Of course he had locked it. He was anal about stuff like this, especially knowing how expensive some of the building equipment was.

That left one alternative. Someone had broken in.

He pushed open the door, flipped the light, expecting to find the place empty, relief washing over him when he spotted everything as he had left it.

A rustling noise to the back of the unit had his hackles rising.

'Who's there?'

Michael's question was met with silence.

Gingerly he stepped forward into the unit, selecting a hammer from the toolbox sat on the table. 'I can hear you back there, so you'd better come out.'

He waited, hammer clenched tightly in his hand, temper rising, annoyed someone had broken in and had been planning to do what... steal or vandalise his stuff? It was probably one of the Osborne twins. They were only thirteen, but had a history of causing trouble, and Alex had hauled them in for questioning on countless occasions. This kind of shit had their name all over it. He pulled the door to the unit closed, wanting to cut off their escape.

'I'm going to count to three. You can come out and we'll discuss what you're doing in here rationally or I can come back there after you. If I do, I'm going to lose my temper.' Michael paused for a second, giving a moment for them to consider his offer. He imagined the pair of them hiding at the back of the unit smirking at each other, and his temper rose another notch. 'Okay, one... two... three...'

Not prepared to wait any longer and ready to give the little shits a scare, he stormed to the back of the unit, hammer swinging, to where he expected to find the twins hiding behind one of the large stacks of bricks.

No-one was there.

Michael huffed, made his way along the back row. God help those kids once he got his hands on them.

A noise behind had him turning, but he wasn't quick enough to see his attacker or stop the blow as the metal bar smacked against his head. He staggered, falling to the floor, his chin hitting the concrete, screaming out as another blow landed across his shoulders then a third cracked into the centre of his back. He attempted to push himself up, his vision swimming, head thumping and blood pouring down his face, focused on a dark shoe that looked too big to belong to a thirteen-year-old. As he tried to look up, needing to know who had attacked him, the bar smashed down into his face and the world turned black.

28

Nell jolted awake at the ringing phone, and took a second to register it was Alex's, not hers. He was already alert, his weight shifting on the mattress as he reached across to answer it.

'Cutler.'

It was still dark out and she glanced at the alarm clock as the caller spoke, noted it was nearly one thirty so assumed it was probably Tommy or one of the other deputies.

'Newt, slow down; you're not making sense. Start from the beginning.'

The mention of her brother's boyfriend's name had Nell bolting up. Why would Newt be calling at this time of night? Neither he nor Michael would call unless it was an emergency, and the fact it wasn't Michael calling had her heart leaping into her mouth.

'What's going on?' she demanded, grabbing Alex by the shoulder, annoyed when he shook her off. 'What's happened?'

He didn't answer her, instead getting out of bed and reaching for his clothes. 'Okay, wait for the ambulance. I'm on my way,' he instructed Newt, shrugging into his jeans.

Ambulance? What the hell had happened?

Nell clambered from the bed, grabbed her robe, belting it as she stalked Alex round the bedroom. He didn't turn to face her until he ended the call.

Dread coiled in her belly as she took in his grave expression.

'What's happened to my brother?' Her voice sounded calmer than she expected, given her insides were like jelly and she wanted to throw up. 'Tell me. What's happened?'

'Someone attacked him over at the storage unit he works out of.'

'Is he okay?'

'Ambulance is on its way.'

Nell sucked in a deep breath and held it. He had to be okay. He just had to. The thought of anything happening to Michael was unbearable. She shuddered, not prepared to even let her mind go there.

'I need to go meet Newt. I want you to stay here and keep the doors locked.'

'What? No... I'm coming with you.'

'Nell, it's a crime scene. I–'

'I don't give a shit. He's my brother. I'm coming with you.' When Alex clenched his jaw and looked ready to argue the point, Nell gave him a steely look. 'If you leave here without me, I'll get in my car and follow. You can't stop me.' She crossed her arms defiantly.

He narrowed his eyes, looking annoyed as he considered her ultimatum.

'Okay,' he relented. 'Hurry up and get dressed.'

They drove out to the site in silence, the only noise coming from the radio. Alex seemed distracted, caught up in his own thoughts, and Nell was conscious of him drawing into himself, shutting her out. Although it bothered her, Michael was her only priority right now, and she pushed the uneasiness aside, focusing on her brother, desperately needing him to be okay.

When they arrived at the site fifteen minutes later, Newt was with the paramedics. Nell was out of the Jeep before Alex had fully pulled to a halt. She grabbed hold of him. 'What the hell happened?'

'Someone attacked him, Nell.' Newt's face was pale, his eyes tear-stained. 'He went to get his jackhammer and when he didn't come home, didn't answer his phone, I knew something was wrong.'

'Where is he?'

As she asked the question more paramedics stepped out of the storage unit carrying Michael on a gurney.

'Michael?'

One of the paramedics caught hold of her arm. 'We need to get him to the hospital.'

'Is he going to be okay? He's not moving.'

'We're doing everything we can.'

Nell glanced back at Alex. 'I need to be with him.'

He nodded, but said nothing, his expression grim and distant. She waited a beat, wanting him to say something, tell her it was going to be okay, but there was only silence. Frustrated by his sudden coldness, dread coiling in her belly for Michael, she made her way to the ambulance.

Alex spoke briefly with Newt and the paramedics before watching the ambulance drive away. Nell had shot him a look before the doors shut, as she sat in the back of the vehicle holding on to her brother's hand. Alex hadn't reacted, knowing she was safe, and he needed time to himself to process everything that had happened. Two of his deputies were waiting inside, having already sealed off the crime scene, and he got them to talk him through what they had so far, pushing all thoughts of Nell from his mind. His best friend had been attacked tonight and the call from Newt had stirred up unwelcome memories of the last time he had received bad news about someone he cared about. He tried to push them away, focus on the job at hand, but the past kept gnawing at him as he worked, grinding on the edges of his temper.

It was almost dawn when he finally left the storage unit and, as he made his way home, the sun rose in a sky of orange and yellow hues. Normally Alex would have appreciated the view, but this morning it only managed to darken his mood.

He walked and fed the dogs, mind working overtime as he tried to piece the previous night's events together. Michael had headed over to the storage unit wanting to load up his truck, which suggested he had disturbed whoever had attacked him.

They would need to do an inventory of the place, but it was looking like the motive had been robbery and Michael had been in the wrong place at the wrong time.

Alex grabbed a shower and a change of clothes before heading into work, stopping to pick up coffee before skulking into his office and calling the hospital. The update did nothing to lighten his mood. Michael had sustained a fractured skull and had swelling on the brain. He was about to go into surgery and the doctor promised he would be in touch as soon as he had any news. He felt guilty not being at the hospital, but it was a waste of his time to be sitting around waiting for Michael to come out of surgery. Better to be working on catching the son of a bitch who did this.

There had been no prints at the scene, suggesting the attacker had been prepared enough to wear gloves, but that was at odds with the amateurish way the lock had been smashed on the door. If it was robbery, the stolen goods would be hot property and word would quickly spread around the island. Nothing about any of this added up.

Needing to focus on something else for a moment to give his addled brain a break he glanced at the jotter pad where he had scribbled the name Sarah Treadwell. He had intended to check her out, if only to put Nell's mind at rest, but things had been too busy. Tommy's reaction had bothered him though. He ran the search, expecting it to offer answers, but instead found himself frowning at the screen. Sarah Treadwell had worked for Bella Golding in the summer of 2005, but after she left the island it was as though she ceased to exist. There were no further employment records, no new addresses. She was a ghost.

Alex turned his thoughts to Nell. Generally when people disappeared it was because they were running from something or someone. Had Sarah been fleeing someone on the island?

His cell phone started to ring. Alex recognised the caller as one of his deputies, Josh Hudson, who had been working with the coastguard. Sarah Treadwell would have to wait. This was more important. He clicked off the screen and answered the call. 'Josh, what have you got?'

The deputy's voice came over the line, sounding excited. 'I think we may have the rest of Penelope Maher.'

'You've found her?'

'We've found more than her. There's another woman's body – well parts of one at least.' Josh paused, catching his breath. 'Jesus, Chief, I think we might be dealing with something big here.'

'You should have called me sooner.'

Nell glanced up at the voice as Luke rushed into the waiting room where she and Newt had spent several uncomfortable hours. As Newt rose, crumpling into fresh tears, Luke hugged him fiercely.

'It was the middle of the night. No point in us all being up worrying,' Nell answered him, getting to her feet and stretching, every muscle in her body aching from both the tension of the situation and the hardness of the chair. Her tone was dull, her mood black, worry about her brother taking precedence, but annoyance and worry gnawing away that Alex hadn't been in touch for hours. She understood he was the chief of police and had to work the crime scene, but the complete lack of contact bothered her. She had felt a wall going up as they drove over to the storage unit and it pissed her off, not so much because Michael had warned this would happen, but because she had told herself it wouldn't matter, and it did.

She didn't protest when Luke pulled her into the hug, tightening his arm around her, appreciative of his support. 'You still should have called. I would rather have been here with you guys,' he told her. 'Is Michael in surgery?'

Newt nodded, stepping back and sniffing. 'Yeah, we're waiting on news. The doctor says he'll let us know as soon as he's out.' His eyes were raw from crying and Nell felt a twinge of guilt that she had yet to shed a tear. It wasn't that she didn't care – hell, Michael was her only family and she loved him to bits; the possibility of losing him terrified her – but she had never been good at expressing emotion, tended to keep her feelings bottled up. Bella had once commented it was a fear of leaving herself vulnerable and exposed and Nell often wondered if that was why she had the panic attacks; that it was those very emotions that she tried to keep in check fighting their way out.

'What the hell happened?'

'Someone attacked him over at the storage unit. It looks like he disturbed a robbery.'

'Jesus, Newt.' Luke scrubbed a hand over his face. 'Who would do something like that?'

'Alex is trying to find out.'

Nell noticed Luke's face tighten at the mention of Alex's name. Although he hadn't said anything on the occasions that she had seen him, since it had become public she and Alex were involved, she couldn't help suspect he disapproved.

Was it for the same reasons as Michael – perhaps he was concerned Alex was going to hurt her further down the line – or had she mistaken his interest in her? She had assumed he was only interested in friendship and had relished the opportunity to get to know him better given their brothers were in a relationship. Had Luke wanted more?

He had been in a relationship when they first met and seemed broken-hearted that Stacey had left him. Nell was tired, she was stressed, and she was misreading the situation. Luke was friends with Alex and his interest in her was platonic. She told herself to chill.

She glanced at her watch, noted it was almost midday. She had been awake for hours and would likely be at the hospital for a lot longer. It was time for another shot of caffeine.

'I'm going to get coffee. Do you guys want one?'

Returning to the waiting room ten minutes later, balancing the three plastic cups between her hands, her heart leapt into her mouth as she spotted Doctor Singh talking to Newt and Luke.

'Has something happened?'

The doctor turned at her voice and gave Nell a warm smile. 'Your brother is out of surgery. We managed to successfully reduce the swelling and he is currently resting.'

'Is he going to be okay?'

'We are going to need to keep him in for a while, but he's stable and we're doing all we can.'

'Can we see him?'

'He's not awake yet, but you can sit with him for a short while.' As Newt grabbed Nell in a hug, she let out the breath she hadn't realised she was holding, relief easing in her shoulders. Michael was going to be okay. Now they needed to catch the asshole who'd done this.

Hunter Stone let out a low whistle at Alex's news, before dropping his own bombshell.

'We have another missing girl.'

Alex's heartbeat quickened. 'From Winchester?'

'This one is closer to home for you, it's East Haven. Caroline Henderson, thirty-six, separated. She'd been reconciling with her husband, but they had a big fight last Sunday. He figured she had gone back to the friend's house where she had been staying. The friend thought the pair of them were still trying to work things out, hence the delay before they realised she was missing.'

'And you're sure it's our guy?' Alex had Hunter on speaker as he drove down to the harbour. 'If she was having marital problems, we've got to look at the husband.'

'I already did. He has an alibi and it checks out. After Caroline stormed out, he went over to his neighbour's, crashed the guy's barbecue and got wasted. A dozen or so witnesses can vouch for him ruining their evening. Meanwhile we have security footage of Caroline in one of the bars in town. She went there alone, got hit on by a guy, and left shortly after. Her car was found in the lot where she had left it.'

'She left with the guy in the bar?'

'Not this time. She left alone, but he followed shortly after.'

'You get him on camera?'

'Not enough to get an ID. He knows where the cameras are and is smart enough to avoid them. Looks like it could be the same guy who was with Penny Maher.' Stone was silent for brief moment. 'I think he's been at it for a while, Alex. He's been going undetected because we didn't have any bodies.'

'Well, we do now. I'm heading out to join the recovery team. We figure out who he's been killing, it'll hopefully get us one step closer to catching the son of a bitch.'

'Okay, in the meantime I'm going to pull police reports on all missing women in the area, see if we get any matches. Call me once you know what we're dealing with.'

'Will do.'

Alex killed the call and pulled into the marina. Relief they had uncovered the killer's maritime dumping ground was tempered with guilt. While they had been desperate for a break in the Maher case, the timing sucked, given what had happened to Michael. The bodies had been found in his jurisdiction though and, much as he wanted to personally deal with Michael's case, this had to take precedence.

Parking up he made a couple of calls, pulling Kyle Mathis, one of the deputies currently following Sam Kent, and reassigning him to Michael's case, then he rang the medical examiner and warned her of the workload about to come her way. As he ended the second call, a text came through from Newt.

Michael out of surgery. Went well and he's stable.

Alex let out a sigh of relief, fired a quick text back, mildly irritated the news hadn't come from Nell.

He spent the rest of the afternoon out on the water with the recovery team and when they returned to shore early evening, they did so with a gruesome catch of severed body parts and weighted-down skeletal remains. The next hour was spent over at the ME's office, Violet Marsden ready and waiting for them, unfazed by the task at hand, but mightily pissed off that a killer had chosen her pretty neck of the woods as his playground.

'Make sure you catch this sick fuck,' she told Alex, seeing him to the door. 'And when you do, you throw away the key. This is a good place and I won't have some asshole running around cutting up girls and ruining that.'

Alex mustered a grin for Violet's potty mouth. She had always been a straight talker and her colourful language belied her prim appearance.

'We're a step closer to catching him. Find me some answers on our victims and I'll do my level best to see they get justice.'

He left her office, bone-tired, wanting nothing more than to drive home, walk Sasha and Teddy, and drop into bed. He could call Newt and Nell, explain about the break in the Maher case. Newt would understand – Nell probably not so much if his experience with women was anything to go by. Plus it would make him a shitty friend. Michael had yet to fully forgive Alex for sleeping with his sister. He needed to repair his friendship, not damage it further.

When he arrived at the hospital ten minutes later, he found Doctor Singh, got a progress update on Michael, learning he was still unconscious, but his vitals were good, the swelling having gone down, and his condition stable. The doctor accompanied him down the hallway to the waiting room.

'Your friends should go home and get some rest,' he told Alex. 'Mr O'Connor is unlikely to gain consciousness for a good few hours. I have told them there's nothing they can do here except wait.'

Alex stepped into the waiting room, found Newt sitting pale-faced and staring into space as he gnawed on his knuckle. On the opposite chairs were Luke and Nell; Luke awake and deep in thought, his arm draped around Nell as she slept against his shoulder.

He glanced up, blue eyes meeting Alex's. 'Hey, Alex.'

He made no attempt to move his arm and Alex felt a flicker of irritation, quickly quashing it down. Luke was just offering comfort. He hadn't been here, so had no right to judge or be annoyed that Nell had taken it.

She stirred awake at the mention of his name, blinked heavily as she took a moment to realise where she was, pulling away from Luke and sitting up, scrubbing her hands over her face. She looked exhausted, her cheeks drained of colour and smudges of grey beneath her eyes. Although she didn't go to Alex, she didn't seem mad at him either.

'You're back,' she murmured, voice devoid of any emotion. She pulled her legs up onto the chair, hugging her knees, looking lost. Her eyes paused momentarily on his face, her expression unreadable, before her focus shifted to the wall behind him.

'Have you found the person who did this?' That was from Newt, who was already on his feet. The worry of the last few hours was clearly etched on his face, like Nell's, and he looked like an extra in *The Walking Dead*.

'Not yet,' Alex told him. 'We're still following leads.'

He had spoken with Kyle Mathis, the deputy he had reassigned, as he drove over to the hospital. With the crime scene clean, Mathis had run an inventory of the storage unit with one of Michael's labourers. Half a dozen items were missing, including the jackhammer Michael had gone over to collect, which suggested the motive had been robbery. Had his friend been so badly beaten just for a few workman tools?

'I still can't believe someone did this to him.'

Alex squeezed Newt's shoulder. 'The doc says he's stable. You should go home and get some rest.'

'I can't possibly sleep. Not until Michael wakes up.'

'Which won't be for hours. You're not doing yourself any favours sitting here. Go home, have a shower and try to sleep.'

'Alex is right.' Luke got to his feet. 'Let me drive you home. We can come back first thing tomorrow.'

Newt glanced at Doctor Singh.

'Listen to your friends. Try and get some rest.' The doctor looked at Nell. 'You too, Miss O'Connor. There's nothing you can do here. Please go home and try to rest. We will call if there is any change in your brother's condition.'

'You promise?'

'I promise. If your brother wakes up we will call both you and Mr Trainor immediately.'

Alex held his hand out to Nell. 'Come on, I'll take you home.' She hesitated for a second, expression stoic, before accepting, and the four of them walked out to the parking lot together.

Newt paused by Luke's car. 'I'll see you tomorrow,' he told Nell, before embracing her in a hard hug. 'He's going to be okay,' he whispered, glancing over her shoulder at Alex. 'And we're gonna find the person who did this to him, right, Alex?'

Alex gave a grim smile. 'Yeah, we are.'

29

Caleb Sweeney sat in his thirty-third-floor office staring out of the floor-to-ceiling window at the night-time view of the Chicago skyline, seeing nothing but Nell's face.

He had returned home nearly a week ago, endured his mother's benefit with forced smiles and gritted teeth, had to face her questions about Nell's absence, swallowing his pride and admitting their relationship was over. Of course, this had given Bitsy something to gloat about. She had always known Nell wasn't good enough for her son and it wouldn't last. She had warned him, and he had been too blinkered to listen, too stubborn to accept his mother was right.

Caleb had reined in his temper, waiting until he returned home before venting his rage. He hadn't wanted his mother to know the truth, but there had been little choice and he hated Nell all the more for putting him in this embarrassing position.

Over the weekend he had used the time to reflect, and now understood his initial rash trip to Purity had been a mistake and he should have taken longer to figure out what he was going to do about the situation.

Although he had checked into the Purity Oaks Hotel under

his stepfather's name, Brooks, it wouldn't be difficult for any investigation to trace the reservations back to him, plus of course the flights from Chicago had been booked in his actual name. There would be no getting round the fact that he had visited Purity Island shortly after Nell left him. The only thing that fell in his favour was that he had caught a flight back. If it came down to an investigation, he would have to admit he had gone after Nell, but would pretend he had approached her and she had officially ended things, say he had accepted her decision and flown back to Chicago and out of her life.

He returned to the office on Monday morning, knowing he needed to create a sense of normality. As he allowed word to filter out about his broken relationship, he sat at his desk and plotted.

He had toyed with killing Nell, had wanted to storm in on her and Cutler, putting a bullet in both of their heads. Such a bold move would have backfired, though, and he would be one of the first people the police would look to. He was a smart man and knew such a scenario would end up with him facing charges of murder. While he wanted to punish Nell, he wasn't prepared to go to jail. She had ruined his life, but she wasn't going to take his freedom.

By Monday afternoon he thought he had come up with an effective plan. The rash Caleb would have acted immediately, but he held back, knowing if he was going to pull this off he would need to exercise caution. Instead he had slept on the plan, running through the details as he dressed for work on Tuesday morning. On his way to the office he had stopped and purchased a disposable phone, paying in cash, then during lunch he made his way to the public library, using one of their computers to run the search he needed. It took about an hour to locate an available cabin that met his requirements: in the heart of New Hampshire, well off the beaten track, no electricity or cell phone access. It was privately owned, and he made a note of the number, knowing this would have to be a cash transaction.

As he walked back to the office he made the call to the owner, giving a fake name and reserving the cabin for a three-week period, agreeing to stop by and collect the keys and pay in full on Friday.

His secretary, Mara, gave him a sympathetic look as he stepped out of the elevator and Caleb knew word had reached her about his break-up with Nell.

'I was sorry to hear about you and Miss O'Connor. Is there anything I can do for you, Mr Sweeney?'

He faked a sad smile. 'I'm okay, thank you, Mara. Adjusting to things. In fact, I'm thinking I may take a break for a few days, head over to New York.'

The city was one of his favourite places and he visited regularly for both business and pleasure. No-one would think it odd if he was vacationing in New York City when Nell disappeared, or that he had chosen to go there to get over their break-up.

'That sounds like a wonderful idea,' Mara agreed, no doubt pleased at the prospect of getting him out of her hair for a few days. Caleb knew he wasn't the easiest man to work for.

'Could you contact the Four Seasons and get me a reservation from this Thursday please? Book it for five nights and I'll need a flight too. One-way for now, in case I decide to stay longer.'

'Yes, of course, Mr Sweeney. I'll get on to it straightaway.'

Caleb left her to make the arrangements, took her call fifteen minutes later to confirm his booking was all in place, then sat staring out of the window as he ran though his plan. He would fly out to New York on Thursday and check into the hotel. Then Friday morning he would find a cheap inconspicuous rental car and make the drive north to the cabin, spending Friday night there to ensure it was all prepared. That would leave a weekend window to get Nell, which was easier said than done. On his previous visit to the island she had never been alone, always with her brother or Cutler.

If he was going to get her by herself, he would have to lure her away.

He mulled over possibilities of how he would do that, knowing there was an element of risk attached to each of them. He needed five minutes alone with her. She wouldn't come willingly, so he would need to subdue her to get her into the trunk of the car. A gun would be easiest. He couldn't take his own weapon, wouldn't be able to get it on board the flight, but he knew a guy in New York who could pick one up, no-questions-asked, for the right price.

Getting Nell off the island was going to be the tricky part and would require sedation or restraints, possibly both, to keep her quiet on the ferry ride back. Once they were on the mainland it should be a breeze getting her up to the cabin and when they were there and alone, he would have the precious time he needed with her to find out if there was anything worth saving from their relationship.

He didn't want her to die, still chose to believe that with a firm hand and time she could be redeemed, but he had to prepare himself for that eventuality, and knew if she refused to see things from his point of view he wouldn't be able to let her walk out of the cabin alive.

And if it reached that conclusion and things were really over between them, then he was going to enjoy killing her.

30

When Alex had said he was going to take her home, Nell assumed he planned to drop her off at the guesthouse. Although they hadn't spent a night apart since the party at Maloney's, something had shifted in the hours since Michael's attack and she figured he wanted time alone, so she was surprised when he drove her back to his place.

She didn't make comment, too exhausted to get into a discussion about how things stood between them, at least for tonight, and part of her was grateful, as, much as she hated to admit it, being alone in the guesthouse after her encounter with the masked intruder still unnerved her. Neither of them had said much on the ride back and after unlocking the door, Alex announced his intention to take the dogs for a walk along the beach.

Nell could tell something was eating at him, didn't doubt part of it was worry about Michael, but suspected there was also something else. Trying to push it to the back of her mind, she helped herself to a beer out of the refrigerator, popped the tab and took a long swig, enjoying the coolness against her dry throat. Beer in hand, she headed upstairs for a shower, keen to get out of the clothes she had been sitting around in all day.

As she stood under the hot spray her thoughts inevitably went back to her brother. The doctor said he was stable, but she wouldn't be convinced he was out of the woods until he was awake. She wasn't a pessimist, but it was difficult to not measure her return to Purity by a series of disturbing occurrences. From the gruesome find of the head on the beach and whoever was trying to spook her at the guesthouse, to Luke being shot and now Michael being attacked, it was hard not to question if they were all somehow connected.

It appeared Michael had disturbed a robbery, but would someone really beat him half to death over building equipment? The question ate away at her as she stepped from the shower.

Not wanting to put on the same clothes she had sat around in all day, she rummaged in Alex's closet and found a T-shirt and pair of sweatpants. Both were too big, but at least they were clean. Towel-drying her hair, she grabbed her beer and headed back downstairs.

The dogs were in the house eating the food in their dishes. Teddy glanced up as she appeared, before turning back to his dinner. Alex wasn't about, or so she thought until she felt the light breeze coming from the open French doors and spied him sat out on the deck looking out over the darkening ocean. Nell went outside, sliding into the bench seat beside him. He didn't look up, instead played with the rim of his wine glass and continued to look out to sea.

'You've been distracted,' Nell commented. She kept her tone light; had no energy for starting an argument.

He was silent for a moment and, despite herself, she felt her hackles rise, convinced he was purposely ignoring her and wishing to hell he had taken her back to the guesthouse.

'We had a breakthrough on the Penny Maher case today.'

The head Nell had found on the beach. 'You did?'

'We found what we think is the rest of her, along with another victim.' Alex finally acknowledged Nell, turning to look at her, his green eyes dark and expression brooding in the fading light. 'Penny wasn't the only one.'

Nell felt her heartbeat quicken. 'How many are we talking about?'

'We're trying to figure that out.'

'Do you think you're dealing with a serial killer?'

'This isn't public knowledge. What I'm telling you is in confidence.'

'I won't breathe a word.' Nell reached across, laid her hand over his and squeezed gently; hurt when he pulled away.

'I had to assign Michael's case to one of my deputies, so I can deal with this.'

'I understand.'

'I wanted to do it myself, but this... this is big. He's a good cop.'

'I'm sure he is. It's okay.'

Alex shot her a look. 'It's okay? You're being very reasonable, Nell.' His tone was dripping with sarcasm. 'This is your brother we're talking about. Don't you care?'

He was trying to pull her into a fight she had no energy for.

'Look, I'm tired. I've been awake for hours and I'm worried about Michael. I am trying hard to be reasonable, but is this why you brought me here, to pick a fight?' When Alex didn't answer, she changed tack. 'This isn't about not being able to work Michael's case or what happened today. You've been cold with me all day. What's going on, Alex? If you want me to go, I'll call a cab, but don't expect me to sit here and beg and plead with you to know what I'm supposed to have done wrong. I've been down that path before and I won't go there again.'

Alex's jaw tightened, but he remained silent.

Nell let out a shaky breath, furious for allowing herself to believe this was different, that he was different. 'Fine, I'm out of here.'

As she started to get to her feet Alex reached out, caught her hand. 'Wait.'

'Why?'

'Just wait, please.'

Hesitantly she sat back down and waited for him to speak.

'I was married.'

Nell's heart caught in her mouth. She waited for him to continue.

'Back in Portland, I was married. Her name was Sophie and we met in college. After we graduated, I joined the force and she trained to become a veterinary technician. We were together for six years before we got married, just after I made detective with the Portland Police Bureau.' Alex angled Nell a look, as though expecting her to come at him with questions. She had plenty, but stayed silent, sensing this wasn't easy for him, and waited for him to continue on his own terms.

'We were married four months when Sophie fell pregnant. Neither of us had planned on becoming parents so soon. We were only twenty-seven, but it didn't matter, we figured we would make it work. I started taking overtime and extra shifts, knew we would need the money, and I guess that's when we began fighting. I was tired, probably unreasonable, she felt neglected, like she was on her own all the time. She was eight months pregnant when we had our last big fight. I was at work and she wanted me to stop by the store on the way home because we were out of pretzels. She'd had this crazy thing for them all the way through her pregnancy. Not long before my shift finished a new case came in. I got off late, forgot to stop by the store, and when I arrived home we had a huge fight over the stupid snacks. I went to bed and let her go out to get them herself. I was awoken a couple of hours later by a phone call. A couple of guys had pulled a carjacking after Sophie left the store. She had tried to stop them and they shot her in the stomach. She died shortly after arriving at hospital. The doctors fought to save our baby girl, but the injuries were too severe, and she died before she was out of the womb.

'I guess I went off the rails after that. I threw myself into work, was hell-bent on trying to track down the guys responsible, I lost my temper a few times in volatile situations. My superiors were worried but cut me some slack given what had happened. Eventually I burned out, hit rock bottom. That was when I knew I had to get out of the city, have a fresh start. I came here figuring small sleepy island, easy pace of life, no drama and no commitments.' He shot Nell a brief look. Despite the bleakness of his words, there was a wry humour in his eyes. 'Guess I got that wrong on all accounts.'

Nell knew Alex had a past, was aware of his reluctance to commit, but she hadn't expected his story to be so tragic. She tentatively reached over and placed her hand on his again, wanting to offer comfort, but certain any words she might offer would seem hollow, insincere. This time he didn't pull away and she tightened her grip.

She understood now the phone call about Michael must have conjured unwelcome memories, wished she had known, and was mad at herself for doubting Alex, for making it about her when he had needed time to deal with the reminder of what he had lost.

They were silent, looking out at the black Atlantic, listening to the rising swell of the waves as they crashed against the shore.

'I never had that,' she said eventually. 'What you had with Sophie. When I met Caleb I was twenty-seven, but still ridiculously naïve. He was this big shot Chicago art dealer and I was flattered he was showing any interest in me. He told me he liked my paintings and also that he liked me. I'm ashamed to say I fell for his bullshit.

'For the first few months he was a gentleman. He wined and dined me, took me to places I never imagined even existed. I was completely in awe and so eager to please. He began to exhibit my paintings, moved me into his home. He sent me flowers, bought me gifts, swooned over me to his friends, my life was freaking Disney perfect and I was so pathetically grateful, I completely missed the cracks.

'It started so subtly. We were out with friends in a bar and he got in a sulk, accused me of not paying him enough attention. Of course, I laughed at him, told him he was being both ridiculous and pathetic. By the time we left the bar he had worked himself up into a rage and somehow managed to convince me he was the victim and I had wronged him. I actually ended up apologising to him.

'Things were okay for a couple of weeks then we were supposed to meet with Michael, to celebrate my birthday. Caleb didn't want to go; he had been dragging his heels. That was the first time he hit me. He punched me so hard I could barely see for three days. Again though, it was my fault. He had been trying to make my birthday special and I had ruined all his plans. My eye healed slowly and he wouldn't let me leave the house, fearful someone would see. At first, I was furious, couldn't believe he had hit me, but he was so contrite afterwards, mortified he had let me push him so far. I wanted to leave, but he begged me to stay. It was an accident, he would never do it again, and he was so sorry. For the next two weeks he was on his best behaviour, a different person. He bought me flowers and gifts I was shallow enough to be dazzled by, and I was stupid enough to believe it had been a one-off, that maybe I had been to blame for antagonising him.

'So we carried on, but more cracks started to appear. He

wouldn't let me see my brother, disapproved of my friends. Gradually he began to cut me off from everyone. It was so subtle I never even noticed until I had no-one else left to turn to. That was when things started to get really bad, when he knew he was in control of my life. A lot of it was psychological. I was clumsy, I was lazy, I was ungrateful, and I wasn't good enough for him. I know it sounds contrived, but when you're constantly being told those things you actually start to believe them. He criticised the way I dressed, the way I ate my food, he even found fault with my work. Meanwhile he was my poor long-suffering boyfriend, and he never missed an opportunity to remind me he paid for everything, that without him I was nothing.

'I learned to walk on eggshells around him, I knew he could lose his temper over the tiniest thing, so I tried desperately to please. Of course, I look back now and realise there was nothing I could have done. At the time I thought it was my actions that led to him hitting me, tripping me up or pushing me down the stairs, but even if I did everything right, when he was in one of those moods, he would find a reason to hurt me.

'It reached a point where I was too scared to leave him. I actually accepted this was my life. He proposed to me and I accepted, not because I loved him, but because I was frightened of him. It took me five years to come to my senses, to understand how fucked up my life was. Bella and Clarke died, and the bastard wouldn't even let me go to their funerals. That was the catalyst; something snapped, and I realised how pathetic I had become. That was when I knew I had to leave him, to get away somehow. And that's how I ended up back here. I've given up everything to get away from him, including my career. I know I can't ever try to sell my work again, because he will be able to find me. But you know what? It's a small price to pay for my freedom.'

As she had done with him, Alex remained silent, no words

necessary. He released her hand, slipped his arm around her and Nell let her head rest on his shoulder.

They remained like that for a while, staring out to sea, both caught up in their own thoughts, while a few miles away a killer sat in his lair, plotting his next move.

31

Newt had barely slept, and Luke picked him up from the beach house, noting his brother looked like death warmed over. His plan had been to drop him off at the hospital then head into work, and he had shown up wearing one of the expensive Italian suits he favoured for the office, before quickly realising Newt was going to require emotional support. Luke put a call in to his secretary and told her he was going to need another day off; he figured he could deal with some of his work-load on his laptop. As they headed down the hospital corridors to find Doctor Singh, his suit caught a few admiring glances from the nurses, stoking his ego.

Michael was still unconscious, but Newt insisted on sitting with him, so Luke took himself off to the waiting room, shed his jacket and loosened his tie, before setting up his laptop, figuring he might as well try and get a little work done. He was busy replying to e-mails when Nell and Alex arrived half an hour later. Alex was wearing his police blazer and Nell was looking fresher than Newt, though there were still dark circles of worry around her eyes.

So far she had shown little emotion over what had

happened. While Newt had been a blubbering mess, Nell had remained dry-eyed and stony-faced as they waited for news on her brother. Luke knew she was hurting as much as Newt, but found it fascinating how she seemed scared to show her true feelings and was curious to know what had happened to make her build her walls so high. In part she reminded him of his cousin, Jane. She had seldom shown emotion. Of course, Nell wasn't a hard-faced bitch like Jane, and she didn't look down on him either. Jane hadn't been capable of showing emotion. It wasn't fair to compare Nell to her.

'Any news?'

Luke set his laptop to one side and looked up at Alex. 'Not yet, but he's stable.'

'Is Newt with him?'

'Yeah, he wants to be there when Michael wakes up. I figured I'd stay out of everyone's hair and wait back here.'

'I should go see him before I go,' Alex said to Nell. Luke noted that as he spoke, he ran a hand down her back. 'Call me if there's any news.'

Nell kissed him goodbye, watching as Alex disappeared down the corridor.

Luke had sensed tension between the pair of them the previous day, but whatever had caused it was gone. He was still struggling with them being together. Nell's involvement with Alex pulled her further from his reach and he didn't like seeing another man's hands on her.

'You manage to get some rest?' he asked, patting the empty seat beside him.

'Yeah, I didn't think my mind was going to switch off, but I was so tired I guess sleep was inevitable.' She sat down and turned to face him. 'How's Newt? Did he get any sleep?'

'Not really. I don't think he'll rest until Michael is awake.'

'Hopefully that'll happen today.' Nell reached out, squeezed his hand, and leant in close. 'You're a good brother, Luke. Newt's lucky to have you.'

Luke swallowed hard and held on to the contact, aware he was growing hard. This close he could smell the scent of her shampoo, feel her warm breath on his face, and it was driving him crazy. She was such a pleasing mix of contradictions, so fragile, yet tough – at times guarded and refusing to show emotion, yet in moments like now, reaching out to offer comfort. He had been a lucky man, able to use his looks and charm to get the women he wanted, but Nell was off limits. It was almost unbearable knowing he couldn't have her.

Something must have changed in his expression, because she was suddenly pulling back, dropping his hand, the look on her face slightly wary, as if she knew what he was thinking.

'Are you okay?'

'Yeah sure, I'm fine.' Nell glanced towards the door of the waiting room. 'I guess I should go check on Newt and Michael. I can bring back coffee. You want one?'

'Thanks.'

She gave him a prim smile, the openness of the moment gone, her walls back in place. Luke watched her leave the room, long legs in worn jeans, her blonde hair spilling over her shoulders in wild curls. He had felt the moment and knew she had too.

He wanted her so badly and he wasn't quite sure what the hell he was going to do about that.

Jenna found Tommy coming out of the Sizzling Griddle, a cup of coffee in his hand as he headed into work. Impatiently she parked by the curb, getting out of her car and hurrying across, casting a quick worried glance around before she approached him, not wanting to raise any suspicion. 'We need to talk.'

His expression was wary, and, like Jenna, he looked around the high street, checking no-one was watching them. 'I'm on duty, Jenna. Can't this wait until later?'

'No, it can't. We need to talk right now.'

Tommy hesitated, his reluctance clear. He glanced around before roughly grabbing hold of her arm and pulling her into the alley that ran down the side of the diner. 'What's up?'

'I heard about Michael O'Connor. He almost died.' Jenna punched her fist hard against the wall of Tommy's chest, frustration bubbling over. 'Is that how you deal with things?'

'What are you talking about?'

'Don't play all innocent, Tommy. I know you did it.'

'No, I didn't.'

When Jenna continued to pummel at his chest with her fists, furious he was trying to deny it, he caught hold of her wrists and forced them down by her sides. 'I didn't do anything to Michael O'Connor. I swear.'

'You said you were going to take care of things. Get us out of this mess.'

'I know I did, and I still plan to, but I promise you I didn't attack Michael. That wasn't me.'

Jenna was silent. She had been so mad when she had found out about the attack, blaming Tommy for getting them further tangled up in this mess. He had assured her he would take care of the situation and it had been easy to conclude he was the one responsible for Michael's attack.

Fresh tears filled her eyes and she swiped them away furiously. 'So, if you didn't put Michael in the hospital, then who the hell did?'

Curtis Milborn was riding his truck down the high street when he saw his wife emerge from the alleyway with Tommy Dolan a few feet behind her. Both of them had a shifty look about them, gave cursory glances up and down the road before heading off in separate directions. Rage burned inside him, fuelled by the flames of Wild Turkey he had drank a few minutes ago. Dolan had been the bane of his life for more years than Curtis could remember and just looking at his face conjured unpleasant memories. Was Jenna cheating on him? The thought played on his mind, making him angry and mean.

They were going to have a little chat about that.

Michael awoke mid-morning on Wednesday. Nell was in the room with him, grateful to be away from Luke, and Newt had gone to fetch coffee and stretch his legs. Nell was holding his hand at the time, a whirlwind of thoughts circulating in her head as she replayed her conversation with Alex from the previous night, mulled over her brother's attack, and now wondered what the hell she was going to do about Luke.

She had dismissed her suspicions, but the look he had given her as they had sat in the waiting room that morning had been unmistakable. He wanted her. And that left Nell feeling uncomfortable and guilty, worrying if she was in some way responsible for leading him on, and also disappointed, as she had believed the pair of them could have been good friends.

Still could be good friends, she corrected herself, though she knew it was difficult once attraction was involved.

She was going to have to talk to him, tell him she didn't feel the same way, though he should know that, damn it. She was sleeping with one of his friends.

More than sleeping with. Last night her relationship with

Alex had progressed to something deeper. Neither of them had defined it, but Nell had felt it, knew he did too, and when they had finally gone to bed, it had been about more than sex.

Her thoughts were still on the predicament when she felt Michael's fingers move gently against her hand.

'Oh my God, Michael, can you hear me? Are you awake?' She grasped at his hand with both of hers, willed him to move. When he did, he squeezed her hand, his eyes fluttering open.

'Nell?' His voice was croaky, weak. 'Water, I need... water.'

Nell glanced around at the pitcher, unsure if he was allowed to have any until the doctors had checked him. 'Let me find a nurse.' She let go of his hand, rushed from the room, colliding with Newt and Doctor Singh, who were deep in conversation in the hallway.

'Michael's awake.'

Newt's eyes widened and he pushed past Nell, the doctor close behind him. Nell followed them back into the room and stood by the door as Doctor Singh performed a few routine checks.

'Water,' Michael repeated.

'Can he have some?' Nell asked.

'Just a few small sips to start off with. His throat will be dry.'

Nell poured half a glass as Newt sat by the bed and tightly gripped Michael's hand. As she helped her brother take a sip, Luke appeared in the doorway, a smile on his face. 'I thought I heard a commotion. Welcome back, buddy.'

'Do you remember anything about what happened?' Newt asked.

'Fucker... hit... me,' Michael managed. He sipped more water. 'That's why I'm here, right?'

Nell grinned; relieved her brother hadn't lost any of his sense of humour. 'You gave us one hell of a scare. I was worried we were going to lose you.'

He managed a smile for her. It was still weak, but the light was back in his eyes. 'I'm not going anywhere.'

Alex headed straight over to the hospital as soon as he got the call from Nell, leaving Violet Marsden and her assistant working on the remains that had been pulled from the ocean. He had spoken with Stone first thing that morning and was expecting him on the midday ferry, so was aware his visit to the hospital would have to be briefer than he would have liked. The most important thing was knowing Michael was okay. For now, it was more about checking in on him as his friend than it was about asking questions as the chief of police. He would send Kyle Mathis over to the hospital later in the day to take a statement and only hoped Michael would be able to remember vital details that would help them catch his attacker.

Newt, Luke and Nell were all around his bedside when he walked in and he was relieved to see his old friend propped up in bed, eyes alert and some colour back in his cheeks. Michael shot him a contrite half grin and looked a little uncomfortable.

'Can you guys give us a moment alone?' Alex asked, thinking it best the pair of them try and clear the air without an audience.

'Sure thing.' Newt got up from the seat he had been occupying beside Michael's bed, pushing Luke towards the door. Nell brushed past Alex and gave his hand a discreet reassuring squeeze before following the others down the corridor to the waiting room.

Alex closed the door after them before taking the seat Newt had vacated.

'How are you feeling?'

'Like someone smashed me in the head with an iron bar,' Michael quipped. 'Oh wait, they did.' He managed a grin and was awkwardly silent for a moment, staring intently at his hands. 'Listen, Alex. I'm sorry I ragged on you about Nell.'

'It's okay. We should have told you instead of keeping it a secret.'

'Yeah, you should have, but I understand why you were reluctant to do so. I was a bit of an asshole about it.'

'Yes, you were,' Alex agreed, his tone dry. 'But we'll move past it.'

'So, are you gonna catch the fucker who did this to me?'

'I'm gonna try. I'm guessing you didn't see who it was.'

'I thought it was kids at first. The door was unlocked, and I could hear someone hiding at the back of the unit. I was convinced it was those little Osborne assholes.'

'And you're sure it wasn't?'

Michael looked affronted. 'Are you suggesting two thirteen-year-olds could kick the shit out of me?'

'I'm just asking the question.'

'I only saw the foot of the person who hit me. Black boot, adult sized. I have no idea who it was. I just know they wanted me to stay down.'

'Permanently, going by your injuries,' Alex agreed. 'You're a lucky man, Michael O'Connor, that whoever attacked you couldn't crack through that thick skull of yours.'

Michael shot him a look. 'Smartass.'

'Kyle Mathis will stop by later, get a full statement from you. That okay?'

'Sure, I want to get this son of a bitch.' Michael looked contemplative for a moment. 'So, have you figured out if you're in love with my sister yet?'

Alex thought back to the previous night and how Nell had opened up to him. He could tell she hated the part of her that had been weak enough to stay with Caleb, that she had been shallow enough to fall for his lies and the materialistic life he had initially promised. She was embarrassed by her past, but she had no need to be, because it had taken courage to leave him. She was far stronger than she gave herself credit for.

'I'm getting there,' he admitted, not yet ready to use the L-word, but aware she was the only woman he had shared his own past with, knew the attraction between them was already something stronger than lust.

'Good,' Michael nodded, seeming satisfied with his answer. 'Because the doctor tells me I'm going to be stuck in this bed for a while longer, so I'm going to need you to look out for her. She's your responsibility now.'

Alex didn't bother to point out he had been looking out for Nell all along. 'You've got it,' he agreed.

'Because it still worries me knowing someone was out there taking shots at her.'

'I won't let anything happen to her; I promise.'

'Good.' Michael smiled. 'I'm counting on it.'

32

'It's going to be near to impossible to get an ID on most of the body parts as they are just bones, and pretty chewed up bones at that,' Violet Marsden told Alex and Hunter without preamble. 'Unless you can bring me a list of names of potential victims we can try to run the DNA against. But I'm not hopeful. Once bodies have been in the water for more than a few weeks...'

'I'm in the process of compiling a report of missing persons from within a 500-mile radius,' Hunter told her. 'Let me cross-check and eliminate then I'll get you a list.'

Violet shot a look at Alex, her lips twisting. 'He's efficient, this friend of yours.'

Her comment brought a chuckle from Hunter who seemed quite taken with the island's ME. 'So, what are you able to tell us at this stage?' he asked.

'Well, you're looking at body parts from multiple victims, most probably. But getting any IDs is going to be near on impossible. Penelope Maher's limbs have ligature marks, suggesting she was restrained. Her body was cleanly cut, most likely with a cleaver or similar, and after death, but you see these slices here?'

Violet lifted an arm, indicating to a series of cuts. 'These were inflicted while she was still alive.'

'Are you able to tell cause of death?'

Violet shook her head. 'I'm still working on that, Chief. These cuts wouldn't have killed, they were meant to torture. Sick bastard made sure he had his fun before he killed her. He seems to like his knives, yet there are no fatal stab wounds on her torso, so my guess would be he slit her throat, though I can't be sure at this stage.'

'How old are the oldest ones we're talking about?' Hunter asked.

'It's hard to say with bones in the ocean; it's not an exact science. Probably none of them are going to be much older than five years before the shrimps and the crabs and whatever else has them down to nothing. Looking at some of the slice marks on some of the fresher bones though, I'd say we have the same guy working his vicious magic. He's obviously weighed them down and dropped them off in the same little dumping ground. And if our divers have found this many, just think how many more could be floating around undiscovered. He seems prolific too, looking at the variety of different corpses we have. Who knows.'

Hunter leant back against the counter, jingling change in his pocket. He glanced at Alex. 'So, we're quite possibly talking at least two or three kills a year. We have to catch this guy, and fast.'

They left Violet with her work. Hunter took half an hour to check into his hotel room, having decided it would be easier to stay overnight, before they reconvened in Alex's office early afternoon to go over the Caroline Henderson file and the copies of the security footage Hunter had brought with him showing the last known movements of both Caroline and Penny Maher. Alex studied the footage closely, agreeing with Hunter it was the same man in both videos.

'The staff weren't as much help in the bar where Caroline was last seen drinking. They didn't even remember her, let alone the guy who had been talking to her. Our first bartender, the one who served Penny Maher, has been the most help. He remembered the guy, had been listening in, amused by their conversation. Said Penny was a little drunk and hitting on our guy. That he had seemed hesitant about leaving the bar with her.' Hunter opened his briefcase. 'We got him to work with a sketch artist. The result isn't great, but it gives us something to go on.'

Alex studied the sketch, noting the man had a distinctive look with light-coloured, shoulder length hair, dark eyes, a moustache and goatee.

'Bartender put him at average height and build; said the hair looked bleached. Had him pegged as a beach bum type.'

'And the staff in the bar Caroline was in, have they been shown this picture?'

'They have. As I say, they didn't remember him. The bar was far busier. I've been working with Buddy Hamilton who pulled the Henderson case. He has copies of the sketch for distribution.'

'So we know he picks his victims up in bars,' Alex mused. 'There's nothing to suggest they have been pre-targeted. And Penny left with him, which intimates he tries to get the women to go willingly. Of course, Caroline doesn't fit in with that, unless she agreed to meet him outside. If not, why did he change his pattern?'

'There also could be an escalation between kills. Judging from the remains we've recovered, this might have been going on for years, but Penny and Caroline disappeared two weeks apart. If the killings had always been that close in the past, we'd have surely noticed all these women going missing.'

'That suggests he's unravelling, which makes him even more dangerous.'

'And unpredictable,' Hunter agreed.

'We need to figure out where he's taking them. His hunting ground covers a couple of hundred miles, so where is the killing carried out?'

'Has to be somewhere mobile.' Hunter furrowed his brow, studying the sketch. 'Ms Marsden said he likes to torture his victims before killing them. That requires seclusion and suggests he uses the same place. Somewhere where he knows he has privacy and can take his time. Somewhere he can also dismember the bodies without fear of being caught, maybe a truck or a van? He goes hunting for a victim, lures her away from the bar, they drive out somewhere nice and quiet in his van, then he gets her in the back, overpowers her, ties her up and has his wicked way with her. If he picks an isolated spot, no-one is likely to disturb him and he can take as long as he needs. Once she's dead he dismembers the body, cleans himself up then heads back to the marina and takes the remains of his victim out to sea. And once on the water he heads to his same favourite spot to throw the remains overboard.'

Alex considered the theory. It made sense and would certainly explain why the killer was able to cover a wide area. That he chose a spot between East Haven and Purity as the dumping ground suggested he was local to the area.

It would mean, as well as a van or a truck, the killer had access to a boat. Hardly a stretch though, as most residents in the area owned a vessel. Purity was predominantly a fishing island and both East Haven and Winchester were coastal towns with marinas.

That was when it hit him. The killer used somewhere that gave him complete privacy.

He looked at Hunter and gave a twisted smile. 'Maybe it's not a van or a truck he uses. Maybe he kills them on a boat.'

After spending an hour with her brother, satisfied he was on the road to recovery, Nell excused herself from the hospital to run some errands. As she left the bank, she walked along the high street back to where she had left her car, enjoying the cool but sunny day, when she spotted Jenna Milborn coming out of the nail salon where she worked. She seemed distracted, checking her phone then lighting a cigarette. As she paced along the sidewalk in front of the salon, Nell saw Curtis striding across the street towards her, and watched as he roughly grabbed hold of her arm, his face red and angry as he swore at her.

Jenna flinched, dropping her cigarette, protesting and trying to pull away as he clipped her around the head before dragging her into the alleyway beside the salon.

'Hey!' Nell didn't even allow herself time to think, sprinting after them, her heart in her mouth. She recognised this scene and, although she had been a victim of it herself, she couldn't stand by and watch it happen to someone else.

As she turned into the alleyway, Jenna had her head ducked and hands raised, trying to shield herself as Curtis screamed into her face.

'You're a fucking liar, Jenna. I saw you with my own two eyes.'

'It was nothing, please, nothing happened.'

'Do you think I'm not good enough for you?'

His fist shot out from nowhere, punching Jenna hard in the gut. She gasped, trying to catch her breath, eyes filling with tears as she sunk to the floor.

'Stop it. You're hurting her.'

Curtis whirled on Nell, his face twisting in disgust as he recognised her. 'Mind your own fucking business, O'Connor. This is between my wife and me.' As though making a point he reached down, grabbed Jenna by the throat, and yanked her to her feet.

Nell took a cautious step forward, aware Curtis was irrational, angry and most likely, judging from the fumes coming off his breath, mean drunk. He squeezed the hand he had clamped round Jenna's throat, lifting her off her feet and causing her to gasp for air.

'Stop it, Curtis. You'll kill her.'

Nell reached for his arm and didn't have time to react when he suddenly backhanded her across the face. Dazed and tasting blood in her mouth, she staggered backwards out of the alley and onto the high street as Curtis advanced on her.

'I told you to stop sticking your nose in private business,' he sneered, his face close to hers, the stale smell of whiskey on his breath making her feel sick. 'You're a pain in the ass. Someone needs to teach you a lesson.'

He poked her hard in the chest. On instinct, Nell grabbed hold of his finger and bent it back hard. Curtis squealed, his free hand swinging at her. This time she was quick enough to duck, but lost her balance in the process, landing uncomfortably on her butt. She was aware of yelling coming from down the street, of people running towards her as Curtis leaned down, grabbed her by the collar of her sweater, and prepared to swing his fist.

Nell went for the nearest target, reaching her hand up between his legs, tightly squeezing him by the balls. He yowled in pain as she twisted hard, releasing his grip on her sweater and stumbling back.

Adrenalin searing through her veins, she clambered to her feet, barely aware of her cut lip or grazed hands. A small crowd had gathered; she was aware of someone's arm slide round her shoulders, and turned to see Antonia. A couple of the women who worked with Jenna had rushed into the alleyway and were helping her to her feet, while two older gentlemen were trying to restrain Curtis, who was still crying with pain, his face red and contorted as he cupped his balls and swore at Nell. 'You fucking bitch, O'Connor. I'm gonna knock your head off.'

'What the hell's going on?'

Nell turned at Alex's voice. He was with Tommy and a guy she didn't recognise. He was sleekly dressed and had chiselled features. The Winchester detective she presumed.

'I want to press charges,' Curtis spluttered, staggering forward.

'Fucking bitch busted my balls.'

'You hit her first,' Antonia pointed out. 'And there are half a dozen witnesses who saw you do it.'

Alex glanced at Nell, his expression darkening as he took in her cut lip.

'Bitch had it coming, poking her nose in my bus–'

He didn't get to finish his sentence, the breath whooshing out of him as, in one fluid move, Alex had him pinned against the wall of the nail salon, his face mashed into the brickwork. As he yanked Curtis's hands behind his back, cuffing him and reading him his rights, Curtis began to protest.

'Wait! She assaulted me. You gonna arrest her too? Jenna will tell you what happened. Jenna?'

Nell glanced over at Jenna Milborn, who was still flanked by her colleagues. Her eyes were tear-stained and she looked apprehensively at her husband. For a moment Nell thought she was going to rush to defend him, but mercifully she remained silent.

Alex handed the still-protesting Curtis over to Tommy. 'Put him in a cell. I'll be back in a bit.'

'Sure thing, Chief.'

As Tommy escorted Curtis Milborn away and the small crowd started to disperse, Alex turned to Nell and ran the pad of his thumb over her cut lip. 'You want to tell me what happened?'

She was still pumped up, the old familiar fear she had of being attacked usurped by the fact she had fought back, giving as good as she had gotten, and although she was shaking it occurred to her for the first time that the panic hadn't taken over. Her anger had been stronger. It felt like a victory. 'I saw him beating up his wife, so I intervened.'

When Alex raised a brow, questioning the wisdom of her decision, she managed a weak smile. 'Don't judge me by my split lip. It looks worse than it is. I did more damage to him than he did to me, I promise.'

'It certainly looked that way as he hobbled off just now,' Alex's detective friend interjected, agreeing with her, humour in his coffee-coloured eyes.

Alex relaxed slightly, though still kept a wary eye on her. 'Nell, meet Hunter Stone. He's the detective who's been working with us on the Penny Maher case. Hunter, this is Nell O'Connor. I'm not sure if you've just seen her at her worst or finest moment,' he joked, sidestepping when Nell swiped at him. 'Hey, I'm staying on your good side. I've just seen what you do to men who piss you off.'

'Good to meet you, Nell,' Hunter told her, shaking her hand.

'It's nice to meet you too. And I'm sorry for what you just witnessed. I don't make a habit of brawling in the street.'

'Looked like he had it coming.' He smiled at Nell, even-white teeth contrasting against his dark skin, kind eyes full of humour, and she warmed to him immediately.

'Hunter's staying on the island tonight. I thought we could take him out to dinner.'

'Sure, that sounds nice. I guess I had better get my lip cleaned up.'

'We've a first-aid box in the diner,' Antonia offered. She had been hovering on the periphery, eyes all over Hunter Stone. 'Coffee's on the house.'

'She makes great coffee,' Nell told Hunter, who looked as though he was wavering.

'Well, then I guess we can't say no.'

Alex caught Nell by the hand and led the way to where Antonia directed them through to the kitchen at the back of the diner. He closed the door, giving them some privacy, before pulling the first-aid box down from the shelf.

'You're sure you're okay?' He ran his hands up and down her arms. 'You're shaking.'

'My lip stings and yes, I'm shaking, but other than that I'm fine. He didn't get the better of me, Alex. I stood up for myself and I didn't have a panic attack. Do you know how good that feels?'

Alex smiled as he cupped Nell's chin with one hand, inspecting the cut. 'It's not deep enough for stitches. You'll just look a little ugly for a while.'

'You're such a charmer.'

She was still spiked on adrenalin, but working her way down, and she appreciated the humour as it helped take her mind off the ugly situation with Curtis. She resisted wriggling as Alex cleaned the wound.

'I can't believe you took on Curtis Milborn,' he commented as he applied antiseptic cream, looking up to meet her eyes as he capped the tube.

'He was attacking his wife. I couldn't walk by and ignore it.'

'I'm not sure your brother will agree. Can you stay away from the hospital until your lip has healed? My neck is gonna be on the line for this.'

He was teasing again, lightening the moment.

'I think he will be more concerned I had my hand on Curtis Milborn's balls,' Nell commented dryly, provoking a laugh from Alex.

He settled his hands on her hips, pulled her up against him, brushing his lips against hers. 'As your boyfriend, I should have more of a problem with that,' he told her lightly. 'The thing is, I've wanted to catch Curtis in the act for a while. Jenna has always refused to press charges, but this time I've got him. As you helped, I'll let the whole ball-touching thing slide.'

'Whoa, back up. Did you just use the B-word?'

'Balls?' Alex asked innocently.

'No, you know what B-word I meant.'

The lines around his eyes crinkled, his cheeks dimpling against that wide cheeky grin Nell had fallen for. 'Ah – boyfriend. Yeah, I did. You have a problem with that, O'Connor?'

Nell slipped her arms around his neck. 'No problem.'

She ran her hands up into his hair, pulled him towards her for another kiss, this one longer, lingering, a little scared by the intensity of her feelings for him. It had never felt this way with Caleb.

Alex broke the kiss first, leaning his forehead against hers. 'We should get back to Hunter. Did you see the look Antonia was giving him? I think she's planning on offering herself up for dessert.'

Nell stifled a giggle. 'We'd better go rescue him.'

33

A lex took great satisfaction in formally going through the arrest procedure. Although Curtis had spent the night in the cells on more than one occasion, it had previously been to cool off, and as Jenna always refused to take things further, they had never taken his prints or a DNA sample.

'I want to press charges against your girlfriend,' Curtis protested as he was locked back in the cell after putting in a call to his lawyer. 'She was the one who assaulted me.'

'You have any witnesses for that?' Alex asked mildly.

'My wife will be my witness.'

'You beat the crap out of your wife. She's hardly reliable.'

'You have no proof of that.'

'But I do have proof that you assaulted Nell and a dozen witnesses who saw you do it. Jenna may not press charges, but Nell will.'

'Nell O'Connor is a troublemaking bitch. Everyone noticed how people keep dying or getting hurt when she is around. It should have been her in the Dolan house that night.'

Tommy picked that moment to walk in the room, visibly flinching at the reminder.

'You agree, don't you, Tommy? Nell is the reason why Lizzie Kent is dead. I wish it had been her in your house that night.'

'I have something you're gonna want to see, Chief.'

Alex scowled at Curtis, glad they were separated by bars. He didn't want anything going wrong with this arrest. Ignoring the man, he followed Tommy out of the cells.

'What have you got?'

Tommy held out the plastic bag containing Curtis's possessions. 'Recognise anything?'

Alex spotted the matchbook right away. It was the same brand as the one they had found outside the guesthouse after Luke had been shot.

'Let's get his prints in the system and see if we get a match.'

It would have been sweet justice to find out that Curtis was the shooter at the guesthouse, so Alex was bitterly disappointed when they didn't get a match. He brooded in his office for a while, annoyed because he knew the assault charge for hitting Nell was unlikely to bring more than a slap on the wrist. It also meant that whoever was harassing her was still at large, and that pissed him off. She had been through enough.

He forced his mind back to the serial killer case and, knowing he didn't have any more time to waste on Curtis, he spoke with Hunter and Buddy Hamilton, the detective working the Caroline Henderson disappearance. Between them they were compiling a list of registered boats in their jurisdictions. He cross-referenced the list for Purity, eliminating several of the smaller vessels and any that didn't have cabins, knowing their perp would need room and privacy to kill and dismember his victims.

As he worked, his mind kept going back to Curtis and the level of vitriol he had shown towards Nell following his arrest. The throwaway comment he had made about Lizzie Kent's murder ate at him. Curtis had said it should have been Nell in the house. Nothing odd there as everyone knew Nell was supposed to babysit, but it was the way he had said that he wished it had been Nell. Although there was nothing incriminating in the words, it was the manner in which he had said them, as though he had been there.

It was stupid. Alex knew he was clutching at straws, that his personal involvement with Nell was clouding his judgement when it came to Curtis. He forced himself to focus, but the comment continued to eat away at him.

Curtis would have been about nineteen when Lizzie was killed. He had always been a man who seemed to believe the world owed him a favour and, in the few years Alex had known him, he had been involved in numerous shady deals. Was it that big a stretch to believe he would have wanted in on a home robbery?

There was no evidence linking him to the crime, just a crazy biased hunch, and Alex had other priorities, but it didn't stop him taking time out to check Curtis's prints against the partial one that had been found on the knife that stabbed Lizzie. He didn't expect a match, and was surprised that there was one, though the print on the knife hadn't been clear, so it wasn't conclusive.

It was still enough to pull Curtis into the interrogation room.

If he wanted to get a confession, Alex knew he was going to have to call Curtis's bluff. The man sat at the table looking cocky as hell, as though he held all the cards. His slimy lawyer, Winston Shakeshaft, had arrived and was by his side.

'You were sloppy, Curtis.'

'How's that?'

'Well, if you didn't keep beating up on women you wouldn't have ended up in jail with your prints on file.'

Shakeshaft was quick to interject, pointing out that his client hadn't yet been found guilty of beating up anyone.

Alex ignored him, aware he had Curtis's attention. 'Now we have your prints we can run them against other crimes.'

'I don't know what you're talking about.'

'You know there was a print found on the knife that was used to stab Lizzie Kent?'

Curtis glanced at his lawyer and swallowed hard. 'What has that got to do with me?'

'You can quit playing games, Curtis. The print is a match. We know it was you in the house with Roy Dolan that night. Your print is on the knife. You killed Lizzie.'

'Don't say a word,' Shakeshaft advised.

Curtis ignored him. 'It wasn't me. I didn't do anything.' But he visibly paled and Alex knew in that moment he might just be guilty.

'Roy came up with a plan to rob his brother. You were in on it and the pair of you broke into the house.'

'I didn't even know Roy.'

'Don't bullshit me. We have a witness who saw the pair of you together.' Alex was clutching at straws now, but needed to get the confession.

'Who?'

'Don't answer, Curtis,' Shakeshaft demanded. 'You don't need to.'

'You broke into the house thinking it was going to be empty, but Lizzie, Tommy and Emily were home. Lizzie saw you and you knew you had to silence her. I'm guessing you killed Roy too, wanting all of the money to yourself. But Tommy saw you and you had to run empty-handed.'

'I didn't kill Roy.'

'You got greedy, didn't you, Curtis? Was fifty per cent not enough? Did you go there on the night planning to kill Roy?'

'I didn't kill Roy!' Curtis pushed back his chair and clambered to his feet. 'Lizzie was the one who killed Roy.'

Shakeshaft gaped, while Alex sat back in his chair, regarding Curtis with a gloating smile.

Got you now, you fucker.

'And how would you know that, unless you were there?'

Realising the magnitude of the situation, Curtis wavered before dropping back down into his own chair. His bottom lip was shaking. 'It was an accident. The house was supposed to be empty. Lizzie had the knife and I was trying to get it off her. I didn't mean to kill her.'

He began to blub.

Alex had no pity for him. Accident or not, he had killed a teenage girl and made so many others suffer as a consequence of his actions. He doubted the confession would ease the burden on those who had loved Lizzie Kent, but hoped it would at least bring them closure.

Nell had gone back to Alex's place to walk and feed Teddy and Sasha, before heading up to the guesthouse to change for dinner. Although she tried to disguise her bloody lip as best as possible, it was still obvious she had been smacked in the face.

Alex arrived at seven and she could tell from his expression the second she opened the door that something was up. Panic bubbled in her throat.

'Is it Michael? Has something happened to him?'

'Let's go sit down, okay?'

'Dammit, Alex. Is it Michael?'

'Your brother's fine, but there's something else we need to talk about.'

'What? Tell me?'

He took her arm and guided her through to the living room. Nell could feel her heartbeat racing, sickness knotting her belly. If it wasn't Michael then what the hell was it? Her legs were trembling, so she didn't protest when Alex eased her on to the couch, sat down beside her and took her hands.

'Curtis confessed to killing Lizzie this afternoon.'

Nell wasn't quite sure she had heard him right. 'What?'

'Curtis killed Lizzie. He's going to jail, Nell. We've got him.'

'I... I...' The words wouldn't come, her head pounding as she tried to process the news. She tightened her grip on Alex's hands, needing to anchor herself to something real, unsure how she was supposed to react. The words came eventually. 'What happened?'

Alex explained about the print on the knife, and the interview with Curtis and his lawyer, and Nell listened numbly, as a surge of emotions rose inside her: relief, guilt, sadness and anger.

'I can't believe you got him,' Nell whispered. 'Thank you. Do her folks know?'

'I just stopped by their place on the way here.'

'How did they take it?'

'They were sad, but relieved. It was a lot for them to take in.'

Nell was quiet for a moment. 'I can't believe it's finally over.' She pulled her hand away, swiping angrily at the tears pricking her eyes.

'I didn't want to tell you over the phone.'

'I appreciate that.'

'You want me to cancel the restaurant? Hunter will understand.'

'No, no.' Lizzie's killer had been caught. Knowing it was Curtis Milborn was a lot to take in, but this was good news. Lizzie would finally have justice. Dinner offered normality and she needed normality right now. 'I'm ready to go. It's just dinner.' Nell forced a smile. 'I'll be fine.'

The three of them went to a fish restaurant along the seafront to eat and although they talked briefly about Curtis Milborn, Nell was aware that Alex and Hunter were doing their best to keep her mind off the subject. Initially she was subdued, unable to get Curtis or Lizzie out of her thoughts, but as Hunter began recounting tales from past cases, including those he had worked with Alex when they had both been detectives with the Portland Police Bureau, she found herself being drawn into the conversation.

Nell liked him a lot, found his stories fascinating, his delivery witty, and she liked learning snippets about Alex's past. Hunter was smooth and laid-back, with an easy-going nature and a dry sense of humour that was similar to Alex's. She understood why the two of them were friends and was glad he was the detective assigned to the Penelope Maher case, giving them a chance to work together again.

She was surprised to find out he was married, had been for several years, to his childhood sweetheart. He struck her as a ladies' man, flirtatious, charming the pants off the waitress who was serving them. She had soon learned though he was like that with everyone and he had even played along with Antonia's little crush back at the diner, turning up the smile and having her giggling like a teenager.

Conversation inevitably turned to the case they were working. Nell knew they were limited in what they could discuss in front of her, and she had been respectful not to push Alex for information she knew he couldn't share, but they did open up about some of the details and she listened with interest as she picked at her lobster, a little unnerved by their theory the killer lived close to home and also that another woman had gone missing – that whoever was responsible for the murders appeared to be escalating their activities.

She couldn't help but think back to the last night she had been alone at the guesthouse and the masked man who had scared the hell out of her before Alex had shown up, though she told herself there was no way the two things could be connected.

Whoever had spooked her that night had to be the person who had shot Luke, and the person who had broken into the guesthouse and left the picture of Lizzie for her to find. It crossed her mind: could it have been Curtis?

'Are you thinking about your friend again?' Hunter asked, filling up her wine glass. He had ordered a good bottle of white to go with the fish platter that he and Nell were sharing, while Alex, who had volunteered to drive, nursed a beer.

Nell sipped her wine, contemplative. 'Yeah, it's a lot to process. And now with everything that's been happening at the guesthouse I keep wondering if...' She trailed off.

Alex caught her hand. 'It's not Curtis. I wish it was, but he's not the one who has been harassing you.'

'He killed Lizzie though and her picture was left for me to find.'

'His prints didn't match the matchbox, Nell. Besides, I checked it out and he has an solid alibi – he was drinking in the bar with lots of witnesses; he even picked a fight with one of them. Curtis killed Lizzie, but he's not responsible for what has been happening to you. I will find whoever is though, I promise.'

'Maybe it's not personally about you, but the house.' Hunter speared a piece of asparagus with his fork, popping it in his mouth as he looked up. They had briefly discussed the incidents up at the guesthouse while they had been waiting for their food. 'If you ask me, I'd be questioning if someone is trying to drive you out of the house and why.'

Alex narrowed his eyes, considering. 'The picture was personal. Whoever left it there for Nell to find was trying to spook her about Lizzie.'

'But were they? Everyone knows about Lizzie Kent's murder, right? And they know Nell was supposed to babysit. What if it was a means to an end to scare her? I mean, has anything else happened to you that connects to Lizzie?'

'Her brother Sam has made it clear he's not happy to see me.'

'He's pretty pissed,' Alex added. 'He certainly didn't hold back when I spoke to him.'

'Pissed, yes,' Hunter pushed. 'He's mad you've come back, and he has anger issues over what happened to his sister. Think about it though. Why would he go to lengths to break into your house and scare you if he's gonna shoot his mouth off to everyone about how much he hates you anyway?'

Nell hadn't looked at it that way, and guessed Hunter had a point.

'So, if it's not about Lizzie, then what is the issue?' Alex's question was as much to himself as it was to Nell and Hunter. 'What reason would someone have to want to drive her off the island?'

'Or just out of the house. You said your brother is in hospital?'

'Yes, he disturbed a robbery where he works.'

'And he has been helping you renovate the house, right?'

'He has.'

'What if the attack on him is also connected to the house? You're living there, he's working there. Someone doesn't want either of you in that place.'

Nell glanced at Alex, curious to know what he was thinking. Hunter had come in with an outside perspective and managed to set her train of thought on a whole new track.

'It's something I hadn't considered,' he admitted. 'The picture, the shooting, the masked intruder – I figured it was all about Nell.'

'And you would.' Hunter took a sip of his wine. 'Because you're blinkered. I get that. She's a pretty lady.' He treated Nell to his killer smile and she flushed, still uncomfortable with receiving compliments. She had never had any from Caleb, who preferred to run her down, and they felt a little alien to her.

They stayed in the restaurant until late, Hunter ordering a second bottle of wine that he proceeded to drink most of, though Nell still felt a little light-headed as they got up to leave their table. They said goodnight to him, watching him walk in a surprisingly straight line across the street to his hotel, before making their way to where they were parked.

'Do you think he could be right about the guesthouse?' Nell asked, slipping on her seat belt.

'Hunter's a smart guy,' Alex mused, backing the Jeep out of the parking spot and heading out towards the coastal road that led up into the hills. 'It's something I hadn't considered, but what he said does make sense. It could be whoever attacked Michael is the same person who shot Luke and tried to scare you.'

'But why though? Why would someone want the house empty?'

'Could it have anything to do with your cousin? He went a little off the rails after your aunt died.'

'I should have come back then,' Nell murmured, hating herself for staying away. 'He should never have been alone in the house after Bella died.'

'There's no point blaming yourself. What happened to Clarke was an accident.' He was right, but it didn't stop the guilt. 'I forgot to tell you, I checked out Sarah Treadwell.'

'You did?'

'There's no trace of her after she left the guesthouse.'

'What do you mean there's no trace?'

Alex briefly took his eyes off the road to glance at Nell. 'I mean there are no addresses, no further employment records and no transactions on her credit cards. She just disappeared.'

'You think something happened to her?'

'Either that or she was running from something and wanted to disappear.'

Nell was silent, her mind churning. Finally, she spoke, 'Do you think Clarke had something to do with that?'

'It's impossible to say, but when I get some free time, I promise I'll look into it further.' Alex reached across and gave her hand a reassuring squeeze. 'Your cousin was a good guy. I'm sure it's nothing sinister.'

They were staying at the guesthouse tonight and Nell found she was now dreading returning. Much as she was tempted to tell Alex to turn the Jeep around and go back to his place, she held her ground and reminded herself the house held happy memories. It looked ominously black as they pulled into the driveway though and she wished she had left a light on downstairs to make their return more welcoming. As soon as she had unlocked the door and reset the alarm, she reached for the table lamp on the reception desk, keen to add some warmth to the place.

Alex tossed his keys on the counter and slipped his arms around her.

'You okay? What Hunter said back there didn't spook you, right?'

'A little,' she admitted. 'Though I know it's stupid. I should be relieved if it's the house and not me I guess.'

'Try not to overthink it, okay. We'll figure it out, I promise.' He kissed her on the nose, swatting her gently on the butt. 'How's your mouth?'

'Sore... and ugly apparently,' Nell pouted, winking at him as she backed away towards the staircase. 'I'm gonna go upstairs and take my make-up off.'

Flicking on the stairwell lights, she made her way up to the second floor. The hallway looked completely different since it had been redecorated, the walls fresher with cream paint, the scent of it still lingering in the air.

She pushed open the door to her bedroom, surprised to find it shut, convinced she had left it ajar, and flicked on the light switch. Written on the wall above her bed, ruining the soft grey paint, were crude red letters.

GET OUT

For a second she was rooted to the spot, unable to take her eyes off the words then she slowly looked around her, half afraid in case whoever was responsible was still in the house. Her eyes went to the bathroom, the door was ajar and the room dark.

Was someone hiding in there? Slowly she backed out of the room.

'Alex?'

He didn't answer immediately so she called again, louder, hating the edge of panic in her tone.

'ALEX?'

This time she heard him on the stairs below. He joined her on the landing 'Nell, what's wrong?'

She couldn't find the words, simply pointed to the bedroom. He strode ahead of her and stepped inside.

'What the fuck? Looks like blood.'

Nell stayed on the landing, her insides knotted with a mixture of fear and anger. She wanted to join Alex, but found she was rooted to the spot, too afraid to follow alongside him and terrified of what might be waiting for them.

34

2005

A week had passed since Jenna's text to Tommy. In the cold light of day when she was thinking more rationally, the plan to get revenge on Sarah seemed a little ridiculous. She didn't like the woman, hated that she was flirting with her boyfriend, but in another couple of weeks Luke would be gone, the temptation removed, and Sarah's summer job would be coming to an end. Jenna hated Sarah for what she had done, but it was easier to live with things knowing she would be gone soon. Or so she thought.

She had finished cheerleading practice one Thursday after-noon when she received a text from Luke saying he was busy packing for college and couldn't pick her up. Jenna offered to stop by and help him; annoyed when he turned her down.

She caught a ride with her friend, Katy, and they stopped off for ice cream on the way home. As they sat outside on the deck at the ice cream parlour twenty minutes later eating sundaes, Paige Whittaker started poking her nose in, asking awkward questions.

'How come Luke didn't pick you up today?' she wanted to know.

'He's busy packing.' Jenna tried to keep her tone nonchalant. 'He has a lot to do before he goes to college.'

Paige was blonde and pouty, and the only girl on the squad Jenna didn't like. It always felt like she was trying to get one up on Jenna or make her look stupid.

'Is that so? I thought you two lovebirds would have been spending every moment you could together before he leaves.'

'I'm seeing him later,' Jenna said tightly. It was a lie, they had no plans, but there was no need for Paige to know that.

She continued to eat her sundae, though the ice cream had lost its appeal, and while she faked a smile for her friends, trying to put on a brave face, she was distracted, the worry about her relationship with Luke weighing heavily on her mind.

Ten minutes later her world hit rock bottom when she spotted his sports car drive by, Sarah Treadwell sitting in the passenger seat.

Jenna dropped her spoon in the almost empty glass, sickness rising into her throat, and for a moment she struggled to breathe.

Pull yourself together, you don't want the others to know.

But it was too late, she realised, as Paige turned to her with a gloating smile.

'I guess Luke got done early with his packing,' she smirked.

Jenna held herself together during the ride home then threw herself on her bed and sobbed.

Barely an hour passed when she received a text message from Tommy.

I heard about Luke and Sarah. Do you want me to come over? Xx

She swiped at her tears, mortified word had already spread; no doubt thanks to that bitch, Paige Whittaker. Furiously she fired a text back.

I wanna be alone.

Her screen immediately lit up with a reply.

No worries. Let me know if you need anything. Xx

She heard from Luke later that night when he showed up on her doorstep. He looked contrite and Jenna realised he knew he had been seen. He didn't try to deny it, but he did spend a few minutes trying to convince her that nothing had happened.

'I had to run to the grocery store,' he told her. 'Sarah was there when I came out and she was having car trouble. I just gave her a ride back to the guesthouse.'

'That was chivalrous of you.'

'Well, I could hardly leave her stranded.'

'So, her car is still there now?'

'We called a tow truck before we left.'

'How convenient.'

Luke let out a sigh. 'You're being unreasonable, Jenna.'

'Am I?'

'Yes, you are. What would you have had me do? I don't know why you're being like this. I try to help someone out and now I'm being made out to be a bad guy.'

He was being frustratingly smooth with an answer for everything and now twisting things around, presenting himself as the victim.

'Maybe I'm being like this because I hate being played for a fool. I know you like her, are you going to deny it?'

'She's a pretty lady,' Luke admitted. 'But you are overreacting.' He picked at an invisible fleck of dust on the comforter and seemed to be looking for the right words for what he wanted to say next. 'I'm off to college in ten days.'

'I'm aware of that.'

'And we're going to be over five hundred miles apart.'

'Your point is?' Jenna asked tartly, ignoring the sliver of dread snaking its way into her belly.

'I don't see how things are going to work between us, especially when you're already paranoid.'

'I'm being paranoid with good reason.'

'No, you're not, and when I'm at Penn you're going to be worrying about all of the girls I am with there.'

'I won't.'

'We both know that's a lie.' Luke looked at her with those vivid blue eyes she loved so much. 'I deserve to have some freedom while I'm at college, Jenna, just as you deserve to have freedom back here. We can't hold each other back.'

'Are you breaking up with me?'

'I think it's best if we have a break from each other for a while.' And in that moment Jenna's world as she knew it, ended.

She spent twenty minutes begging him to change his mind, even saying she would overlook the whole Sarah thing. When Luke refused to reconsider, told her his mind was firmly made up, her tears turned to anger and she kicked him out of the house.

Over the next two hours she went from shock and sadness to self-pity and mortification. How was she going to face her friends? They all knew Luke had cheated on her and now he'd dumped her. The self-pity and mortification soon manifested into bitterness and rage. She needed a target for her anger and focused on Sarah Treadwell, convinced if she hadn't shown up in Purity, her relationship wouldn't have fallen apart.

Sarah would pay for what she had done.

Jenna spent the next two days in her PJs, refusing to leave the house, not ready to face anyone and desperate to plot her revenge against Sarah. She considered and discounted a dozen possibilities, knew she wanted to cause the woman pain and humiliation, but not actually hurt her. The idea of using the pills came to her when she was looking in the medicine cabinet for painkillers, needing to numb the blinding headache she had from her continual crying.

She looked at the bottle of laxatives, her mind working overtime, considering how she would be able to get Sarah to digest them. If they were crushed up small they could probably be disguised in food, but how would she make this work? She could hardly show up at the guesthouse bearing food gifts. She had never spoken to Sarah before and the woman probably knew she was Luke's girlfriend, so would automatically be suspicious.

After giving it more thought, she picked up her cell phone and texted Tommy.

Are you still up for helping me? xx

It took only seconds for him to reply.

Sure. What's up? Xx

Can you come over? xx

Fifteen minutes later she opened the door to him, forcing a bright smile.

She told him her idea as they drank from bottles of soda in the backyard.

'I can't do it without your help, Tommy.'

He was immediately attentive. 'What do you need me to do?'

'If I make the brownies, can you get them to Sarah?'

'I can try.'

'She likes chocolate, right?'

'Yeah, I guess she does.'

'So if I make a batch, crush in the pills, and give them to you, you can take them over to the guesthouse, make sure she eats one?'

'Are you sure this is safe? We don't want to put her in the hospital or anything.'

'It's perfectly safe. My mom sometimes takes them and she's a nurse. I don't want to hurt her, just give her an upset belly, maybe make her a little sick.'

Jenna thought of Luke and wished there was a way she could do the same to him, make him suffer for hurting her, but he would never accept brownies from her. He hadn't been in touch at all in the last couple of days, ignoring all of her texts and calls, and she suspected she wouldn't see or hear from him before he left for college. She would have to focus her revenge plans on Sarah.

She made the brownies on Sunday afternoon while her mom was on shift. The directions on the bottle said to take one pill, but she wanted to be sure they were effective and also that Sarah suffered a little, so she crushed four into the dough mix, sprinkling plenty of cocoa powder in and adding extra chocolate to try and disguise any taste. When they were in the oven baking, she texted Tommy and told him to come over.

'Something smells good,' he told her by way of greeting when she answered the door.

'That's the idea, but I wouldn't recommend you eat them.'

'You're sure you want to do this?' he asked as she scooped the brownies up from the oven tray and laid them neatly in a Tupperware dish.

'Absolutely,' Jenna told him, sealing the lid. 'Why? Are you having second thoughts?'

'No.' Tommy looked annoyed she was doubting him. 'I already said I would help you. I just wanted to check you were definitely cool with it before there's no turning back.'

Jenna leant back against the counter and gave him her most beseeching smile. He was growing into his looks and she didn't doubt he would break hearts one day, but he was no Luke. She knew he adored her though and for that she was grateful. She was willing to throw him a carrot now and again.

'I am definitely cool with it, if not I wouldn't have spent the morning baking. I want you to know that I appreciate your help with this, Tommy.' She reached up to caress his cheek and turned up her smile. 'You're such a good friend and I don't know what I would do without you.'

She reached up on tiptoe, brushed her lips against his cheek, and felt him inhale sharply.

Yes, he was worth keeping around.

Tommy had been staying over at the guesthouse and Jenna got his message a little after five. As she got in her car she felt both giddy and nervous, the idea of finally meeting Sarah face-to-face making her palms clammy.

She rang the front doorbell and waited as the seconds ticked by, listening to the sound of the waves crashing on the rocks below, relieved and disappointed when it was Tommy who opened the door.

He must have sensed she was nervous and gave her a reassuring smile. 'It's all good,' he whispered. 'I showed her the brownies, told her to help herself. She said they smelt great.'

'Where is she?'

'In the kitchen. Why don't we go upstairs? It will seem less suspicious if we're not hovering around.'

Jenna peered down the hallway in the direction of the kitchen, keen to see if the brownies had yet been touched. She guessed Tommy was right though, and she followed him up the stairs to the second floor, a little dubious when he opened the door to his bedroom.

She didn't want him getting the wrong idea.

Fortunately, Clarke heard them and came bumbling down the hallway.

'Whatcha doing?'

Tommy looked annoyed, but Jenna was relieved to see him. She never thought she would say that about Clarke Golding. The guy was odd and hard work to be around, but she figured safety in numbers. At least with Clarke present Tommy wouldn't try anything.

'We're just hanging out,' she told him, forcing a bright smile. 'You wanna come join us?'

Tommy's expression darkened, but Clarke seemed delighted. 'We can play video games?'

'Sure, why not?' Jenna agreed, the idea of spending her evening in a geek pad about as appealing as visiting the dentist. It beat the alternative of trying to fend off Tommy if he tried to hit on her though. She wanted that like she wanted a hole in the head, but needed to keep him on her side. If he tried to kiss her and she rejected him, he could turn spiteful and tell Sarah about the brownies. She didn't need that.

Clarke fetched his Xbox and set it up to the television in Tommy's room. Jenna tried her best to feign interest in the racing game on the screen, but her mind kept wandering back to Sarah and whether the woman had yet sampled her brownies.

'We should go check,' she urged Tommy, as Clarke ejected the game and was preparing to insert another disc.

'I guess we could go get a drink.'

They left Clarke to set up the new game, made their way down the hallway towards the stairs. Before they reached them, a gut-wrenching scream pierced through the old house.

Sarah?

Jenna paled. She wanted to see the woman vomiting or at least stuck on the toilet, but the scream didn't sound good. It was pure agony.

Tommy's eyes widened. 'What's happened? You said this was safe.'

'It was. I swear it wasn't supposed to hurt her.'

He raced down the stairs and Jenna followed, her legs shaking.

What if Sarah was badly injured or dead? She had baked the brownies, laced them with laxatives. Would she go to jail?

The scream had come from the basement where Bella Golding housed the laundry facilities. The door was already ajar, and Tommy reached it first, peering down the steps.

Jenna noticed his face drain of colour and his chin start to wobble.

'What is it?'

When he didn't reply she tried again. 'What the hell is it, Tommy?'

He had no words and, as Jenna joined him in the doorway, neither did she.

Lying at the foot of the stairs, her neck twisted at an unusual angle, was Sarah. She wasn't moving, her eyes staring towards the ceiling, blood pouring from a wound in the back of her head.

'Shit, Jenna,' Tommy whispered, trying to take in the scene. 'What have we done?'

35

After Nell had calmed down from the initial shock, anger had taken over that someone had broken into the house, had violated the place where she slept. They had moved rooms for the night and Alex took a sample of the blood from the wall with him when he left the following morning. He was annoyed about the security system, keen to know how someone had managed to bypass it. Before going to bed he had checked all of the doors and windows, finally concluding the intruder had entered through the unlocked conservatory window on the ground floor.

Nell had promised him she hadn't left it open and could only think that maybe one of Michael's labourers had. Both men showed for work ten minutes after Alex had left. Nell had wondered if they would appear, given that Michael was in the hospital, but they seemed to know what they were supposed to be doing so she left them to it.

Shortly after they arrived there was a loud knock at the door. Nell glanced back at Carlos, who was painting the hallway, hesitant to open it after the previous night's scare, then told herself to pull it together.

Pete Moorhouse, one of her brother's old friends, stood on the front step. Behind him two men sat perched on the hood of a truck, having a smoke while they waited.

'Miss O'Connor.' Pete raised his cap, shuffling from foot to foot.

'Hi, Pete, how are you?'

'Uh, good, thanks. I was sorry to hear about what happened to Michael.'

'Thank you.'

'Anyway, thing is, we've been to visit with him, the boys and I...' He hooked a thumb in the direction of the two men waiting behind him, who both waved a hand in greeting. 'We want to try and help. We're between jobs at the moment so I told Michael we would come over and put in a few days' work on the guesthouse for you. Try to keep things ticking over while he can't be here.'

Nell's jaw gaped before she found a smile, surprised and touched by the offer. 'Thank you. That's so kind of you. I don't know what to say.'

'No thanks necessary, Miss O'Connor. Your brother is a good man and I know he would do the same for any of us. We're all mad as hell about what happened to him and we want to do our bit to help.'

'It's Nell, please, and thank you so much.'

She wouldn't have had the first clue to tell them what to do, but fortunately Michael had been clear in his directions when he spoke with Pete at the hospital and his guys brought in the jackhammer, ready to tackle the concrete floor in the conservatory, where the pool was going to be.

Feeling redundant, Nell made coffees for everyone then took herself upstairs with a tin of paint to sort out the damage to her bedroom. Alex had already cleaned the blood off the wall as best as he could, but the words were still visible and Nell wanted them gone – though even with the wall freshly painted her bedroom still felt violated.

Someone had been in here, possibly going through her stuff, kneeling on the bed where she slept. It left her feeling uncomfortable and the sooner the attic was converted and she could move upstairs, the better.

Figuring she should visit Michael, she changed out of the old paint-splattered cargo pants she had been using to work in, assessed her reflection in the bathroom mirror, scowling at the bruising around her cut lip. She spent a few minutes attempting to disguise it with powder, knowing her brother would go nuts when he learned about her fight with Curtis Milborn. He was still recovering and she didn't want to do anything to risk raising his blood pressure.

Her efforts were wasted as her face was the first thing Michael zoned in on when she walked into the hospital room. He had been mid-conversation with Newt, who was sitting loyally by his bedside and they both glanced up hearing Nell's footsteps.

'Did you walk into a door?' Michael asked sharply.

'It's a long story and perhaps better saved for another day.'

Newt shot her a knowing glance and she guessed he already knew some of what had happened. Word had spread quickly, probably thanks to Antonia. Her old high school friend had a heart of gold but did love to gossip. She wasn't sure if he yet knew about Curtis being charged with Lizzie's murder.

Michael held up his hands and glanced down at the bed. 'I have time.'

Nell pulled up a chair and explained as casually as she could about confronting Curtis. She played down the swing he had taken at her, instead focusing on the part of the story where she had left him writhing in agony.

She could see Michael's face reddening, a vein throbbing in his forehead. 'Did you know about this?' he fumed at Newt.

'No, of course not... well, I might have heard a rumour.'

'Great, just great, so you're all keeping me in the dark again. And you both wonder why I worry.'

'He killed Lizzie, Michael.'

'He what?'

'Alex arrested him and ran his prints against the knife used to stab Lizzie. He did it. He's guilty. He confessed.'

She could see Michael needed a moment to process the news. Newt looked shocked too. 'Curtis killed Lizzie?' he questioned. 'Curtis Milborn?'

'He did. It's crazy, isn't it?'

'So, you didn't just confront a wife beater. He's a murderer too.'

'Look, I know you're mad at me for getting involved between Curtis and Jenna, but if I hadn't Alex wouldn't have been able to link Curtis to Lizzie. He's gonna go to jail, Michael, and the Kents finally have some closure.'

She could see her brother was torn and although he was still mad about her intervening he also understood how big a deal it was to her knowing that Lizzie's killer had been caught after all this time.

Nell kept her visit brief, aware that just looking at her bruised face was annoying him. Thankfully she hadn't told him about the break-in at the guesthouse last night. He didn't need any other surprises to raise his blood pressure.

She would feel safer being alone if she had a gun for protection, but Alex wouldn't hand over the weapon he had bought her, and she couldn't blame him given her terrible aim. He had promised to take her back to the range for another practice, but he was so busy with work that Nell didn't like to push the issue. She supposed there was nothing to stop her going by herself.

She wasn't much use at the guesthouse at the moment and had the time to spare.

On a whim she turned the car around, heading down to the ferry port. She found the range okay, feeling nervous when she first walked in, but the guy on the front desk was friendly, renting her a gun and ammo, asking her if she had been before and talking her through everything. She thanked him and waited until he was gone before firing the gun, not wanting him to see her embarrassing aim. Safety glasses on, ear protectors in place, she positioned herself as Alex had taught her, lined the gun up with the bullseye and squeezed the trigger, cursing in frustration when she completely missed the target.

How could this be so difficult?

She finished the round, missing every shot, frustration bubbling up into anger. Part of her wanted to have a petulant fit and walk away, accept she couldn't do this.

You won't ever do it if you give up now. Don't be a quitter.

Nell drew in a deep breath, trying to ease the knot of tension between her shoulder blades.

She wasn't a quitter.

Forty minutes later she hit just inside the target and fist pumped the air, doing a little dance of satisfaction. She left the range knowing she wasn't quite there yet, but her aim was improving. Unfortunately, her bank balance had taken a hit, as she had recklessly ploughed her way through ammo, but it didn't wipe the smile off her face as she followed the country road that wound through forestland back up to the main highway.

She was singing along to the radio, a couple of miles from the shooting range, her mood brighter than it had been all day, when her tyre blew, and she gripped both hands tightly on the wheel as she lost control of the car, veering sharply from one side of the road to the other, wrestling for control and swearing loudly as she edged closer to the trees at the side of the road. There was nothing she could do to avoid the collision and she squeezed her eyes shut, bracing herself for impact, jolting forward hard against her seat belt as she crashed.

Everything went still, the awful sound of scraping metal followed by an eerie silence. She cracked open an eye, found herself face-to-face with a large oak tree, the hood of the car crumpled up, almost beyond recognition. Letting out a shaky breath she glanced down at her body, wiggled her toes, barely believing she was okay and had no apparent injuries, especially given the messed-up state of the car. As she reached for her purse, figuring she had better call for a tow truck, her car groaned loudly and something inside the engine began to hiss.

Maybe she would call for a tow truck from the side of the road. Neither the driver nor passenger door would open, so Nell wound down her window, clambering out. As she landed on her knees with an ungraceful thud, she heard the sound of an engine in the distance and looked up to see a dark car on the road approaching from the direction of the shooting range. She started to get to her feet, hoping to wave the driver down, but he hadn't spotted her and took a turn off the road before she could alert him.

Her legs were shaking as she brushed her palms down her jeans and her head was starting to throb, so she sat down on the side of the road. With trembling fingers, she pulled her cell phone from her purse deciding she would call Alex instead, needing to hear a familiar voice.

He sounded in a good mood when he answered the phone, though that changed when Nell told him about the accident.

'Where are you?'

Her location brought an exasperated sigh, but he didn't make comment, seeming more concerned she was okay.

'I bashed my head on the steering wheel, but I'm okay. Nothing is broken and no body parts have fallen off.'

'It's not funny, Nell. I'm calling an ambulance. What happened to the airbag?'

'I guess it didn't go off. I'm fine, honestly, just a little shaken up.'

'Have you reported it to the local police?'

'Not yet. I called you first.'

'Okay, let me make a couple of calls. I'll call you back.'

'Alex, there's no need to–'

He had already hung up and Nell threw the phone back into her purse, frustrated.

She glanced at her watch, wondering how long she would have to wait; hungry, thirsty and needing to pee. Fifteen minutes passed; her phone buzzed with a text alert. She fished it out of her purse, expecting it to be Alex.

The number showed as 'unknown' and she frowned, opening the message.

I'm watching you.

A trickle of fear ran down Nell's spine and she warily glanced around at the empty road and woods. The afternoon sun cut through the trees, the sky a vivid blue, the only noise coming from the birds chirping overhead. She had managed to crash in a beautiful spot. It should have felt peaceful, but instead it now felt plain creepy.

Hesitantly, she made her way to the trunk of the car, her heart thumping hard in her chest. She popped the lock and reached into the dark space for the lug wrench, the only potential weapon at hand. As she closed the trunk and started to turn away, another text arrived on her phone from the same number.

Look behind you.

Nell swung around, eyes scouring the forest.

At first she saw nothing, only the trees, then a glisten caught her eye and her focus was drawn to the steely sharp blade and the figure holding it. He stood about thirty feet away, partly hidden by the trees, and was dressed in black, wearing a white mask. The same mask she had seen pressed against the kitchen door. Realising he had her attention, he took a step forward, raised a gloved finger to his lips.

Nell froze, the lug wrench tightly gripped in one hand, her cell phone in the other, panic clawing its way into her throat. Her heartbeat quickened, as the familiar dread squeezed against her chest.

Not now. You can beat this, O'Connor.

She forced herself to focus, Alex's voice in her head urging her to control her breathing.

The man stayed where he was, made no further attempt to move towards her, and she weighed up her options, keeping her eyes on him, fearful for the slightest movement.

Her legs were leaden, but still she could attempt to get back in the car and wind up the window. Doing so would make her a sitting duck though and he could easily smash the glass if he wanted to get at her. The only other option was to run back to the shooting range. It was about a mile away, but if the panic really took hold, she would never outrun him.

As though her body wanted to taunt her, a wave of nausea swept over her and her breathing threatened to spin out of control.

Focus. Damn it, Nell.

As she continued to watch the masked man, wanting to make a move, but terrified that if she did, he would too, the familiar sound of an engine cut through the silence. Nell took her eyes off the man long enough to see a vehicle heading towards her. Finding her feet she ran down the middle of the road, waving frantically for the car to stop, collapsing to the ground in relief as it slowed to a halt and an older woman got out, concern etched on her face.

'Are you okay?'

Nell nodded, struggling for breath. 'I had an accident and there was...' She glanced towards the trees, to where the masked man had stood, but he was no longer there.

She met the woman's kindly eyes. 'Can you help me, please?'

36

It was after seven when Nell finally arrived back on the island. Alex had collected her from the East Haven Police Department, where he had talked with the police chief, Rick Winslow, and a deputy had been dispatched to the scene of her accident. When they learned of the man with the knife in the woods, two further units had been sent, though as Nell suspected, they found nothing. Despite her protestations, Alex insisted on taking her to the local ER to get checked over and she headed home with a diagnosis of concussion and a course of painkillers.

'I don't need these, I feel fine,' she grumbled on the ferry ride back to the island.

He cut her a look. 'You might have a different view about that tomorrow.'

She was tired, hungry and cranky, the adrenalin that had kicked in straight after the accident having ebbed away, and she could tell Alex was annoyed with her for coming over to the shooting range alone and without telling anyone, though he hadn't said anything as of yet.

'Or I might feel fine,' she pouted, trying to bait him, annoyed when he didn't respond. Deciding to get the fight out of the way sooner rather than later, she added, 'Look, I know you're pissed at me, okay, so you might as well go ahead and say what it is you've got to say.'

Alex's jaw tightened. 'I already told you I would take you back to the shooting range.'

'You were busy with work and I was at a loose end. I wouldn't have gone if I'd have known I was putting myself in danger.' Nell tried to keep her tone calm.

'There was a guy in a mask following you, who had a knife.'

'He wasn't following me. He was in the woods. If my tyre hadn't blown, I wouldn't have even seen him.'

'You think it was a coincidence he happened to be there? That he happened to have your cell number?'

Nell was silent for a moment, feeling stupid for not seeing the obvious. 'You think he caused my accident?' she asked quietly.

'Rick is going to check the tyres of your car. See if they were tampered with.'

'Do you think he followed me across on the ferry?'

'I think it's likely, yeah.'

'So, he was waiting for me to come out of the shooting range?' Nell's stomach dropped, the idea terrifying her.

'You're sure there were no cars following you when you left?'

'I don't remember seeing any.'

'Focus, Nell, think back. The woman who stopped for you, hers was the only other vehicle you saw on the road?'

Nell tried to recount her journey. She had been ecstatic when she had left the shooting range, so pleased with herself for hitting the target. She remembered turning onto the country road, listening to the radio. It was their Throwback Thursday segment and she had been singing her heart out to 'My Sharona' when the tyre blew. She couldn't remember seeing any other cars on the road at all.

'No, it was definitely just me, I...' She paused, recalling the dark coloured car she had seen in the distance as she was climbing out of her busted up Ford. 'Wait, there was one car. I saw it after I had crashed. It was on the road behind me, quite some distance away, though it turned off before it reached me. I was going to try and flag it down.'

Alex gave a tight smile. 'Perhaps it's best you didn't.'

'You think that was the guy?'

'It's possible.'

A shiver of fear trickled down Nell's back. 'Oh.'

'Did you see what kind of car it was or get the licence plate?'

'No, it was too far away. I couldn't even be certain what colour it was. I'd just crashed the car and my mind was all over the place.'

'It's okay.' Alex brushed his fingers through her hair. 'It seems like whoever he was he was playing some kind of game. I don't think he actually wanted to hurt you, just scare you.'

'He messed with my tyres. I'd say that was trying to hurt me.'

'Yeah, it was a dangerous game, but he had ample opportunity to get you if he wanted. Think about it. Deserted road, you had just crashed. He could easily have pulled up alongside your car and attacked you with the knife, but he didn't.'

'That's a comforting thought. Thanks for that.' Nell turned towards the railings, looking out across the water to home. Hunter Stone had suggested whoever was trying to scare her had been doing so because of the guesthouse, but this felt personal. The idea she had been followed all the way to the shooting range, that her tyres might have purposely been tampered with, was a lot to take on board.

Alex slipped his arms around her waist. 'You get now why I don't like you sneaking off? I know you don't want a babysitter, but until we figure out who the hell is harassing you, I don't like the idea of you being alone. I need to know you're safe, Nell. I won't lose you.'

And suddenly she got it, understood things from his point of view. He had lost so much already. This was his second chance; one he had thought he wasn't going to get. The weight of that slammed hard in her chest and, in that moment, she understood the depth of her own feelings, realised she had fallen head over heels in love with him.

She turned in his arms, hugging him tightly. 'You won't lose me. No more running off, I promise.'

They picked up Teddy and Sasha on the way back to the guest-house. It had been Nell's idea they come along, saying she wanted the canine company. Alex wasn't sure Michael would be happy having them running amok in the place he was renovating, but he agreed anyway, liking that Nell wanted to include his dogs. With both of them sat in the back of the Jeep, seeming delighted to be along for the ride, Teddy's big shaggy head poking out of the window, they stopped off to collect pizza, both hungry and neither wanting to cook. As Alex pulled into the driveway of the guesthouse, he was surprised to see Pete Moorhouse's truck still there.

'He works harder than your brother does,' he quipped, killing the ignition.

'I'll tell Michael you said that,' Nell warned, stifling a smirk.

Another engine sounded on the road behind them, head-lights beaming brightly as the car turned into the drive and pulled to a halt behind the Jeep.

Luke climbed out; concern etched on his face. 'I heard about what happened.' He wore one of his expensive suits and looked as though he had come from the office.

'News travels quickly,' Nell commented dryly, lifting the pizza box out of Teddy's reach as he made a lunge for it. 'Michael, I'm guessing.'

Alex had updated both Michael and Newt from East Haven, figuring word would quickly spread and it was better for Michael to hear what had happened from him first. As expected, Michael had blown a gasket. Alex didn't blame him as he had been pretty mad at Nell himself.

'I got a text from Newt. Are you okay?'

'I'm fine, honestly, but thank you for asking. How come you're out this way? You didn't drive all the way up here just to check on me, did you?'

'I was over at Bob Pilgrim's place when I got Newt's message, so I thought I'd stop by, see if there was anything I could do.'

'I'm all good. But thank you.'

'You want to come in for a coffee or beer?' Alex offered.

'Actually, I'm beat,' Nell interrupted. 'I just want a soak in the tub, some pizza and a glass of wine.' She slipped her free arm around Alex's waist and looked at Luke. 'I hope you don't mind.'

Luke hesitated, the smile he gave was a little tight around the edges, which had Alex narrowing his eyes, wondering what he had missed. 'No, of course I don't. You've had a shock.' He lingered for a moment, seeming reluctant to leave. 'I see you already have company anyway.'

Nell glanced at the work truck. 'Did Newt not tell you Pete Moorhouse is helping us out while Michael is in the hospital?'

'No, he didn't. I assumed work would be postponed until Michael had recovered.'

'Pete insisted on helping. I can't believe how sweet he is giving up his time like this.'

'Yeah, it's nice of him. He's a good guy.' Luke hesitated. 'Well, if you're sure there's nothing I can do.'

'There's nothing. We're fine, honest.'

He was offered a reprieve when the front door opened and Pete Moorhouse stepped out, his expression troubled.

'You okay, Pete?'

'Chief Cutler, you need to come inside. There's something you should see.'

Alex exchanged a look with Nell. When she shrugged, he turned and followed Pete into the house. He heard footsteps and paws following.

'What is it, Pete?'

Moorhouse led them down the hallway, walking quickly as though worried whatever he needed to show them might disappear.

'We've been working on pulling up the conservatory floor. It's where Michael wants to put the pool. We got the concrete up and figured we may as well get a start on the digging. Well, we, uh...'

'What is it?' Alex repeated, keeping his tone patient. The man was spooked.

'I think it's probably best if we show you.'

He took them through into the conservatory, where his two men had downed tools and were waiting. Alex recognised Jeff Hooper and Kevin McKinnon, noted both wore similarly shocked expressions.

'It's down there,' Pete pointed to a mound of freshly dug earth.

'Jeff thought it was stones at first.'

Teddy eased his nose into Alex's hand, whining, and Alex gently pushed him away, grateful when Nell caught hold of his collar, keeping him back. He climbed down into the wide hole the men had created.

'What is it?' Nell asked. There was a note of apprehension in her voice.

Alex didn't answer straightaway, recognising the skull lying part buried in the soil as human. He got down onto his haunches, brushed dirt away to reveal more bones.

'Alex, what is it?' This time it was Luke asking.

He glanced up at Pete, ignoring the question. 'You say you just uncovered this?'

'Yeah, not even five minutes ago.'

Brushing his palms on his jeans, Alex stood up, looked at Nell and gave a tight smile.

'We're gonna have to put a hold on that pizza.'

Nell had turned white when she had seen the skeleton. Alex had tried to stop her looking, but she had pushed past him, needing to see for herself. Luke guessed it was a lot for her to take in learning a body was buried under the floor of the house she was living in.

Alex had acted quickly, clearing the scene and calling for backup, before ushering the group into the kitchen, asking them to wait in there.

Nell made coffee for everyone, though left hers untouched, and she refused to sit despite Luke's best efforts to get her to slow down.

'It's a lot to take in and you're probably already in shock from everything that happened earlier,' he told her gently, rubbing his hand on her arm, irritated when she pulled away.

'I'm fine,' she snapped, before softening her tone slightly. 'I would rather keep busy.'

He watched her find a bowl, filling it with water for the dogs, and told himself the slight was nothing personal. She had been through a lot the last couple of days, learning that Curtis had killed Lizzie. Now the car accident and this. Still he found it frustrating that she wouldn't settle down or let him touch her.

Jeff sat quietly, his pallor grey, though he was trying to put a brave face on the situation, while Kevin whined continually about needing to get home as his girlfriend was coming over.

Luke listened to his grumbling while clenching and unclenching his fist, wishing he could punch it into Kevin's nose and shut him up. From the look on Pete's face, he was having similar thoughts.

'Text her,' he had suggested, sharply. 'I'm sure she will understand.'

Luke could tell Kevin didn't like Pete's idea, probably because then he wouldn't have anything to whine about. He shut up momentarily before locking his eyes on the pizza box sat on the counter. 'Is anyone going to eat that?'

Nell didn't even bother looking at him, fetching a plate and shoving it in his direction. 'Help yourself.'

Kevin glanced around the group, looking sheepish. 'Anyone else?'

When no-one replied, he pulled the box towards him and started tucking in. Teddy moved to sit beside him, staring up longingly and growing frustrated when he was ignored.

It was too crowded in the damn kitchen, Sasha slurping water from the bowl, Teddy whimpering over the pizza, Jeff clearing his throat every few minutes, trying his best to be discreet, but becoming more irritating each time he did it, and Kevin cramming pizza into his mouth, sounding more disgusting than a pig. Luke actually preferred it when he had been whining. And then there was Nell, wired and pacing. He needed her to be still, needed some calm and quiet in the room so he could take everything in. After a busy day working and now this, was it too much to want some downtime, to be alone with his thoughts?

Tommy Dolan and Dwight Halloran had both arrived within fifteen minutes of Alex's call, accompanied by Violet Marsden. Tommy hadn't missed the opportunity to scowl in Luke's direction as they made eye contact and then he was gone, locked away in the conservatory with Alex, Dwight and Violet, leaving the others to wait.

It was forty minutes later when Alex eventually came through to the kitchen. He wore a scowl, peeling off latex gloves and tossing them in the trash, before accepting the coffee Nell poured for him.

'I want you to take Sasha and Teddy and go back to my place,' he told her quietly.

'I can wait here with you.'

'I'm gonna be a while. Luke will give you a lift home.' Alex shot a look at Luke. 'That okay?'

'Yeah, of course it is. No problem.'

Nell looked like she was going to argue the point.

'This place is a crime scene and I'd rather know you are safe out of the way. Go pour that glass of wine, try and get some rest. I'll be home as soon as I can.'

She had pouted a little at Alex, but reluctantly agreed, disappearing upstairs to throw a few things into an overnight bag.

'Is she okay?'

Alex shot Luke a look. 'She was in a car crash, terrorised by a guy with a knife, and now she's come home to find a dead body in the house. Would you be okay?'

Luke must have looked visibly shocked, because Alex immediately softened his tone. 'I'm sorry, that was unnecessary,' he apologised, raking his hand back into his hair. He looked tired. 'It's been a hell of a day. She's holding up, but I don't think she can take too much more. Thanks for agreeing to give her and the dogs a ride.'

'It's not a problem. Anything I can do to help.' Luke was aware his words were a little stiff, but he was still bristling, despite Alex's apology. 'I expect she's going to be feeling sore in the morning,' he added, trying to push past it. Seeing Nell with Alex should be getting easier, but it wasn't, and that probably wasn't helped by Nell's coolness towards him, which he suspected had nothing to do with the day's events.

'Yeah, she will.'

'You think this guy with the knife was personally harassing her or was it a case of wrong place, wrong time?'

Alex cut him another look, ignored the question. 'I'm just glad another car showed up when it did and got her out of there.'

He was just being cagey because it was an active investigation.

Luke tried to ignore the slight. 'Yes, I bet Nell was relieved when the woman stopped. I can't imagine how scary it must have been for her. You know I can stay with her tonight. I don't mind keeping her company.'

Something passed over Alex's face, suspicion, annoyance, realisation, and he narrowed his eyes.

Luke's heartbeat quickened.

He knows how I feel about Nell.

It was stupid. He was tired and reading too much into the reaction. It was an innocent offer and there was no way Alex could pick up from it that Luke wanted his girlfriend.

'That's not necessary.' Nell's voice had both men looking up, to where she stood halfway up the stairs, a canvas bag in her hand. She smiled stiffly. 'I just want some time to myself. It's been a long day.'

'Of course,' Luke agreed lightly. 'I can just drop you off and make sure you're safe, if that's what you want.'

'Actually, on second thoughts I think I'm going to head home for a quick shower and a change of clothes. I'll take Nell myself.' Alex's tone gave nothing away. 'There's no need for you to wait about. You might as well go home too.'

'Are you sure? I don't mind.'

'I'm sure.'

Luke glanced from Nell, who looked relieved, and back to Alex, his expression unreadable, and a queasy feeling rose in his belly. He had always been so good at covering his true feelings, at painting on a mask, having learned from a young age it was the only way he would survive life with his grandmother, but somehow the mask had slipped and Alex had figured out how he truly felt about Nell.

They had been friends for the last five years. How would this affect things between them going forward? Would Alex tell Michael and Newt?

He had driven home, his head pounding as he replayed the scene in his head. Nell knew and now Alex had figured it out too. How was he going to fix this?

When he arrived home, he went straight to the cupboard where he kept the Jim Beam, poured himself a large measure and downed the drink in one. The alcohol burned his throat, put welcome fire in his belly, and he refilled the glass, still reeling from the shock of the past two hours.

He couldn't stop thinking about the body that had been uncovered at the guesthouse, how cool Nell had been towards him, and the look Alex had given him before he had left. And yet Nell still consumed his thoughts and he wanted to know how she tasted, how her flesh would feel beneath his fingertips, how she would react to the things he longed to do to her. The fact she had cooled towards him made him want her even more, and he cursed himself, aware that he could have very well just lost Alex's friendship.

He had drained his second glass when his phone rang, jarring him to his senses.

'Hello?' Luke didn't recognise the number and figured it could be a work call.

'Is this Luke Trainor?'

'Speaking.' He scrubbed a hand over his face, trying to shake off where the alcohol was already blurring the edges. 'How may I help you?'

'My name is Doctor Karen Lockwood. I was wondering if Stacey Monroe is with you.'

Luke squeezed the bridge of his nose between his thumb and forefinger, the reminder of Stacey conjuring unpleasant memories.

'I'm afraid she isn't. You said doctor, right?'

'That's correct. I'm sorry to be calling you so late, but I'm worried about Stacey.'

'Why? What has she done?' Luke asked dubiously.

'She hasn't shown up to her last three appointments.'

'Okay.' Luke was silent for a moment. 'I didn't realise she was seeing a doctor. Is everything all right?'

'Forgive me, Mr Trainor. Your number was down as her emergency contact. I didn't realise though that she hasn't spoken to you about our sessions. Perhaps you could ask her to call me?'

Sessions? Why had Stacey been seeing a doctor for sessions?

'We broke up,' he said abruptly. 'She moved out.'

There was a pause. 'Oh, I'm sorry.'

'What kind of doctor are you? Why is she seeing you?'

'I'm sorry, Mr Trainor. I can't discuss Miss Monroe's case with you. Doctor and client confidentiality.' Karen Lockwood was quick to end the call, thanking him for his time and apologising for disturbing him.

Luke immediately googled her name, curious to know what kind of doctor Stacey was seeing. He found her straightaway, an attractive older blonde who might have been his type if she had been twenty years younger. He read a couple of articles on her, curious to know why Stacey had been seeing a psychiatrist. He noted Doctor Lockwood specialised in anger management; Stacey had been prone to unreasonable fits of rage and jealously. It was what had driven them apart. Had she been seeking help for it?

He poured a third glass of the Jim Beam and then a fourth, before he stumbled through to the bedroom, pulling off his shirt and pants, dumping them on the easy chair in the corner of the room, and crawling into bed.

The alcohol was meant to numb, but there was so much raging in his head right now: the currently inaccessible Nell – not being able to have her was driving him crazy; then there was the discovery of the body at the guesthouse, something he couldn't manage to shake from his mind; and now Stacey and her doctor. Why had Stacey been seeing a doctor and why the hell, when he was trying his best to get past her, did he keep being reminded she was gone? Luke had worked so hard to build this life for himself and he felt like it was slowly being taken away from him, despite his best efforts to make things work out for the best. He knew he probably shouldn't have had the alcohol, that it would have been wise to keep a clear head, but for now he needed numbness to quieten the thoughts in his head. He would figure things out in the morning.

He had barely drifted off to sleep when he felt a dip in the mattress behind him and for a moment in his dreams, he believed it could be Nell. He felt fingers run up the back of his neck into his hair and he rolled over, startled as someone climbed on top of him, pinning him to the bed.

Luke sucked in a breath, pain searing through the shoulder where he had been shot. As he struggled to fully focus, long hair trailed across his face.

'Surprise.'

Luke sucked in a breath, recognising Stacey's voice. She had gone, she had left him. What the hell was she doing back here?

'Stacey, what are you doing?'

'I missed you.'

'You missed me?' He felt his heartbeat quicken, recalling his conversation with her doctor. Stacey hadn't been attending her sessions she had said.

A week ago he might have been relieved to have her back. He had missed her so much and had nothing but regret for the way things had ended. But time had passed and he had reflected, come to terms with the fact she was gone forever, had moved his attentions on to Nell. This wasn't good.

'Stacey, you can't be here. You need to go.'

'Why? Is there another woman warming your bed?'

There it was: the jealous streak that had driven a rift between them.

'Why were you seeing a doctor?' he blurted, needing to know.

'That is none of your business.'

'She's a psychiatrist. What were your sessions about?'

'I told you it's none of your business,' Stacey repeated more heatedly. 'If you cared you would have paid more attention when I was here.'

'You're here now.'

'That's to torment you.' She linked hands with him, pinning his arms above his head, and leaning down to kiss him, trying to slide her tongue into his mouth.

Luke tried to resist, eventually yielding, and to his annoyance felt himself grow hard. He kissed her back deeply, her perfume clouding his senses and lust taking over from the anger he felt. For a moment it was perfect, then Stacey bit his tongue hard and he yelped, pulling back, pushing her off him as he tasted blood.

'What the fuck is wrong with you?'

'What is wrong with me?' She laughed incredulously. 'Sweetheart, look closer to home. You're the one who broke us. You made me this way.'

'So why the hell are you back? Just go? Leave me alone.'

'Leave you alone?' Stacey shook her head, her eyes dark and her smile malicious. 'Oh, Luke. You don't get to have it that easy. I'm not going anywhere.'

37

Caleb arrived in New York late Thursday afternoon, checking into his suite at the Four Seasons before going out to dinner with friends. It was supposed to be a vacation after all, to get over his break-up, and he needed to be seen in public.

He took his group to one of his favourite restaurants, ordering several bottles of champagne and tipping generously, before heading on to a club. Caleb made sure his friends had a good time, that they were seen by lots of people, buying drinks for everyone he talked to throughout the night, though he was careful to make sure he himself stayed sober, was aware he needed to be up early the following morning and that he had a lot to do.

He sloped back to the hotel around two thirty with two call girls, a voluptuous redhead and a skinny Asian chick, who had arrived at the club courtesy of an old friend. After indulging in a threesome, he left them to snort coke and watch TV, and retired to the master bedroom where he had a fitful night's sleep. They were both out of it and sprawled on the couch when he left the following morning, discreetly heading out of the hotel wearing a baseball cap, jeans and a lumberjack shirt, different and low-key to his usual sharp suits. He met his friend, Jimmy Rubenstein, who had supplied the two call girls, over coffee in a downtown diner. Jimmy was a fixer and the pair of them went way back. Caleb knew he could count on his friend to be discreet and ask no questions, and he gladly handed over an envelope of cash in exchange for the sports bag he knew would contain the unmarked revolver and the other items he had asked for, plus the set of car keys.

'Dark blue Volvo, parked in the bay across the street,' Jimmy told him.

'The girls will stay put, they won't leave the hotel?' Caleb checked, wanting reassurance. They were going to be his alibi and he needed to be sure they didn't fuck this up.

'They know the score. The suite is theirs and they can order as much room service as they like on your tab, but they mustn't leave, mustn't let on to anyone that you're not there.'

Satisfied everything was in order Caleb downed the rest of his coffee, thanked Jimmy, and got up to leave.

'Good luck, my friend. Give me a call if you need anything else.'

Jimmy didn't know Caleb's plans and was smart enough not to involve himself in his client's business. He was just the yes man, getting people what they needed at the right price.

The Volvo wouldn't be Caleb's preferred mode of transport, but he had to admit it was perfect for the job. It was subtle, easily blending in, and not obviously recognisable, and it had a generous sized trunk. As he made his way across the state line from Massachusetts into New Hampshire, he felt confident everything was going to plan.

It was a little after three when he stopped at the Meredith residence, needing to pay for the cabin and collect the key, and he spent a moment in the car donning sunglasses and pulling his cap low, careful to conceal his identity.

He needn't have worried. Dolores Meredith, who owned the cabin, was in her late seventies at least, possibly older, and from what he could tell, the thick-rimmed bottleneck glasses she wore did little to help her sight. He paid cash, took the key and set of directions she gave him, aware she seemed thrilled he had rented the cabin.

He got the impression she didn't have many people interested in it and wondered what kind of hellhole he was about to walk into. With a pit stop at a local convenience store to pick up basic supplies, he drove the rest of the way out to the cabin, turning off the main road and following dirt track lanes for a good twenty minutes before he laid eyes on the place.

It was perfect, standing alone in the woods and miles from anywhere.

Tired from driving, Caleb heaved his overnight bag and the sports bag from the trunk of the car, unlocked the door to the cabin and stepped inside.

The place was basic with no heating, a sparse and antiquated kitchen, and only one cold water tap, but it would serve its purpose and there was something homely and rustic about the wooden beams and the various animal heads adorning the walls. He assumed Dolores and her husband had been hunters in their day and the cabin had mostly been for their personal use. There were three rooms, the open plan kitchen cum diner cum living room forming one large area downstairs, while upstairs was one generous sized bedroom with a bathroom that had seen better days.

Caleb dumped the bags on the bed before heading downstairs to fetch the groceries from the car. He made coffee using the kerosene stove then sat out on the porch, watching as the sun started to set, and drank two cups before returning upstairs and emptying the contents of the sports bag on the bed.

Jimmy had come through for him, as he always did, and everything he had asked for was there, including the unmarked gun and box of ammo. He put them to one side, starting a pile of items he would need to take with him in the morning. A little bottle sat in the middle of a coil of rope. It was filled with clear liquid and he picked it up, uncapping the lid and sniffing. The contents were odourless, the bottle unmarked, and Caleb wasn't sure what it was, but Jimmy had assured him it would do the trick, had told him one syringe full would knock a grown man out in two to three minutes and keep him under for at least an hour. He rummaged through the items on the bed, found the syringe and added both to the pile.

An hour should be enough time to get Nell off the island, but he couldn't risk her waking up on the ferry. Knowing he would have to suitably restrain her he added a couple of pairs of cuffs and duct tape to the growing pile. Once he was certain he had everything he needed for his trip he put the items back in the sports bag, zipped it up and set it at the foot of the bed ready to grab the following morning, scooping the remaining items up and sitting them on an old wooden dresser.

He peered out of the bedroom window, the sight of never-ending trees pleasing him. Out here, far from civilisation, he would have the precious time alone he needed with Nell to see if their relationship could be saved, and with no other distractions she would have little choice but to hear him out. She would have to understand that she had betrayed him terribly and she would have to be punished, but he was a fair man and once he had taught her a lesson, he was prepared to give her a final chance. He hoped and prayed she would eventually see sense and realise they were supposed to be together. Understand that he couldn't live without her.

Confident he was prepared both mentally and physically for the task ahead, he made another cup of coffee, settled down to eat the sandwich he had earlier purchased, then hit the sack wanting to get another good night's sleep ahead of his reunion with Nell.

This time tomorrow night she would be here with him, back where she belonged.

38

2005

Sarah Treadwell made the decision to move to Purity Island the day her divorce papers came through. Knowing she needed to have a fresh start, she had studied her map, considered a number of places, throwing up arguments against each one before finally settling on Purity, where she remembered visiting as a kid on a family vacation.

The place held fond memories and, even though the vacation had only lasted a week, she clearly recalled the bright boats bobbing on the water, the vast expanse of sand where she had built castles with her father and strolling along the marina eating double-scoop ice cream cones. While she wasn't fool enough to believe the place was as good as her memories allowed her to believe, she desperately needed to get away and she knew Purity Island would offer her the chance of a fresh start.

The place was smaller than she remembered, but she guessed everything seemed bigger when you were looking at it through a child's eyes. It seemed comfortingly familiar though, even if it was years since she had been there. She took time reacquainting herself, checking into a cheap hotel, walking along the marina, paddling in the surf, enjoying her first weekend, knowing that by Monday she would need to find both a job and somewhere to live.

The two came to her as a package.

Sarah had exhausted the main street and marina, asking in the bars and restaurants if anyone was hiring before approaching store owners. Most places had already hired for the summer and she was worried she had left it too late, that perhaps she wouldn't find anything, when she entered the little bookstore at the end of the main road.

She enquired politely, her smile that had started the day so bright and earnest now wilting, expecting a no before the woman behind the counter had spoken. She was already learning from the way people looked at her as she asked, that they were readying themselves to deliver bad news.

The 'no' came and, confidence ebbing, Sarah thanked her before turning to leave the store.

'Wait a moment. Bella, didn't you say your help had fallen through?'

Sarah glanced up, spotting the middle-aged blonde woman who looked over at the counter clerk.

'You mean Daphne? She quit on me last week.'

'This lady here is looking for work.'

Bella gave Sarah an appraising look. 'Have you ever worked in a hotel before?'

'No,' Sarah admitted. 'But I'm a fast learner.'

'It would involve mucking in. We're a small guesthouse, so it's all hands on deck.'

'I'd be happy with that.'

'It's sometimes long hours, hard work. One day you might be cooking and serving guests in the restaurant, the next you might be cleaning windows and scrubbing out toilets.'

'I'm not shy of hard work or getting my hands dirty.'

'Where have you worked previously?'

'I just left my job in Richmond. I was a legal secretary.' At Bella's raised brow, she quickly added, 'But I worked in a bar all through college and I've waitressed before.'

'You're new to the island?'

'I arrived a couple of days ago.'

'Why here? What brought you to Purity?' Bella was direct, blunt almost, but Sarah didn't mind, preferring to know where she stood with people.

'I've just got divorced and I need to make a fresh start. This seems like a good place to do it.'

Bella studied her. 'What's your name?'

'Sarah. Sarah Treadwell.'

'I can give you a room at the guesthouse, and meals, twenty-five per cent off your salary. I will need details of your former employer for reference purposes and I'll warn you now, I can only offer summer work. We don't get many guests once the tourists have gone, so you would need to find something else come end of September.'

'Okay, that's fair enough.'

'You drive a stick?'

'Yes, ma'am.'

'Good. And it's Bella.'

'Okay, Bella.'

'Why don't you come on up to the guesthouse tomorrow and I'll show you around. We can both be sure you're the right fit.' She gave Sarah the address and directions.

'So, did he cheat on you?'

Sarah's mouth gaped at the directness of the question. 'Yes,' she said, finally finding her words. 'With my best friend.'

'Asshole. Men – trust me, you're better off without them.'

Sarah had fallen in love with the place the first time she saw it, set back from the clifftop, nestled amidst pine trees and approached by a steep driveway that overlooked a more rugged part of the coastline. It was perfect.

Within two months of living there she felt like part of the family. Bella had a sixteen-year-old son, Clarke, and Sarah bonded with him quickly, soon learning he was a gentle giant, incredibly intelligent, but socially awkward. He had kind eyes and a big heart, and, after some initial wariness, he welcomed her into his home, as did his mother. Bella was a straight talker, but one of the least judgmental people Sarah had ever met. She proved to be a fair boss and gradually became a friend. Sarah was true to her word, putting in long hours and working her butt off to help keep things running smoothly, and for the first few weeks she was the happiest she had been in a long time.

It was while she was food shopping that she first ran into Luke Trainor.

She had just left the store and was making her way back to the car when the bag split, and her groceries spilt everywhere. Flustered, she had quickly bent to retrieve the lost items and he had suddenly been there, helping her scoop everything up and fixing her with a wide grin, his striking blue eyes intent on hers.

'Thank you.'

'You're welcome. It's Sarah, right?'

'It is,' she confirmed, amused everyone seemed to know who she was. Beauty of living on a small island, she guessed.

'I'm Luke.' He offered his hand and held on a second longer than necessary. 'It's nice to meet you, Sarah.'

He insisted on helping her carry the groceries to Bella's car, winked at her as she pulled away, making her grin like a loon on the drive back to the guesthouse. She had received a fair amount of male attention since arriving on Purity Island, guessed maybe the fact she was getting her confidence back may be behind it.

Luke Trainor was the first man to flirt with her though, who she wanted to reciprocate with. Therefore, it embarrassed her when she learned from Bella, later on that evening, that he was only eighteen, having just graduated high school.

He had looked older and, although eighteen wasn't breaking any laws, flirting with a kid who wasn't yet even in college felt wrong.

The age gap didn't appear to bother Luke and it seemed from that moment on he was everywhere she was, trying to get her attention, flirting outrageously with her and trying to charm her into a date.

Sarah had laid her cards on the table with him, told him she was uncomfortable with the age difference, that the flirting was going nowhere. He had smiled and agreed, made a joke about how he would keep pushing his luck and he would get a kiss out of her before he left for college. She played along. It was all harmless fun and she had no intention of letting him get his way, especially when she learned he had a girlfriend.

It had never occurred to her he might be involved with someone and it sat uncomfortably with her, especially after she had been cheated on herself. She made a point of cooling her friendship with Luke after that point, avoiding places she knew he might be, even changing the times she did the grocery trip.

Even though nothing had happened between them, never would happen, she would not be responsible for hurting his girlfriend. Her plan seemed to work, and the rest of the summer passed without incident.

As September arrived and the guests dwindled, Sarah began hunting for a new job. Bella offered her a brief reprieve when the hospital appointment she had been waiting for came through. As the timing clashed with the scheduled building of the new conservatory, she asked Sarah to stay on while she was away, to keep an eye on things and look after Clarke.

It was a couple of days after Bella had gone into hospital that Sarah left the grocery store to find the car wouldn't start. She had been fishing in her purse for her phone to find a number for the local garage, when Luke had appeared, coming to her rescue. Although she had been avoiding him, she had to admit she was grateful when he looked at the engine for her.

'I'll give you a ride home,' he told her when he couldn't get it started.

'You don't have to do that. I can wait for the mechanic.'

'The mechanic could be hours. Haven't you got stuff that needs to be refrigerated?'

He had a point. She couldn't risk the food she had bought spoiling. 'Well, I guess okay then.'

Luke had grinned like a Cheshire cat and warily she had transferred her groceries to his car and climbed into the passenger seat.

She told herself to stop being stupid. He was helping her out and she would have been in a muddle if he hadn't have shown up. He was giving her a ride and it was in no way a betrayal of his girlfriend.

And she was right; it had been an innocent ride home. He had joked with her, making her laugh and talked about his plans for college. As they pulled up in the driveway of the guesthouse, Sarah had relaxed and was annoyed she had overreacted.

But then he had leant over, catching her off guard as she turned to thank him and to say goodbye, and he had kissed her, snaking his hand into her hair and holding on tight when she tried to break away.

Eventually he released her, and Sarah pulled away, shocked.

'What the hell are you doing?'

'Kissing you.' He grinned. 'I told you I would before I left for college.'

'You have a girlfriend.'

'Jenna?' He looked a little surprised it was a problem. 'I'm about to break-up with her. We've been coasting along for far too long and now I'm off to college...' He trailed off, seeming distracted for a moment. 'I should have ended it a while back, but you know how it is, these things are never easy to do.'

Sarah stared at him for a moment, still reeling that he had kissed her and feeling sorry for Jenna that she had such a shit of a boyfriend, that he would disrespect her like that.

'I have to go.'

'I'll help you with the groceries.'

'Don't bother. I've got them.'

Luke started to get out of the car anyway, but then the front door opened and Clarke ambled out. 'Hey, Sarah, you're back. Hey, Luke, how are you?'

'Fine.' Luke scowled at Clarke and slammed his door shut. He waited, and Sarah was aware of him watching her as Clarke helped her with the groceries. Without glancing back at him she kicked the door shut.

She kept herself busy in the house that evening and the following day, not wanting to venture out for fear of running into Luke. He would be gone to college soon and at least the problem would have removed itself.

Tommy showed up later that afternoon. He had been staying at the guesthouse as company for Clarke. 'How are you?' he asked, finding her in the kitchen where she was busy scrubbing the floor. 'You seemed a little sad when I saw you this morning.'

Sarah glanced up, surprised a teenage boy would have picked up on her emotions. 'I'm okay. Nothing for you to worry about.' She wondered if Clarke had said anything to him about seeing her with Luke.

'Well, I brought you these. My friend baked them earlier.'

Sarah glanced at the box of brownies. 'That's sweet, but they're yours.'

'I've already had about six. I can't eat anymore. Please help me out.' When she hesitated, he smiled. 'Tell you what, I'll leave them on the counter, and you can help yourself if you change your mind.'

'Okay, thank you.'

She indulged in a couple of brownies with a cup of coffee that afternoon while taking a break from housework. It wasn't until about an hour later she started to get belly cramps, but she didn't connect it to the brownies, assuming maybe she was getting her period early.

The cramps grew in intensity and another hour passed before she decided to give up on cleaning. She had one more load of washing to collect from the machine then she would go and lie down. Tommy and Clarke had a friend over. She had heard them answer the door a while ago and knew they were upstairs, no doubt playing video games. She would take a break while they were busy, before starting dinner.

Not that she thought she would be able to eat anything as the pains in her stomach seemed to be getting worse. Maybe it wasn't period cramps and she was coming down with a bug.

She hit the light to the basement laundry room, descended the stairs and switched off the machine, keen to stop the annoying beep. As she opened the door and started to pile damp clothes into the basket, she heard a click behind her, then the sound of footsteps.

Sarah started to turn, felt someone grab her from behind. Startled, she screamed, but the sound was muffled as a hand clamped over her mouth.

'Hush.' The voice brushed against her ear as a gleam of silver flashed in front of her and something sharp pressed against her throat. 'We don't want to disturb the kids.'

39

'Was everything okay with Luke tonight?' Alex asked, his tone deceptively casual as he started the engine.

Nell thought back to the time they had spent waiting in the kitchen. She knew Luke wanted her, was aware at some point she would have to broach the subject with him, tell him she didn't feel the same way, but tonight hadn't been the right time.

And it wasn't anything she needed to involve Alex in. She knew Luke was his friend and didn't want to cause a rift between them. Luke might have feelings for her, but he hadn't acted on them. Although she felt uncomfortable around him and knew they needed to clear the air, he was still a nice guy and she didn't want to hurt him.

'Yes, of course,' she lied. 'Why?'

'You seemed uncomfortable around him and you pretty much balked at the idea when I asked him to give you a ride home.'

Had she been that obvious?

It would explain what had happened between them while she had been upstairs because Alex had abruptly changed his mind about Luke giving her a ride home, leaving the crime scene to take her himself. He had been cagey with her about it though and she had known there was more than he was letting on.

'I'm fine, Luke is fine. I'm just tired and jumpy, and I didn't want to leave you.'

'Did you guys talk about what happened on the mainland today at all?'

'No, I think we were both too shell-shocked by tonight.'

Alex had seemed satisfied with that, dropping her off at his place, checking all of the locks were secure and she had her cell phone close by, before heading back to the guesthouse. Although Nell understood why he was being over-cautious, it did nothing to soothe her already frazzled nerves. She drew all of the blinds before pouring a large glass of wine and curling up on the couch, jumping at every little sound, knowing it was going to be a long night.

Tommy didn't arrive home until two in the morning, physically exhausted, but his mind far too alert to sleep.

He had lived in fear this day would come eventually and had spent the last twelve years bitterly regretting what had happened, wishing they had called the police the night Sarah had died. He was still angry he had allowed himself to be talked into covering her death up.

Sure, there would have been consequences, but nothing like the shitstorm that was about to unfold. They had been stupid kids, knew nothing about covering their tracks, and burying all of Sarah's belongings in a suitcase beside her meant she had already been identified. It would be a day, maybe two if they were lucky, before Alex started to connect the dots.

Tommy had worked the crime scene, saying little, part of

him wanting to confess, to get it over with, but the words wouldn't come. Instead he dutifully followed instruction, feeling numb as Sarah's skeleton was removed from the grave they had made for her, helped bag the items he had long ago helped pack in the suitcase, all the time thinking about his parents and his sister, and how disappointed they were going to be when they learned the truth. Alex had cut him a glance when he had looked at Sarah's driver's licence, and, although he hadn't said anything, Tommy recalled pretending that he hadn't known her. He could tell that Alex knew it was a lie.

As he drove home it occurred to him that he could pack up his things and leave the island, get away before he was found out, but he was smart enough to know it would never work out. He would get caught eventually. Running away would only make things worse.

He called Jenna from the car, figuring he should warn her that Sarah's body had been found.

She was already in a mess and still trying to come to terms with the news that Curtis had been charged with Lizzie Kent's murder. The discovery of Sarah's body just about tipped her over the edge.

'Oh my God, Tommy, what are we going to do?'

'I think we should turn ourselves in.'

'Are you crazy? We'll go to jail.'

'I don't see where we have a choice. Maybe the courts will go easy on us. We were just kids at the time.'

Jenna started to cry. 'I can't go to jail, Tommy. I can't. After everything else that has happened, I really don't need this. You have to make it go away.'

'We killed a girl.'

'It was an accident.'

'It was a prank and it went wrong. We buried her, Jenna. We

hid her body and made it look like she took off. We have to pay for that.'

'I can't.'

'Look, I'll call you tomorrow.'

Tommy ended the call before she could protest, not in the mood for her whining and self-pity. He had loved Jenna once, but now he found her self-obsessed and pathetic. He had thrown his life away to help her that night and all she could focus on was her own fate. What he would give to go back and redo things. He would have refused to go along with her stupid prank and never would have found himself in a position where he was helping to get rid of a body.

He cursed Nell O'Connor too, wished to hell she had never come back to Purity Island. If Clarke had still been alive and living in the guesthouse, everything would have been okay, but instead Nell had returned and started renovating the place. She was going to be the one responsible for destroying his life a second time round and he wished to hell he had never laid eyes on her.

Nell had been unable to sleep after Alex dropped her off. She was still trying to come to terms with Curtis killing Lizzie, and today had brought fresh shock.

The skeleton that had been found at the guesthouse threw up a dozen new questions and, as she sipped at her wine, the alcohol soothing her frazzled mind, easing knots in her neck and shoulders that were there partly due to her accident, partly from tension, niggling doubts ate away at her over the identity of the bones and whether Aunt Bella had anything to do with it. She dismissed the idea almost as quickly as she thought of it, feeling terrible for even considering it, knowing her aunt had

had a heart of gold and couldn't possibly be capable of such a thing.

She was beginning to feel like she was a curse for this island. Lizzie had died because she had covered a babysitting shift for Nell. Now she was back and bodies seemed to be cropping up everywhere. Was it possible the skeleton under the house was connected to the serial killer case Alex was investigating? Probably not. Penelope Maher's killer was active now and favoured dumping the remains of his victims at sea, while the body under the house could be years old and hadn't been dismembered. Weren't serial killers supposed to use the same method?

Shivering, not sure if it was the temperature or thinking about serial killers, she finished her wine and double-checked all of the doors and windows, before swapping her empty glass for a bottle of water and heading upstairs.

Although she closed her eyes and attempted to sleep, her mind wouldn't shut down; every tiny sound had her on edge. Her mind was awash with images of her car crash, the masked man standing in the woods, and then Pete Moorhouse's face when he had come outside to tell them about the body under the conservatory floor. She remained on edge all night, relieved when Alex finally arrived home.

'You're still awake?' he questioned when she propped herself up on one elbow as he slipped into bed beside her.

'I've got too much going on in my head to sleep. I can't stop thinking about Lizzie, then there's everything that happened today, and now there's a body buried beneath the guesthouse. It's too much. I keep thinking that if I hadn't come back then none of this would have happened.'

'You can't think like that. If Curtis hadn't attacked you yesterday, we wouldn't have taken his prints. You played a part in catching him, Nell. I know you blame yourself for what happened to Lizzie, but it was Curtis who killed her and it's thanks to you that her family will finally have some peace.'

Nell was silent for a moment. 'I guess, but how could we not have known? And what about tonight? I've been living in a house with a body buried under it. Will you be able to identify who it is?'

'We already have. There was a suitcase buried next to the body. It was full of clothes, a cell phone and driving licence.'

'It's Sarah Treadwell, isn't it?' Voicing her suspicions out loud sent a chill through her.

Alex nodded. 'I had my suspicions as soon as I saw the skeleton. Of course, it's unofficial. The ME will still have to formally identify the body, but it's her. Someone wanted all trace of her gone.'

'Do you think Bella was somehow involved in this?'

'It's too early to say what happened. When she disappeared, everyone assumed she had found a new job and moved away.'

'But she hadn't. She was murdered and buried under the house.'

Alex propped himself up to face her, the shadows of the dark room cutting across the lean planes and angles of his face. 'I want you to move in here. At least until Michael is out of the hospital. Hunter was right. Someone didn't want you in that house and now we know why.'

'You think whoever killed Sarah is the same person who's been harassing me?' Nell hadn't considered that possibility and it left her feeling sick. She thought of the man in the woods, the same man who had tried to get into the house. She had assumed he was trying to scare her, but maybe he did mean to hurt her?

He shot Luke. Of course he is trying to hurt you.

And Michael? Alex and Hunter had suspected he had been attacked by the same person.

'Yeah, I do, and I don't want you going back there alone.' He ran his hand gently down her arm. 'Okay?'

She drew out a shaky breath. 'Okay. I need to get more stuff though. I only brought an overnight bag.'

'I'll get someone to drive you up to the house tomorrow.'

'Thank you.'

Nell settled back down against the pillow and was silent for a moment, considering, as she stared up at the dark ceiling. Had she been watched from the moment she arrived back on the island? It was unnerving thinking of all the times she had been alone in the house in the first couple of weeks.

'Alex?'

'Yeah?'

'You're gonna get him, right?'

He slipped his arm around her, pulling her close, and she rested her head against his shoulder, breathing in his now familiar scent, her hand resting against the hard muscles of his chest. Beneath her palm she could feel the methodical rhythm of his heartbeat.

He turned slightly, pressed his lips against her forehead. 'Yeah, we're gonna get him, Nell. I promise.'

Jenna paced relentlessly after hanging up from Tommy, tears streaming down her face, fingers raking through her hair. She was shaking, felt sick, and she desperately wanted someone to come and save her.

She had tried to pay for what had happened to Sarah. Had taken her beatings from Curtis without complaint, accepting it was her penance for what had happened.

Now he was in jail, awaiting an appearance in the court-house for Lizzie Kent's murder, and she couldn't help but relate the two things, thinking that if he were here with her now then Sarah's body wouldn't have been discovered.

She couldn't go to jail, she just couldn't.

Eventually she grabbed her keys, got in her car and drove across town. It was the middle of the night, but she didn't care. Her world was falling apart, and he would have to see her.

He opened the door wearing just a pair of low riding sweatpants, rubbing at his eyes, suggesting she had awoken him, but unsurprised to see her on the front step. When he shrugged, turned and walked back down the hallway to the kitchen, she followed, closing the door behind her.

'What are we going to do?' she asked tearfully.

Despite the lateness of the hour, he pulled two glasses from a cabinet, filled them both with whiskey and handed her one. 'We're going to fix this. That's what we're gonna do.'

'How?'

He stared at her, his eyes hard. 'Leave that to me. Drink up.'

Jenna gulped down the whiskey and pushed her glass forward when he offered her more.

'I'm sorry,' she sobbed. 'I'm so sorry for all of it. I have done some terrible things. Please forgive me.'

He held her as she cried, before plying her with more drink. Eventually she passed out and he carried her out to her car, drove her across town, back to the house she shared with her husband.

Curtis might be in jail, but he was still quiet as he unlocked the door and carried Jenna inside. Her dog was waiting, tail wagging, and he spent a couple of moments making a fuss of the mutt. He found treats in a jar on the counter, put down a handful, aware a barking fit might alert the neighbours. While the dog ate, he carried Jenna upstairs, carefully undressed her, sat her in the bathtub and filled it with water. Leaving the faucets to run, he fetched a bottle of Curtis's bourbon, filled a glass half full and set it by the tub, then he found a razor in the medicine cabinet and used it to slice her wrists.

She remained unconscious throughout and, while that made things easier, he almost regretted that she hadn't woken; he would have liked to see the last struggle for life before he took it from her.

Leaving her bleeding in the tub he rummaged through her purse, found her lipstick, and crudely wrote across the mirror.

Tell Sarah I'm sorry.

With one last look in Jenna's direction, pity mixing with loathing for the pathetic creature she had become, he let himself out of the house.

It was all to play for now and only the strong would survive.

40

Alex had been right about the painkillers. When Nell awoke the following morning, she could barely move her neck and it took a couple of minutes before she managed to roll over in bed, pulling herself up into a sitting position.

'You okay?' he asked, stepping through into the bedroom, a towel wrapped around his waist, hair damp and curling from his shower.

She grunted, rubbing gingerly at her neck. 'Can you get me my painkillers? They're in my purse.' She didn't miss the look he gave her as he found them for her. 'And don't tell me you told me so. I felt okay last night.'

He sat on the bed beside her, green eyes intent on hers as he took her hand and dropped two pills into her palm. 'It was the adrenalin. Now it's worn off, your muscles have stiffened up.'

'Thank you, Doctor Cutler.' She uncapped her bottle of water and took a sip to wash down the pills.

Alex grinned and pressed a kiss against her forehead. He smelt fresh and citrusy from his shower and the scent jarred pleasantly with her senses. 'I'd take it easy today. Try and get some rest. I can always bring you some more stuff down from the guesthouse.'

'I'd rather go myself. It'd be easier.'

'Okay. I'll get someone to stop by this afternoon, give you a ride up there when we're done.'

He placed his hands on her shoulders and kneaded gently at the knots, and Nell closed her eyes. 'Hmm, that feels good. Don't go to work.'

'You know I have to. Someone has to catch the bad guys.'

'Yeah, I know. Purity Island, murder capital: who'd have thought, huh?'

He left her with Teddy and Sasha, making her promise to keep the doors locked and her cell phone close by, answer the door to no-one but him, and telling her he would have a patrol car drive past hourly. Nell had no issue with any of that, figuring she had experienced more than enough drama in the last twenty-four hours. She lounged around watching daytime TV, drank coffee then called her brother.

He already knew about the body at the guesthouse, word travelled quickly, and he seemed to be taking the news better than she had expected, probably because he knew she was out of harm's way and staying with Alex. He wasn't happy about her car accident though – and even less so about the man she had encountered in the woods – and she held her cell phone away when he started ranting at her for going over to the mainland unaccompanied.

Nell put him on loudspeaker, brewed a fresh pot of coffee and poked her head in the refrigerator, feeling hungry, only half listening to what he was saying.

'... So, do you promise then? Nell? NELL?'

'Huh? Yeah, okay. Sure.'

'Are you even listening to me?'

She closed the refrigerator door and scooped up her phone. 'Yes, of course I am.'

'So you won't then?'

'Won't what?'

'I knew you weren't listening. I don't want you going back up to the guesthouse.'

'I need to go up there, Michael. I left in a hurry last night and I have to get more stuff. Alex is going to send someone up there with me later though. You don't have to worry.'

He grumbled a bit, made her promise to call him when she arrived so he could see for himself she was okay. Nell agreed – anything to keep the peace – and ended the call, returning to the refrigerator. She pulled out eggs, cheese and ham and made an omelette as Teddy sidled up to her, licking his lips hopefully. Sasha was by the French doors, head on paws, and she raised her head as Nell emptied the pan onto a plate. She sat down and picked at her food, aware both dogs were watching her every move. Feeling guilty she shared the last quarter with them.

Her cell phone rang as she was clearing away the plate and she grabbed it, assuming it would be Alex or Michael, frowning at the unknown number and leaving it to go to voicemail. When the phone beeped alerting her she had a message, she dialled her server to listen.

'Hello, Miss O'Connor. This is Christopher Daley. I'm Judy Davenport's assistant.'

Nell's heartbeat quickened as he continued. 'Ms Davenport would like to meet with you if possible, to discuss purchasing some of your paintings. Could you please call me? She's going to be over on the east coast for the next few days on a buying trip, but then back in Chicago next week and we can set up a meeting.'

Judy Davenport owned some of the biggest galleries in Illinois. Tempting as it was, Nell couldn't strike a deal with her, aware that if she did it would leave a trail of breadcrumbs for Caleb to find her.

Her career in the art world was over. She had accepted that the day she'd left him.

She couldn't be rude though, so she called Christopher Daley back, apologised and said she wasn't interested.

'Ms Davenport's in a place called East Haven this week, but she'll be back in the city from next week.'

'East Haven?' For a moment she wondered what harm there'd be in arranging a meeting with the woman. She could say it was a coincidence that she was up in New England too. But then she realised there was every chance it would get back to Caleb and, although it wouldn't matter too much that he knew she'd been in East Haven, it wouldn't be smart. She could do without giving him any clues as to her whereabouts on Purity.

'Yes, East Haven, that's right.'

'No, I'm sorry. I'm not selling any of my work at this time. Thank you for the call though.'

'You do realise who Ms Davenport is, don't you?'

'Of course,' Nell hissed, annoyed at his attitude. 'But I'm no longer actively painting. I'm sorry, please thank Ms Davenport, but the answer is no.'

He started to give her a lecture and Nell hung up midway through, figuring she was better off without the business anyway. Screw Christopher Daley.

Alex called to check on her early in the afternoon.

'Everything okay there?'

'I'm fine. I'm going stir crazy, but fine.'

'I've asked Tommy to take you up to the guesthouse. He's just finishing up on another job and I've given him your number, told him to give you a call when he's on his way.'

Nell screwed up her nose, remembering how uncomfortable things had seemed on their previous encounters. She didn't protest though; she knew Alex was short-staffed and having to free up someone to babysit her. It was a ten-minute ride up to the house to get her stuff. She could be back at Alex's inside forty-five minutes. 'Sure, that's great. Thanks.'

'How's your neck?'

'Stiff, though I think the painkillers have helped a little.'

'Have you been doing the exercises the nurse gave you?'

'Yes,' Nell lied. She had forgotten all about them. 'What time do you think you'll be home?'

'I don't know yet. As soon as I can, I promise.'

She made an attempt with the exercises after she got off the phone, twisting her head from side to side then rolling her shoulders, feeling slightly stupid in front of her canine audience, before heading upstairs to take a shower.

Tommy called late afternoon, the conversation lasting all of ten seconds, and when he showed up half an hour later he seemed distracted, skipping over any pleasantries. 'Are you ready?' he asked, already glancing at his watch as if he had to be somewhere else before she had even stepped out of the house.

'Yeah, let's go.'

The ride was as uncomfortable as Nell had expected and after one lame attempt to make conversation she had given up, and they had spent the rest of the journey in silence. He pulled up the steep driveway to the guesthouse and Nell got out, unlocking the front door and disabling the alarm. She glanced back to the car where Tommy sat looking at his phone, completely preoccupied.

'Are you coming in?'

He shot her a brief look. 'I'll wait here.'

'I'm going to be about twenty minutes or so.'

'I said I'll wait.'

'Suit yourself,' Nell muttered under her breath, pushing the door shut. She didn't bother to lock it or reset the alarm, in case he changed his mind. Avoiding the conservatory, she headed upstairs to pack.

Tommy tried Jenna's number, frustration growing when she didn't pick up. He had sent her three texts over the course of the day and all of them had gone unanswered.

Was she being difficult because he had hung up on her last night? He hadn't changed his mind and still planned to turn himself in.

He didn't want to do that though until he had spoken with Jenna.

He glanced up at the guesthouse; saw the light on in the bedroom he knew belonged to Nell. Alex had wanted him to chaperone her, not leave her alone, but then Alex was being overprotective because he was sleeping with her. It would take Tommy eight minutes to get to Jenna's. He could get there and back, and Nell wouldn't even notice he was gone.

He was in limbo until he talked to Jenna and it was driving him nuts.

Making a decision, he started the engine and reversed back down the driveway.

Caleb was in a foul mood by the time the ferry arrived on the island. He had been so convinced Nell would respond to the call from Judy Davenport's office and hop on the ferry across to East

Haven. It would make things infinitely easier, as he wouldn't have to worry about getting her off the island.

Of course, there would have been no meeting with Judy Davenport, just as the phone call hadn't come from her assistant, Christopher Daley. Caleb had called in another favour with Jimmy, had someone make the call to Nell, hoping to lure her away.

For whatever reason though she had turned the offer down and Caleb found himself heading back across the water to Purity Island. He figured he would chance the guesthouse first and ducked down in his seat when the police patrol car pulled out of the driveway and headed on down the road that led into town.

For a moment he thought the place was empty as there were no other cars in the drive, but then he spotted Nell at a second-floor window and his heartbeat quickened.

She was home.

Of course, he couldn't be certain she was there alone, so he continued down the road, parking the Volvo in a secluded spot hidden behind the trees about half-a-mile away. He would go back to the guesthouse, spend a little time making sure she was by herself, then once he had her subdued he could jog back to fetch the car, get her loaded into the trunk, and be on his way.

Adrenalin pumping through his veins, he hoisted the sports bag over his shoulder and started the short hike back to the guesthouse.

~

It was by chance that Nell found the journal.

She had gone up to the attic to collect her art equipment and had been gathering her paints and brushes, packing them neatly away in a box when she had dropped one of the smaller brushes, swearing under her breath as it rolled across the rickety wooden floor, disappearing between two of the panels. Knowing how expensive it was she was reluctant to leave it.

'You are such a klutz,' she muttered to herself, dropping to her knees, wincing when pain shot up through her neck as she bent to try and retrieve it.

The gap between the panels was wide enough for her to slip one finger into. Wiggling around she could touch the tip of the brush and was able to move it slightly but couldn't pick it up.

Frustrated she sat back on her haunches. She couldn't really afford to replace the brush and she couldn't paint without it.

Twisting her hand at an angle, she forced two fingers into the gap, managed to catch hold of the tip of the brush but dropped it almost immediately. She tried again, this time her fingertips catching the edge of something else. It felt like a book. Both curious and annoyed, she tried to wiggle her fingers further into the gap, realising too late that her hand was stuck.

Way to go, O'Connor, you damn idiot.

She gave her hand a test yank, feeling a slight edge of panic when it didn't move, tried again, this time pulling much harder, and the whole panel of wood came away.

Gingerly Nell rubbed at her hand; her momentary feeling of relief quickly replaced by curiosity when she spotted the leather-bound journal lying in the hole beneath the floorboards. She retrieved her brush and dropped it into the box then turned her attention to the book, picking it up and brushing a film of dust off the cover. Carefully she opened the journal, recognising the handwriting of her cousin. The entries were marked by dates, the first one in January 2005.

So, Clarke had kept a diary. Why, she wondered, had he hidden it away?

She glanced through the first few entries. They were sporadic. He had written every day and some entries were brief, while others took up a whole page. It seemed mostly monotonous stuff, documenting what he had eaten, his school grades and the scores he was achieving on his favourite video games. She flicked randomly through the book, spotted Tommy's name a handful of times, then she came across an entry that was a little deeper, where Clarke seemed to be opening up through the diary and talking about his feelings. It made her uncomfortable, knowing that she was snooping. This was his private stuff. She was about to close the book, replace it under the floorboards, when she spotted another familiar name.

Sarah.

Sarah, whose name Clarke had written on the wall and whose bones had been discovered under the conservatory floor.

Intrigued, Nell studied the entry more carefully. It was tame stuff. It had been Clarke's birthday and Sarah had made him a chocolate cake. In the evening she and Bella had played video games with him.

Sarah had died in 2005. Did Clarke know what had happened to her? Was that why the journal was hidden? Nell flicked through a few more pages, saw Sarah's name appearing more frequently. Alex needed to see this. It could be important.

She packed the journal in the box with her paints and brushes, and took it downstairs, setting it beside the bag of clothes and toiletries she had packed, then went back up to the attic for her easel and paper. Satisfied she had everything she opened the front door, surprised to see Tommy's car was gone. She stepped outside, glanced around, part of her wondering if it was a stupid prank, but he was nowhere in sight.

Had he seriously driven off and left her?

Nell pulled her cell phone out of her pocket, was about to call Alex but faltered.

If he knew Tommy had ditched her, he would go nuts. Tommy already had a problem with her, and she didn't want to make things worse between them. She had his cell number from when he had called her earlier. Finding it up she pressed dial, waiting as it rang.

Where the hell are you, Tommy? Pick up, dammit.

The phone rang a dozen times before he answered. 'Yes?'

'It's Nell. Where are you?'

'I had something I had to do.'

'Okay, well are you done? I'm ready and waiting.' She heard him sigh loudly, sounding exasperated. 'Tommy?'

'I'll be there in a bit.'

'Look, I don't want to put you out. If it's that big a deal I can call Alex. I've found something he needs to see anyway.'

'What have you found?'

'Clarke kept a journal. He talks about Sarah. He might have known what happened to her.'

There was a period of silence. 'Look, give me ten minutes. I'll be there as quickly as I can. We'll go to Alex together, okay? There's something I need to tell him myself.'

'Okay, ten minutes.'

Tommy slipped his cell phone back into his pocket. 'This has to end. Right now, it has to end. I'm not doing it anymore.'

'You think it's going to end by turning yourself in? You're crazy.'

'The truth is going to come out anyway. It's only a matter of time before they link it back and figure out what happened.'

'Not necessarily, Tommy. It's been a secret all this time. We can keep it that way.'

'And what about Jenna?' Tommy said her name bitterly, still reeling after finding her in the tub full of blood. He wasn't sure if he felt sad, guilty or angry. She had taken the easy way out, left him to face this alone. That was why he had driven here. He had nowhere else to go.

'What about Jenna?'

'She's dead, damn it. Does that mean nothing to you?' Tommy looked at the familiar face, the penny dropping as he suddenly realised the train of thought. 'You want to let her take the fall, don't you?'

'Well, she's confessed. And she's already gone. It would be a waste for her to drag us down with her.'

Tommy shook his head in disbelief. 'You're an asshole.'

'No, I'm a survivalist.'

'You think Jenna's confession is going to stop them coming after us? Clarke kept a journal. He's written all about Sarah. Nell has it and plans to give it to Alex. He is going to find out we were involved.'

That brought a satisfying flicker of uncertainty. 'Nell has the journal?'

'She said just now on the phone that she has found Clarke's journal and that Alex needs to see it.'

'You're lying.'

'You know I'm not. It's over. I'm going to turn myself in, confess about what happened. You should too.'

Tommy turned to walk away, hadn't reached the front door when the blow struck him hard on the back of the head. He staggered forward, attempted to reach for his sidearm, but a second blow knocked him clean off his feet and he tumbled to the floor in a pool of blood.

Michael was getting frustrated being stuck in a hospital bed. He was feeling much better and didn't understand why he couldn't recuperate at home. Instead the doctors insisted on keeping him hooked up to stupid machines he was quite certain he no longer needed. Too much was happening. The serial killer case, the discovery of the body at the guesthouse, the incident with Nell on the mainland. He felt like he was losing control; if he was at home he could keep on top of things more easily.

He glanced at his watch, annoyed Nell hadn't called him. She had said she was going up to the guesthouse in the afternoon and it was already after five. He picked up his phone ready to fire off an angry text then reconsidered, deciding he would Facetime her instead, his anger ebbing when she answered, her face appearing on the screen. He hadn't seen her since the accident and was relieved to see she looked okay. Her lip was still a little puffy from where Curtis had hit her, and he could see the darkening bruise on her forehead from the car accident, but other than that she seemed bright-eyed and in good spirits.

'I thought you were going to call me?'

'I planned to. I was just getting my stuff together.' He could see she was in the kitchen, could hear the coffee pot hissing in the background.

'Is Alex there with you?'

'No, umm, Tommy is.'

Something registered as off. It was the way Nell diverted her eyes away from the camera when she answered him.

'Is that so? So, where is he? Put him on so I can say hi.'

'He's waiting outside.'

'Nell, where's Tommy?'

'I told you he's—'

'He's not there, is he?'

'He had to go into town for a bit.'

'Does Alex know you're up at the guesthouse alone?'

'Look, Tommy, he had... a thing. He's on his way back though, should be here any second now, I promise.'

Michael guessed he must have looked pissed because she

continued to babble. Something his sister didn't do unless she knew she had been caught out.

'Don't tell Alex, okay? Things have been a little off with Tommy and I don't want him getting into trouble over this. It will make it more awkward. I spoke to him a minute ago and he's on his way back. I am fine. I've been packing my stuff and you can stay on the line and keep me company until he gets here if you like.'

Nell gave a bright smile. It looked a little forced and it was obvious she was trying to get things back on a more light-hearted level. She set her phone down on the counter, propped up, so he could see her as she made her coffee.

Michael was still vexed and made a mental note to lay into Tommy Dolan when he saw him, but for the sake of his sister he dropped the subject for now.

'So, you're moving in with Alex then?'

'It's just temporary. You're in the hospital and I don't want to be up here at the moment. I'm sure he'll want me out of his hair at some point.' She shrugged, trying to give the impression she was fine with that, picking up her phone and heading back into the hallway towards the main living room.

'Things okay with you two?'

'Yeah, they are.' She sipped at her coffee, smiled again, this one full of genuine warmth. 'In fact, they're more than okay. I know you guys talked. You're cool... about us, now, right?'

'Yeah, we're good.'

'I'm glad.' There must have been the slightest hesitancy in his voice, because she added, 'Don't screw this up for me, Michael. He makes me happy.'

'I won't screw it up. Happy is all I ever want you to be. So, what's happening with my pool?' he asked, changing the subject. 'I suppose it's a crime scene.'

'To be honest, I've avoided going in there. What the hell happened to that poor girl?'

'Hopefully now she's been found there will be some answers.'

'She just disappeared, and no-one even noticed or cared.' Nell was silent for a moment. 'You know, Clarke wrote about Sarah in his journal.'

'He kept a journal?'

'Yeah, I found it hidden under the floorboards in the attic.'

'You've given it to Alex, right?'

'I plan to. I only just found it.'

Nell set down her coffee cup and wandered back out into the hallway heading down towards the reception desk, and Michael saw the camera lower as she fished in a box. 'See.' she held up a thick leather-bound book in front of her phone. 'It's full of diary entries from 2005. It might have some clues as to what happened to her.'

'Get it to Alex ASAP. This could be important, Nell.'

'I'm going to. Tommy should be here in a few minutes and we're going to drive straight into town to see him.'

'Where the hell did you say Dolan was?'

'He didn't say, only it was important. He was on his way back though when I spoke to him.'

Michael noted he had been talking with Nell over ten minutes. 'I should call him.'

'You don't need to. I'm fine.'

'I'm gonna kick his ass for leaving you up there alone.'

'Michael!' Nell rolled her eyes. 'You're being an idiot.'

As she berated him, she wandered back into the kitchen, the camera up high enough for him to see the view behind her and the figure standing in the shadows behind the kitchen door.

Michael's heart leapt into his mouth, his eyes widening.

Caleb.

Nell was still talking about Tommy, though she sounded distracted. Michael heard the faucet running.

'Nell!'

She didn't seem to be able to hear him over the running water. Michael sat up in the hospital bed, screamed at his phone as he saw Caleb approaching her from behind.

'NELL! GODDAMMIT, BEHIND YOU!'

Caleb must have spoken to her, because he saw her face pale, her eyes widen in horror. As she started to turn, the phone slipped from her hand. He heard and watched as it hit the floor, the screen turning black.

'NELL!'

41

'Mr O'Connor, you need to get back into bed.'

The grey-haired nurse was doing her best to stop Michael, who had unhooked himself from the machines and was currently skulking around the room wearing just the skimpy hospital robe and a bandage on his head. 'Where the hell are my pants?'

'Mr O'Connor, please. You're not well enough to leave.'

'My sister's in danger. Don't tell me what the hell I can and can't do. Now get me my damn clothes.'

Yelling didn't help and brought on a head rush that left him feeling dizzy, like he was about to pass out. He grabbed the railing at the end of the bed, attempting to steady himself.

Another nurse and two orderlies arrived.

'Let me go,' Michael yelled at them, trying to jerk away as they wrestled him down onto the bed. 'My sister's in danger. I have to help her.'

The two nurses exchanged a glance, the older one filling a needle.

'You need to rest, Mr O'Connor. This will help you.'

'No! You don't understand.' He flinched away as the needle

came towards him, struggling as the orderlies pinned him down and the nurse looked for a vein. 'Please, help her. Her name is Nell O'Connor and she's in Bella Golding's old guesthouse. She's in danger. Please call Alex... Chief Cutler, right away and tell him.'

He made eye contact with the younger nurse, the only one who seemed to be listening to what he was saying. 'His number is on my cell. Alex. Tell him Caleb is there.'

She gave a hesitant smile, nodded.

Michael felt the needle sink into his arm, was aware of the drug starting to take effect. 'Just help my sister, please.'

'Hello, Nell. Did you miss me?'

Nell recognised the soft deep voice and she froze at the kitchen sink, the hairs on her neck standing on end. Barely daring to breathe, she slowly turned around, vaguely aware of Michael calling her name.

Caleb stood before her, his posture relaxed, the hint of a smile touching his lips. In his hand he held a gun that was pointing at her.

She couldn't speak and was aware of her cell phone slipping from her shaking fingers; it crashed against the floor, the sound slightly muted by the rush of water as the sink filled.

He had found her.

Oh, dear God, he had found her.

They stood facing one another, the only sound coming from the running faucet. Nell's legs were leaden, her throat dry as fear clawed inside her. She had built herself up, was proud of her independence, her moments of bravery, but in that second it was all undone and she hated herself for how scared and pathetic she suddenly felt, aware of what Caleb was capable of and knowing she didn't have the guts to stand up to him.

His demeanour suggested he was relaxed, but she knew better than anyone it was a mask, that he wanted to fool her into believing he was being reasonable so she would be unprepared when he decided to strike.

He took a sudden step towards her and she flinched, stepping back into the counter. She gripped it tightly with both hands, her eyes never leaving his – those cold dead eyes she remembered and feared so well. He was mean and he was unpredictable, and that made him dangerous, and she could tell from the way he was looking at her that he wanted to hurt her.

'Do you have nothing to say to me? After what you have done, what you have put me through these last few weeks, you have nothing?'

'I... I... How did you...?'

The rest of the words wouldn't come and those that had sounded pathetic. She'd been so strong and in five seconds he had reduced her to a quivering wreck. Nell couldn't hate herself anymore if she tried.

'How did I find you? It took some work, but I guess you're not as smart as you think you are. What I don't understand is why you did it? I gave you everything!' He raised his voice on the last word, smiling cruelly when she visibly flinched. 'In return you made me look a fool, completely betrayed my trust.'

He sneered as she started to hyperventilate. 'You're not going to pull this shit again, are you?'

'One-hundred, ninety-nine, ninety–'

He moved before she had time to react, pinning her against the counter, the tip of the gun pressed against her chin, forcing her head back, his face inches from hers. 'One-hundred, ninety-nine, ninety-eight,' he mocked. 'Listen to you, for fuck's sake. Do you have any idea how weak and pitiful you are? I mean, look at you, you're a thirty-four-year-old woman and you can't even fucking breathe properly.'

Nell gasped for air, her legs now shaking so badly she was sure she would collapse to the floor if he wasn't pinning her with his weight. 'Please,' she managed.

He traced the gun along her jawline before reaching behind her with his free hand and turning off the faucet. 'You are going to have to do a lot better than please. This is bad, Nell. I don't know if I can forgive you this time.'

He took a step back releasing her, though kept the gun pointed at her chest. Rummaging in his pocket he pulled out a pair of handcuffs.

'Turn around.' When she didn't immediately obey, he barked the order louder. 'TURN AROUND!'

'Please don't—'

She didn't have time to react as he lashed out, smacking the gun across her cheek. Pain shot through her face and she tasted blood as Caleb caught hold of her again, twisting her around so she had her back to him. He forced her head down onto the counter, sending a fresh wave of pain shooting up through her neck where she had hurt it in the car accident, and she cried out in agony. Feeding on her reaction, he caught a fistful of her curls, twisting viciously as he leant forward to whisper in her ear. 'How badly I hurt you depends on how well you co-operate. Do you understand?' When she didn't immediately reply, he screamed the words. 'DO YOU UNDERSTAND?'

She was still fighting to breathe and struggled to get the word out.

'Yes.'

He caught hold of her right hand, slipped the cuff around her wrist and locked it.

'You don't want to be testing my patience at this point, Nell. You're lucky I didn't walk in here and shoot you dead after I found out you've been sleeping with another man. How fucking dare you let someone else touch you? You're mine.'

Nell froze. How did he know about Alex?

How long had he been on the island? Had he been watching them?

As he reached for her left wrist, something inside her snapped. She couldn't let him destroy the life she had built. At the very least she had to try and fight back.

Pulling her hand away from him, she drove her elbow back against his belly, hearing a grunt as it made contact. He temporarily released his grip and she swung around, using her cuffed hand as a weapon, swinging the loose metal cuff hard into his face.

Caleb yelped, stepping back and putting both hands to his eyes. Nell didn't wait to see what damage she had inflicted, pushing past him, her legs rubbery and threatening to collapse as she ran out of the kitchen, heading down the hallway to the front door. She tried to focus, still counting in her head, trying to get her breathing under control.

He was quick to follow, catching hold of a handful of her hair and yanking her back. She lost her balance, stumbling to the floor and, hand still knotted in her hair, he dragged her back along the hallway into the kitchen.

Nell screamed in agony, fought to get free.

Where the hell was Tommy? Tommy should be here by now. Caleb threw her down on the kitchen floor and attempted to straddle her, and she kicked out like a wild animal, catching him first in the knee then the chin, desperately trying to stop him from gaining the upper hand. Her foot connected with his hand, knocking the gun from his grip, and she heard it clatter as it landed in the hallway. With both hands free he found it easier to field off her blows, pinning her arms down as he climbed on top of her.

'Get off me!' Nell spat in his face, earning herself a hard slap. She managed to get her left hand loose and swiped out at him, but he caught it easily, twisting her fingers back and making her cry out in pain.

'You fucking bitch. Just wait until I make you pay for this.'

He eased his weight off her, rolled her onto her belly and grabbed for her hands again, yanking them behind her back.

A gunshot rang out and Nell jumped. For a moment there was silence and she half wondered if she had been hit – couldn't understand why she felt no pain – then Caleb's grip on her wrists loosened and she felt him collapse on top of her.

She lay there for a few seconds, adrenalin still pumping, her breath coming in erratic spurts, then his weight shifted.

'Nell?'

She managed to roll over, to look up at Luke. The gun was slack in his hand and he was looking down at Caleb who laid face-down on the floor, the back of his head missing.

As she didn't trust herself to stand, she drew her knees up to her chin, focused on getting her breathing under control. 'Sixty-three, sixty-two, sixty-one...'

'Who is this guy?'

Nell didn't answer until her breathing steadied. She looked up at Luke and saw he was watching her curiously.

'He's my ex-boyfriend.'

'Jesus Christ. He was trying to kill you.'

'He's dead.'

'I know. I shot him.'

Luke offered her a hand and Nell took it hesitantly, aware her legs were still shaking, nausea still swirling in her belly. For a few seconds she continued to draw in deep breaths, trying to calm her nerves.

She glanced around for her cell phone, spotted it was on the floor in front of the sink where she had dropped it. She had to call Alex, needed him here with her. Numbly she bent to retrieve it, noting the screen was smashed. She tried to turn it on, but it wasn't working.

'Can I borrow your phone please? I need to call Alex.'

'What's this?' Luke asked, ignoring the question.

Nell glanced at Clarke's journal sitting on the counter. He went to touch it.

'Leave that,' she told him, grabbing it from him. 'It's evidence.'

'Why? What is it?'

'Clarke kept a journal. I think it might reveal what happened to Sarah. Can you please call Alex?'

'Really? Let me see.'

When he reached for it, she held it possessively to her chest. 'It's evidence,' she repeated. 'Tommy will be here in a minute. We're going to take the journal to Alex.'

Luke hesitated and nodded slowly, a tight smile on his face. He reached up with the tip of the gun and used it to casually scratch the side of his head. 'Yeah, here's the thing. Tommy's not coming.'

Something in his expression unsettled Nell. 'What do you mean, he's not coming? I spoke with him ten minutes ago.'

'Give me the journal, Nell.'

'No.' She took a cautious step back. Why did Luke want the book so bad?

'Okay.' He chuckled to himself and smiled broadly at her as though there was a joke he knew, that she wasn't a part of. 'I tried to be nice, play along.' He raised the gun and pointed it at Nell's chest. Something in his expression had shifted, his face hardening, the familiar vivid blue eyes lacking warmth. 'Now give me the damn journal.'

It had been a slip of the tongue that had roused Alex's suspicions.

He had been talking with Luke while they waited for Nell to pack a bag and Luke had mentioned the woman driver who had stopped after the accident.

Alex had never told him that the driver was a woman.

Of course, it was plausible there was an explanation, possibly Nell had mentioned it to Luke while they had been waiting for Alex in the kitchen, but it was still enough to set off alarm bells and there was no way in hell Alex was letting Nell get in the car with him.

He was glad he had made that decision when Nell confirmed on the ride home that she hadn't talked to Luke about her accident. She already seemed spooked about Luke, which had him wondering if anything else had happened.

He hadn't shared his suspicions, didn't intend to say anything to Nell until he'd had a chance to investigate further. Luke had been his friend for five years and he was Newt's brother. There was no way he was going to accuse him of any wrongdoing unless he had the evidence to back it up.

He had a morning meeting at the ME's office with Hunter Stone, so it was mid-afternoon before he was able to focus his attention on Luke. Luke had told them he had come from Bob Pilgrim's place and Alex had called the cranky old farmer, who confirmed that he hadn't seen Luke in weeks.

So Luke was lying about where he had been and he knew about the woman driver. If he had been stalking Nell, what was his end game?

Had he killed Sarah Treadwell?

It was a stretch, but he had seemed genuinely shaken last night. Maybe it was because he knew he was close to being caught. Sarah had disappeared in 2005, Luke had moved to the island a year before. He would have been eighteen at the time she disappeared.

Alex felt a stab of guilt. It was bad enough accusing Luke of being a stalker, but now he was pushing it to murder. He hesitated for a moment before running the search. It felt like a betrayal, but he knew he had no choice. It was his job and he couldn't let his friendship with Luke sway his judgment.

He didn't expect the search to throw up anything suspicious and had hoped it wouldn't, and his heartbeat quickened as he read about the string of cautions sitting on Luke's record. He had been a minor at the time and it had happened in the summer before he had moved to Purity. The cautions, mainly for harassment, all related to a woman called Marla Jefferson, who had been a neighbour of the Trainors.

Alex made a couple of calls and finally got to speak with Marty Womack, one of the officers who had been involved.

'Yeah, I remember Marla Jefferson and Luke Trainor. The trouble started after she moved into the neighbourhood. She was a pain in the ass, calling us out, all the while claiming he was following her or leaving creepy things for her to find. One time she claimed he had stolen her panties from her clothesline.'

'And had he?'

'We never found any evidence to back up her accusations. We spoke with the kid and his brother. They seemed like nice people. Trainor said Jefferson had it in for him, claimed she had hit on him and was bitter, looking for revenge because he had rebutted her advances. It wasn't a stretch to believe it could be true.'

'It says on his record that a restraining order was filed.'

'Initially she was calling us out over petty stuff, but then she accused the kid of breaking into her house while she was asleep, claimed he had sexually assaulted her. We investigated it, but there was no evidence to back up her story, so no charges were ever brought, but she went to court and had the order filed. Shortly afterwards Trainor and his brother moved away, claiming Marla Jefferson had driven them out of the neighbourhood.'

'You think he was innocent?'

'The way I see it, he was a good-looking kid. Why would he need to go after a crazy lady fifteen years his senior?' Womack was silent for a moment. 'Of course, that's just my viewpoint. You ask my partner and he would tell you the kid was guilty.'

'Why is that?'

'Kid didn't have the easiest start. Parents killed in a plane crash, raised by his grandmother. I met the woman a few times before she died, and I imagine she wasn't easy to live with. I think they had problems.'

'What kind of problems?'

'The kid's older brother, the one who became his guardian when the grandmother died, he said she used to pick on Trainor, that she resented looking after him and would look for excuses to punish him. He asked us to go easy on him with the whole Marla Jefferson thing, said he had been through enough. I guess I felt sorry for him.'

'And your partner?'

'He thought he was broken, found him arrogant, self-absorbed, said he had dead eyes.'

Alex thanked Womack for his time. Nell had been followed, had her house broken into and her stalker had left creepy mementos. Had Marla Jefferson been telling the truth?

The call that came in from Doctor Karen Lockwood added an extra layer. Alex was about to head out when Ruby transferred her through.

'I'm sorry to disturb you, Chief Cutler. I know you must be busy.'

'How can I help you, Doctor Lockwood?'

'I work in East Haven and I've been treating Stacey Monroe? I have her address as living on Purity Island.'

Alex's ears pricked up at the mention of Luke's ex-girlfriend. 'Go on.'

'Miss Monroe has missed her last three appointments. I've tried calling her cell phone, but there's no answer, and I have to admit I am concerned.'

'Can I ask what you were treating her for?'

'I'm sorry, Chief Cutler, that's doctor patient privilege.'

'Okay, but can I ask why you are so worried about her?'

'Because the last time I spoke with her she said there was something big she needed to talk to me about. Something she had found out. She said she needed to see me urgently, so I brought her usual Monday session forward, came into the office specially to meet her on a Saturday. She didn't show.'

A gnawing feeling ate at Alex's gut. 'If you've been treating Stacey you'll know she has mood swings, can be irrational, unpredictable.'

'Yes, I'm aware of that. I think she's still on the island.'

'Really? How so?'

'It's just a hunch, based on how our last conversation went.'

'Which you can't tell me anything about because of doctor client privilege,' Alex spoke the last three words sarcastically.

'I'm sorry to be so vague, Chief Cutler, but I have a bad feeling about this.'

So did Alex.

Stacey Monroe didn't have many friends on the island, tending to spend most of her time with Luke, but he knew she did sometimes hang out with Autumn Eastman. After ending the call with Karen Lockwood, he grabbed his jacket and headed over to the salon where Autumn worked. The place was almost empty with just one woman having her hair styled. Autumn and her colleague, Louise, were behind the desk chatting. They both glanced up when Alex entered, Autumn's face turning a deep shade of red. She had been giving him a wide berth since finding out he was involved with Nell.

'Have you got five minutes?' Alex treated her to a wide smile, hoping to ease any awkwardness, but only succeeded in making her look more uncomfortable.

'Umm, yeah, I guess.'

She led him into the back room of the salon and Alex didn't miss Louise's grin as he followed her.

'How can I help you, Alex?' Autumn was wringing her hands together, looking like she would rather be anywhere but here.

'You're friendly with Stacey Monroe, right?'

'Yes, I guess. I style her hair and we sometimes hang out. Why?'

'When was the last time you saw her?'

That threw Autumn. Whatever the reason was Alex wanted to see her, he guessed she hadn't counted on it being about Stacey.

'Not in a while.' Autumn bit into her bottom lip as she pondered.

'She never came to Michael and Newt's barbecue, so I guess the last time would have been when I styled her hair, so maybe a month ago.'

'She's not called or texted you?'

'Nope, though she's not big on texting. She had a fight with Luke and I heard they had split up, that she went back to the mainland. I did send her a text saying I was around if she wanted to talk, but I never heard anything back.' Autumn frowned, making eye contact for the first time. 'What's this about? Has something happened to her?'

'I'm sure she's fine. I'm just checking up on something.' Alex hesitated, the guilt creeping back in. 'Has she ever talked to you about her relationship with Luke?'

'Sure, all Stacey ever talks about is Luke.'

'He says she's jealous.'

'I think obsessed is the correct word. Stacey is paranoid about other women and constantly worried about them stealing him away.'

'They fight a lot then?'

'Oh yeah, but that is just them. They're both headstrong characters and I think they like the drama. Stacey always says they like to fight in and out of the bedroom, though I think sometimes he takes it a bit far.'

'Luke takes things a bit far in the bedroom? How so?'

Autumn's eyes widened, her cheeks coloured again as she realised what she had said. 'Well, I shouldn't really say. It's private between them.'

'It's important, Autumn.'

'Well, umm...' The poor girl looked mortified at the idea of talking about sex with him and Alex had to admit it wasn't a conversation he particularly wanted to be having with her either, but it was important. Sarah was dead, Stacey possibly missing, and a stalker had been targeting Nell. He needed to get to the truth.

'He likes it rough.' Autumn made a point of studying her nails, her cheeks on fire. 'And I don't just mean hair pulling and a bit of spanking. He likes choking and knife play. Stacey is pretty much up for anything, but she says he gets carried away sometimes. He also likes her to wear this wig and it's been pissing her off. Like I said, she is already jealous, and it just adds to her insecurities.'

'Did she say what this wig is like?'

'Yeah, it's blonde. She's a brunette and he makes her wear this blonde wig during sex. It upsets her.'

Sarah Treadwell had been blonde, so was Nell.

And so were Penny Maher and Caroline Henderson.

Alex quashed the thought, thanked Autumn, and left the salon. There was still nothing substantial to connect Luke to anything, but lots of potential red flags.

He found Hunter waiting for him back in his office, his friend immediately picking up that he was distracted.

'You look like a man with something important on his mind.'

'I guess you could say that.'

Hunter was a good detective and Alex trusted his instincts. More importantly, he didn't know Luke or have a vested interest in Alex's close circle of friends. Alex decided to use him as a sounding board, wanting to know if he was nuts or genuinely on to something.

'There's nothing concrete,' Hunter agreed after the evidence had been presented. 'That said, you add all those warning signs together and they give a very good argument. Does he own a boat?'

'This is Purity. Everyone has a boat.'

'And you say he works on the mainland? That gives him easy access to our victims. He doesn't match the guy in the security footage though.'

'Yeah, I've been thinking about that. We know he already owns a wig because he likes his girlfriend to wear it when they have sex, so is it that big a stretch to think he might have more than one? He's not a stupid guy. He picks women up in bars and knows there are going to be cameras, so he alters his appearance.'

Stone nodded. 'That would make sense. What about alibis?'

'He lived with Stacey, but since she disappeared he's been on his own.' Alex thought back to the night Nell had been terrorised by the masked intruder. Luke had been at the guest-house with Michael and Newt. It was the night after Stephanie

Richardson's party and he had known Nell was going to be on her own until Alex had finished his shift. It would have been easy for him to return to the guesthouse after Michael and Newt had dropped him off. 'I think there's enough for me to go have a chat with him.'

'Mind if I tag along?'

Alex glanced at Hunter, not sure if it was a good idea. Luke was supposed to be his friend. Did he not owe it to him to have this chat privately?

'I know you feel a loyalty to him, Alex, but don't lose sight of what we're dealing with here,' Hunter reasoned. 'If he is guilty then he's not your friend. He's a sick son of a bitch who has been butchering women.'

Always the voice of logic. Alex smiled tightly. 'Let's go.'

They pulled up outside Luke's townhouse ten minutes later and Alex's gut knotted further when he spotted the patrol car parked in the driveway.

'That's Tommy's car. He's supposed to be with Nell up at the guesthouse.'

Hunter's jaw tightened. 'Let's go see if Luke's home.'

Alex knocked on the door, waited a beat, trying again when there was no answer. If Tommy's car was here it made sense he would be inside, so why was no-one answering?

Splitting up, they walked the perimeter of the property, meeting round the back of the house. There was no sign of anyone being home, then Alex glanced in the kitchen window and spotted the spattering of blood up the wall, the further trail leading across the kitchen floor. He exchanged a glance with Hunter, unholstered his weapon, and tried the kitchen door. Finding it locked he stepped back and gave it a hard kick.

The door flew back on its hinges. Weapon drawn he entered the kitchen.

'Luke? It's Alex. Are you home?' There was no answer.

The trail of blood led from the hallway, across the kitchen, to the closed door that led to the basement. Whose blood was it? Did it belong to Luke or Tommy? And if Tommy was here then where the hell was Nell?

Hunter signalled for Alex to check out the basement, while he did a sweep of the first floor.

Alex twisted the knob to the door, pulled it open and flicked on the light. The blood trail led all of the way down the stairs.

From below came the sound of groaning.

He descended the stairs, gun aimed and ready to fire if necessary. Tommy was sprawled on the basement floor, blood gushing from a wound in his head. He was barely conscious, and Alex radioed for backup and an ambulance as he knelt beside him.

'Who did this to you, Tommy?'

Tommy mumbled something, but it was barely legible.

'Where's Nell? Is she here?'

'Sorry... I'm... sorry.'

'Tommy, where's Nell? Did Luke do this?'

This time he didn't get any answer as Tommy slipped back into unconsciousness. Alex removed his jacket and used it as a pillow, placing it under Tommy's head and trying to make him as comfortable as possible. 'Hold tight. Ambulance is on its way.'

He heard footsteps on the stairs and glanced up to see Hunter joining them.

'We're all clear upstairs.' He glanced at Tommy. 'What happened?'

'He's not lucid enough to say. I've radioed for an ambulance.' Alex glanced around the basement that served mostly as a laundry room. It was sparse in furnishings and he found his attention drawn to the large chest freezer. It was old-fashioned and looked out of place with the more modern washer and dryer. Luke was a gadget freak, always liked to have the latest appliances. Why would he have an ugly old freezer in his home?

Weapon still in hand, he approached the freezer with a sense of trepidation, his head telling him he was being stupid, his gut suggesting otherwise.

As he yanked up the lid, the odour hit him and, although it was faint, he recognised it as death.

Two bodies were inside, both female. The top victim, her eyes still wide in terror, was familiar from her photograph: Caroline Henderson. Her body hadn't been found with their killer's other victims. Her throat had been cut and other knife wounds on her body seemed similar to those of the victims they had pulled from the ocean grave. Beneath her was the body of Stacey Monroe, Luke's girlfriend. She was still partially dressed, her body in a more decomposed state than Caroline's with vicious bruising around her throat suggesting she had been strangled.

Luke told everyone she had left him three weeks ago, carried out a charade that he was heartbroken, yet all this time she had been lying dead in his freezer. Doctor Lockwood said Stacey had called her, saying she needed to see her urgently. Had she discovered the truth about her boyfriend or did she suspect he planned to kill her?

'Jesus!' Hunter stood behind him and let out a low whistle. 'If you had any doubts you shouldn't have now.'

Tommy mumbled something as he came to again, but it was barely coherent. Alex recognised one word.

Nell.

Dread coiling in his belly, he went back to the fallen officer.

'Tommy, talk to me. What about Nell? Where is she?'

'Guesthouse,' Tommy managed. 'Luke wants... journal.'

'What?'

His cell phone chose that moment to ring. Alex grabbed it from his pocket, recognising Michael's number. 'Michael, this is not a good time.'

'Is this Chief Cutler?' It was a woman's voice.

'Who is this?'

'My name is Georgina Walker. I'm a nurse over at the hospital. Michael O'Connor asked me to call you.'

'Where is he?'

'He's currently sedated. He was getting agitated. He asked me to call you, said to tell you his sister, Nell, is in danger. He mentioned the name Caleb.'

'When? When did this happen?'

'Maybe ten minutes ago.'

Alex ended the call abruptly, the growing dread inside him now spilling over into genuine fear. He recalled the night he had lost Sophie. This wasn't going to happen again. He gently slapped Tommy round the face. 'Tommy, where's Nell? Is she at the guesthouse? Tommy?'

It took a moment. Tommy was drifting in and out of consciousness.

'Tommy, is Nell at the guesthouse?'

Eventually he registered.

'You've gotta... stop... Luke.'

42

2005

It started the day Sarah died. That was when Luke Trainor first discovered exactly who he was. He had wanted her, was used to getting what he wanted, and her rejection had left him reeling, reminding him of his prudish cousin, Jane, and that bitch, Marla Jefferson. They had rejected him too, both tried to humiliate him. Sarah was no better.

That humiliation and the frustration balled into rage that slowly built inside until it consumed him. He had never had the opportunity to get even with Jane and had spent years dreaming of ways to get retribution. He hadn't made that mistake with Marla though. He had made her pay and he would make Sarah pay too. They all thought they were better than him and he needed to show them they weren't.

Sarah hadn't seen him, had her back to him as she pegged up sheets. The back door was open and he slipped inside the guesthouse. He had never been inside before, and he found himself in a large kitchen. Another door on the far wall appeared to lead into the heart of the house and he crossed the room, keeping his movements quiet, aware Bella Golding's idiot son and Tommy were probably upstairs.

The hallway was long and spacious leading to the front of the property and what he assumed was a reception area. In the space in between stood a grand staircase leading to the second floor and archways on either side leading to both a living room and a dining area. There were two other doors and Luke checked both, finding one was a cluttered cupboard, while the other, which stood ajar, led down to a basement. He could hear the whir of a washing machine and guessed that was where Sarah was doing the laundry.

It was the perfect place to hide and wait.

She came downstairs twenty minutes later as he stood in the shadows watching her through the eye slits of the cheap mask he had bought, the anticipation that had been building now at an unbearable level, reminding him of the night he had broken into Marla's house. She had been terrified when she woke up to find him in her bedroom and he had soon wiped that stuck-up look off her face.

As Sarah unloaded the machine, refilling her basket, he crept up behind her, pulling his knife out of his pocket and flicking the blade. She must have heard him because she started to turn and then he had hold of her, clamping his hand over her mouth as she tried to scream.

'Hush.' He pressed the knife against her throat. 'We don't want to disturb the kids.'

She had frozen in his arms, a whimper escaping through his fingers and he had pressed the knife tighter, aware the tip was cutting into the delicate skin of her throat, growing hard when she tried to squeal and struggled against him. Marla had struggled, but no-one had believed her, just as no-one would believe Sarah. He was aware of her sweet perfume, the scent of her shampoo, the racing of her heartbeat and of her intense fear, and he fed off of it, pushing the knife deeper as he allowed his free hand to roam over her breasts.

He wanted her so bad.

'You and I are going to have some fun.' He bit her earlobe hard enough to make her flinch. 'So you do as I tell you, okay.'

She nodded and he felt her body quiver in fear. It was amazing how compliant the knife had made her. But then she startled him, stamping hard on his foot and driving her elbow back into his belly. The breath whooshed out of him and he dropped the knife, momentarily losing control, and losing that precious second that allowed her to break free of his grip and make a mad dash for the stairs.

She was screaming and he panicked, chasing after her.

He caught her as she neared the doorway, grabbing her arm and pulling her back towards him, and she swung around, lashing out. As he tried to subdue her, she made a grab for the mask, knocking it back off his face. It clattered down the stairs as she stared at him in horror.

'Luke?'

He only meant to put his hand over her mouth, but it ended up against her throat and then both of his hands were there and he was squeezing harder, aware she was thrashing against him and fighting to breathe, her eyes widening as they stared into his. Her face had briefly morphed into Jane's. Pretty, blonde, stuck-up Jane, the favoured cousin who could do no wrong and who had lauded it over him. He squeezed harder and felt Sarah go limp.

A noise came from above, footsteps on the stairs from the second floor. Luke let go of Sarah, watched her body tumble down the stairs and heard a loud crack as her head hit the concrete floor. He followed quickly, grabbed his knife and the mask, hiding in the shadows as he saw Tommy appear at the top of the stairs.

'What is it? What the hell is it, Tommy?' Jenna? What the fuck was she doing here?

And then they were descending the stairs and Luke saw his whole life flashing before him, knew he couldn't go to jail.

Tommy was crying. 'Jesus, Jenna, you've killed her.'

'I didn't mean to.'

Why did Jenna think she was responsible?

'What the hell are we going to do?'

'I'm sorry.' Jenna had her hands on her head, tears streaming down her face as she turned, in that moment spotting him. 'Luke? What are...?'

The fear of being caught manifested itself into anger. 'What the fuck have you done, Jenna?'

He stepped out of the shadows, ignoring Tommy's look of shock, his focus solely on Jenna, aware she was the one he needed to manipulate.

Her bottom lip trembled. 'It was an accident, I swear.'

'This doesn't look like an accident. What the hell did you do to her?'

'She was only supposed to get a little sick.'

'She's dead! That's not sick.'

'I know, but it was an accident... I swear.'

The story of the brownies came spilling out between sobs and Luke felt his heartbeat quicken. Jenna and Tommy believed they had killed Sarah, that they had somehow poisoned her.

'This is bad. I can't believe you fucking killed her.'

There was more wailing from Jenna. 'What are we going to do, Luke? I can't go to jail, I can't. I have my whole life ahead of me.'

'So did Sarah, but you've taken her life from her, haven't you?'

'Please help me.' She grabbed at the front of his T-shirt. 'Please, it was an accident. You have to believe me.'

'Why should I help you? You did this. It's nothing to do with me.'

'Why are you here, Luke?' Tommy questioned. 'What were you doing in the basement with Sarah?'

Luke looked across at him. Tommy's tone was accusatory and had Jenna looking up. She had been so preoccupied with finding Sarah, convinced she was responsible for killing her, she hadn't stopped to consider why Luke might be there. Now she did and her eyes hardened slightly.

'You were seeing her, weren't you? I knew I was right.'

He had to think quickly if he wanted to get out of this mess. Right now, Jenna's anger that he might have been seeing Sarah behind her back was the least of his problems.

'Yes.'

'You're a bastard.'

'And you're a killer. You murdered the girl I was in love with.'

The jab hit and brought with it a fresh bout of tears.

'We need to call the police,' Tommy mumbled, pulling out his cell phone.

'But what are we going to tell them? It was an accident, Tommy. What if they don't believe us though?'

Tommy hesitated and looked at Jenna. 'We don't have a choice.'

'But I can't go to jail. I can't.' Jenna looked tearfully at Luke again. 'What am I going to do? You have to help me, Luke.'

'How am I supposed to help you, Jenna? Are you asking me to help you get rid of the body?'

He floated the question out there, left it a moment, watching as the idea registered with both Jenna and Tommy.

'We can't do that,' Tommy shook his head, his tone suggesting he was appalled by the idea. 'We have to turn ourselves in.'

As Luke suspected, Jenna was immediately on board. 'She's already dead, Tommy. It was an accident and I don't see why we should go to jail.' She looked at Luke, her eyes pleading. 'Would you help us?'

'Why should I help you? You killed her. I didn't do anything wrong.'

'Luke, please. I know we're no longer together, but you loved me once. Please don't let me go to jail. You have to help me. Please, I'm begging you.'

They had buried Sarah in the backyard where the new conservatory was to be erected, knowing the earth had been freshly dug over and that the concrete floor would shortly be laid.

It had taken a while to convince Tommy. Luke knew he had a crush on Jenna and played on this knowledge, while Jenna did her part, pleading and begging with him, until eventually Tommy had agreed.

It would have been easier if it had been the three of them, but Clarke Golding was upstairs. Luke knew he was unpredictable, could be a liability. He persuaded Jenna to try to keep him occupied. She seemed happy with the idea, not wanting to get her hands dirty, but then Clarke appeared at the top of the stairs.

'Why are you and Tommy taking so long?' he had accused. 'I have the next game ready.'

'I'm coming. Tommy's a little busy.' Luke had listened as Jenna had tried to usher him up the stairs, but Clarke had pushed past her.

'What are you doing, Tommy?' His face crumpled when he spotted Sarah's limp body. 'Sarah? What have you done to Sarah?'

'It was an accident, Clarke.' Tommy had tried to reason with him, his face pale and his eyes looking unconvinced by his own lie.

'Is she dead? Sarah can't be dead.'

Clarke rushed to the foot of the stairs, dropping to his feet and sobbing over Sarah's body.

Luke scowled at Jenna as she joined them. 'You'd better sort this out. Calm him down.'

It took much persuasion, but eventually Jenna managed to get Clarke out of the way. Luke didn't trust he wouldn't talk though and pulled him to one side after the body was in the ground and Jenna and Tommy were scrubbing up the blood. He had to be sure he had Clarke's silence.

'You can't ever tell anyone what happened here tonight.'

'But what about Sarah?'

'If anyone asks, she left the island and has gone back to the mainland.'

They had cleared her room, piling her belongings into her suitcase, switching off her cell phone, burying everything in the ground beside her. She was due to finish working at the guest-house as soon as Bella Golding was out of the hospital and had been looking for another job. It should be easy to convince people she had just left.

'But she hasn't. She's still here. People are going to find out.'

'They won't if we don't tell them.'

'But...'

'And I need you to promise me, Clarke, that you won't ever tell anyone, because if I ever find out you breathed a word I am going to have to come back here and hurt you, do you under-stand? You saw how we made Sarah disappear. There's plenty more room down there in the dark next to her. You ever tell a soul and I will make you disappear too. No-one will ever know what happened to you. You and Sarah in a dark hole together in the ground.'

He saw Clarke's bottom lip wobble.

'Promise me, Clarke.' When the boy wavered, Luke pulled out his knife, flicked the blade and jabbed it against his chin. 'Promise me. Unless of course you want me to put you in the ground now. That will be easier. If I kill you and make you disappear now, I won't have to worry about you telling anyone what happened.'

'No, please. I won't tell anyone I promise. Please don't hurt me.'

'No second chances. If I find out you've talked, I will come back and kill you.'

'I won't tell.' A tear spilled down Clarke's cheek. 'I won't say anything. Please don't kill me.'

Luke put the knife away, stepped back, noting the kid had pissed himself. 'Good,' he told him, patting him on the cheek. 'I knew I could count on you.'

The next couple of weeks passed and Luke was on tenterhooks, fearful something could go wrong and he would somehow be found out. The concrete floor was laid at the guesthouse, the conservatory erected, and Bella Golding returned from the hospital.

Word was she was pissed at Sarah's sudden departure and for giving no warning she was leaving, but everyone seemed to buy the story that she had left the island of her own accord. Some folks remembered she had interviewed for a job on the mainland and it was assumed she had decided to take it. By the time Luke left for college, everyone had pretty much forgotten about Sarah Treadwell.

She remained alive in his dreams though and he continually replayed that evening in the basement of Bella Golding's guesthouse, recalling the fear that had radiated off of Sarah when he had attacked her. He had lived that high before when he attacked Marla, but the feeling of omnipotence he had experienced when he had choked the life out of Sarah was on another level.

He made his first premeditated kill seventeen months after putting Sarah in the ground. Her name was Amber, and she was a perky blonde he had followed from a bar. He liked the blonde ones. They reminded him of Sarah, and they reminded him of Jane. He had snatched her from a secluded street as she walked home, pulling her inside the back of the van he had hired specially for the occasion. Then he had driven her to an isolated wooded spot, discovering that night how much he enjoyed knife play. When she was dead he had wrapped her in the plastic sheeting he had used to line the van and buried her in a shallow grave.

With each kill he evolved. By the time he graduated college he had murdered six women, had learned that by donning a disguise he didn't have to be so fearful of security cameras and could go into bars, even talk with potential victims. He played with different looks, found the blonde beach bum wig and moustache worked best. The interaction appealed to him and he liked being able to flirt with the women he chose, have them willingly accompany him, particularly enjoying that moment when he had them all alone and they suddenly realised his true intentions.

After college he took a graduate job with a law firm in Philadelphia for a couple of years, before transferring to a renowned company in East Haven. He had initially planned to stay on the mainland, figuring it would be easier for hunting, but he missed island life and his brother, and eventually relented, buying a property back on Purity. Little had changed on the island. Jenna, Tommy and Clarke still lived locally; Jenna now married to

Curtis Milborn, while Tommy had joined the police. Something Luke found a certain irony in.

The three of them barely spoke, the secret that bound them together pushing them further apart, and life went on, Luke killing when the urge took over, always taking victims from the mainland and making sure they were from different towns, knowing this gave him anonymity. He had bought a second car, an inconspicuous Toyota he kept in a parking lot in East Haven, and used to hunt for his prey, keeping the tools he needed in the trunk.

One of his first purchases when he returned to Purity was a boat. The cabin cruiser he chose allowed him the freedom to leave the island whenever he wanted, and he kept a second mooring spot in a quiet location not far from his workplace. The boat offered an ideal place to be alone with his victims and he spent time adapting the cabin, ensuring that it could quickly be adapted into the perfect kill room.

Luke settled back into island life, enjoyed both his work life and his hobby. He met Stacey Monroe, moved her into his townhouse, and to the outside world they were the model couple, but then the cracks started to appear. Stacey began to show a jealous streak and grew suspicious when Luke disappeared on all night fishing trips; meanwhile, Jenna's marriage was in a bad way and she kept trying to turn to Luke for help when he wanted nothing more to do with her.

The real problems started when Bella Golding died though. The woman had been unwell for a long while, finally succumbing to a stroke, leaving Clarke alone in the guesthouse.

Clarke Golding had always been the weak link and his mother's death seemed to tip him over the edge. Luke's concern grew when he overheard people talking about how he wasn't coping living up in the big house alone. It was driving him

insane, they said, and he kept repeatedly proclaiming his innocence, though no-one knew what for.

Luke had driven up to the house purely wanting to talk to
him, needing to find out how bad the situation was.

'I'm going to tell,' Clarke had announced as soon as he had
opened the door. 'You made me do a bad thing. I'm going to tell.'

'You can't do that, Clarke.'

'You can't stop me. I have a journal. I wrote it all down.'

'Where is it?'

'I'm going to give it to the police. You made me do a bad
thing and I'm going to tell them.'

Panic rose inside Luke. He had been so careful since Sarah,
but there had always been a lingering fear that she would
somehow be his undoing.

He had tried to reason with Clarke, but the man was irrational, a simpleton. He kept talking about a journal. Luke wasn't
sure if he was making it up, but if there was a book, he needed to
find it. He followed Clarke upstairs, attempting to talk sense into
him, growing frustrated when he didn't even appear to be listening. He had grabbed at his arm, only intending to get his attention, startled when Clarke lost his balance and tumbled
headfirst down the stairs. It was a repeat of Sarah and brought
the memories rushing back.

Luke had checked for a pulse but could see from the
awkward way the man's head hung that he had broken his neck
and was already dead. He had spent the best part of an hour
hunting through the house, looking for any existence of a journal, eventually giving up and going home.

Three days later Clarke's body was discovered and shortly
after word began to spread that Bella Golding's niece had inherited the place. It went on the market soon after and Luke had
tried to juggle his finances, wondering if he could afford to buy
it. If the house was his, it would certainly solve all of his prob-

lems. He had managed to gather enough money together to put in an offer when it was taken off the market.

Six weeks later Nell O'Connor arrived on Purity Island, looking to make a fresh start.

Luke had never met her, but his brother, Newt, was dating her half-brother, and he found a twisted irony in the fact the security of his future now laid in her hands.

The night he first met Nell was the night Stacey found his collection.

Things had been turbulent with her for months. Stacey was out of work and boredom had led to paranoia, and she was becoming obsessed with trying to find proof he had cheated on her. She had gone snooping through his things, finding far more than she bargained for when she discovered the box where he kept the Polaroid souvenirs of his victims. She had been in shock when he had arrived home from work and luckily hadn't called the police, instead deciding to confront him.

Luke didn't want to kill her, but she had left him with little choice, and the moment after he had choked the life out of her was when he had realised his own life was starting to spiral out of control. He had left her dead on the bedroom floor, pulled the mask in place, knowing if he didn't show up at Newt and Michael's barbecue, questions would be asked. He needed to put on a show of normality, while he decided what the hell he was going to do about Stacey.

When he returned home that evening he had moved her into the basement freezer, but she had returned to haunt his dreams that night, taunting and goading him, accusing him of wanting Nell, pushing him further over the edge, until he felt his sanity crack and he was no longer sure if she was dead or alive.

Standing here in the kitchen at the guesthouse, he could see her standing next to Caleb's dead body. She tutted at him. 'Oh, Luke, what have you done? You're getting in deeper.'

He twitched, cut her a look. 'Shut up!' he barked.

'So, this is the bitch you've been lusting for?' Stacey glanced at Nell then back at Luke. 'You're going to kill her, right? Same as you killed me?'

'Shut the fuck up.'

'If you don't kill her, she will tell. You know you have to do it.'

Nell gave Luke a wary look and clutched the journal tighter. He felt himself slip a little further over the edge, the line blurring between reality and insanity, knowing he needed that book, that he had to figure a way to fix this mess.

He clutched at his shoulder with his free hand, at the wound where Jenna had shot him, and poked his finger against it, grimacing at the stabbing pain, using it to draw himself back from the edge, relieved when Stacey disappeared. She wasn't gone forever though. She had threatened to stay with him, to make his life hell, and he wasn't strong enough to completely drive her away.

It had been driving him crazy trying to figure out who had taken the shot at him that night at Nell's; his money had been on Sam Kent, as he knew Lizzie's kid brother still held a grudge against Nell. But Jenna had confessed it had been her when she had shown up at his house the previous night, begging for his forgiveness and then for his help.

It had been jealousy. She had admitted to that. She had seen him in the grocery store buying flowers and wine, and followed him up to the guesthouse, consumed by rage, scared he was cosying up to the one woman who could end up destroying their lives. In the heat of the moment she had fetched Curtis's air rifle from the back of the truck. She hadn't meant to actually hit him she had told him. She had been aiming for the wall behind Nell, wanting to scare her.

She had been so sorry for what she had done and she had sobbed and begged for his forgiveness. He had held her and soothed her, told her everything would be okay, before plying her with drink, driving her home and slitting her wrists, aware she had just given him a get out of jail card.

Luke would tell the police she was obsessed with him and had been for years. She had killed Sarah because she was jealous and then she had taken the shot at Nell.

He wished he could figure a way to tie her to Stacey. But that was still a problem to be resolved, as was the woman currently standing in front of him.

He had wanted Nell, had resisted because she was Michael's sister and because, since Sarah, he only killed strangers. It was safer that way.

But he had already broken his own rule when he had killed Stacey. Of course he had been left with no choice. She knew too much, just as Nell now knew too much. Maybe it was fate, maybe he was meant to have her.

Regardless, he had no choice and Stacey was right. Nell O'Connor had to die.

43

L uke twitched.

'Shut up!' He glared at the wall, behind where Caleb was sprawled. 'Shut the fuck up.'

Nell watched him warily, wondering who he thought he was talking to. For a moment he had a glazed look on his face and appeared to have gone completely over the edge. She hesitantly took a step back as he jabbed his finger against the wound where he had been shot, yelling out in pain.

Had he killed Sarah Treadwell? It was the only explanation she could think of for why he would want Clarke's journal so badly.

She eyed the gun, aware his mind seemed to be wandering. Would he notice if she tried to slip away? But then he was back, his focus returning, and she was aware she once again held his full attention.

'Give me the journal, Nell.'

When she ignored the request, he fired a shot at her feet. She jumped, scuttled back another step, her legs shaking. How had she never noticed this dark side to him?

'The next bullet goes in your head. Give me the journal, now!'

He looked irrational, dangerous. Crazy even. Not daring to call his bluff, quite certain he would shoot her, she handed the book over, and quickly took another couple of steps back. He didn't lower the gun.

'Cuff your wrists together.'

Nell glanced at the loose handcuff dangling from her right wrist and swallowed hard. 'What are you going to do, Luke?'

'Cuff your wrists together,' he repeated.

She weighed up her options, realised she had none. He had said Tommy wasn't coming. What the hell had he done to Tommy?

Michael was her only hope. He had been yelling at her when she had dropped her phone. Had he seen Caleb behind her, been trying to warn her? She could only hope he had and that he had called Alex. The only thing she could do at this point was keep Luke talking.

'You don't need to do this. You have the book, so why not just let me go.'

'I can't do that. Now cuff your wrists together. I won't ask you again.'

Nell hesitated, her gaze dropping to the gun where Luke's finger was twitching over the trigger. She swallowed hard and reluctantly slipped the loose cuff onto her left wrist and locked it in place.

Luke nodded and to her relief put the gun away. He rummaged in Caleb's sports bag, fished out the keys to the cuffs and slipped them in his pocket, before grabbing hold of her arm and pushing her towards the back door.

'Where are we going?'

'Just keep walking.'

He led her outside, his grip on her arm tightening as he

guided her across the backyard towards a pathway that cut through the trees.

'You don't have to do this. I gave you the book.'

He laughed; the sound hollow. 'You think this is just about the book?'

'You killed Sarah, didn't you?'

She took his silence as affirmation.

'It would have been okay if you hadn't decided to dig up the damn conservatory floor.'

'You're the one who's been trying to scare me into leaving, aren't you?'

He didn't answer.

'Did you attack my brother? He's supposed to be your friend. He's Newt's boyfriend.'

'That was unfortunate. I didn't expect him to come over to the storage unit while I was there.'

'Unfortunate? You almost killed him.'

Luke shrugged. 'Like I said, I didn't expect him to show up. I should've killed him, but I felt bad for Newt.'

Nell sucked in a deep breath, anger battling against the fear. She stopped walking, wanted to hit out at him with her fists. How dare he so casually disregard Michael's life?

'You're an asshole,' she spat at him.

He actually smiled at her accusation. 'Oh, trust me, Nell. I am far worse than an asshole. Now keep walking.' When she didn't move, he pressed the butt of the gun into the small of her back. 'Keep walking.'

Grudgingly she complied, her legs rubbery as dread coiled in the pit of her belly. Where the hell was he taking her?

'What happened to Sarah?' she asked, slowing her pace, still trying to stall for time. 'What did you do to her?'

Luke didn't answer the question, instead roughly pulled her forward. He ducked her head under a low bush, pushing her through into a clearing to where his car was parked. He unlocked the passenger door, threw the journal on the back seat then sat her inside, fastening the seat belt over the top of her cuffed wrists.

'Where are you taking me?' She asked as he got in the driver's seat.

'Somewhere we'll have some privacy.'

Nell felt a shiver of fear trickle down her back, the familiar dread tightening in her chest. 'We had privacy at the guesthouse.'

'I've somewhere better.'

She gulped for air as nausea and the familiar blackness threatened to sweep over her.

Luke regarded her with something close to fascination as she started to count. 'I watched you at the hospital. You didn't shed a single tear for Michael. I know you were scared and worried for him, but it's like you have this wall and you're scared of showing your emotions. But this, what is this, a panic attack? This is a treat. We're going to have some fun, you and I.'

'Don't... don't do this, Luke. Please... let's talk. I... know you... don't want... to hurt me.' It was getting harder to breath.

He paused, his hand on the ignition and he looked at her, those vivid blue eyes that had been cold and emotionless now filled with a predatory hunger. 'Oh, but I do, Nell. I'm looking forward to it.'

Sam Kent was in the cabin of his boat, drinking a cold beer and watching the sunset when he heard the car engine then foot-steps on the dock, and he peered out of the porthole window, curious who it was. There were only a handful of other boats moored at this spot and most folk had finished on the water for the day. He tended to come down here for peace and solitude, needing to be alone with his own thoughts after the revelation that Curtis Milborn had killed his sister, and it pissed him off a little that someone was intruding on that.

He saw the feet first, a woman's sneakers and a man's black boots, and as they passed his boat, heading further along the dock, he saw the rest of them come into sight, and realised it was Luke Trainor and Nell O'Connor.

He rolled his eyes and was about to reach for his beer, when the pair of them appeared to struggle, Nell trying to shake off Trainor's grip on her arm. He caught her roughly, making her squeal, yanking her against him and covering her mouth with his hand, and at that moment Sam spotted the handcuffs on Nell's wrists.

What the fuck?

That had his attention and he discreetly headed onto the deck, curious as to what the hell was going on. He watched as they reached Trainor's boat; saw Trainor pushing Nell down into the cabin.

Something wasn't right here, and it looked like Nell could be in trouble.

He shouldn't care. Curtis may have been the one who plunged the knife into Lizzie, but Nell had placed her in the house in the first place. After everything she had put him through, he should pick up his beer and turn a blind eye. Except he couldn't.

Picking up his cell phone he called the police.

Nell wasn't in the guesthouse, but her ex-boyfriend was, half of his head splattered up the door of one of the cream cabinets; it was clear from the contents of the sports bag lying on the floor beside him that he had come to the house intending her harm.

Had she shot him? If so, where the hell was she now? She had been in the house, her stuff was packed and waiting in the hallway.

Alex recalled Tommy's words. He said Luke had also been on his way to the guesthouse. Had he been here at the same time as Caleb? Did he now have Nell? Alex was unable to call her, having found her smashed cell phone on the counter, but he'd called Luke, repeatedly going to voicemail.

The fact that the man he had considered a friend for the past five years was responsible for murdering dozens of women seemed surreal, but there was no getting away from the truth. Luke Trainor was a cold-blooded psychopath. He had killed his own girlfriend too, suggesting he was starting to go off the rails. That made him unpredictable and even more dangerous, and if he had Nell, she didn't have much time.

'We will find her, Alex.'

Hunter's words didn't help. Alex was furious with himself for not acting sooner. Luke had given him cause for suspicion last night, but he had been hesitant, wanting to gather evidence and be sure he wasn't making a mistake before he pointed the finger at a friend. He should have told Nell of his suspicions. If anything happened to her, this one was on him.

The thought of losing her terrified him. He couldn't – he wouldn't – let it happen.

Dammit, focus, Cutler.

Luke had a cabin cruiser that he kept docked down by the marina. That's where he had taken his other victims and that was where he would take Nell, out on the water where they would have privacy.

His cell phone bleeped and he glanced at the screen, recognising the number.

'Ruby, what's up?'

'Chief, I've just had a call from Sam Kent. I think you're gonna want to hear this.'

'What are you going to do to me?'

Luke was in the kitchen area of the boat and glanced back at Nell. She sat on the floor, arms cuffed overhead to the stair rail, and he heard the tremor of fear in her voice, fed on it.

Her panic attack in the car had been a delight. After witnessing her bottling up her emotions for the past few weeks, watching first-hand as anxiety took over and exposed her weaknesses had given him an overwhelming sense of satisfaction. The attack had lasted several minutes and by the time they had reached the dock she was drained of energy. She had still managed to put up a fight though as he dragged her from the car to the boat, but now he had her restrained she was watching him with quiet trepidation.

He found her intriguing, her reactions fascinating him. Usually by this point his victims were crying and pleading with him to free them. That was what had drawn him to Nell. He knew she had already experienced terror at the hands of her ex-boyfriend, had seen that emotion was something she didn't give into willingly. She thought her panic attacks made her weak, but she was actually tougher than the others he had killed, and that made her more of a challenge. He was looking forward to seeing how far he could push her, curious to know how much it would take to completely break her.

'You want me to tell you and ruin the surprise?'

She visibly gulped but tried to keep up a brave front. 'You won't get away with any of this. You might kill me, but Alex is already on your trail. He will catch you.'

'Trust me, Nell. I'm smarter than your boyfriend. I won't get caught. Michael, Alex, we're all friends and they trust me. Hell, your dumbass brother even showed me the code to the new alarm system, that's how much he trusted me. I have wanted you from the moment I first met you, but I kept telling myself it would never work. You were Michael's sister and it was too dangerous. When Tommy told me you had the journal though, that's when I knew this was meant to be.'

'Meant to be? You're going to get caught. You won't get away with it.'

'Sure I will. I've been getting away with it for years.'

'What do you mean, "years"?'

'Do you think Sarah was the only one?' He let that sink in, satisfied when the shock hit and realisation dawned.

'You killed Penelope Maher and the other women?'

He simply smiled at that. 'As I said, I've been getting away with it for years.'

'What the hell is your brother going to think of you?'

'He won't ever find out.'

'You're wrong. He will, and he's going to have to live with knowing you're sick, that you're a fucking monster who kills women for pleasure.'

'Shut up! Stop talking about my brother.'

'You are going to get caught. You might be too arrogant to believe it, but it's going to happen. And your brother is going to be so disappointed when he learns what a pathetic excuse for a man you are.'

'I told you to shut up.'

'She's right.'

Luke glanced up and scowled when he spotted Stacey peering down into the cabin. She descended the stairs, slowly walked towards him.

'About what a pathetic excuse of a man you are.'

Luke stepped back, pointed his finger at her. 'You go away. Leave me alone.'

'Now why would I want to do that?'

'Just go away, Stacey! You're supposed to be dead. I killed you, so leave me the hell alone!'

'You killed your girlfriend?'

Luke glanced at Nell and blinked hard.

'She doesn't know? Go ahead and tell her how you put your hands around my throat and choked the life out of me.'

'Shut the fuck up, Stacey!'

'Wow, you're a bigger loser than I realised.'

Luke swung around, feeling a chill at the familiar voice. Prissy Jane sat on the kitchen counter, her legs swinging off the edge, her clothes perfectly neat and that smug, condescending smile on her face. She hadn't aged.

'How did you get in here, Jane?'

Jane picked at an imaginary fleck of dust on her sleeve.

'Grandma always said you were a waste of space. I guess she was right.'

'Get out!'

'Loser Luke, you really are pathetic.'

Luke lashed out at her with the knife, hitting air.

'Loser Luke, loser Luke, loser Luke...'

He turned around. Jane stood beside Stacey and they were both taunting him.

He put his finger against his wound, pressing hard, trying to focus on the pain and blot them both out. It worked momentarily, but then they were back and crowding in on him, the taunting ringing in his ears.

'Loser Luke, loser Luke, loser Luke...'

In desperation he pulled out his pocketknife, flicked up the blade and stabbed it into the wound, screaming out in agony as white-hot pain shot through him. He breathed deep and hard, relieved as his focus came back and both Stacey and Jane were gone.

Nell was staring at him, her face drained of colour, her golden eyes wide. He could tell she was scared, but she was angry too. He wanted to see her suffer another panic attack, needed to get back that edge of control, but she stuck her chin out defiantly, the anger stronger.

'You're talking to your dead girlfriend,' she pointed out sarcastically. 'Great! You're not just sick, you're crazy too.'

'Shut up.'

'I thought being a murderer was bad enough, but you're a real whack job, a proper Norman Bates. Yeah, your brother is gonna be so proud of you.'

'Shut up!'

'And you're cutting yourself too? What the hell is that all about?' She was pushing his buttons intentionally, he got that, but it irritated him it was working. Picking up a reel of duct tape, he went to her, pressing it across her mouth and winding it around her head.

She glared up at him, grunted something unintelligible and rattled her cuffs in frustration.

Luke turned his back to her, ran his fingers through his hair, forcing himself to breathe deeply, to focus. It was all going to be okay. Jenna would take the blame for Sarah and, although the police had found the bodies of his victims, there was no way of tracing them back to him. Nell was the last loose end and one he was going to take great pleasure in tying up. Come morning she would no longer be a problem.

Leaving her in the cabin, he went up on deck, untied the boat and started the engine.

$\sim$

Sam watched Luke's boat head out across the water, and he glanced at his watch, noted it had been nearly ten minutes since he had called the police. Where the hell were they? He had told them what he had seen, explained that Nell O'Connor appeared to be in trouble. Given that she was dating the chief he had expected the dock to be swarming with blue lights two minutes after his call.

Sit down and finish your beer. It's not your concern.

It wasn't and shouldn't be, but what had Luke done with Nell and where was he taking her?

He watched the lights of the boat fade into the distance, telling himself he had already done the right thing by calling the cops. There was nothing else for him to do.

Pulling another beer from the cooler he popped the tab, took a healthy swig, ignoring his guilty conscience. Nell O'Connor was not his problem.

Nell yanked at the handcuffs, hoping if she pulled hard enough, she might be able to loosen the stair rail, but it wouldn't give. Annoyed, she took a moment, tried to calm her frazzled nerves, before attempting again. Sweat rolled down her sides and beaded on her forehead, as much through frustration as through physical exertion. It didn't help the angle at which her arms were pulled was putting pressure on her neck. She twisted her head from side to side, trying to ease the pain, not wanting her muscles to seize up, aware she needed to keep as much strength as possible.

She wasn't sure where Luke was taking her, but knew she had to get herself free before they reached their destination, understanding that once they were there she would have little chance to fight back.

And she intended to fight. She hadn't come this far, hadn't finally plucked up the courage to stand up to Caleb, only to give in to another woman-hating sicko. No-one knew she was out here with Luke, no-one was coming to rescue her. She had to stay strong, knew she could only help herself at this point.

She was pretty certain Luke was on the verge of losing it. He had already been having conversations with his dead girlfriend and someone called Jane, and he was clearly on the point of some kind of breakdown. She had seen the way he had reacted to her jibes, growing frustrated and annoyed with her, and she wished she could get this damn tape off her mouth, certain if she continued to taunt him, she would push him closer to the brink.

It was her fear he wanted, and she would try her hardest not to show it to him. Anger would work better for her than fear.

She rattled the cuffs, frustration building. There had to be a way out of this, there had to be.

Think, Nell. Focus.

Luke hadn't left a light on in the cabin. It had been dusk when they had left the island and the only light that now remained came from the moon, casting silvery shadows through the porthole windows. Her eyes had adjusted though, and she could see the cabin was sparse. Other than a small kitchen area there was a slim built-in couch and what appeared to be a fold-away table set into the wall.

How many women had he brought out here, she wondered, and what had he done to them before they had died? Alex would know. He had seen the body parts, but he had never shared with her the cause of death and she had never asked, understanding it was his job and it was probably confidential.

An image flashed in her mind of Penny Maher's severed head, and a sudden wave of nausea washed over her, followed by uncontrollable shaking.

Don't think about it, she ordered herself, pissed off that her mind had wandered and terrified she might bring on another panic attack.

Focus and pull yourself together. Think about Alex and Michael. You want to see them again. You need to be strong and do this for them.

The anger slowly built. She was finally happy, had met someone she was in love with, and she had reunited with her brother. How dare Luke try to take that from her?

Using that anger she attempted to change her position and managed, with some effort, to get onto her knees. Although it wasn't comfortable, it gave her arms a little more leverage, allowing her to pull harder at the railing she was cuffed to. After several attempts she felt like it was starting to loosen against the wooden step. She tried again, blinking hard as perspiration dripped down her forehead, stinging her eyes. Drawing in a deep breath through her nose she paused and attempted to rub her face dry on her arm. Every muscle ached, a result she knew was from her car crash, her fight with Caleb and no doubt the tension of her current predicament.

You can do this, O'Connor. You want to see Alex again, don't you?

God, she desperately wanted to see him, wished she had never insisted on going up to the guesthouse. He had offered to bring her stuff down to her, but no, she was the one who had to go. Why the hell was she always so damn stubborn? If she hadn't gone to the guesthouse, if Tommy hadn't ditched her, she would be back at his place with Teddy and Sasha right now, waiting for him to come home.

A fresh wave of anger had her yanking hard at the railing. This time it definitely moved. Nell's heartbeat quickened, a sense of hope creeping in, and then the boat's engine spluttered to a stop and everything was quiet for a long moment. She heard Luke moving about above deck, realised time was running out and renewed her efforts to free herself, pulling frantically at her wrists and grimacing against the pain shooting through her limbs.

The door to the cabin opened and Luke climbed down the steps, the smile he gave her as he turned to face her chilling her to her soul. He went into the kitchen, fumbled in a drawer, pulling out a knife, the blade wide and sharp glinting in the shadows. Nell froze and she felt herself start to tremble.

Pull yourself together, O'Connor. He wants to see your fear. Don't give it to him.

She forced herself to take deep breaths in and out through her nose again, trying to calm herself, counting backwards in her head.

To her relief he laid the knife down on the kitchen counter, reached back in the drawer for matches. She watched as he lit half a dozen candles that sat in glass jars. They bathed the cabin in an eerie light that, were he not planning on killing her, might have almost been romantic.

She continued to pull at the railing, trying to be discreet, not wanting him to realise what she was doing. It was getting looser. If she could just work it free. Her hands would still be cuffed, but if she could grab the knife or the gun, catch him off guard. Nell realised she was clutching at straws, but knew she had to take any chance possible.

Warily she watched as he opened a cupboard, pulled out a metal box, sitting it on the counter with the candles and knife, then he set about opening out the table that was folded into the wall. Her eyes widened as he unlocked the box, took leather cuffs out, attaching them to hooks on each corner of the table, and she yanked harder, not caring that she was no longer being discreet.

He shot her a glance, gave a creepy smile as he pulled a plastic white sheet from the box, unfolding it over the table, and it was when she saw the stains on the sheet, realised it was blood from his previous victims, that she completely lost it, fighting to free herself at any cost, her screams muffled against the tape.

She frantically kicked out at him when he approached her, knowing she would fight him to the death before she would let him strap her down to that table.

He tried to grab her legs, to steady her while he reached for her wrists and Nell managed to catch him hard on the chin with the heel of her sneaker. She heard his teeth snap, saw she had drawn blood.

'The more you fight me the worse I will make you suffer,' Luke growled. He managed to get his arm around her waist, forcing her back onto the steps. Nell struggled against him, but he was far stronger and held her easily. As he reached for her wrists, someone else was suddenly in the cabin, catching hold of Luke in a headlock, pulling him off of Nell. The pair of them struggled, crashing back into the table and in that instant she recognised the man fighting with Luke was Sam Kent. She watched, feeling helpless as Luke overpowered Sam, pinning him down on top of the table, hands around his throat squeezing, then a gunshot rang out, making her jump, and Luke slumped on top of Sam.

For a moment she thought they were dead then both bodies moved and Luke fell back across his death table, blood spurting from a bullet wound in his belly as Sam clambered to his feet.

Nell drew in a deep breath, never so relieved to see Lizzie's younger brother. He dropped to his knees beside her, set the gun down on the floor, and pulled out a pocketknife to cut the tape off her mouth.

'Are you okay?'

Nell greedily sucked in air. 'How did you know we were out here?'

'I was on my boat and I saw him dragging you along the

dock. It looked like you were in trouble, so I thought I'd better follow.'

Nell swallowed hard; surprised Sam had tried to help her. She had been convinced he hated her, had believed he may have been the one stalking her. 'Thank you.'

He looked at her and she could see there was a still a conflict, that he was torn over whether he should hate her or not.

She rattled the cuffs again, anxious to be free. 'Can you get these off me, please?'

'Is there a key?'

'I think it's in Luke's pocket.'

He nodded, returned to Luke's body, checking the pockets of his jeans and his jacket. He turned to Nell. 'Are you sure–'

Nell saw it before Sam, and screamed out as Luke lunged forward, grabbing him in a choke hold. Sam dropped his pocketknife, but managed to elbow him in the gut, earning himself a loud scream when he caught the gunshot wound, but then Luke had hold of him and they were rolling back over and off the table, crashing to the floor.

Nell pulled the railing, this time hearing the wood splinter as it started to break. She pulled again, tried to lower the chain between the cuffs to fit through the gap she had created, but it held fast.

Sam and Luke were both on their feet, Sam seeming to have the upper hand this time as he threw a punch at Luke, sending him stumbling backwards into the kitchen area. Luke felt out for his knife, knocking one of the candles to the floor before his fingers made contact. The jar smashed, the flame igniting the wooden floor.

Nell jerked her hand again. The wood gave a little more. Her heart was racing, her mouth dry as she watched the fire start to take hold. She gave another tug, this one even harder, crying out as pain shot through her arms. The railing snapped out of the wood and she stumbled forward landing uncomfortably on her cuffed wrists.

Hearing an agonising scream she looked up as Luke stabbed the knife into Sam's chest. He drove the knife in deep, held it there as Sam dropped to his knees, before pulling it free, kicking him to the floor. As he turned towards Nell, the bloody knife dripping in his hand, she scrambled for the gun, her hands shaking as she tried to aim it at him and squeezed the trigger. The bullet missed him completely and he laughed at her, skulking his way around the table.

'You'll have to do better than that.'

The second bullet grazed his arm. Luke's eyes narrowed as he glanced down, brushing his fingers over where it had passed. Without warning he lunged at her with the knife.

Nell squeezed the trigger a third time, saw the momentary look of shock on his face as the bullet caught him clean between the eyes. He staggered towards her, the knife dropping from his grip, before he followed, collapsing to the floor.

She managed to get to her feet, tapped his body with her sneaker, relieved when he didn't move.

'I didn't miss that time, you fucker.'

Sam was still slumped on the floor of the cabin, flames licking around him. Nell was aware she needed to get off the boat before it exploded, but she couldn't leave him, not after he had saved her life. She stumbled over to him, felt for a pulse. He was still alive but had lost a lot of blood. She tapped him on the cheek.

'Sam, wake up. We have to get out of here.' At first he didn't move, but then he stirred when she slapped him harder. 'We have to go. The boat's on fire.'

He was groggy and mumbling, but conscious enough to help her get him to his feet.

'I can't support you with my wrists cuffed. Can you put your arm around my shoulder and hold on?'

He nodded, flinging his arm around her, his full weight pulling her down as she tried to half drag, half carry him towards the stairs. They faltered a couple of times, Sam's grip slipping, and Nell glanced around at the growing flames, aware time was running out.

They reached the cabin stairs and Nell's heart sunk. How the hell was she going to get Sam up them? He had lost consciousness and she propped him up on the bottom step, choking on the smoke, sweat pouring down her face, and aching from head-to-toe.

'Sam? Sam? I need you to help me. I can't get you up the stairs without your help.' She tapped him lightly against the cheek, panic and desperation clawing at her throat. 'Please, Sam. I can't have you on my conscience as well.'

Something registered and his eyes fluttered open.

Nell managed to twist him onto his belly, clambered up the first three steps herself and reached down, grabbing his arms, trying to pull him up behind her. He was a dead weight though and she wasn't strong enough to do it without him.

'Please, Sam. I need you to be strong for just a little bit longer.'

He stirred again, her words seeming to get through, and he managed to get a foothold on the bottom step, attempted to push his way up. Nell pulled at his arms, hanging on for dear life when he slipped, waiting for him to find his footing. With his help she dragged him the rest of the way up the steps.

The deck was already on fire and to her dismay the flames had already spread onto Sam's boat, which he had tied to the side of Luke's before sneaking aboard.

She glanced around, realising it was too late to get a life jacket or flare, and understood if they were going to have any chance of survival they were going to have to get in the ocean.

She had always been a strong swimmer, but right now she was physically shattered, her wrists still cuffed, and Sam was practically unconscious and in dire need of medical attention. While she didn't fancy their chances, she figured they had to be better than burning to death on the boat. She pushed Sam in first, jumped in after him, grabbing hold of him and managing to slip her arms over his head, holding his head back against her as she trod water.

She lost track of how long she held him, her muscles cramping as she tried to keep the pair of them afloat, knew it was probably only about ten minutes at most, though it felt a lot longer. When she spotted the lights heading towards them and realised it was another boat, she could have cried with relief. A wide beam of light cut across the water in front of them, blinding her.

'Nell?'

She heard Alex's voice, was too exhausted to reply, then she heard a splash and he was swimming towards her, covering the distance between them with powerful strokes. He eased Sam out of her arms as the boat pulled up alongside them, and she recognised Hunter Stone as he leant over the edge to help Alex get Sam on board. 'He looks like he's lost a lot of blood. Get an ambulance on standby.'

Alex turned back to Nell, pulling her close against him, and she slipped her wrists over his head, held on tight, the relief of knowing she was finally safe almost too much to take in.

'I thought I had lost you,' he admitted.

'You can't get rid of me that easily.' She managed a shaky smile, kissed him hard on the mouth, before giving in to the tiredness and letting him take her full weight.

He tightened his arms around her, brushed his lips against her temple. 'You're okay, Nell. We're gonna be okay.'

EPILOGUE

Alex made Nell go to the hospital, more for his own peace of mind than anything. Although her injuries appeared superficial he knew she had been given one hell of a scare and he wanted to know she was okay. Armed with a further dose of painkillers he drove her home, taking the doctor's recommendation to run her a hot bath, then followed his own by pouring her a large glass of wine.

She kept up the bold front, attempting to shrug off the nightmare she had been through by using nonchalance and humour, trying to make out it was no big deal, and he remained patient, waiting for the cracks to appear, knowing they would eventually. When the initial shock wore off, giving way to tears she fought so hard to hold back, he held her close, stroking her hair, telling her she was safe and promising her everything would be okay.

And it would be. She had been so brave, so strong, and, had it not been for her actions, Sam Kent would be in the morgue right now instead of the hospital. Alex had spoken with the doctors, who had told him Sam was in a critical but stable condition, but they were quietly confident he would pull through. Although Curtis Milborn had killed Lizzie, he knew

Nell felt responsible for what had happened to her. By saving Sam's life he hoped she would stop being so hard on herself.

Likewise Sam had helped save Nell, thwarting Luke's plans and buying her extra time. Alex dreaded to think what the outcome might have been had Sam not followed the boat, the realisation of how close he had come to losing her knocking it home how much she now meant to him. Something Michael addressed with him the next morning.

'You manage to figure out if you're in love with my sister yet?' he asked when Alex stopped by to see him in the hospital.

Alex had left Nell at home sleeping, knew she needed the rest. Michael had been frantically calling; needing to know everything was okay. He would see her for himself soon enough, but until then Alex wanted to give him some reassurance.

'Yeah, I am.'

Michael clearly hadn't been expecting that response, the grin he broke out in stretching from ear to ear. 'Really?'

'Yeah, really.'

'She's gonna be okay, right?'

'She's gonna be fine. How about Newt? How's he doing?'

'He's in shock,' Michael admitted. 'We both are, but I guess it's harder for him. Luke was his brother and he loved him, but it turns out he was also a monster. How is he supposed to get his head around that? He feels guilty, blames himself for not picking up on the signs. He thought I was going to hate him for what happened, and he is dreading seeing Nell.'

'She will be fine with him. It's difficult for her too, knowing she shot his brother.' Alex shoved a hand back through his hair. 'Give them both some space to work it out. They're both level-headed enough to get past this.'

'Yeah,' Michael gave a pensive smile. 'Hopefully you're right.'

. . .

It took a while for Newt to come to terms with everything that had happened. Michael had been discharged from the hospital two weeks after Luke's death and the pair of them had immediately taken an extended vacation down to Mexico, partly to aid Michael's recuperation, but as much to give Newt time away from Purity, a place that held so many memories.

Nell didn't get to see Newt before they left, and was certain he was avoiding her.

Alex had told her to give him space, promised her he didn't blame her for his brother's death, but still she felt guilty. Luke had deserved to die and she didn't regret shooting him; she knew she would be dead if she hadn't, but she hated what that did to Newt and was worried it would change their relationship forever.

She spoke to Michael a handful of times while he was away, and they agreed the guesthouse held too many raw memories, so they had decided to put the place on the market. She had already moved the rest of her things into Alex's place and he had made it clear he wanted her to stay. Nell wasn't sure if they would get a buyer for the guesthouse, though at this point thought it might be a good thing if the building was razed to the ground.

Clarke's journal had been found on the back seat of Luke's car, shedding light on what had happened at the guesthouse the night Sarah had died. Nell had been relieved to learn he had played no part in her death, though hated that Luke had threatened him into silence.

With both Luke and Jenna dead, only Tommy could be held accountable for what had happened to Sarah and he had slipped into a coma shortly after arriving at the hospital, staying unconscious for several weeks. When he eventually came to, he had tearfully confessed to everything that had happened. Jenna's prank hadn't killed Sarah Treadwell though. She had been Luke's first victim, and because of that the DA had reduced the charges. Tommy Dolan would have to turn in his badge, and he would stand trial for trying to cover up Sarah's murder, but he wouldn't take the full heat for Luke's crime.

Sam Kent was also out of the woods, making a full recovery and recuperating at his parents' home. He hadn't made contact with Nell and she had been reluctant to get in touch with him, still unsure how things were between them. He had saved her life and she had saved his back, but did he still bear a grudge about Lizzie?

So, it surprised her when he had shown up on the doorstep one Sunday afternoon while Alex was at work, Sasha and Teddy going crazy when the buzzer sounded, Nell immediately on guard, still wary whenever she was on her own. She had invited him in, conversation between them awkward at first, but then they had both opened up. Feelings had still been running high over Lizzie, but recent events had changed everything, and they talked things out, took the first tentative steps to repairing the damage between them. When Sam left, Nell felt like a weight had been lifted and she was finally able to start moving forward.

As fall turned into winter, a cool front, bringing with it icy winds and the first flurries of snow, Nell felt her life was returning to normality. She started painting again on a regular basis, had taken a part-time job in one of the craft stores in town. Caleb's death had made waves in the society columns of the Chicago press and, while she had faced the wrath of Bitsy Sweeney Brooks, who had made her intentions clear in both a letter and a voicemail, as well as numerous newspaper quotes, that she held Nell responsible, with Caleb gone there was no longer any need to hide and she could start selling her work again. It felt good to be paying her way and gave her a purpose, plus the painting was therapeutic and it helped to relax her.

Two weeks before Christmas Alex's brother and sister announced they were planning to visit. Nell had answered the phone a couple of times to his sister, Cassie, and knew from snatches of conversation she overheard that she was curious to know who Alex was shacking up with.

'I think they want to check you out?' he admitted a couple of days before they were due to arrive, as they walked the dogs along the beach one evening.

'Okay,' Nell replied, feeling a little apprehensive. Having grown up with such a dysfunctional family unit she always felt uncomfortable in these situations. 'So, no pressure then?'

'Cassie's a headcase, so you two will get on great, and Joe's a lush. Ply him with alcohol and he won't notice you're certifiable, trust me.'

When she pulled a face at him, he grinned, leaning in and giving her a kiss.

The pair of them, along with Joe's wife, Lacey, were planning on staying at the Purity Oaks Hotel and Alex had invited them over for dinner on the Saturday night.

'I guess I should decide what to cook,' Nell announced, picking up a pebble and throwing it into the surf. Teddy darted after it, disappearing into the freezing water.

Alex shot her a look. 'You want to poison my family?'

'Hey, my cooking is not that bad.'

'Yeah it is, Nell.' He arched a brow. 'I've tried it. And yes, I know I'm still alive to tell the tale, but that is down to a strong stomach and pure luck.'

'Oh, stop being so dramatic. I don't mind cooking.'

'But I do.' He grinned slyly. 'I want them to like you, remember? We'll order something in.'

As they walked back to the house, the dogs running on

ahead, Nell spotted a figure standing on the back deck. She gripped hold of Alex's hand.

He glanced over to where she pointed, squinting. 'It's Michael.' Nell felt her heartbeat quicken and she let go and hurried back towards the house. 'Michael?'

He spotted her, stepped down onto the beach and started running across the sand. They met halfway and then he was scooping her up in a bear hug, arms tightening around her.

'I have missed you so much.'

'Yeah, me too,' he told her, swinging her around.

As they walked back to the house, Nell realised Newt was also standing on the deck, looking out to sea. She glanced at Michael then Alex, her expression a little wary.

'Go on,' Michael urged her. 'It will be fine.'

Hesitantly Nell approached Newt, leaving Alex and Michael talking down on the beach.

'Hey, Nell.' Newt's tone was light, but he sounded awkward, a little uncomfortable even.

Nell stepped onto the decking, went to him. 'Hey, Newt. How are you doing?'

'I'm okay.' There was a long pause. 'Well, no, I'm not okay, but I'm getting there.' He paused. 'I'm sorry for what Luke did.'

'It's not your fault.'

'No, so people keep on telling me. I guess he was my brother though, so I have to figure out a way to convince myself of that.' He gave a sad smile. 'I'm getting there though, I promise. As long as we're okay.'

'We're more than okay.' Nell stepped forward, slipped her arms around him. 'We'll get through this, together.'

Newt hugged her back and nodded as he pressed his head against her shoulder, and they stood there for a few moments until Alex and Michael rejoined them on the deck.

'Have you guys eaten?'

Michael shook his head at Alex. 'Not since this morning.'

'I'll order in pizza.'

Michael glanced at Newt; got the okay. 'Yeah, sure. That would be good.'

Alex unlocked the French doors, let Michael and Newt inside. He looked back at Nell and held out his hand. 'You okay?'

She smiled. 'Yeah, I'm okay. In fact, I'm more than okay.'

She took his hand, brushed a kiss against his lips, and led him inside.

Her brother was finally home, things were going to be okay with Newt, and she had Alex by her side. Everything was going to be fine.

THE END

ACKNOWLEDGEMENTS

I may write the story, but as always there are a number of people who help make the finished article what it is and I would like to take a moment to thank them.

To my beta team, Jo, Andrea, Paula, Sally, Christine, Jeff and Janet, I say a huge thank you. Your support, encouragement and honest feedback makes my job so much easier. To Jeff and Janet in particular, my US angels, who checked my manuscript for any inconsistencies and patiently answered all of my questions, you did a wonderful job and I am in your debt. Any mistakes in the finished book are mine, not yours. And also to Jo, who has to take credit for Purity Island. I may have set the scene, but she came up with the name.

To Antonia Richardson, the winner of my competition to have a character named after her – thank you for entering.

I doubt I will ever write a book without calling on my police detective sister, Holly Beevis. Thank you for always answering my (often bizarre) questions.

Finally, to my wonderful readers: without you I am nothing. Thank you for your continued support of my writing and especially to those of you who take the time to engage with me on my Facebook page, send me pictures of my books in some wonderful locations and poses, and who spread the word to other readers. You really are the best bunch of people a girl from Norfolk, UK, could ever hope to have on her side.

Made in the USA
Middletown, DE
18 April 2020